In The Face Of The Foe

The Jock Mitchell Collection

Nathaniel M Wrey

Waterman Books

This collection published in 2025 by Waterman Books

Triumphant Where It Dares Defy

A Place More Dark

For All the Treasures Buried Far

ISBN Hardback: 978-1-7394144-2-9

ISBN Paperback: 978-1-7394144-0-5

ISBN Ebook: 978-1-7394144-1-2

Book cover design by Milbart

Acknowledgements

With thanks to my family, John McGee, Mary Whinder, Leon Chambers, Gwen Cushen, Zoe Ward, Charlotte Ward and to my editor, Lee Dickinson.

Dedication

To the Spirits that opposed and the victorious dead.
For my grandparents.

Triumphant Where It Dares Defy
1941

Book One

Prometheus

By Lord Byron (George Gordon)

And Man in portions can foresee
His own funereal destiny;
His wretchedness, and his resistance,
And his sad unallied existence:
To which his Spirit may oppose
Itself—and equal to all woes,
And a firm will, and a deep sense,
Which even in torture can descry
Its own concenter'd recompense,
Triumphant where it dares defy,
And making Death a Victory.

Chapter 1

"That's quite a shiner you have there, private," observed Colonel Brook, rocking back on the only chair in the hut.

Private Robbie Hyde, his disinterested eyes wandering, shrugged. "Yes, sir."

"It's the least you deserve, you damn fool!" cursed Brook, slamming forward on his chair, his moustache twitching in agitation. "What possessed you, man?" Silence followed. "Well?"

"'Abit," conceded Hyde with his East End accent, his interpretation of standing to attention accommodating a slouch.

"Smoking or thieving? Oh, don't bother answering. You're a lost cause." Brook shook his head in disappointment. "We're prisoners of war, for God's sake! The enemy wear the swastikas. We don't steal from each other; we stand together. I hope those cigarettes were worth it?"

Hyde's toothy grin answered. "Sorry, sir."

"Oh, get out of my sight!" ordered Brook, his checks flushed red.

Hyde sniffed, gave a half salute, and strode away with his distinct swagger between the rows of bunk beds.

"A scoundrel!" cried the colonel to those in earshot. "Who signed him up for the army in the first place?"

"They don't ask many questions in times of crisis," remarked Captain Maddox from his top bunk.

"The wee Ned enlisted tae escape the police," said Lance Corporal Richard 'Jock' Mitchell.

"Doesn't surprise me," replied Brook. "Had we still been fighting, I'd have thrown him in the glasshouse. Not much I can do when incarcerated myself. The men's rough justice seems the most fitting sentence." He paused, pursing his lips. "Not that I like indiscipline anywhere. Don't want Jerry thinking we're a rabble."

"I'll have a quiet word with the men," offered Maddox. "I can guess who meted out the punishment."

"Aye, all punches tae the body in the future, so nowt shows," laughed Jock in his thick Ayrshire brogue.

"Now, now, lance corporal," chided Maddox with a wink.

"Sorry, sir." Jock's smile remained. He enjoyed the informal relationship forged with the officers since their arrival at Stalag XXA. The strict hierarchy when under fire in France and on the journey into captivity across Germany and deep into occupied Poland, evaporated amid the chaotic reality of prison life.

"You seem to know something of the boy, Jock," said Colonel Brook. "What's his background?"

"Nae, nawt much, other than what the lads tell me. Crime runs in his blood. A street urchin. Already served time in borstal for burglary."

Brook tutted.

"Nawt a bad wee fighter though," continued Jock, always keen to offer a rounded opinion. "Took oot a machine gun post at Clery."

"Hmm, suppose that's the beast in him," mused Maddox, sitting up and swinging his legs over the side of the bunk. "Although, a touch longer on the parade ground and he'd soon get some discipline knocked into him."

"Quite," agreed Colonel Brook. "That's all they need: a good dose of army discipline."

Maddox pushed himself off his bed, falling to the ground with a controlled crouch. "We'd better get the boys ready for parade. Work parties are due out in half an hour."

"Aye, sir," said Jock, his tall, wiry frame rising to look down on his superior.

"What have you volunteered for this week?" asked Brook of Captain Maddox.

"I'm looking after the commandant's potatoes and carrots."

"How they coming along? Planted a little late in the season, eh?"

"Not bad at all, sir," said Maddox, straightening his collar. "Our first crop is due in about a fortnight's time. I must say, I rather enjoy seeing the fellas grow."

"Excellent, keep up the outstanding work."

"Aye, beats working in the fields," added Jock, his tone obscuring any bitterness at the officers' exemption from working for their captors, never experiencing the backbreaking work on the farms or in the factories of Thorn.

"Chin up, Jock," chirped Brook. "This war won't last forever. You'll soon be back with your chrysanthemums."

Jock sniffed an acknowledgement as he walked to the door. He loved his garden, but an image of his wife and sons floated into his thoughts. He prized them above all else.

"Try to get more information on the Russian campaign," urged Maddox, tucking to the side of Jock as they exited the hut together. "It'll do the boys' morale wonders if the bear has taken a bite out of old Boche."

"I'll try, sir," answered Jock, "but the locals' German is as bad as mine. We spend most of our time gurning, attempting tae understand each other."

"I can't understand you half the time," ribbed Maddox. "Do your best. It's good you've built a relationship."

"I pity them. Jerry's stolen their land and then forced them tae work as slaves on it."

"This Hun is a loathsome creature. Has the arrogance of a Greek god and the cruelty of a Roman tyrant! Shouldn't have let them climb to their feet after the Great War."

"Things weren't so rosy for ourselves after that one."

"True," said Maddox. "If only this war wasn't over for us. We'd show Jerry a thing or two!"

Jock rolled his eyes at the young captain's naivety. Their chance to show Jerry a thing or two floundered in France because of inadequate training and equipment. He recalled the order to stand their ground at Albert, west of the Somme, and the shock and incomprehension that followed. How did they expect an ill-prepared territorial battalion from the Royal West Kent Regiment to hold back the Wehrmacht juggernaut? A sacrificial lamb was how his mate, Toby, described them before a German bullet entered his skull, one final erudite view of the debacle. Sacrificed so that the cream of the army might escape via Dunkirk. And that gave Jock an idea. "What aboot escape, sir?"

"Escape!" echoed Maddox, restraining his shock to a whisper. "We're in the middle of Poland, with Berlin between us and Blighty. Moscow is closer than London, and I don't fancy walking into Uncle Joe's fight with Hitler."

"There's Sweden."

"Do you know the way to Sweden?"

Jock shrugged. "We cannae sit on our bloody arses for the rest of the war. Ma bum's already gone numb after a year in this place!"

"Jock, language!" teased Maddox. "And you a staunch Presbyter-ian."

"Och, that Hyde's rubbing off on me."

"I've heard much worse in this army, I can tell you," chuckled Maddox. "Listen, we'll not sit still for the rest of the war, but we need to consider the big picture before constructing a plan. The whole of Europe is under Hitler's control. If the Russians stop the advance, the Germans may fall back, and options appear. That's why gleaning intelligence from the Poles is so important."

"Aye, I said I'd try," said Jock, wondering how soon the war would be over. Would victory for Hitler send him home? In that dark moment, even that felt preferable to another week in the camp. With a touch of his cap, he split from the captain and headed to his own hut with his languid gait, ready to rouse the men for a hard day's work in the fields.

Chapter 2

J ock wiped a layer of sweat from his brow and rubbed his sore back. Each time the sun broke through the clouds in the early autumn sky, the temperature rose. Bound with sleeves round his waist, his tunic hung flapping against his trousers. A bronzed, grimy torso showed off his gaunt frame and ribs. With a glance at the sky, Jock tried to gauge the sun's position. It told him little other than time crept forward. Despite a recent water break, he craved another precious ladle. His tongue licked at cracked lips, while their solitary guard lazed by the water bucket under the shade of a solitary tree, his rifle resting against the trunk. Overpowering him would not take much, considered Jock, but then what?

"Arbeit! Vork!" cried the guard, noticing Jock's eyes on him.

He allowed his bitter gaze to remain a moment longer, prompting another cry from the guard. But it never paid to irritate their overseer, not unless you wanted to miss the next water ration. With feet straddling the neat line of turnips, Jock bent his tired back once again, gripping the cluster of leaf stems, waggling the root. The fine, loose soil released its captive, and, with one brisk shake, he dislodged the mud. Jock shuffled forward, flinging the vegetable into the wicker basket at his feet, seeking the next.

At staggered points in adjacent rows, prisoners and local Poles laboured as Jock, sullen, gaunt faces reflecting their reluctance and fatigue. Whenever the occasion allowed, Jock glanced sideways, observing his fellow harvesters. Five rows to his right, a young Pole named Antek worked. About the same age as Jock's eldest, a slight deformity to his foot prevented an alternative captive life, or death, as a Polish soldier. Once the pair had swapped pleasantries in a mess of broken English, German and hand signals, a friendship formed on nothing more than adversity. Jock now stood over a full basket, biding his time, ignoring the diktat to empty it into the cart at the side of the field. With no more room in his basket, he discarded his pickings to the floor, hoping the sentry's eyes looked elsewhere.

Finally, Antek waddled towards the cart, lugging his overflowing basket. With a casual swing of his boot, Jock spread the unloaded turnips out and heaved his basket up. He staggered along the rutted channel heading for the cart, weighed down with his basket, his muscles cramping.

"Aw right!" greeted Jock as they arrived at the cart together, his face now red from the effort. "How are ye?"

Antek replied with a flurry of indecipherable words, but his smile translated all. He dropped his basket to the ground, continuing to chatter at Jock in the futile hope that bombardment would furnish some understanding.

"I cannae understand a word ye say, lad," explained Jock with his own smile. He pointed towards Antek's basket. "Let me help ye with that." Jock put his basket down and grasped the edge of Antek's.

The Pole nodded with enthusiasm. "Tak! Tak! Mein freund."

They lifted the container to shoulder height, tipping its contents with ease. A familiar rumble of turnips rolling on turnips echoed in the cart. They did the same with Jock's basket, its load stirring a dusty odour, reminding Jock of harvest time on his smallholding in Kent.

"Good lad," praised Jock, slapping Antek on the back.

The Pole leaned against the cart, wiping both hands across his brow, conveying his discomfort.

"Aye," concurred Jock with a nod. "It's probably raining at home. Any news aboot the war?" Aware that his words meant nothing to his young confidante, he tried again. "WAR. RUSSIANS. GERMANS. BOOM. BOOM." Hand gestures accompanied the pantomime, his fingers spread in explosive animation. At the performance's end, Jock waggled one hand, uncertain the Poles shared the sign for 'in the balance.'

Antek nodded, the crude communication triggering some response. With his bottom lip protruding, he shook his head. "Nie. Nein." Lifting one foot off the ground, he tapped his battered boot. "Germans." Then he spat, stamping his boot down on the spittle and dirt, grinding the heel in. "Russians."

"Och, nae," lamented Jock. "It'll be over before the winter, and that was Uncle Joe's best hope."

Antek reached into his pocket, sensing the Scot's disappointment, retrieved some cherries, and offered them to Jock.

"Ye're a fine man," remarked Jock, "for a Catholic." Laughing at his own joke, he took two cherries, folding Antek's fingers around what remained. "Ye need these as much as I do. Thanks, lad." He placed one cherry in his mouth, allowing his tongue to run over the shiny surface, eking out a hint of what was to come. Then, with eyes closed, Jock bit into the fruit, savouring the juice and flavour. Manoeuvring the stone to the tip of his rolled-up tongue, he spat it to the ground and stamped on it. "Germans!"

Antek mimicked his companion and burst out laughing as he added a burst of crushing jumps on their vanquished enemy.

"Steady there, lad," cautioned Jock. "We donnae want Fritz taking an interest. Best get back tae our turnips." He glanced towards the guard, grateful to see his interest elsewhere. His empty basket collected, Jock considered putting the remaining cherry in his pocket as a treat for later at the camp. His stomach, stirred by the itch of the pitiful consumed morsel, clamoured for more. The gut's argument proved persuasive, and Jock flicked the fruit into his mouth, enjoying the moment, forgetful of the torment to suffer when his unsated stomach demanded still more. "Cheerio the nou," he called to Antek, making his way back down his row.

Chapter 3

"Jock! Jock! Wake up!"

"We'd better have won the bloody war!" cursed Jock, his eyes creeping open to inspect the private looking down at him.

"Colonel Brook's asking for you," said Harry Packham, a young farm labourer from Tonbridge.

"Och, does the man nawt get I've been toiling in the sun all day? I need ma rest!" Jock rolled out of bed, stamping his feet on the floor in protest.

"It's been cloudy all day," teased Packham.

"Then ye won't mind running ten laps of the camp, will ye, private?" Jock eased his sore feet into his boots, letting Packham stew over whether or not he joked.

"I've been out in the sun too," stated the youngster. His eyes urged Jock to smile.

"So ye have," said Jock, rising to his feet, his face still sombre. "What kind of fool says 'oot in the clouds?' Did the colonel say what it was aboot?"

"No. Lieutenant Morbin called me from the door. Asked me to go find you."

"Fine, ye grab yerself some shut eye. Ye need yer rest too." Jock ambled off, clocking Packham flop onto his bed, adding in a private whisper: "And I'll bloody wake ye from yer slumber on ma return!"

On entering the officers' hut, Jock found a small group congregating around the colonel. Maddox sat on his top bunk, Lieutenant Morbin and Captain Butler perched on the bed below. By their side, Lieutenant Harcourt stood leaning against another bunk, his pipe's smoke drifting with cigarette fumes in the dusty air.

"Sir, ye wanted tae see me?"

"Ah, Jock. Excellent," answered Colonel Brook, having made the one chair his own. "Come, sit on Harcourt's bed. Light up if you have any."

"Aye, I will. But ma baccy's getting low."

"We have just the man to get you some: no questions asked," joked Maddox.

Harcourt laughed. "Careful, Tom. Stealing from Peter to pay Paul. Could be your stash Hyde takes!"

"I'll fight any man who approaches." Maddox raised his fists.

"A glass jaw, I'm told," teased Butler, pushing Maddox's swinging leg from his face.

"But my parrying technique is flawless. The only person I let touch this chiselled masterpiece is the missus."

"I bet her right hook ain't half-bad," quipped Harcourt.

"Gentlemen," interrupted the colonel. "As much as I enjoy the banter, this meeting is for more serious matters. Here, Jock." Brook held out his own cigarette between finger and thumb, the lighted tip kissing Jock's rolled fag.

"Thank ye, sir."

"Okay, Maddox, the floor's yours," began the colonel. "Tell them what you told me earlier."

"Of course, sir." Maddox shuffled an inch forward on his bed. "The carrots and potatoes are in good health, but as I tended my patch, a conversation between the camp commandant and his good lady wife drifted in my direction: rude not to listen in. Their kitchen window overlooks the vegetable patch. They didn't notice me kneeling to weed."

"What were you doing?" exclaimed Harcourt with a melodramatic look of shock.

"Weeding, man. Weeding!"

"Sorry, the man's got a very weak 'dee'," quipped Harcourt, before noticing the Colonel's stern glare. "But you were saying…"

Maddox grinned and continued. "They weren't arguing. Rather, moaning about an impending visitor. My German's strong enough to get the gist."

"If you can understand Jock, you can understand anyone," teased Harcourt, risking Brook's glare again.

"Jakey nyaff," mumbled Jock, with a smile in Harcourt's direction.

"What's that Jock?" enquired Brook.

"Och, nowt. I'm just reminded of a lass from school who married a German."

"Gentlemen! If we can focus," sighed the colonel. "Maddox, please continue and no more interruptions!"

"The cause of their unhappiness? They've orders to billet an SS officer for a night: on his way back from the Russian front. Old Skull and Crossbones accompanies a special shipment."

"The 'what' remains a mystery," cut in Brook, using the privilege of rank to ignore his own order.

"That's right," continued Maddox. "But I inferred they're moving something precious. Marked for Himmler himself, with an all-night SS guard posted in a village."

"A village?" queried Butler, playing with his ring-framed glasses in his nervous manner. "So, the shipment's not staying with the officer within the prison walls?"

"I guess not," answered Maddox. "Odd, as a prison affords natural security."

"Not if they don't want the eyes of prisoners on it," mused Brook. He sucked on his cigarette, blew the smoke upwards and smiled. "This reinforces my summation." The British commander leaned forward. "Now, we're out of the fighting, but not the war. Intelligence is a powerful weapon, and if Jerry doesn't want us to see this shipment, then I goddamn want to see it!"

Butler cleared his throat, as he always did when challenging the colonel. "Even if we found out, what good is intelligence if we can't get it to the boys back home?"

"Well, I err…" A flustered Brook took to puffing on his cigarette.

"The Poles," said Jock.

"Yes, the Poles," repeated Brook. "Go on, Jock!"

"Well, ye've heard of their resistance movement: one that's in touch with the British. The local peasants may nawt be members, but they may know who is."

"That's a fair few 'mays' for my liking," said Harcourt. "They took a fair beating from both the Hun and the Ruskies. Takes some organisation and guts to set up resistance after that."

"They've guts aplenty," growled Jock. "They'll help. Organised resistance or nawt."

"Hmm, righto, let's not worry too much about that aspect," pondered Brook. "We need to gain worthwhile intelligence first. Any thoughts?"

"The obvious answer," proffered Butler, "is to get a sight of the orders Herr Commandant received. I presume he took them home to show Frau Commandant."

"I suspect he did," chuckled Maddox. "You don't force an unwanted guest on your wife without being able to blame someone else."

"We must break into their house," stated Harcourt.

"Oh dear," said Brook, brushing his moustache. "I suppose we must. Maddox, your role gives you opportunity. You up for it?"

Maddox spluttered in disbelief. "Me? With all due respect, sir, I'm not equipped for such stealth. And anyway, in daylight when I'm under the scrutiny of a watchtower? They'd shoot me dead if I went near the doorknob."

"Perhaps you're right," conceded Brook. "Any of you other chaps have the balls for a night-time visit?"

Maddox huffed at the slight but perked up when no one answered.

After an embarrassing silence, Butler piped up. "Is it not rather an issue of skill than bravery?"

"Hyde," said Jock.

"Sorry?"

"Hyde," repeated the lance corporal. "He has the skills."

"Well, yes, but, no," stuttered Brook. "The man's a rascal. We can't trust him with such a delicate operation."

Harcourt stepped forward. "You're right, sir, but he has the perfect attributes. He's a housebreaker by profession. If anyone can navigate their way out of here, it's Hyde. What we need is for someone to accompany him: someone to keep him under their beady eye and who understands what they're looking for."

"Who do you suggest?" pressed Brook, enlivened again.

"Well," considered Harcourt, tapping his pipe stem against his lips. "We need someone we can trust, but someone Hyde can work with. There's only one suitable man."

Jock grimaced as all eyes fell on him.

"Yes, you're spot on, Harcourt," trilled Colonel Brook. "Well, Jock? Think you can persuade Hyde?"

"Aye, jakey nyaff. She were a bonnie lass," muttered Jock, much to the bemusement of the others.

Chapter 4

"Rather than slouching with a smug grin on yer face," moaned Jock, "how aboot saying something!"

Hyde remained silent, grinning for a few seconds more. "A man's entitled to enjoy these moments. Not every day one's betters come crawling for help. In fact, I'm disappointed the Colonel didn't ask me himself."

"Yer damn country's asking for help," snapped Jock. "Do ye nawt possess an ounce of patriotism in that scrawny body?"

"I'm sure the Colonel would have been a lot politer."

"Well, ye got me," retorted Jock. "And if the rumours are true and they're moving officers tae separate camps, I'll be in charge. Then ye'll see how polite I can be!"

Hyde's demeanour remained unaffected by the threat. He leaned back on his elbows, chewing on a stalk of grass. "So, what's in it for me?"

Jock rolled his eyes. Within the seclusion of a rare quiet area of the prison yard, a ruined section of the old fort, he fought the temptation to hit Hyde. "If ye get us intae the house ye're nawt tae take anything." Jock jabbed a finger at Hyde's chest. "We donnae want the Germans getting suspicious. Take nowt! We only collect intelligence."

"Well, I'm not interested then," answered Hyde.

Jock screwed his fist up. "Cigarettes. Will ye do it for cigarettes?"

Hyde straightened; his interest piqued. "Hmm, dangerous job. I might get shot."

"Aye, I know. I'm going with ye!"

A sly grin formed on Hyde's face. "Oh, dear. More dangerous. I work alone. You're a liab... lia..."

"Liability?"

"That's what I said," sniffed Hyde. "Okay, if you supply me with baccy to the end of the war, I'll do it."

"What!" exclaimed Jock. "Who knows how long this war's gonnae last? Maybe years: that's hundreds, thousands of cigarettes!"

"But you said this operation might help shorten the war," countered Hyde, his eyebrows rising in haughty triumph. "If that's true, I'll be doing myself out of baccy."

"Fine! Ye'll get yer cigarettes." Jock smiled, determined not to show how much the lad got to him. Anyway, he pondered, he'd owe nothing when the Germans shot them dead. "So, tell me your thoughts on how we do this?"

Hyde lay flat on the sandy soil, looking up at the sky. "You're lucky. I've already cased this joint. Not much else to do in camp, and I've no intention of staying locked up forever."

"So, is it possible?"

"Listen, Jock..." Hyde paused. "What's your actual name? Do you even like 'Jock'?"

The question surprised Jock, never having given the topic a thought. "Richard. I've nae problem with either name."

"Ha, recall a copper called Richard," mused Hyde. "Gave me a good old beating. I'll stick with Jock... or what about Mitch?"

"Jock will be fine!"

"Yeah, well, I'm Robbie. As I were saying, the art of housebreaking ain't no walk in the park. You've got locks, walls, dogs, witnesses, stupidity; any one of those can bugger up the job."

"Didn't ye get put inside for burglary?"

Hyde rolled onto his side to give Jock a withering stare. "Luck's the other factor, and I ran out of that."

"If that happens tae us, we're dead!" stated Jock.

"Who can tell me about this house?" asked Hyde. "I'll need details on the layout, doors, locks and how many guards in the area. Any kids inside?"

"Captain Maddox's yer man. Donnae know aboot any kids."

"Mmm, they can be erratic, so best if there ain't any. Now, there ain't no lock I can't pick, so getting into the house won't be a problem, but walking from the hut to the house won't be no picnic. We've got to stay clear of any searchlights, get through the gates and pass through enemy territory."

"Can't ye pick the gates?"

"I could, no problem," answered Hyde. "But prison locks are never on the inside, which makes things a lot harder. It'll take time. Something we don't have with those nosy guards. A key would be much better."

"How do ye propose getting one of those?"

"House breaking ain't my only talent," bragged Hyde. "I can pick pockets too."

"Yer mother must be proud," sniffed Jock. "Won't they miss them?"

Hyde sat upright, flicking the chewed grass away. "They will, unle ss... hmm, risky, but if we took copies." A smile formed. "We'd need to make moulds and cast new ones. Our materials are shoddy; they won't come out well."

"If ye can get the keys, others have the skills tae cast decent copies. Larry's a smithy," said Jock.

"I won't steal his ciggies again." Hyde rubbed his black eye.

"What aboot when we're through the gates?"

Hyde laughed. "That's always the fun bit. We get to dress up and play Germans. People take no notice of you if you don't appear out of place."

"And ye're gonna steal some uniforms, are ye?"

"No, I'm going to let you into a trade secret," whispered Hyde. "The brain's a lazy fella: don't take much fooling. I've got into a house showing a homemade police card. You wear a nice suit and talk with authority, and most people won't challenge you. We just need some minor adjustments to our uniforms. At a glance, we'll look like a guard. It'll be dark, remember."

"And ye speak German?" asked Jock, feeling less confident with each passing minute.

"Hardly a word," chirped Hyde in answer. "But we'll manage. Trust me!"

"Ha, I ain't trusting ye."

"You must if you want to succeed," laughed Hyde. "Now, how about a fag."

Chapter 5

"This donnae look anything like a guard's uniform!" moaned Jock, as Captain Butler tugged on his needle and thread, admiring the strip of black material around Jock's waist.

"Squint and look at me," suggested Hyde. "A belt in the blur, eh?"

"Aye, only tae a blind drunkard in thick fog."

"It looks fine," said Colonel Brook, observing from the side. "You're even the same age as some guards."

"Thanks, sir. That's reassuring."

Maddox gave Jock a furtive wink, rewarding his sarcasm.

"Now, if we can get the hat looking right," continued Brook, "you'll be all set. Splendid idea one of you pretending to be an officer. Less chance they'll challenge you."

"The hat's straightforward," said Hyde. "Just need a circle of wood for the top and material to cover it."

"That's 'sir' when you address the colonel, Hyde!" snapped Maddox.

Hyde's head crept up, a disinterested, rebellious stare responding to Maddox.

Jock held his breath, unsure if the rascal would follow orders, now that he held a strong hand.

"Yes, sir," answered Hyde through an ambiguous smile. "You got anything we can use that looks like a medal bar... sir?" His eyes fixed on the colonel's chest. "Don't worry, you'll get 'em back... if we survive."

Brook hesitated, caught between reluctance to give up his prized First World War ribbons and not wishing to appear uncooperative. "Oh, very well. Don't get caught or killed! That's an order!"

Hyde sniggered in his unnerving manner. "Oh, very good, sir. I like that."

"And if we have tae talk?" Jock returned to his most pressing concern.

Maddox shuffled around on his bunk, crossed arms leaning over the side. "What about: Nicht jetzt! Muss der kommandant uns sehen?"

"Meaning?"

"'Not now! The commandant vishes to see us,'" explained Maddox, in his finest German accent. "It's perfect. A phrase for every situation."

"What aboot in response tae 'stop or we'll shoot'?" challenged Jock.

"Almost all situations," corrected Maddox with a grin. "Go on, try it! Nicht jetzt..."

"Nie jets," repeated Jock.

"Okay," said an unconvinced Maddox. "Interesting with the accent. Let's you and I practise some more - lots more - when the tailors have finished."

"Och, nae!" cried Jock. "How did ye talk me intae this?"

"Stop fretting, Jock," said Brook. "The guards won't be expecting anyone to break into the commandant's house. They're only on alert for escaping prisoners."

"You got everything you need from me regarding the house, Hyde?" asked Maddox.

"The proof's in the pudding," answered Hyde. "If I come back as a ghost to haunt you, you'll know you forgot something... sir."

"Oh, jeez," wailed Jock, ignoring Butler's attempts to pin the medal ribbon on his breast.

Harcourt burst into the hut, startling the plotters, causing another whimper from Jock. "Got a circle of wood! Used the top of a stove as a template. Wasn't easy cutting. Will this do?" He passed it to Brook, who nodded, passing it on to Hyde.

"It's good enough," opined Hyde. "Who's sacrificing some of their sheeting?"

"Only fair an officer contributes that," said Brook. "I've given my medal ribbon; Harcourt has found the wood. How about you, Maddox?"

Maddox sighed. "Of course," he answered through gritted teeth. "Won't it be too light to fool the guards?"

"Not once I've trampled it in ash and dirt," said Hyde. "Brown's as good as black at night... sir."

"Wonderful!" declared Maddox, rolling away from the bunk edge to wallow in annoyance.

"Someone's swiped one of my epaulettes!" complained Harcourt, peering at his shoulder.

"Don't look at me," said Jock, pushing out his chest. "Got all the decorations I need."

"Perhaps it just fell off from wear and tear, sir," suggested Hyde, his tone deferential for a change.

"Possibly," considered Harcourt. "Though I could have sworn I had it firmly attached this morning."

"Stop whingeing, man," demanded Brook. "You still have one, and we're all aware you're a lieutenant."

Chapter 6

"Are ye ready?" asked Jock, pacing by the hut door.

Hyde sat composed on his bed, adjusting the rim of his fake German cap. "Sure, what's going on outside?" He remained unmoved.

"Infrequent sweeps by the searchlight," answered Jock, in no hurry to leave but desperate for the night's end.

"Well, chaps," said Hyde, rising to his feet. "How do I look?"

"Like Adolf bleeding Hitler himself," called out a wag in the darkness.

"I'd mistakenly shoot you if I owned a gun," joked another.

"I'd shoot you whatever uniform you wore, Hyde!" This last quip caused the whole hut to burst out in laughter.

"Keep it down, lads!" urged Jock in a hushed tone. "Don't want tae give Jerry an excuse for getting suspicious." The laughter faded until only Hyde's footsteps and Jock's whispered practice of his German phrase drifted in the air. "Nich jets mus das commandant... Nicht jets mus das commandant uns sehen... uns sehen."

"It's 'der' not 'das'," whispered Hyde, as he strode past Jock, out into the prison yard.

"Wait for me, ye rocket!" Jock's exit lacked the confidence of his partner in crime.

Despite the mild night air, sweat soaked Jock, clinging to his clothes as he skirted round the hut, following in Hyde's wake. An old fort housed their camp, one of many surrounding the north Polish town of Thorn, holding the human plunder of Hitler's successful campaigns across Europe. While saving the Germans the effort of constructing a prison from scratch, the fort offered plenty of shadowy recesses for those seeking cover.

The pair scrambled from one shadow to another, taking a long, wide route towards the inner gate. Light clouds blocked the moonlight and hid the stars Copernicus once studied from the town. The open space on their right afforded time to avoid a sweeping searchlight. Twice they scrambled for cover from its burning inquisition, but little slowed their progress.

"Well, now things get interesting," whispered Hyde, rummaging in his pocket as they hung back in sight of the gate. His pickpocket boast proved well-founded. A light brush of the German sergeant on daily inspection dispossessed him of his keys. Hands relayed the prize to a hut, each pressed into a block of clay, returned to Hyde and, finally, back to their ignorant owner's belt in a seamless operation. Smelting metal proved a tougher proposition. To the lasting detriment of a stove, they produced something resembling a key, but did it have the strength to turn a lock?

Hyde ran the teeth of each key between his fingertips. "It's this one," he declared in Jock's ear. "You stay here until I give the signal!" Without noticing Jock's gaping mouth, poised to ask a question, the thief dashed off.

"What's the signal?" mumbled Jock to himself, crouching in the shadows. He stared into the charcoal night, able to make out Hyde loitering by the gate. A gentle snort of laughter left his nostrils. He does look like a German guard in this light!

Close enough to pick up the off-duty revelry from the guards' barracks, Jock drew in the Germanic ambience, whispering his rehearsed line over and over.

"Psst… psst."

Jock looked up to see a shadow gesticulating in his direction. With a brief glance around to check for the searchlight, he sprinted forward, his long legs carrying him to Hyde's side. "Ye call that a signal?" he hissed.

"I've been waving for a minute!" retorted Hyde. "Now, shut up! Silence from now on."

Strangler's hands morphed behind Hyde's back as he pushed open the first gate, but Jock let his annoyance dissipate with a deep breath.

They walked down a fenced path, their pace measured and slow. Jock yearned to search around, to spot the spotters, but he recalled Hyde's instructions: "You must convey yourself with the arrogant authority of a Nazi officer."

Without warning, Hyde grabbed his partner's shoulder, pulling him down. Jock tried to speak, but Hyde lifted a finger to his lips, gesturing left. A guard paced along the fence, nearing the next gate in their path, too close for their bluff to work. To their horror, the guard stopped, turning towards them. He shook the gate's frame, testing the lock. Hyde's grip tightened on Jock's shoulder. Jock held his breath; frightened breathing would expose them. Each second felt an eternity. Until, with a carefree whistle, the guard turned, continuing his patrol. Jock's bursting lungs savoured a rush of fresh air, as Hyde's hand slipped from his shoulder.

Hyde gestured with a wipe of his brow before raising his other hand to show off a makeshift blade.

"What have ye got that for!" spluttered Jock, struggling hard not to shout out in anger.

"Dead men tell no tales," whispered Hyde, straightening to full height.

"They do when the only suspects are prisoners!" hissed Jock. "They won't have any qualms aboot executing ten innocent men for one dead guard. We're tae leave nae trace we were here."

"Quit yacking and get moving before another guard comes round!" huffed Hyde.

As Hyde wrestled with the gate lock, Jock shuffled behind, his eyes scanning every angle for the enemy. Two watchtowers loomed within sight, their searchlights scanning only areas they expected prisoners to be.

Jock cringed at the clang and screech of the lock and bolt moving, sure all the camp heard. Silence prevailed. Hyde pulled the gate open, motioning his companion through. As Jock passed, Hyde held up the key, buckled at a right-angle. Their luck held.

Clear of the fences and within the German quarters, they marched forward in synchronised step, something Hyde never managed on the parade ground. A guard hut stood a mere 10 yards away, with only a pair of boot toes visible. Jock adjusted his hat until it sat straight and lifted his chin. He may not be an officer, but aping one was easy. As they strode past the hut, maintaining as much distance as possible, Jock turned his head away, mumbling nonsense, pretending to be in deep conversation with Hyde. He dared not glance towards the guard.

"Ja, kapitan," said Hyde, loud enough to reach the guard.

The ad-lib surprised Jock, but the latent actor within warmed to his role. "Gut," he replied, not as loud or confident as Hyde, but from the corner of his eye he saw the thief's mouth curl to a smile. No challenge emerged from the sentry, and, with the success of their charade, Jock grew into his part.

They entered an open stretch of grass and avenues. Germans on their regular business speckled the outer reaches of their vision. Ahead lay multiple paths. Maddox had provided clear directions, but with the reality of choice, Jock questioned his memory. Was it right or straight ahead before bearing right? His steps fell out of sync with Hyde's as he hesitated, when two Germans appeared from the right. He veered away, taking the path in front. A hand grabbed his tunic, yanking him back to Hyde's side and over to the right path.

"Bravado!" hissed Hyde from the side of his mouth.

The guards weaved along the path, supporting each other, beer bottles in hand. "Die nacht is jung und die mädchen sind wunderschön," one called out.

Jock's mouth remained taut in fear. An elbow struck him in his ribs. "Err... Nic jets der sehen commandant."

"Sieg Heil," added Hyde, with a Nazi salute.

The drunk soldiers attempted to salute, but found the action further hindered their balance. Their faces, mouths ajar with muddled confusion, followed the two strangers as they passed with purposeful haste. "Kann ihr bier nicht halten!" commented one with a shake of his bottle.

Hyde risked a peek, then smiled at Jock. "Our luck's in. Pissed as a newt! Could have been Churchill and they wouldn't have cared."

With a grimace, Jock held a finger to his lips.

They took the next trail left, past empty stables and, after 20 yards, looked onto a neat, cultivated garden and cottage. Hyde gave a thumbs-up and reached into his pocket, withdrawing a thin stick of metal. "Lights are out," he whispered. "All's good. Keep a watch out while I try the lock!"

Jock nodded, following Hyde up the path to the door.

"Not here!" Hyde waved Jock away. "Back at the corner. If we're disturbed, I want some notice."

Retreating down the path, Jock inspected the vegetable patch, keen to see the famous carrots. He crouched at the corner of the stable wall and removed his hat to scratch his head. Distant, faint carousing carried on the wind every now and again, but otherwise silence hung over the night. Jock spared regular backward glances, checking on Hyde's progress. The youngster's hunched figure showed no sign of movement in the poor light, but, after a minute, the shade of the door changed. It was open.

Jock scurried back up the path to find Hyde sitting on the ground. Not daring to talk, Jock signalled his confusion. With a roll of his eyes, Hyde lifted a foot and waved it, then removed his boots. The logic dawned on Jock and he followed suit.

With footwear discarded, they crept into the hall of the cottage, its homely smell bringing a cruel reminder of better times. Jock remained a yard back, allowing his companion space to move and inspect their surroundings: the only familiar room, the kitchen, observed by Maddox from the garden. All four other doors led to the unknown; all four other doors looked identical. Behind one slept the commandant and his wife. Behind another, their target: the study.

As Jock struggled with uncertainty and anxiety, Hyde circled the hall, spending a moment assessing each option. Then, with serene confidence, he gripped the handle of the far-left door. Jock held his breath.

In the blink of an eye, Hyde disappeared into the room, leaving his companion flushed with angst. Jock edged towards the room, his eyes flicking both ways in anticipation of discovery.

Since no commotion stirred within, Jock slipped through the door, sighing on discovery of a serene drawing room. Hyde stood before an open desk, under a sliver of moonlight, rifling through a pile of papers.

"That's ma job!" hissed Jock, hurrying across.

A condescending finger lifted to Hyde's mouth.

"Ye've nae clue what ye're looking for," continued Jock, unperturbed.

Hyde lifted a piece of paper and smiled. "This?"

Jock grabbed the sheet, squinting to read it, but failing in the poor light. He shuffled across to the window, glancing out for signs of movement, holding the note in the moonlight. A crude grasp of German allowed him to make out one in every five words, but he recognised it as a telegraph. Running his finger across each word, he made out the commandant's name, dates and times, some locations and the identity of an SS officer. How Hyde identified the correct scrap of paper remained a mystery. If only he could understand more.

Hyde leaned across and whispered in his ear. "Goldbarren." In reply to Jock's quizzical face, he tapped the paper.

With a further scan, Jock discovered the word at the end of the telegraph. "Gold?" he blurted, a little too loud.

Hyde cringed. "Gold bullion and keep it down!"

"How do ye know?"

"Dunno," he whispered. "You pick these things up..."

A soft creak from the hallway froze the intruders. Jock stared towards the drawing room door, awaiting company. He noticed Hyde edge sideways, the makeshift blade in one hand, the other reaching for a figurine above the desk. The door crept open, but no face appeared. Jock blinked in surprise before refocusing downwards. With thumb in mouth and sleepy eyes, a girl of four stood in the doorway. Hyde lifted the statue above his head, stepping towards the child.

"What are ye doing?" hissed Jock, his fingers clasping Hyde's raised wrist.

"Let go!" Hyde moved the blade up to Jock's chest.

Jock's grip remained tight. "She's a wee bairn. Ye'll nawt touch her!"

"She's a witness." Hyde pressed his face up to his comrade's. "Or do you want to be shot? She won't feel a thing."

"Have ye ever been tae Glasgow?"

"No, why?"

With a jolt of his neck, Jock sprung his forehead against Hyde's face, sending the lad to the floor with a crash. "That's their special greeting."

Hyde sat in stunned silence as the little girl sobbed.

"Hey, donnae cry," urged Jock, bending to stroke her cheek, his ears alert for any movement caused by the rumpus. "Let's get ye back tae bed. Do ye have a doll?"

"Ye stay there!" Jock turned and glared at Hyde before guiding the girl to her room without another sound uttered.

"Put everything back as we found it and let's get oot of here!" commanded Jock on his return.

"You've signed our death sentence," stated Hyde, back on his feet and clasping his throbbing nose.

"I can live with that."

Hyde's stern face broke into a smile, the aggression gone. "Ha, I like that."

"Just put it all back!" Jock passed the telegraph to his companion and returned to the hall.

When Hyde emerged, he nodded at Jock, confirming all was back in place, and thumbed towards the front door. The house remained as silent and peaceful as on their arrival.

The journey back possessed all the risks of their escape, but with the job done, it felt somehow easier. Perhaps with a boost in confidence, they fitted the part so much better, strolling along like proper German soldiers. The keys bent but did their job, and within ten minutes they slid into the hut, welcomed by a chorus of snores.

"Forgot to ask Maddox about the kids!" cursed Hyde, kicking off his boots.

"What did ye plan tae do tae her?" demanded Jock, glaring at his companion.

"Calm down! I was just going to threaten her, not hit her. You know, 'tell anyone, and we'll be back to get you.'"

"Ye can threaten in German, can ye? That's nawt how it looked tae me. Ye are some lowlife scum, Hyde," hissed Jock. "That uniform suited ye."

"Keep it down!" came a mumbled complaint from the darkness.

"She'll wake up in the morning," continued Jock, his tone lowered, "thinking it was a dream. All forgotten by breakfast."

"Mmm," mused Hyde, as he slid under his blanket, the Scot still towering over him. "And if she doesn't and tells Daddy?"

"Then Daddy will tell her it was a dream. Och, ye donnae have kids. Ye probably did nae have a childhood." Jock wandered back to his own bunk and dropped onto his straw mattress.

"I'm not a Nazi or evil, Jock," whispered Hyde. "I just do stupid things."

"Aye, I know, lad. Now, go tae sleep."

Adrenaline coursed through Jock's body and, as he collapsed backwards with boots still on, an overwhelming weakness swamped every part. Not since being taken prisoner had such a sensation engulfed him. Despite his fatigue, his racing mind would offer little sleep.

Chapter 7

"Take the hat off, Hyde!" ordered Colonel Brook. "You're not a Nazi anymore."

"Ja, mein Führer," responded Hyde, clicking his heels together and removing the cap.

Captain Maddox, standing behind the jester, clouted the back of Hyde's head. "Your deeds last night saved you from something more severe, you insolent idiot. What happened to your nose?"

"Bumped into something. It were very dark." Hyde smiled, milking his newfound credibility, the clash with Jock forgotten.

"You don't look so good yourself, Jock," observed Maddox. "Everything all right?"

"Och, aye," answered Jock, fighting off a yawn. "Lack of sleep."

"You can catch up on some later, while the men have their recreation period," offered Brook, tending his moustache with a thoughtful stroke.

"Bullion," uttered Lieutenant Morbin, echoing an earlier discussion with an intrigued lilt. "But how much, well, that's a mystery."

"There's lots we donnae know, sir," said Jock, content with his night's work but uneasy now his colleagues tried to fill the blanks in their knowledge.

"Gold from the east can mean only one thing," mused Brook. "They're shipping Russian loot to the Fatherland."

"They say Belgium was stripped of its art and treasures," offered Harcourt.

"So, lots of gold," stated Hyde, with eyes aglow.

"I fear you're right, Hyde," said Brook. "All helping to finance the war. Damn! If only we could do something. There's no way to get the information to Blighty in time to make a difference."

"That's if our interpretation of the date of arrival is correct," chimed in Jock.

"I'm sure it is," said Maddox. "You saw no other date on the telegraph?"

"Nae, 2nd October and nowt else."

"Two weeks away and staying for one night only," mused Harcourt. "Even if our boys sent a bomber, what would they bomb? If the bullion's kept in the town or a village, the Poles are in danger, and if in the prison, we are!"

"Yes, I fear we must face the truth," sighed Brook, turning to Jock. "You risked yourselves in vain. I'm sorry we put you through that. At least you're sure no one saw you or suspected anything?"

"Aye," said Jock, his tone far from convincing as he recalled the little girl.

"He's a natural at it," chirped Hyde. "After the war, I might employ our Jock."

As Jock sat sullen, nervous laughter moved around the circle.

"There's one thing we ain't considered," added Hyde.

"And what would that be?" asked the colonel, trying to hide his indifference at the vagabond's opinion.

"We steal the gold ourselves. What better alibi does a thief need than being couped up in prison?"

A shocked silence followed until Harcourt began to chuckle. "This isn't a high street bank in Chipping Norton, my good fellow. Nazi thugs with machine guns guard it, for starters."

"Not forgetting we're locked up!" threw in Butler, his first contribution to the de-brief.

"It would be like breaking out of Brixton prison to steal the crown jewels," said Brook. "And then breaking back into Brixton. Impossible!"

Hyde shrugged. "You not heard of Tommy Keeler?"

"Was he at Lord Collingwood's garden party in the spring?" quipped Maddox.

Through a mischievous smile, Hyde responded. "Maybe, but not by invitation nor for the drinks. Nah, he broke out of Wandsworth to do a jewellery heist."

"Then broke back into prison for an alibi?" queried Harcourt with a disbelieving frown.

"Sort of," chortled Hyde. "Getaway car broke down, and he got caught in the act. Earned another seven years to his sentence."

"Well, there you go," exclaimed Brook. "Can't be done. Ridiculous notion."

"But Tommy weren't the brightest."

"You don't say!" spluttered Harcourt.

"What I mean is, with better planning it could have worked," pressed Hyde.

"Enough!" demanded Colonel Brook. "Thank you for last night, Private Hyde, but I'm drawing a line under this. You can return to your hut. Go shave and keep out of trouble!"

Hyde rose and shook his head in disappointment. "Shame, 'cause they never found Tommy's diamonds. They'll be awaiting him when he gets out."

"Out!" shouted Maddox.

"Sorry to have to lumber you with our problem child, Jock," said Brook, as Hyde departed. "Hope he didn't take too many risks last night."

"The lad knows his business," confessed Jock. "Don't suppose anyone taught him right from wrong."

"I suppose not," admitted the Colonel. "But I do wish he'd pronounce his aitches! Now, try catching up on some sleep."

***

The noise of laughter and idle chatter greeted Jock as he entered his hut. A morning of sport and exercise awaited the men, who buzzed with anticipation. Hyde, less enamoured of the prospect, stood within a small group trading cigarettes. He caught Jock's eye and wandered over.

"You didn't have a lot to say," he said.

"Said all I needed," replied Jock. "I reported back on what we found."

"No, I mean about stealing the gold," said Hyde. "The colonel's got no balls. Didn't give it a second thought."

"It's called brains," retorted Jock. "Ye shouldnae be disrespectful of him."

"Jock," began Hyde with an almost mature air, "we're not with the officers now. Come on! What did you make of my idea?"

"Ye really think it's possible?"

"Nothing worth having can be got without taking risks," answered Hyde. "Haven't worked out how yet, but you never start with the how."

"I'm all for giving Jerry a bloody nose while having a concrete alibi, but the 'how' does seem rather important."

"That's the spirit," said Hyde. "The glitter of gold does wonders for my imagination. I'll conjure something up."

"The motivation of greed," sighed Jock with a plaintive shake of his head. "Ye planning on posting the gold home?"

Hyde laughed. "I'll do what Tommy Keeler did: make it vanish and return later."

"Schnell! Schnell! Auf parade." The summons alarm clanged, accompanying the shouting from outside.

"Bloody hell!" cursed Jock. "We're nawt due roll-call. What's Jerry up tae?"

"Perhaps Little Miss Commandant spoke to Daddy," suggested Hyde, prompting Jock's eyebrows to rise in horror. "Ah, don't worry. I do denial rather well. Just stay relaxed."

"What if she points us oot?"

"Last night you said we were actors in her dreams."

"Are German girls different tae British ones?" Jock edged to the door to watch the prisoners run out onto the parade ground. "Och, come on, let's see what they've got in store for us!"

They joined their colleagues in the practised formation, Jock craning his neck to inspect the Germans from their position at the rear. Hyde slouched with his usual disregard for authority, while Jock fidgeted, his mind racing with negative possibilities.

"Relax!" said Hyde. "I've never seen a more guilty face."

"Easy for ye tae say," retorted Jock. "Ye've practised."

"Aaa-tenn-TION!" came a command, followed by a sharp straightening of the ranks and a thud of boots.

Jock spied the broad hat of the camp commandant. As his face came into view, Jock recognised the resemblance to his daughter. She was her daddy's girl.

An aide-de-camp placed a soapbox on the ground, allowing the commandant to rise above his captive audience. "Gentlemen, my apologies for interrupting your Sunday leisure." The commandant's accent hinted at time spent in England, the hard, Teutonic edge smoothed. "Officers, step forvard! Sergeants, step forvard"

Confused expressions passed along the line of officers. Colonel Brook took the initiative, striding forward, followed by the others, the sergeants making their way through the ranks.

"Your time here is at an end," announced the commandant. "You are to be transferred to a new camp…"

While each expected such news, a hubbub broke out among the lined-up prisoners.

"SILENCE!" yelled the aide-de-camp. The guards behind the commandant tightened the grips on their guns. Before the situation got out of hand, Colonel Brook signalled silence and the uproar subsided, military discipline returning.

"You are to be transferred to a new camp," repeated the commandant, "for officers and sergeants alone." The German laughed. "This is gut news, nein? Rank and file stay behind mit no vone to boss them, ja!" His laughter grew louder in the following silence.

"They're trying tae hamstring us," muttered Jock.

"You'll be in charge, corporal," whispered Hyde.

"I've always been in charge, laddie," said Jock. "Now, I'll just have no one tae give orders tae!"

Those within earshot sniggered, misleading the commandant as to the success of his joke.

"Collect your belongings," instructed the commandant. "Trucks vill be here in thirty minutes to transfer you."

"Half hour?" An anonymous voice sprang from the ranks, expressing the disbelief felt by all.

The aide-de-camp readied himself to bellow again, but the commandant stopped him with a raised hand. "No time for goodbyes. Pack now or you loaded onto trunks vith no belongings. You may dismiss your men, colonel!"

Brook looked shell-shocked, his mouth wide in disbelief. "C... Herr commandant, a word if you will!" His raised hand dropped to his side in dejection as the German vanished without acknowledgement. "Damn!"

Lieutenant Morbin sidled across and whispered in the colonel's ear.

"Quite right!" announced Brook. "Like minds and all that. Sergeant Bellows, keep the men on parade a little longer, please. I want to address them."

"Stand at attention!" yelled Bellows. "No one dismissed you."

"Thank you, Bellows," said Colonel Brook, before clearing his throat. "Now, men, it would appear our captors fear us. They have taken away our guns, marched us halfway across Europe and placed us behind wire, but still old Tommy gives them the jitters. They want to divide us, remove your leaders to pacify the lions. Once again, Jerry fails to appreciate who he's picked a fight with. The cast that made us all includes British spirit, mightier than steel and longer lasting. We will not bend under their torment, but like the sword under the blacksmith's hammer, grow stronger with each hit, ready to strike back at the first opportunity. I expect you all to uphold the standards of the British army and do me proud. God save the king!"

"God save the king!" cried every prisoner.

"Three cheers for Colonel Brook!" urged a solitary voice. "Hip hip…"

"Hooray!"

As the third and final cheer faded, the Colonel gave a curt nod and departed, his bottom lip firm in resolve.

"That's the man ye disrespected earlier," commented Jock. "Had he ordered the men tae attack the guards, they would have done so."

"He has a fine way with those words," replied Hyde. "I'll give him that. But words don't get things done."

"Dismissed!" cried Sergeant Bellows, causing the lines to disintegrate in a flash.

"Some do," observed Jock with a wry smile, as Hyde dashed off, happy to follow the latest order.

Chapter 8

The black exhaust fumes hung in the air as the truck pulled away. Jock observed from the hut steps, his heart sad, his mind daring to wonder if the officers' departure meant more food for those left behind. Constant hunger occupied the men's thoughts from when they rose to when they laid their heads on a pillow at night, and on into their dreams. But other worries preoccupied Jock: no one stood above him in rank now. Would order in the camp disintegrate? Who would he turn to for advice? It felt lonely at the top.

As the deep roar of the truck engine faded, a flurry of activity consumed the German guards. Shouts and commands echoed across the parade ground. The rhythmic stomp of marching men emerged, and through the gates of the prison a column of shabby, captive soldiers entered. Intrigued, Jock stepped forward onto the sandy earth to inspect. They were not British. Gaunt, haunted faces occupied emaciated bodies, clothed in oversized uniforms of the Polish army. Jock rubbed his chin. This would add an interesting dynamic to the camp.

"That didn't take long!"

Jock turned to find his pal, Archie Peters, addressing him. "Aye, I guess they've planned this all along."

"Poor bastards look in need of a meal," commented Peters.

"Suspect we'll all be like that in a few months."

"The walking dead."

Jock raised an eyebrow. "What d'ye mean by that?"

"Being stuck in this place is only going to lead to one thing," answered Peters.

"Hmm," pondered Jock.

"How's your Polish?"

"Non-existent," admitted Jock. "But ma gut says we're gonnae get along."

"Oh, why's that?"

"We both hate the Nazis!"

Peters laughed. "A universal tongue. Perhaps we should say hello?"

"Let them settle, lad!" said Jock. "Last thing they need now is a Scot and a Yorkshireman making strange noises at them."

"I might teach them cricket," quipped Peters. "Yes, a Test match on the manicured grass of Stalag XXA."

"Och, nae! They're supposed tae be our allies. I wouldn't wish that even on the Germans."

"You philistine," ribbed Peters. "I'll have you converted by the end of this war."

"Will that give us time tae finish the game? I've heard it drags."

"You've never seen my googly!"

About forty Poles stood in formation on the parade ground, twice the number of the British just departed. Despite their sorry state, all stood proud, unwilling to let their captors see them any other way.

"Math ain't my strong subject," said Peters, as he lit a cigarette. "But where are they going to fit? They'll have to build another hut."

"They've nae intention of making us comfortable," said Jock, sitting down on the bottom step.

"Does that mean less food as well?" Peters spat some loose tobacco to the ground.

Jock held his tongue. Discussions of German cruelty and neglect did no one any good.

"You were right!" declared Peters in disgust as the Poles broke their formation. "They're putting them all into the officers' hut. What do they expect them to do, sleep two to a bed?"

"They donnae care," mulled Jock. "The more successful the Hun is on the battlefield, the cosier it'll get in here."

"What about the Geneva Convention?"

"As meaningless as the Munich Agreement tae Herr Hitler."

"Jesus, I'd like to give him a bloody nose," exclaimed Peters.

"Aye," said Jock, nodding. "Take care with the Lord's name though."

"Sorry, Jock. I sometimes get carried away when thinking about the war."

"Aye," repeated Jock, his mind drifting off elsewhere.

Chapter 9

A droplet of water, building at the point of a leaf, conceded defeat to gravity and fell on Jock's forehead, mixing with the layer of drizzle and sweat. He wiped a sleeve across his brow, preventing it from trickling and tickling down his nose. Blowing out his lips, Jock re-gripped the saw handle and nodded to the man holding the other end. This weather was not conducive to cutting down trees. The rain on the steel clung to the flesh of the tree. Only with a steady rhythm did they make progress. Jock rolled his eyes to the heavens.

"Cholera!" uttered Jock's companion, as the blade's teeth jammed again. He kept repeating the word, and Jock soon recognised it as a Polish curse. Without speaking, the pair extracted the tool, easing it back into the narrow cut, building up their rhythm as they reached the uncut flesh again.

Jock took an instant liking to the Pole. Despite a row of crooked teeth, he possessed a warm smile, and beyond the tired eyes, Jock recognised a kind soul. He introduced himself as Piotr, his English quite sufficient to make himself understood. "Piotr – you say Peter, no?"

"Aye, I'll call ye Peter. Ma name is Jock. Nawt sure Jock has a Polish equivalent."

Piotr repeated his name "Yok."

"Good enough," laughed Jock.

The first days with their new camp companions resembled the first days at school. Old friends stuck together, assessing the newcomers, avoiding communication beyond a shy acknowledgement. Only when thrown together with the work parties did the frost thaw. Photos of loved ones, their corners battered, the images marred by folds, emerged from pockets, shared to start a conversation, a common ground discovered through their sweethearts and families.

Although under the watchful eye of the sentry, the work allowed for chat.

"What did ye do before the war?" enquired Jock.

With a hesitation as he translated in his mind, Piotr replied. "University sdudenk. From Kraków. In south."

"What were ye studying," asked Jock, impressed by his companion's education.

"Err, I..." Piotr searched for the English. "Prawo: law."

Jock straightened, observing Piotr. "And ye didn't become an officer?"

Piotr frowned.

"Why nawt an officer?" Jock touched his sleeve, saluted and pointed at the Pole.

Piotr's smile carried regret. "No time. Vor over for Polska.

"Vhat about you, Yok? Vhat did you do?"

"Gardener."

Piotr nodded, but Jock, sensing doubt, mimed digging and pruning to clarify.

"Ogrodik!" exclaimed Piotr, holding a make-believe flower to his nose, his eyes drifting off with nostalgia.

Each with a smile, they repositioned the saw and began pushing and pulling until the satisfying grate of teeth through wood announced progress.

***

As the cry for lunch sounded, the rain stopped, a partial rainbow failing to lift spirits. The soaked workers queued to collect a dry chunk of bread and an apple, before splitting into groups, prisoners into their nationalities, reclining on the grass just beyond the woods, the local peasants separate among the pack animals.

"Got a damn blister!" moaned Jock.

"I got blisters on my blisters," countered Peters, examining his hands.

"Aye, but ma hands weren't like a bairn's bottom."

"I've suffered my share of paper cuts over the years," quipped Peters, drawing in a lungful of smoke from a cigarette. "Us clerks get no sympathy."

"That's cos ye donnae produce anything... except delays!" Banter was their best weapon against the drudge and despair.

"You wait, Mitchell. When this war is over, I'll make sure each marrow you grow requires a completed form before you can harvest your crop."

"I'll have tae learn tae write then," said Jock, introducing the self-deprecating element of their act. A curl of cigarette smoke leaked through his smirk.

"Oh, I was looking forward to reading your memoirs: check if I get a mention." Peters ripped off a piece of bread with his teeth, following with a chomp into the apple.

"Ye're supposed tae save the apple for dessert, ye fool!"

"Mmm." Peters tried to answer through stuffed cheeks, encouraging his own chewing with rippling fingers. "It helps soften... mmm... the bread."

No stranger to stale bread, Jock restrained himself from following Peters' example, dipping it in a small pool of rainwater and moulding each bite into a doughy lump.

"They seem a good bunch." Peters nodded at the Poles. "My one doesn't speak a word of English, but he's a good worker."

"Suppose that's why they've paired us up," said Jock. "Thought we couldn't communicate. Mine's a wee blether box. Cannae be over 19 though."

Peters pushed himself up, his attention caught by something. "What the hell's Hyde up to? He's having a confab with the Poles. I've seen him try it on with the girls before, but those folk are somewhat hairy."

"They won't own anything worth stealing," said Jock, looking across at Hyde in discussion with two men. "But I bet he's scheming up something."

"Eh up! Here he comes," said Peters. "Business is concluded."

"Looks like he's coming tae chat tae us!"

Hyde paused before them, his crooked smile greeting curious eyes.

"What are ye up tae, Hyde?" asked Jock, crunching into his apple. "I hope ye're nawt letting His Majesty's diplomatic service down."

"On the contrary," answered Hyde, lowering himself to a crouch. "I've been building bridges."

"In fluent Polish?" queried Peters.

"Nah, in the tongue of His Majesty. Quite a few of them speak English."

"Better than you then," teased Peters, getting a withering look in reply.

"Ignore him, Hyde," said Jock, appreciating the need for some ego massaging. "The king donnae understand a word I say either."

"I've got it, Jock!" declared Hyde, a glow of enthusiasm bursting from his eyes.

"Got what?"

"A plan to steal the gold."

"Och, what ye talking aboot!" exclaimed Jock. "We put that tae bed when Brook and co left."

"What gold?" piped in Peters.

"That's just it," continued Hyde, ignoring Peters. "With the officers leaving, a solution is presented. They didn't have the balls for starters, but with our new inmates we can communicate with the locals."

"You mean the Poles?"

"What gold?"

"Yes, we now have our inside man!" enthused Hyde. "They'll get messages out to the peasants, who will organise things."

"What makes ye think they'll help us?" pressed Jock. "Or that we can trust them? They'll as likely tattle on us for a reward."

"Jock! Jock! My dear friend," cooed Hyde. "We have something on offer far more precious than a piddling reward. It corrupts the purest of souls. Gold!"

"WHAT GOLD?" yelled Peters.

Heads turned and Jock cringed. "Keep yer voice down, ye damn eejit!"

"Tell me what you're talking about!" demanded Peters.

"I'll give ye the details later," reassured Jock. "We may get tae kick Hitler in his one good goolie, and Hyde's gonnae convince me it won't get us killed. Aren't ye?"

"Well," began Hyde with a grin, "if you do as I say, you should be okay."

"Doesn't sound too convinced to me," said Peters.

"Nae," agreed Jock. "Like a politician! Wants us tae trust him, while being untrustworthy. The Hyde I know won't even be willing to split the spoils with our Polish brethren."

"Hear me out!" pleaded Hyde, appearing needy for the first time since crossing paths with Jock. "Listen, I'll confess I'm not in this for king and country. But the gold ain't everything for me, neither. It's the challenge. The kudos I'll have when home will last a lifetime. Gold can't buy that where I'm from, though I'll take my share. The Poles can take their cut too. Now, will you let me tell you how we're gonna pull this little beauty off?"

Jock glanced at Peters, who returned a bemused expression and shrugged. "Okay, but ye'd better hurry. Before old Fritz warms up his throat to order us back tae the woods in a few minutes."

"Excellent!" exclaimed Hyde, rubbing his hands together. "You're going to love this."

Chapter 10

"Our SS visitor is here," remarked Peters, bending to tie a shoelace by the barbed-wire perimeter. "No question."

"Aye," replied Jock, turning away from the Germans and towards their hut with a nonchalant air. "Never seen the guards so smart."

"Or alert," added Peters.

"Hmm, that's ma concern. Last thing we want is Jerry paying us too much attention."

"Oh, the irony!" lamented Peters with dramatic flair as he climbed to his feet. "To be under watch seven days a week and never noticed! Crushes a man's ego."

Jock laughed in appreciation. "They can check under ma bed or beneath the floorboards. As long as they've been neglecting ma face."

"'Tis a noble face, Jock. One worthy of a statue and, without question, Ayr has room for one."

"Shut up, ye fool. Nae pigeon's landing on ma head."

The summons alarm clanged.

"Well," said Peters, "here we go. If we don't have time to speak later, good luck."

"Thanks. Where's Hyde? He'd better nawt be bottling oot!"

They sauntered to the marshalling zone, joining the column forming two by two with a mix of British and Poles. Jock acknowledged Piotr and his friend Jan with a subtle nod and glanced backwards, seeking Hyde. The rascal had convinced him with his plan, made him do all the arrangements and now... Jock sucked in a lungful of air as he caught sight of Hyde emerging from the hut with his casual, slinking gait. Releasing the breath, Jock winked at Peters.

The guards shouted commands in a tone fiercer than usual, haranguing the column onwards as the gates opened. Jock pushed his cap forward, lowering his head.

"The Rubicon!" whispered Peters, as they passed through under the stern inspection of the guards and barking hounds.

Under a grey sky, they marched along a narrow road, away from Thorn, into the open countryside. Peasants labouring in the fields spared them a glance before returning to their backbreaking work. Flat and expansive, the landscape lacked the beauty of home for Jock: neither the rugged coastline of Ayr where he grew up, nor the green valleys of Kent where he now lived.

Over the grinding wheels of the tool cart following behind, a prisoner began whistling a familiar tune. Soon the whole column joined in — the Poles, new converts, but no less tuneful. Even the guards, more relaxed away from the camp, appreciated the lift in mood, oblivious to the portent of rebellion.

Jock walked with a lighter step, his nerves somehow under control. Even when Hyde conveyed his plan a week ago, Jock accepted all the foolhardy elements without a blink. The officers' departure did signal a watershed and, for Jock, it symbolised another defeat, reinforcing their helplessness against the whim of the Germans. No news filtered through of a fightback since Dunkirk, and even the Russian campaign appeared an inevitable victory for Hitler's troops. When the fox raided his chicken coop at home, Jock took the fight to the fox.

Two young boys, about 11, cycled down the road. They pulled up and pushed their bicycles onto the grass verge, allowing the prisoners to pass.

The Polish prisoners called out to them. "Dzień dobry." "Jak się masz?" "Błogosław ojczyznę!"

One boy blushed; the other, less inhibited, hollered back a greeting. Jock doffed his cap, eliciting an intrigued stare. The scene brought thoughts to the surface from his youth, of cheering the exotic circus folk as they passed through his village, fascination and fear combining in his innocent eyes.

After ten minutes, the column turned off the road onto a field, tramping across sticky mud until the sentry ordered a halt. Jock bit his lip, a wave of concern washing through him. The open landscape provided little cover. A band of trees lay about 100 yards south, but their immediate surroundings offered nothing more than crops, mud and ditches. Jock sought Hyde, discovering him approaching with similar apprehension.

"This ain't good!" whispered Hyde. "The one day we need a hiding place, and we're as exposed as Lady Godiva!"

"Perhaps we should cancel?" suggested Jock.

"Let me think!" snapped Hyde.

Jock refrained from clipping his ear, instead joining the queue for a tool. "What they got us doing taeday?" he asked the man in front.

"We're to dig up the old crops and burn them. Get the field ready for the winter and planting in the spring."

With a nod of his head, Jock surveyed the field of sorry-looking potato plants. Another day of strenuous work awaited.

From the corner of his eye, Jock caught Piotr jogging to catch up with the other prisoners. Beyond, loitering at the field's edge, stood the two boys on their bikes surveying the activity. They must have followed the column. A guard spotted them and shouted a threat. The boys lugged their bikes around and pedalled away.

After Jock selected a battered, blunt spade, he assessed the head with a thump to the cart, then stood at the end of a furrow, awaiting orders. A hand gripped his shoulder, causing him to swing around in alarm.

"Calm down! It's me." A furtive Hyde stood behind, as though about to offer stolen goods. "We're all good. Your mate Piotr has fixed things."

Jock looked across to see Piotr loitering behind Hyde. "How?"

"The lads on the bikes are part of the network," explained Hyde, his words spoken to the open sky, though heard by Jock. "Our comrades passed a code to confirm all was good when we passed on the road. They carried word to our outside contacts. Piotr proposed some practical changes. You don't mind getting wet?"

Unable to help himself, Jock turned to glare at Hyde. "What does that mean? I donnae have time for games!"

"The ditches," said Hyde. "The one behind the cart. We nip in between to change. Ain't perfect, but with the lid of the tool crate raised, we'll have some protection from Jerry's roaming eye. The tufts of grass should hide us when we're in the ditch."

A sentry shrieked at the malingering Hyde, ordering him to the cart.

"We must build the fire tae the side of the cart!" gabbled out Jock. "Use the smoke for additional cover."

"Nice one," mumbled Hyde, as he gave the guard a cheeky wave and ambled off to collect a spade.

Jock caught Piotr's fear-filled eyes as he followed Hyde and nodded in appreciation.

***

A cold, autumn wind cut across the exposed land, drawing the prisoners together around the raging fire consuming the morning's harvest of withered potato plants. Some slipped half-rotten potatoes into the edges, where the embers of stems glowed, hoping to add to their meagre lunch.

"It's only going to get colder," said Peters. "Damn cold!"

"Aye," agreed Jock. "Let's hope some Red Cross parcels arrive soon with woollies." Then with stoic resignation he stripped off his tunic, folded and laid it over the cart's wheel. He placed his cap on top.

"You going to be okay?" enquired Peters.

"Sure, once I get working again," said Jock, rubbing his hands together, a vest the only thing keeping the cold from his chest.

None of the other prisoners paid his contrary action any attention, while three others - Hyde, Piotr and Jan - followed suit. The two Poles shivered in the wind, their ribs protruding through their vests.

"Wouldn't take much to blow them over," observed Peters.

"Ye can understand why they volunteered," remarked Jock. "Jerry's stripped them of their homeland, their freedom, and is now trying tae destroy their souls."

"But their spirit burns stronger."

"Aye, that it does. Come on! I need tae get working again."

***

The afternoon dragged, but Jock worked with an enthusiasm unbecoming of a POW. His labours kept his mind occupied and body warm. As soon as the order to finish came, he walked down his furrow, mixing with the other prisoners crowding around the tool cart.

Jock sidled up to Peters, passed his spade to his friend, then slipped to the back of the group. The wind swung round, blowing the smoke from the dying fire across the cart. A promising omen. Both sentries, as expected, sought warmth by the fire, their view disrupted through a haze, as the prisoners, their manner clumsy and slow, milled about stacking the tools.

"We set?" whispered Jock to Hyde, as the latter wormed his way through the crush to the rear. Piotr and Jan emerged a second later.

"We are now," answered Hyde, coughing as the smoke caught his throat. "Pete, you go first! Give the signal and convey any necessary instructions. And remember, be fast... Oh, remind them to turn their backs." Hyde began unbuttoning his trousers.

Piotr frowned.

"When they re-emerge," clarified Hyde. "Keep their heads away from the guards. They'll be close."

"Tak," answered Piotr with a display of his wild teeth. "Yes, yes!" He vanished behind the cart.

"I'll go next!" said Jock, his own trousers loosened, ready to take off. "Then you and finally you, Jan. Okay?"

"Tak," answered Jan.

"Tak," said Hyde. "Eh, the first is done!"

Over the heads of the crowd, through the smoke, an unfamiliar face appeared in a Polish uniform.

"Wish me luck!" urged Jock, as he disappeared behind the cart. Aligning himself to obscure the guards' view, Jock undressed. He noticed the tunic and hat left on the wheel had vanished. As he kicked off his boots and eased his left leg out of his trousers, he sensed movement to his right. He continued freeing his right leg, holding his trousers aloft as a figure approached wearing his familiar tunic and hat. Without a word, Jock handed over his trousers, receiving a pile of clothes and sandals in return. Only as Jock tugged down his new top did he ponder the size of his replacement. His tunic hung loose on the gaunt figure, and Jock estimated he stood an inch shorter. He tugged up a pair of baggy trousers, tying a rope around the waist to hold them up. A cold sensation tickled his ankles. He looked down, cringing at the gap between trouser bottom and foot. He hoped the sandals would fit.

Jock's double stood fitted out in his British uniform; a hand outstretched towards the Scot. The hundred words Jock wished to say, conveying his gratitude, remained unspoken. He grasped the hand and shook hard. The man turned, leaving Jock to duck, grab the sandals and dash to the ditch. He rolled onto the ridge of tufted grass, finding a row of hands reaching out to pull him down.

A cold, damp squelch welcomed Jock's feet at the base of the ditch, forcing him to bend his knees. He looked around to survey the lair. Piotr's smile greeted him to the right. To his left, two unfamiliar faces etched with terror watched him. The bare legs and ill-fitting military tunics betrayed their status as doubles.

"Iść!" whispered Piotr, spurring the man to Jock's left to scramble out of the ditch.

With his departure, a new face came into view: Antek, the young farm labourer befriended by Jock. Dressed in his own peasant garb, Jock surmised he would be their local guide. With a nod and a smile, they greeted each other.

A mass crashed down at the lip of the channel, and Hyde's body rolled over the edge. Jock reached out to yank his partner down. Hyde's knee clipped his brow, stunning him. The cry of pain, desperate to escape, remained bottled inside. As Hyde straightened himself and discovered the water-filled bottom, he gave a thumbs-up. He's in his element, thought Jock, rubbing his brow.

Jock listened to the noisy chatter of their fellow prisoners around the cart as the damp worked its way through his clothes. They understood their role: present normality while causing a distraction. Their biggest challenge awaited: to incorporate four Polish peasants into their ranks and get them back into the camp without raising suspicion. For a day, the peasants would pass themselves off as POWs. Their task, to be counted but remain anonymous.

"Iść!" whispered Piotr again. The last doppelgänger propelled himself up, one leg slipping on the bank, his hands grabbing at the grass to steady himself. Antek caught his foot and heaved it up.

"Beeile dich! Schneller!" The guard's command silenced the chatter.

Jock winced, their time up. The clatter of lobbed tools, followed by the slam of the toolbox lid, confirmed his fears.

However, a commotion stirred among the men. Shouts erupted, and the familiar sound of a fight reached Jock's ears. He smiled, recognising the drastic tactic to squeeze out more time. A second later, Jan's body rolled into view, and they pulled him down into the channel.

As the shouting died, only the sharp commands of the guards broke the silence. Jan manoeuvred himself around, his back pressed to the slope, his bent legs clinging to the far bank. The others copied him, their backsides hovering just above the pool of water at the base of the ditch. There was nothing more to do other than remain still and quiet until alone. It felt like an eternity.

Only when they heard the distant grate of a wheel on the road did they dare put their heads above the parapet. The coast was clear.

"We did it!" said Jock, surprise in his voice.

They exchanged glances and laughed, a release of tension. With a helping hand, they eased themselves out of the ditch, examining each other.

"You remind me of a schoolboy who's outgrown his uniform," teased Hyde.

"Ye still look like a thief," rebutted Jock. "Yer replacement possessed an uncanny resemblance tae ye."

"A handsome fellow," concurred Hyde. "What now, Pete?"

The Polish soldier spoke to Antek, before translating for the British. "Ve to vait here. Transport arranged. They bring news of vhere gold is."

"Let's hope it's nawt too far away," said Jock, impressed by the organisation. "I hope the names I got from the telegraph helped."

"Ve vill see," commented Piotr.

"Potato, anyone?" Hyde withdrew a handful of spuds from his pocket.

Jan laughed, withdrawing his own collection. "Is better than prison food!"

"It's a feast!" added Jock.

Even Antek, who struggled to understand the conversation, laughed.

Though stifled by a sprinkling of dirt, embers still glowed in the fire. They sat around it, enjoying its meagre heat, their supper sizzling within the ashes.

"It'll be good tae go over the plan; ensure we're as ready as we can be," suggested Jock.

Hyde nodded. "Yes, if they're transporting bullion and stopping over for the night, the gold will remain in the truck. It's too much effort to unload and reload."

Piotr translated for Antek as Hyde continued.

"So, we steal the truck. I'll drive as I've started a few cars in my time that weren't my own."

Piotr frowned at Hyde, struggling to comprehend.

"Ne'er mind, lad," said Jock, imitating the use of a steering wheel. "Hyde will drive."

"Everyone else pile into the back... Gets in the back," Hyde continued, correcting his vernacular for the benefit of the Poles. "What's unclear is the environment housing our truck and its gold. Let's assume that, as it ain't parked in the prison camp, they've been complacent, and we won't have wire and guard towers to overcome. However..."

"Slow down!" cut in Jock. "Let the lad catch up."

Hyde huffed as Piotr caught up. "Okay? Right, as I were saying, with the SS accompanying it, we must assume it'll be well guarded. While overnight there may be only a couple of sentries on duty, it is likely they'll have dogs – woof, woof. A bark from them and jackboots will swamp us."

"Svamp with jackboots?" queried Piotr.

"More Germans will come," explained Jock. "A sound by anyone and more Germans come."

"That's right," pressed on Hyde. "Therefore, we have to silence everyone at the same time."

As Piotr translated, Jan ran his finger across his throat.

"Nae, laddie, nae way," stressed Jock, shaking his head. "We cannae kill the guards. We do that, and they'll take revenge on the locals."

"Tak," said Jan with a sigh. "You right. I see vith my own eyes."

"We bludgeon... knock them all out," added Hyde, with a quick mock demonstration of a swipe to the back of Jock's head. "We'll need to find some weapons."

"No problem," said Piotr, whose explanation to Antek received an eager nod. "But vill they not take revenge for loss of gold?"

Hyde smiled. "Leave that to me."

The conversation lulled. They sat with their own thoughts, rolling the potatoes as they browned, the light of the day fading.

"I don't know about you guys," said Hyde after a while, "but my stomach tells me those spuds are ready."

Jock suspected the embers lacked the heat to roast the potatoes, but his stomach also called out for food. He plucked a spud from the ash. It was warm rather than hot but smelt appetising. With a crunch akin to that of an apple, he sank his teeth in. The texture felt wrong, but the taste right. The group nodded in satisfaction as they sated their hunger.

"Quiet!" hissed Jock, his mouth half-full. "Listen!"

A faint, repetitive squeak carried on the wind.

"Lie flat, quick!" urged Jock.

Instead, Antek stood.

"Does he nawt understand?"

Piotr rattled off a question to his countryman, who replied with confidence. "He say our transport is here!"

Before Jock could question further, three boys, two familiar from earlier, rode into view. "Bikes!"

"That's our transport?" queried Hyde.

"Tak," answered Piotr with a smile.

"Three bikes for five men?" queried Hyde with a raised eyebrow.

"Is faster than horse with cart, no?" said Jan.

"Come! Ve go!" urged Antek, waving for the others to rise and follow him.

"Last time I shared a bike, ma brother fell off and broke a tooth," confessed Jock as he climbed to his feet.

The boys held their bicycles with an air of pride, glossing over the fear they might never see them again.

"How will the boys get back?" asked Jock, casting an eye over one of the black-framed bikes.

"They young," said Piotr. "They run."

"How far do we have to pedal these things?" questioned Hyde.

Piotr began a fast and furious conversation with the boys and Antek, everyone having their say.

"Sounds like it's getting complicated," observed Jock.

"Not too complicated, I hope," said Hyde. "You can carry me on your bike."

"Don't ye want tae pedal yer own one?"

"Nah, best to leave it to a local," answered Hyde.

"Ye scratch yer cheek when ye lie," said Jock. "Ye cannae ride a bike, can ye?"

"Dunno, never tried," mumbled Hyde, flexing his neck back and forth, agitated at his damaged pride.

"Is there a problem?" Jock now addressed Piotr, whose conversation faded to silence.

"Nie, all is good. Ve have… err… good intelligence… Is that the word?"

Jock nodded.

"Yes, good intelligence of vhere is gold," continued Piotr. "At village called Lubicz. Err, it is east. About 5 kilometres."

"Why there, I wonder?" chipped in Hyde.

"Um, yes. Ve believe they plan to… to load onto boat. Lubicz is on small… err, small rezeka. How you say?" Piotr waggled his arm like a snake.

"River?"

"Tak, rivier," repeated Piotr. "Joins vith Motlawa river and up to Danzig." He motioned the route with another wave of his hand.

"Makes sense if the load is heavy," contemplated Hyde, with a glint in his eye. "Some roads out here ain't good enough. The autumn rain's made the ground wet."

"Aye, probably suffered a wretched time. Does Antek know the way?"

"Of course, Yok," declared Piotr. "Ve must go before dark. You pedal, Hyde?"

"I'm with the big Scot. I want someone who knows which side of the road to ride on."

Piotr shrugged.

"They drive on the right oot here," said Jock, waggling the bike's seat to its maximum height.

"That's what I meant," answered Hyde. "My yokes don't translate, Yok."

"Just get on the back and shut up," commanded Jock, shuffling on the hard seat, his knees bent but feet still resting on the ground.

"Those trousers go with the bike," teased Hyde, as he straddled the carry frame and put his arms round Jock's waist. "I always suspected you were a kid at heart."

"I'll throw ye in another ditch if ye donnae shut up!" growled Jock, pushing off, trying to get his balance with the undersized bike and the extra weight.

"Understood, sweetheart," said Hyde, squeezing his companion.

Chapter 11

U nder the wide-open sky, the autumn sun lingered, giving light enough to cycle. A flock of migrating geese headed due south, honking their farewell, while the cumbersome bikes, heading south-east, shuddered along the neglected roads, a distinctive noise disturbing the serene evening.

"Stop dragging yer bloody feet!" snarled Jock over his shoulder. "Ye're slowing us down."

"I cannae help it," replied Hyde with a mocking accent. "My legs are cramping."

Jock's own body struggled with the lung-busting exertion, but he pushed on. Despite the regular toil in the fields, a starved body soon weakened.

They passed a clump of run-down peasant dwellings, spotting an armoured German car parked off the road. Its occupants leaned against their vehicle, cigarette smoke wafting upward, following the cyclists with a curious gaze. Jock fought the urge to pedal faster, noticing Hyde's grip tightened a fraction.

Few Poles ventured outside at this hour, most seeking early sanctuary indoors. Curfew approached, with little required to provoke their occupiers.

Away from the scrutinising Germans, an odd cyclist passed them, calling out a greeting, sparing a wry smile at the ill-fitting bikes, reassuring Jock their own presence was not anything unusual.

"How's that arse of yours?" asked Hyde in Jock's ear. "Mine's numb!"

"And yet ye can still talk through it!" Jock smiled, pleased at the joke, his own backside aching like hell. He tried standing but quit as Hyde struggled to hang on.

"What will you do with your share?" asked Hyde with a change of tact.

"Give it back tae its owners," stated Jock, his muscles straining from a gentle incline. "As ye should, too!"

"Yeah, ain't gonna happen," said Hyde. "I've earned my cut. Who came up with this plan?"

"Stealing donnae entitle ye tae anything. Ye've nae right tae what isnae yers!"

Hyde fidgeted for the hundredth time, causing the bike to wobble. "I just follow a popular British tradition."

"How d'ye work that one oot?"

"Ain't that how we won the Empire? India wasn't ours to take, but we took it."

"Och, nae man," said Jock. "Ye donnae break intae a pauper's house and improve the place. That's what the Empire does."

"That diamond on the king's crown didn't come from no pauper's house."

"Ye cannae judge in terms of money," insisted Jock. "Empire's aboot civilising: teaching them a better way of life."

"Yeah, well, that's what I do. Teach the posh folk not to leave their jewellery lying around!"

With Hyde's laughter ringing in his ear, Jock tried to restrain himself, but he recognised a good joke. Soon the bike wove from one side to the other as Jock lost focus. The Poles looked with bemusement, before the infection spread and they laughed along, no wiser on the source of the merriment.

An unseen pothole caught Jock by surprise. The bike dropped, catching the rim hard, causing the front wheel to waggle out of control. "Hang on!" Squeezing the brakes, Jock steered the bicycle as best he could. A lake lay to the side, and they headed straight for it. As they mounted the grass verge, Jock lost all control. Hyde slipped off the back, the change in weight tipping the bike forward, sending Jock over the handlebars.

With a screech of brakes, the other two bikes came to a standstill, their occupants watching the drama unfold in horror.

"Yok!" cried Piotr.

"I'm okay!" replied Jock, face down on the grass, a foot short of the water. He rolled over. "Nae harm done tae me. What aboot the bike?"

"'Eh! What about me?" Hyde climbed to his feet, rubbing his behind.

"Ye didnae have far tae fall," moaned Jock, sitting upright to rub his knee. "And ye caused the crash with yer joshing!"

"I wasn't driving," retorted Hyde.

"Ye donnae drive a bike; ye ride it."

The three Poles waited on their bikes, listening to the strange conversation.

Jock stood, picked the grass and soil from his hands, and examined the bike. With a shake of his head and a tut, he knelt and squeezed the tyre. "Nae puncture. Let's have a closer look at ye." He lifted the frame, placing the bike down on its wheels. The handlebar swung loose. "Och, the bolt's sheared." He pulled the handlebar section out, confirming his diagnosis.

"Can you still ride?" asked Jan.

"Only in circles," answered Jock, scratching his chin. "We need something tae hold the pole in place, so the wheel turns when I rotate the handlebar. Any ideas?"

The five men surrounded the patient, hoping for inspiration.

"Can't we leave someone behind and the rest travel on two bikes?" proposed Hyde.

Piotr shook his head. "Certain death. Germans vill find him; everything find out!"

"What about him with the dodgy foot?" Hyde nodded at Antek.

"Ye know the way, do ye?" challenged Jock. "We stick together!"

Antek muttered something to Piotr.

"What'd he say?" asked Jock.

"Mud," answered Piotr. "He suggest ve fill vith mud. Make sticky."

Jock glanced across at Antek. "Worth a go. Plenty aboot."

The peasant scraped a handful of dirt from the bank of the lake, picking out any large stones. He held the prize up for all to see, pointing to the fine grit within. "Good."

"Sounds like ye've done this before," said Jock with a grin. "The grit hinders movement."

Piotr translated, and Antek nodded an enthusiastic head.

"Come on, Hyde!" urged Jock, as he pushed Antek's mud down the pipe. "Get yer hands dirty. I'll need more than this, and ye'll think twice aboot suggesting we leave anyone behind again!"

"If it works," replied Hyde with a huff, before kneeling to harvest some mud.

Jock's long fingers suited the task of working the grime deep into the hollow shaft. He held two together and pushed down, limiting the space for mud to overflow. Everyone contributed, and soon they were ready to attempt the next stage.

"Pass me the handlebars," requested Jock. "I hope we've nawt over-filled."

"God is vith us," said Jan.

"Aye, that he is," said Jock, aligning the inner and outer shafts. "Though he never helped me with a puncture before. Here goes!"

The handlebar shaft sank down a couple of inches without issue, the grit scraping between metal, before halting. "Give us a hand!" grunted Jock. "Feels sticky, but it's nawt going down."

Antek grasped the other handle and added his weight. As the mud compressed, the shaft became harder to insert.

"A wee bit more and it'll be passable," suggested Jock, testing whether the handlebars affected the wheels. "Someone, push down at the centre!"

Piotr squeezed between Jock and Antek, pressing down with his palms on the shaft.

"That'll do," gasped Jock. "Let's have a test." Remounting, he placed his fingers around the handlebars. "Ha, the height's better." He pushed off and, with a delicate tilt, turned the bike. "That's good enough for me," he declared. "I donnae want tae be doing any sharp turns, but it'll do. Hyde, ye had better ride with Antek."

Hyde stood pondering the suggestion.

"We must go!" urged Piotr. "Getting dark."

"Ye'r too heavy, lad," added Jock, pushing off down the road to give Hyde little choice.

"Not far. Few kilometres," said Antek, as Hyde straddled his luggage frame.

"I hope not," whined Hyde. "My arse can't take much more."

"Arse?"

"Yeah, like bottom, backside, rear, butt, posterior, ass, rump…"

As Hyde persisted with his bargain-basement English lesson, Antek pushed off, content to leave his passenger to his unintelligible rambling.

Jock shook his head, watching his compatriot before him. "Ye're right," he called across to Piotr and Jan. "God is with us. I won't have tae put up with Hyde for the rest of the journey!"

Chapter 12

Chimney smoke gleamed in the faint moonlight, vanishing as the wind dispersed it into the darkness. Amid a small copse, three bicycles rested against a stump, while Jock paced at the edge of the tree line, inspecting the silhouetted village across the field. The hour was late, the temperature low, and he moved to keep warm. Beside the bikes, the Poles huddled together, chatting in their own tongue, vapour escaping through their mouths. Hyde reclined against a tree, not long returned from a brief, solo reconnoitre, his eyes closed, his face relaxed.

Trudging back to the group, Jock examined Hyde. Part of him wanted to kick the still body, stir him from his tranquillity, make him count down the agonising, crawling hours with the rest of them. However, a grudging respect grew within him for the lad. He recognised Hyde as a survivor, almost envied him. Nothing would compel Jock to leave Jane and the boys, but Hyde exuded a freedom he would never achieve. He cared only for himself; no one told him what to do, and if they did, he ignored them. Jock slid down the opposite side of the trunk. He closed his eyes and shuffled his back into the most comfortable position available.

"Is that the cold or fear?" Hyde spoke with a soft timbre, his eyes still shut.

"I though ye slept," said Jock, conscious of his chattering teeth. "Sorry if I woke ye."

"I wasn't asleep, just waiting."

"Are ye nawt cold?"

"I'm cold," said Hyde. "But you get used to sleeping outdoors."

"It was a bit of both," confessed Jock.

"Eh?"

"Ma teeth."

"Oh, don't worry about it. We're all scared."

"Even ye?" asked Jock.

"Terrified," admitted Hyde. "On the streets, you never let your fear show."

"Why are ye telling me now?"

Silence lingered until Hyde answered. "Cos, I trust you, and I've trusted no one before. You don't have a fag?"

Another shiver passed through Jock, but absent of cold or fear. It was an emotional charge, the same he experienced when Jane announced she was pregnant or when his youngest, Tom, uttered his first words. "Ye're a good lad, Robbie," said Jock, breaking a lifetime of side-stepping sentiment, ignoring the request for a cigarette. "Life's dealt ye a lousy hand, but ye've done all right. There's a good heart in there."

"What do you suppose our friends are talking about?" asked Hyde with an abnormal serenity in his voice, as though a valve released.

"Maybe family, a girl back home or better times," suggested Jock. "What most soldiers talk aboot. Have ye got a girl waiting for ye?"

"More than one!" answered Hyde.

"Och, get away with ye! Pick one and settle down. She'll make an honest man of ye."

Hyde laughed. "Not these ones, Jock. Anyway, I have a local girl I'm kinda fond of."

"Ye taking her tae the cinema for the weekend?" Jock patted the youngster on his shoulder, shaking his head at the imagination and fabrications woven through the boy's world. "I meant tae ask earlier, what did ye mean when ye said ye would make sure the Germans donnae blame the Poles?" Jock turned his head, awaiting the response.

"Ah, another trick of the trade," said Hyde. "Always leave bread-crumbs to confuse and divert old plod, or Jerry." He reached into a pocket and withdrew something, showing it to Jock on the palm of his hand.

Jock chuckled. "So, ye stole old Harcourt's epaulettes! Good on ye."

"If I drop it for Jerry to find, they'll suspect a British raid," explained Hyde.

"There ain't nae officers left in the Thorn camps, so it must be a commando raid," surmised Jock. "Brilliant!"

"Of course," added Hyde, "it won't mean squat if we leave something incriminating behind."

"You mean like a body?"

Hyde let the question hang unanswered.

"If I don't make it, I've left a letter with Peters tae send home tae Jane," said Jock.

"What did you write?"

"Private stuff, but I wrote I love her and the boys. I donnae fear death, but I do fear dying. Does that make sense?"

"Not in the slightest," admitted Hyde. "What's the difference?"

"Death is finding peace; dying is the turmoil of getting there and what it leaves behind: the suffering of ma family."

"I guess I've got nothing to fear, eh?" said Hyde.

"Ye've nae family at all?" asked Jock.

"None who care about me or deserve my love," confessed Hyde.

"I'm sorry."

"Don't be, I…"

Piotr's face appeared to their side. "Antek say the time is here. Ve must go."

"Good," said Hyde. "This tree is bloody uncomfortable!"

"Is everyone happy with the instructions?" asked Jock, peeling wet trousers from his backside.

The group nodded, before exchanging handshakes as though last farewells.

***

Hyde led the party across the field, retracing his earlier route. Each carried a makeshift weapon: a bulky stick, a sock full of stones. They first encountered a shed, cut firewood stacked under the rafters, the noise of clucking chickens filtering through the walls. Hyde motioned them to skirt round left, stopping only to retrieve a discarded, broken spade handle, missing the digging end. He assessed it with a firm pat to his palm before emptying his stone-filled sock.

A low-lying fence posed no obstacle, leading them into a backyard. As though on business down the Old Kent Road, Hyde ducked, slinking beneath the windows of a peasant's hovel. Jock's frame, not designed to slink, bent as best it could. They emerged by the principal thoroughfare, an unimpressive dirt road lined with a mix of shacks and more substantial stone buildings. One hundred yards before them stood their destination, the village inn.

A two-finger signal from Hyde prompted him and Piotr to stroll out onto the road. The others waited, crouching in the shadows, watching the pair cross the unlit street and amble towards the inn. This couple of 'drunks' faced better odds if challenged than a group of five after curfew. Once the darkness consumed the vanguard, Jock and Jan rose to their feet to follow, leaving Antek to provide the rearguard.

Jock's sandals, though a better fit than expected, struggled in the churned mud. Autumn rains, combined with the flow of horses and carts, left the surface a sloppy, pockmarked nightmare. No wonder the Germans headed for the river. On the far side, the ground evened out; only faint footprints marked the surface. They found Hyde and Piotr crouching behind a water trough, 40 yards from the inn. The only prominent light and noise in the village leaked from the tavern.

"Just one guard by the gate," whispered Hyde, as Antek joined the group.

Jock peeked across, making out the faint upright body in front of the two large wooden gates, a dot of intermittent light revealing the guard's cigarette.

"They're bolted on the inside," explained Hyde, pointing at the gates, "and lead into the courtyard. The stable's on the right, the truck on the left." Hyde mapped the scene with his hands. "There are also a couple of light armoured vehicles. Perhaps a Kfz 13 and 222. Most importantly, only two men guard the truck. Others will be asleep or drunk."

Despite having heard it before, Hyde's retelling in sight of the inn brought it to life. Piotr whispered a translation into Antek's ear.

"We've no idea when the guard might change," continued Hyde. "We'll need lady luck with us."

"And God," added Jan.

"Anyone who'll help," said Hyde. "Our way in is down the side. We cut across this garden," he motioned behind, "through the shadows, out of sight of the guard. One at a time."

When Piotr finished translating, Hyde shot off, hurdling a small wall, disappearing into the cover of the darkness. One by one they followed, the guard oblivious to the movement. A cellar door lay to the side of the inn, beneath an open window. Distant singing carried into the street. The five men lined up against the building, hunched and tight against the wall. They waited in silence, listening for nearby voices above the singing. Hearing none, Hyde leapt over the cellar door to where the padlock lay open, jimmied earlier by his own hand. After easing it from the latch, he lifted one door, peeked down, then nodded.

Jock led. One hand gripped the doorframe as he swung onto the chute. His feet struck a sandbag placed at the bottom, bringing him to a stop. Before he climbed to his feet, he felt the soft impact of someone behind. One by one they descended until safe inside. Last down, Hyde, turned, reaching up to pull the doors closed, bringing near darkness. Only slivers of light reached the cellar through the floorboards above. Again, they waited in silence, listening for signs of company; awaiting until convinced they remained undiscovered.

"Each man, hold another's shoulder!" whispered Hyde. "I'll lead you through to the stairs."

Jock pictured those eerie images from the Great War of blind chains of gassed soldiers, as Hyde guided them into the dark interior, weaving around crates and boxes.

The noise from above filtered through, the darkness fomenting the imagination. Jock's perception of SS troops formed by the propaganda films: blonde, chisel-jawed Goliaths, dressed in black, brutal and formidable.

They stopped at the base of the stairs, light seeping around a door at the top.

"Through that door," murmured Hyde, "is a corridor leading to the inner courtyard. There's a closed door on the left, an open one to the right. Leads to the kitchen... probably. At the top of the stairs, when the coast's clear, we go one at a time. Walk past the open door with your head turned away. If Jerry comes your way, attack before they can blink."

"Everyone knows yer jobs once in the courtyard?" pressed Jock.

Whispered affirmations replied.

"Then lead on, Hyde."

Jock followed Hyde, step by step, noticing the muddy footprints his partner left. Five stairs from the top, Hyde jerked to a halt, his fist raised. A voice filtered through the door, then footsteps. The handle turned. Jock heard a whispered prayer from Piotr and muttered one himself.

The door swung open, light flooding through, blinding the raiders. A silhouetted figure stood motionless before them. Hyde raised his weapon and leapt up two stairs at a time.

"Przyjaciiele!" hissed Piotr, as loud as was sensible. "Milcz ze względu na ojczyznę. Stop, Hyde!"

The spade handle hovered over the cringing figure, frozen in a dramatic silhouette.

"He's Polish," whispered Jock, recognising the loose trousers.

Hyde's arm shot out, grabbed the man's collar and dragged him inside, his other hand pulling the door shut. Jock dashed forward, his hand smothering the man's mouth, pushing him against the wall. Terrified eyes stared at the five bodies crowding round.

"I talk to him please!" urged Piotr.

Hyde stepped back, allowing Piotr to sidle up to the man's side. Jock held his palm firm as the Pole whispered into his compatriot's ear. A mumble escaped, followed by a nod of the head.

"No hand, Yok," asked Piotr.

Jock released his palm, his eyes remaining locked on their captive.

A stream of hushed Polish flowed from the man's mouth, conveying fear and confusion, but no threat.

"Chichy!" hissed Piotr, before turning to the Brits. "Inn his. He not like Germans, but no choice and no happy at losing money."

"Aye, that sounds like a landlord tae me," said Jock, unable to contain the observation.

"He tell to no one ve here," continued Piotr. "But is vorried about his family if Germans blame him."

Without warning, Hyde lashed his spade handle against the landlord's head. The body crumpled under the disbelieving gaze of the others.

"What d'ye do that for, ye numbskull!" hissed Jock.

"I solved his and our problem," said Hyde. "He can't tell and isn't to blame."

There was some logic to Hyde's actions, considered Jock, though he wondered how forgiving the Germans might be, regardless of how innocent.

"No time to debate," added Hyde. "He may not talk, but they'll notice his absence soon."

"Then get moving!" growled Jock, noticing a trickle of blood running from the man's hair to the ground.

Hyde edged the door ajar, took a breath and vanished through.

To the side of the prostrate man, Antek leaned forward to nurse his wound. They didn't have time, but Jock froze with guilt, unsure what to do. Jan yanked the peasant up, whispering firm commands in his ear. He shoved Antek towards the door, waving for him to go through. Jock rested a reassuring hand on the youngster's shoulder and eased him on.

"Does he recognise him?" whispered Jock, as Jan readied to go.

"Tak, friend of cousin. He vill be okay." With that, he vanished through.

"Don't vorry, Yok," said Piotr, noticing the guilt in Jock's eyes. "One day he vill tell grandchildren about this day vith pride, no?" He slid out into the corridor.

Jock nodded, hoping it was true. He stood alone with the unconscious body, wishing he were anywhere but there. With a deep breath, Jock glanced down the corridor and stepped out. The noise through the open door seemed excessive; boisterous, drunken sounds that pierced his nerves. He turned his head away and marched on as instructed. The door to the courtyard stood hooked open, allowing a fresh breeze to mix with the stale, beer-soaked air of the inn. Four huddled figures awaited Jock's arrival.

A finger pressed to Hyde's lips, and Jock nodded in understanding. Beyond the grey armoured vehicle they crouched behind, stood armed and alert German guards. Hyde raised two fingers, then mimed holding a gun. He bared his teeth, pawing with a hand, lifting one finger.

Jock shook the image of Christmas charades from his head, chilled by the realisation that a dog might sense them before they moved an inch.

Formed in a tight circle, Hyde tapped Piotr, Antek and Jock on their shoulders, pointing down the side of the wall, then directing them to cut in. He tapped Jan's shoulder and his own chest, pointing between the vehicles. A swipe of his spade handle conveyed their next instruction. All nodded, understanding the grim task.

The sickening taste of fear returned to Jock as he broke away with his two associates. A pungent smell of urine seeped from the wall, yet he clung tight, stooped down to escape observation from the window. The vehicles provided cover, as long as no one else emerged into the courtyard. Jock gripped his stick with clammy fingers. In the heat of the attack, it seemed a pitiful weapon, his doubts growing with the beat of his heart.

They cut in at the end of the vehicles, in sight of the tall gates, each step a delicate exploration forward. The sound of a panting dog reached their ears. Jock took the forward position, squatting behind the bulky engine of the armoured car. He eased his head forward, inch by inch, trying to secure sight of the guards and Hyde at the other end. Three horses watched them from the other side of the courtyard, stabled for the night, frisky and alert at the late hour. Jock edged forward another inch, sighting the source of their excitability. The snout of an Alsatian appeared; the smell and noise of the horses, the distraction saving Jock and his colleagues from discovery. Beyond, the shiny black boots of a guard emerged, followed by the trousers, trench coat and helmet of an SS soldier. Jock dared another inch forward, hoping to spot Hyde to orchestrate a dual assault.

The second guard came into view. He leaned into the truck, stretching his legs. In the space between his body and the vehicle, Jock looked on the face of Hyde, mirroring his own intense appearance. Their eyes locked on one another. Hyde nodded, and Jock returned the gesture. On the count of three, Jock, his heart racing, raised an arm behind him to signal to Piotr and Antek.

With a sharp crunch of feet pushing off the sandy gravel, Jock sprinted at his prey. Time slowed. The drumbeat of his heart pounded; the hard breaths of his companions followed in his wake.

"WOOF!" The dog, its teeth exposed in a snarl, pulled at its lead towards the attackers.

Jock swung his foot, kicking the Alsatian's head, triggering a pained yelp. His momentum carried him past, onto the guard, whose own face hung in shock. With one more stride, Jock threw himself at the stunned German. The stick slipped from his fingers; useless against a helmet. Instead, the dark arts of the rugby field surfaced, as Jock executed a full-blown, neck-high tackle. He felt the rigid discomfort of the guard's gun cut into his stomach as they collapsed to the ground. The grunts and groans from struggles elsewhere never reached Jock. Fear dissipated under the adrenaline. Only the precious divide between life and death mattered now.

As Jock manoeuvred off the winded guard, one arm still hooked around his neck, Piotr crashed atop the German's lower half. Back on his knees, Jock pulled the flapping body up, squeezing his arm to cut off the air, his other hand covering the mouth. The guard's fingers scrambled at the vice-like grip, a pitiful gargle escaping his throat. Piotr, now sitting on the German's thighs, whacked the desperate hands with his stick, then pulled them away, pinning them to the ground.

Jock's grip slackened as the suffocated body fell limp. He collapsed his exhausted face into the German's helmet, a passive regret for his minute of brutality. The world around came into focus: the agitated horses, Antek standing over the unconscious dog, Jan and Hyde dragging a blood-stained guard under an armoured car and the stars blinking through the broken clouds above.

"Qvick, Yok," whispered Piotr, on his feet and clasping the unconscious guard's boots.

Jock pushed the body off, wiping a sleeve across his cheeks. A pain surfaced in his ribs, the memory of hitting the gun surfacing. With no time to check for damage, he climbed to his feet, gathering up the wrists of their fallen foe. For the first time, he examined the guard. What normal features, considered Jock, the face not unlike those within his or any regiment; better fed perhaps, but just a normal lad.

As Piotr and Jock lugged the German to the front of the second armoured car, Antek dashed to the gate, standing ready to lift the wooden bar holding them shut.

"In the back!" hissed Hyde, ushering the others on to their next felonious act.

Jock bent down, collecting the guard's fallen machine gun. Jan gripped the other, his eyes scanning the courtyard, ready to meet unwelcome guests. Their attack, swift and effective, was not without noise. The horses reared in distress, their neighing enough to draw a curious peek from a window.

As Hyde climbed into the driver's seat, Piotr locked his fingers together and helped Jock and Jan climb into the back of the truck.

"Jesus!" gasped Jock, breaking a lifetime commitment not to use the Lord's name in vain. He stood staring at row upon row of gold bullion: six deep, perhaps twelve wide and two high. Jan staggered to his side, spluttering his own curse.

"Pssst!" Piotr's hands waved in the air, expecting help into the truck.

Jock shook his distracted head and turned, grabbing at Piotr's wrists and pulling.

"This is the... Jesus Christ!" Hyde, having turned to warn his passengers of some imminent noise, caught sight of the gold. "I've... I've never seen so much. We've struck the jackpot!"

"Get this truck going! Get us oot of here!" hissed Jock, still struggling with Piotr.

A guttural roar erupted as Hyde somehow ignited the engine, a puff of smoke spewing from the exhaust. He pumped the choke, making the engine growl and hum in response. With a crunch, Hyde moved the gear stick into reverse and pressed down on the accelerator.

As they jerked back, Jock stumbled, grabbing the roof framework with one hand to steady himself. The other shot out, grasping hold of Piotr, who hung tottering off the rear.

At the gate, Antek lifted the bar at the first sound of the engine. The muffled voice of the sentry outside enquired about the unexpected activity. Antek whispered a prayer and swung the bar across. He pushed against both doors, keeping them shut, fighting against the efforts of the guard outside. With a glance back, he saw the truck reversing at speed, stirring the horses to a greater state of anxiety. Faces appeared at windows. A man in a vest, braces dangling down, arrived at a doorway, his perplexed expression turning to alarm.

"Chroń mnie, Matko Maryjo!" cried Antek. He pulled the gates and ran, letting their weight carry them open.

Hyde drove forward, leaning across to open the passenger door. Shouting flared all around, the call to arms stirring the soldiers. Gasping, Antek leapt into the cab and slammed his door shut. The first sound of gunfire erupted.

"Get down!" yelled Jock, finding his face pressed to the gold.

The truck crept forward, Hyde racing the engine but controlling the speed with the clutch. He awaited the gates to open a fraction more. Bullets whizzed around. In the gap between the parting gates stood the sentry, his rifle aimed at the cab.

"And now for the fun bit!" cried Hyde, easing off the clutch. The truck lurched forward to the sound of breaking glass as the sentry fired his rifle. Instinct forced Hyde to veer right, hoping not to provide a sitting target. The truck ploughed through one gate, ramming it shut, before shattering it off the hinges. With one further squeeze of his trigger, the sentry leapt out of the way as the truck hurtled through onto the road.

Hyde spun the wheel, skidding the truck to face down the road, then pressed hard on the gas again. As the engine roared, the wheels span, sliding in the mud, failing to grip. Their load weighed them down. Hyde tried a different tack, easing the accelerator out, acquiring some traction, before building speed as the shouts and bullets intensified.

"Step on it!" screamed Jock, still prone atop the gold. "Ma granny walked faster."

As they sped up, Jock dared a peek over the rear. Bullet holes littered the wooden barrier, and he thanked the heavens for his good luck so far. Behind, Germans, in an array of dress and readiness, poured onto the street. Some continued to fire; others shouted insults or commands.

"Come on, man!" urged Jock. "We need to be oot of here before they fire up the armoured cars." The truck veered to the right, sending Jock crashing against Jan. "What're ye doing up there?" He scrambled over the gold, sticking his head through the hole in the canvas separating cab and rear. "Is everything all right?"

"Sorry," groaned Hyde. "I'm avoiding the mud. Means some gardens will need replanting."

"At least drive with both hands on the wheel," chastised Jock. "We donnae..." He stopped, spying Hyde's left arm limp to his side, a patch of blood growing through the sleeve. "Laddie, ye've been shot!"

"Hmm," replied Hyde with no sign of pain.

"Antek, help him oot!" urged Jock. Wrap something around the wound. Make it tight."

Piotr appeared on Jock's shoulder, shouting a translation over the noise of the engine.

No reply came.

"He's dead," said Hyde, his voice breaking. "One in the head."

"Och, nae!" wailed Jock. "He were just a wee nipper."

The Poles made the sign of the cross, cursing their comrade's misfortune.

"I'll climb through," said Jock. "Help ye drive this thing."

"No!" snapped Hyde. "Stay where you are. I'm fine for the moment. I need to think."

"Think aboot what?"

"We have a dead Pole on our hands. If Jerry finds him, they'll suspect the Poles. And Antek knew a good hiding place for the gold."

Jock sat down, his back to Hyde, rocking as the truck fought along the uneven road, speeding away from Lubicz. They had come too far to lose the gold back to the Germans. If Antek's death was to mean something, they must see this through to the end. "Any ideas? Jan? Piotr?"

"Sorry, I not know these roads," said Piotr.

Jan confirmed his own ignorance with a shake of his head. "Ve dig. Put both Antek and gold in ground."

"With what?" sighed Jock. "We donnae have any spades and nae time either." Lady Luck, a welcome companion until now, appeared to have deserted them. "Perhaps a barn or wood?" suggested Jock aloud.

"The Huns will scour every inch to find the gold," called out Hyde. "They're too obvious."

"Back in our camp?" proposed Jan, before dismissing the ridiculous notion with an angry tut.

At a suitable distance from the inn, with no pursuers in sight, Hyde switched off the headlights, content to drive almost blind. They made good progress, returning down familiar roads. Without warning, he slammed on the brakes.

"Hey!" cried Jock. "What's happening? Are ye all right?"

"Get out!" yelled Hyde. "I've got a plan. Get out!"

"What plan?" Jock squeezed his head through the divide.

"Best you stay ignorant," said Hyde, his sleeve now bright red with blood. "If Jerry captures you, they won't force the gold's location from you."

"But we all have tae get back tae the camp or the game's up!" pressed Jock.

"Yok's right," agreed Piotr.

"Make your way back to the potato field," instructed Hyde. "I'll meet you there at daybreak."

"Nae, lad," mused Jock. "We should stick together."

"Trust me, Jock."

Something in the way Hyde uttered the words made Jock trust the most untrustworthy man he had ever met. "Okay, but let me look at that arm."

"Come around the front, but be quick about it! Jerry may not be far off."

Jock helped Jan and Piotr down from the truck's rear, accepting their offer to support him as he pushed himself off to the ground.

"Can ve trust him?" asked Piotr with a furtive whisper.

"Ye can trust me," said Jock, "and I trust him, but I'm nawt letting him go on his own in that state."

The Pole nodded, accepting but not convinced.

As they walked down the side of the truck, Hyde's head appeared through the window. "I'll see you in the morning!"

Before anyone reacted, the truck pulled away, leaving the three men, mouths agape, standing in the road.

"Bampot!" yelled Jock. "Does he think he donnae need help? He'll bleed oot!"

"Yok," said Piotr. "He vent vith gold and guns. Ve vill not see him in morning."

Similar thoughts crossed Jock's mind. "Nae, ye're wrong. I don't understand the lad, but he's more than a thief."

"Hmm, I hope you right," said Jan. "He take vhat is ours. I not forgive."

"We should walk through the fields," suggested Jock, eager to change the subject. "The Germans won't be looking for us there."

Their anger simmered through the silence, but with a curt nod, the two Poles followed Jock off the road. They had a long walk ahead of them on this long night.

Chapter 13

"Get much sleep?" asked Jock of no one in particular.

The bedraggled spectre of Jan emerging from his straw cocoon answered the question. Piotr appeared moments later, dark bags under his eyes.

"Szczury!" exclaimed Jan, measuring out a foot with his hands.

"Rats," explained Piotr. "Rats, fleas, cold. Not good for sleep."

"Aye," said Jock, scratching an itch on his shin. "But nae Germans." That he had slept at all surprised him. With his racing mind alert for pursuers, and the discomfort of a ramshackle hut, the night seemed a long one.

The warm orange glow of the rising sun brought light enough to make out their surroundings for the first time. Walking in the darkness proved a dangerous venture, straying from the familiar route, slipping in the mud, becoming entangled in thorny undergrowth. Fortune delivered the feeding station on their path, a place to shelter and find warmth amid the straw. A mist now hung above the ground, lending a false sense of serenity.

Jock stood, stretching his aching muscles, surveying the horizon for signs of the Germans. Vehicles prowled through the night, but they required daylight for a full-scale search.

"Hyde did us a favour," commented Jock, a cloud of vapour escaping from his mouth in the chilled air. "Jerry is looking for a large truck, knowing we'll stick with the gold."

"I not sure," responded Piotr. "They think ve unload gold by now. May be anyvhere. They vill search everyvhere, including barn."

"Aye, I suppose ye're right," admitted Jock. "We'd better get moving. Get as far away as we can. Give ourselves time tae find the work party."

"If vork party out today," pointed out Piotr. "They may stop all..." He flailed, unable to articulate his point.

"Damn!" cursed Jock needing no explanation. "We didnae think this through, did we?"

"If gold not found," said Jan, "ve successful. Ve give lives to Motherland."

"Speak for yerself! I've nae intention of giving ma life tae anyone. Jane would kill me if I gave up."

The Poles nodded, understanding the gist of Jock's declaration, if not the humour. "Ve must trust in... vhat vould Hyde say?" mulled Piotr. "Lady luck?"

"Aye, we're in her debt."

The hum of a distant plane broke the peace.

"They're hunting us from the skies," said Jock, squinting at the vast milky-blue expanse above. "The sooner we find a place tae lie low for the day, the better. We're too vulnerable here. Hyde will also be at the potato field."

"If he still live," said Jan. "Or..." He left the sentence hanging with a snort, his doubts about Hyde's integrity clear.

"I've underestimated the lad before," remarked Jock. "He has a habit of surprising ye."

"Ve should go now!" urged Piotr. "Another plane."

They marched at a good pace despite the sticky mud, the distant, medieval spires of Thorn guiding them. Already, the local peasants emerged from their homes, making their way to the fields. Under suspicious eyes, Piotr assured Jock that no one would betray their presence to the Germans.

After an hour, they found the potato field as they had left it: empty.

"No Hyde," commented Jan.

"Hmm," mulled Jock, his mind's eye seeing images of Hyde with the gold. "Let's give him some time. We donnae know how far he's got tae come."

"Ve should hide in trees." Piotr pointed to the south. "No one see us, but ve see all."

"Good idea," said Jock, glad to be getting some warmth from the sun.

Under the cover of the trees, with time reluctant to advance to his liking, Jock chewed on a stalk of grass. "I'm parched."

"Sorry, Yok?" queried Piotr.

"Thirsty. Water."

"Oh, yes. I too parched."

"What d'ye call that hat of yers?" asked Jock, hoping to make small talk.

Piotr removed the soft, round cloth cap with its short, hard peak. "Ve call Maciejówka. Popular here."

"Aye," said Jock, the conversation fading to awkward silence.

After a few minutes, Jan broached the topic, becoming ever more realistic. "Vhat ve do if no vork party?"

"I donnae know," confessed Jock.

"If they vork, ve not know vhere," added Piotr.

Jan released a flurry of Polish, Jock recognising the anger and frustration within. A heated exchange followed between the two Poles. Jan stormed off to sulk behind another tree.

"Everything okay?" asked Jock.

"He not want give his life to Motherland now," explained Piotr, shaking his head. "Don't vorry."

"I donnae blame him for being angry," said Jock. "We shouldnae have dragged you into this mess. Poor old Antek. I cannae help but fear for those in the camp too. Are they dead already?"

Piotr surprised Jock by laughing. "We have saying in Poland: 'Nieszczęścia chodzą parami'. Which translates, 'misfortunes come in pairs'. We underestimate, no?"

"Ha, you could say that. I..." Something in the distance caught Jock's attention.

"Vhat?"

"Someone's at the edge of the field!"

Piotr joined Jock in straining his eyes to make out the figure.

"That ain't Hyde," commented Jock. "I'd recognise his walk anywhere."

"Too small," concluded Piotr. "Maybe is child. Tak! Boy vith bike from yesterday."

"Ye're right! Does he want his bike back?"

"I go and talk," said Piotr. "Best one go."

Jock followed Piotr's progress towards the boy, slow and suspicious.

"Vhat... er..." Jan reappeared, waving his hand at the field, struggling to find the word.

"We hope it's one of the wee lads from yesterday," explained Jock. "Might help us find the work party, if they're oot there."

"He alone?" Jan's voice reflected an upturn in mood.

"Aye," Jock peeled some bark off a tree as he looked on. He made out an animated Piotr ruffling the boy's hair, before the youngster dashed off with a friendly wave. "Looks like all went well."

"Polish children truthful. You can trust," said Jan.

Jock bit his tongue. He had defended Hyde enough, and more pressing matters loomed.

"Well?" he asked, as Piotr slunk back into the woods.

"He unhappy ve not have his bicycle," joked Piotr, "but I explain he important for Motherland."

"The lad can have a medal," huffed Jock. "Can he help us?"

Jan added his own question in Polish.

"He not see other prisoners, but many Germans," explained Piotr for Jock's benefit. "But I ask him to find."

"How did ye do that?" asked Jock.

"New bicycle promised!"

A fresh voice cut into their laughter. "The gold'll get him a 100 new bikes."

"Robbie!" cried Jock, swinging round to find a pale, bedraggled Hyde leaning against a tree. "Man, are ye all right? Ye look terrible."

"We just got away with millions of pounds of gold," said Hyde, his voice weak. "Of course, I'm all right. Your lookout's terrible, by the way!"

"Sit!" urged Piotr. "Your arm."

"I may do that," said Hyde, sliding down the trunk in exhaustion.

"Ye've lost a lot of blood," remarked Jock, as they crowded around. "Take off that top! Let's examine that wound."

"Vhere is gold?" asked Jan, receiving a disapproving glare from Jock.

A feeble smile formed on Hyde's face. "Safe."

"You tell us vhere!" demanded Jan.

"Leave the boy alone!" growled Jock. "He explained last night it's best we donnae know until we're beyond suspicion."

"Arr! You Inglish vont gold for yourselves."

"I'm nawt English! And remember who came intae this bloody war for ye!" The two stood face to face, an inch apart.

"Dead man say nothing," hissed Jan. "Then nobody find gold!"

"Whoa," croaked Hyde. "I'm not dead and won't be dying soon. Calm down, mate. It's an arm wound. With a bit of food in me, I'll be right as rain. You'll get your gold. You not heard of honour among thieves?"

As Piotr uttered soothing words to his compatriot, leading him away to cool down, Jock knelt by Hyde's side. "Honour among thieves! Ye're still a cheeky scallywag. What happened last night?"

"I got a little lost," confessed Hyde. "It ain't easy finding your way with no lights in a foreign land."

"I wasn't sure you were gonnae come back," admitted Jock. "Ye weren't tempted to hide the gold, then escape tae Sweden?"

"And miss out on all those cigarettes you owe me! Nah, not with this wound or driving a stolen German truck. Best thing to do after a job is lie low. No better place than the camp. You didn't consider escaping too? Still an option."

Jock ignored the suggestion. "Where's the truck and Antek's body?"

"They're safe too," answered Hyde. "Everything is safe. Jerry will have fun looking but won't find nothing."

"So, what's the truth with yer arm?" pressed Jock. "I don't want any of yer bollocks!"

Hyde grimaced. "It hurts like hell. The bullet's still in there."

"Damn! Ye gonnae make it back tae camp?"

"Oh, sure," answered Hyde with his usual confidence.

"It's good tae see ye," said Jock, patting Hyde's other shoulder, further concerns left unspoken. "Now get some rest."

***

Waiting, doing nothing, felt wrong, but there was little for Jock to do. He maintained a vigilant watch across the fields, his interest occasionally straying to a bird in the sky. It was a glorious autumnal day, the air fresh, the sun's rays invigorating. Back home, such weather would entice him into the garden; late autumn always a busy time, tidying and preparing for winter. He pictured the scene, imagining the aroma of Jane's baking drifting out the open kitchen window, as he rested on his spade. A fire would await him indoors, the dogs lying at his feet, while he read or dozed.

"I sorry, Yok."

Piotr's approach startled Jock. He blinked the daydream away. "For what?"

"You right about Hyde. I should trust you. And for Jan. He, err... passionate man."

"Robbie and Jan are much alike," suggested Jock. "They're eyes get drawn tae shiny things, but when the chips are down, they come good."

"I understand you," said Piotr. "Like fox and volf."

"Err, well, I donnae know aboot that. We've another problem, though." Jock checked to ensure Hyde remained out of hearing range. "Ye got any medics in yer lot?"

Piotr frowned. "Doctors are officers, Yok."

"Nae, I mean anyone trained tae do frontline stuff. Knows something aboot first aid."

"I not sure. This is to help Hyde?"

"Aye," answered Jock with a drawn-out sigh.

"He is bad?"

"If someone doesnae take oot the bullet and treat the wound, an infection will kill him."

"And you have no one?"

"Nawt anyone I would trust," replied Jock. "If Jerry finds oot one of ours has one of their bullets in him, they'll work everything oot."

"Even if someone help, they not own... err... tools," added Piotr.

"If we can rob this gold from under their noses, we can steal a knife. Well, Robbie could." Jock leaned his head into his folded arms resting on a trunk. "If we get the bullet oot, we might get him in the hospital: let Jerry look after him. Claim something else caused the wound. Thing is, it's got tae be done quickly, cos he can't work with that arm."

Piotr looked less than convinced.

"Well, we can worry aboot it later," said Jock, his head peeking round the tree. "Here comes yer boy!"

Breathless and excited, the young Pole tried to convey his message amidst a battle for air. Piotr calmed with soothing words and a pat on his shoulder. With hands on knees, the boy sucked in long breaths, until a smile formed. A torrent of words spewed from his mouth, Piotr and Jan nodding in response, asking the occasional question. Hyde and Jock watched with impatience.

"And?" asked Jock, as the boy stood beaming a smile, his performance over.

"He found them," declared Piotr. "Not far. About 1 kilometre to east in vood."

"Excellent!" exclaimed Jock. "If they're carrying on as normal, they've nawt discovered our replacements."

"What else did he say?" enquired Hyde, looking up through tired eyes. "Sounded like Reverend Pendry down at the old soup exchange. Never stopped talking if he cornered you."

"Nothing," said Piotr with a chuckle. "He tell story of all he did. Speak to family and friends. They all help find soldiers. It is Polish vay to, err... honour people in story."

Jock grinned, recognising something familiar between his kinfolk and the Poles.

"He also ask me about bicycle," added Piotr.

"Well, that's all lovely," remarked Hyde, easing himself up, ignoring the laughter. "But we need to get going and check out the woods."

Jock ruffled the boy's hair. "What's yer name, lad?"

He stared back, wide-eyed.

"His name Antek," advised Piotr.

Jock gulped, a sense of guilt flushing through his body. "Any relation?"

"No, is common name."

"Aye, well, thank ye, Antek. Ye're very brave. After the war, ye can tell everyone all aboot taeday."

As Piotr translated, the boy's chest and smile grew with pride.

"Goodbye, Antek," whispered Jock, with a wistful sigh, as the boy sprinted off with the determined vigour of youth.

"Reminds me of myself at that age," commented Hyde, a hand resting on Jock's shoulder. "Running messages; avoiding the authorities."

"It's nawt the same!" snapped Jock, shaking the hand loose. "The boy will get shot if caught. Ye were just up tae nae good!"

"You're a surly old bastard sometimes, Jock."

"We've lost a good man. His family donnae know what happened tae him. I'm allowed tae be surly. Och, come on! Let's get going."

Chapter 14

"Hmm, the problem with them being in the wood," mused Jock, finding himself squatting in a ditch again, "is they've taken the best hiding place. I'm nawt lying in here for half a day and we canna watch them from elsewhere withoot being exposed."

From their sodden vantage point, the rhythmic noise of sawing drifted in their direction. A carthorse, uncoupled from its load, stood chewing a clump of grass at the wood's edge.

"Should we retreat tae another group of trees?" added Jock, throwing his thoughts out to all. "But how do we contact our doubles?"

"Perhaps we swap over on the march to camp?" proposed Hyde, lying with his back to the ditch bank, his eyes closed.

"Too difficult," rebutted Jock. "How'd we change clothes or alert them we planned tae do so? We have tae access the woods at some point."

Jan, sticking with his native tongue, conversed with Piotr.

"Tak, tak," responded Piotr. "Robbie, you can vork vith good arm?"

Hyde's eyes flicked open. "Why?"

"Jan has good idea," said Piotr. "Ve... err, how you say, creep into vood as peasants. Guards not care or see peasant if they vork hard. Ve change clothes. At end of day, ve to return to camp, peasants return home."

"Ha, I like!" exclaimed Hyde. "Bold as brass."

"One minute," countered Jock. "Ye struggled to walk this far. Chopping or moving wood is hard work for any man, let alone one with a bullet wound."

"Jock, you old mother hen," said Hyde. "If anyone's suited to shirking his work duties unnoticed, it's yours truly. Many a sergeant major can vouch for me."

"Ye're incorrigible," laughed Jock.

"That's a big word for a corporal."

"That's lance corporal tae ye, private," replied Jock, pleased the lad was fit enough to partake in barrack-room banter again. "Okay, if ye're nawt gonnae collapse on us, let's go play in the lion's den."

"Take my koszula!" Piotr removed his direct-covered shirt, passing it to Hyde.

"Good idea. The blood's a giveaway. Give us a hand putting it on!"

With a sharp tug, Jock ripped off a clean section of the old, bloodied top and redressed the wound, applying a tight knot. He fed Hyde's limp arm into the sleeve, eliciting groans and gritted teeth as he pulled it over his head.

"What'll ye do if a guard discovers the wound?" challenged Jock.

"Lie."

"Hmm, best if we make sure ye get yer clothes back first. Ye'll lie so much better back in army uniform."

They walked up to the woods in character, their scrawny bodies matching the locals. Only their age, old enough for army service, might raise eyebrows. To avoid scrutiny, Piotr or Jan stood prepared, if challenged, to spin a tale.

The horse looked up at the strangers, assessing them, deciding the grass offered more rewards. At this range, the dappled light penetrating the wood exposed the men and ponies working within. A faint odour of cut timber stirred the senses, reminding each of past days under the German yoke.

They lingered behind the beast, readying themselves. With a nod from Jock, they took a step forward, when a face appeared before them.

"Bloody hell, Joc...!"

Jock whipped his finger to his lips, curtailing the man's sentence. "Hello, Archie," he whispered. "Is everyone okay? Are we prepared tae swap back?" Jock studied the surroundings. "Continue as though we're nawt here!"

"Yes, worked like a charm," muttered Peters from the side of his mouth, his hands rummaging through the tool cart.

The others hung back behind the horse, appearing busy doing nothing.

"We're gonnae melt intae yer group. Stick with Hyde! He's a bullet in his arm."

"Bloo..." Peters restrained his shock, his eyes flicking sideways to assess Hyde.

"Just change him intae his uniform and oot of the sentry's sight! What they got the locals doing?"

"They're working the ponies, carrying wood."

"How many guards?"

"Four: positioned in a square. One's paying us attention." Peters pointed a discreet thumb. "From the hubbub among the Germans this morning, can one assume you were successful?"

"Aye," replied Jock with no enthusiasm. "We'll talk again back at the camp. Spread the word among our men. The odd distraction may be helpful."

Peters held a splitting wedge in his hand, his journey's purpose achieved. "Good luck."

They watched him vanish into the woods; a guard's sharp "Raus!" hurrying him on.

"We shouldnae use the same path as Peters," whispered Jock.

"Tak," agreed Piotr. "Ve must pick vood qvick. Look like ve vorking long time."

"Let's just get this over!" urged Hyde, fatigue etched on his face.

"This way!" Jock led them left, into a small, overgrown salient of trees, providing some cover. Twigs and branches tugged at their clothes as they clambered through, the ground an uneven mess of animal burrows and foliage.

As larger trees dominated, the undergrowth thinned. Fallen leaves and seeds littered the floor, their beautiful autumnal colours at odds with their decaying state. Discarded limbs from storm-damaged trees allowed the temporary peasants a rich bounty of wood. Each carried their load mounted on one shoulder, a single arm wrapped around it. They tramped deeper into the woods until the work party came into view.

"Hey, was machst du?" A guard spotted them. "Bleib im umkreis!" He waved his gun in their direction, ushering them towards the other workers.

Adopting a deferential bow and with logs shielding their faces, they jogged into the midst of their comrades. Their ploy had worked. Jock restrained a cheer, aware they still had some way to go.

The tired eyes of other prisoners glinted in welcome. A triumphant rhythm sang out in their work, replacing the words they dared not speak.

Jock recognised his double, the baggy uniform flapping as he grappled with a rope, tying it around a tree to control its descent. Relief flooded the man's eyes at the sight of Jock.

The guard continued to shout in their direction.

"He say ve take big trees from vood, not small sticks." Piotr showed off his grasp of German with a whispered translation.

"Tak, tak," called out Jock, stretching his Polish to the limit.

The pungent odour of the working ponies reached Jock's nostrils. In a despondent stoop, the beasts stood awaiting their loads. Peasants scrambled behind, trimming off branches from a fallen tree, attaching chains.

Jock spilled his pitiful collection of sticks to the floor, pretending to check the wooden yoke harnessed around a pony's neck. It seemed impossible such a diminutive creature could pull such a load, but Jock possessed a newfound faith in the impossible.

As Jock stole a glance around, he spotted Jan and Piotr taking an unorthodox route. Each sang a soft refrain, veering as close as possible to the peasants disguised in British and Polish uniforms. Without understanding a word, Jock understood all. He sought Hyde, hoping to offer a reassuring nod but the man had vanished. A knot formed in Jock's stomach.

"Jesteśmy gotowi. Poprowadź konia!" A peasant called to Jock, waving his hand forward.

Jock understood. "I donnae know if ye speak English, but it's time tae go," he whispered in the pony's ear, encouraging her forward with a push on the harness. The horse remained still.

"Przenieść! Przenieść!" cried the peasant, assisting with a smack to the creature's hind.

Without complaint, the pony took a step forward, followed by another. The chains straightened until taut. As the horse took the strain of the trunk, the peasant repeated his command, cajoling her forward with further smacks.

"Ye poor thing," whispered Jock, stroking her mane. "Better do as ye're told."

The mulch-covered surface aided the log on its way, and soon Jock walked at a slow but steady pace alongside the beast of burden. He risked another sweep of his head in search of Hyde. The criss-crossing trees and patchy light hid the occupants well, but on one side of a fallen tree, gripping a saw with lazy intent, stood Hyde, already back in his uniform. Peters worked the other end, his face full of contentment, unconcerned at taking on the burden of their task.

"Good old Archie," whispered Jock to his equine friend, shaking his head in disbelief at the speed and guile employed. The woodland provided the perfect environment for the switch.

Chapter 15

At day's end, as they shuffled into marching formation, Jock cast an eye back on the departing peasants. They led the working ponies away into the diffused light of the sinking sun: four in their midst among the bravest men Jock had met. He sniffed at his uniform's collar, distinguishing the odour of its former occupant from the accumulated dirt and his own sweat. This nameless man, humble and unrewarded, who tomorrow would take to the fields again, slaving for no return or gratitude, was a hero.

The guards wandered down the line, counting off the prisoners before the march back to camp. As one passed Jock, a subtle frown crept onto the German's brow.

"Good evening, mein herr. The weather's been glorious taeday," said Jock, addressing the guard.

"Nicht sprechen!" snapped the guard. But the distraction worked. He continued down the line, paying little heed to the pale Hyde; any suspicion at unfamiliar faces dissipating with the sound of a fluent English speaker.

"Well played," murmured Hyde, one place in front of Jock.

"Ye gonnae make it?" whispered Jock.

"Hope so," replied Hyde, the vigour gone from his voice, a damp film of sweat clinging to his forehead. "I don't know what I want first: sleep or food."

"Try both together," joked Jock, hoping to keep his companion's spirits up. "If ye need support on the march, just ask."

Despite the still brilliant blue sky, the temperature dropped. Grateful to have trousers that once again reached to his ankles, Jock trooped down the country lane in his watertight boots with one eye on Hyde. The man never marched with a rigid soldier's pride, but today all his strength went into holding himself upright, fighting the urge to collapse.

"How ye doing?" asked Jock for the fourth time.

Hyde grunted his acknowledgement.

"What's that noise?" A low rumble invaded the peace of the countryside.

The guards started shouting commands, corralling the prisoners to the roadside. Hyde stumbled at the sudden direction change, drifting back into the road. With a sidestep, Jock caught Hyde's elbow, guiding him to the verge.

"What is it?" a breathless Hyde asked, his eyelids hanging heavy.

"I donnae... Oh, damn!"

The once empty vista came alive with Germans, hundreds in number. Stretched out across the fields, as far as the eye could see, a line of soldiers advanced in steady formation. A puff of black smoke accompanying the roar signalled a column of armoured vehicles approaching down the road.

"They're searching for the gold!" whispered Jock. "We're lucky we didn't meet them earlier taeday." He looked along the row of prisoners, searching for Piotr and Jan. "D'ye think they'll be able tae recognise us?"

"Why?" Hyde lacked the energy to say more.

"I donnae know," answered Jock. "What aboot the sentry on the gate? He would have been looking straight at ye when ye drove at him."

Hyde tapped the arm of the prisoner to his right, holding out his hand. "Glasses, please." The man handed his wire-framed glasses across with the minimum of curiosity. "There!" announced Hyde, resting them on his nose.

Jock restrained a laugh. "The Scarlet Pimpernel has met his match!"

"Who?"

"Never mind, try looking like a soldier for a minute!"

An eight-wheeled, heavy armoured vehicle led the convoy, an SS officer perched in the turret. It jerked to a stop halfway along the row of prisoners, a plume of exhaust smoke triggering an outburst of coughing. The officer yelled questions at a prison guard, his tone as abrasive as if addressing a peasant.

Jock listened, trying his best to understand the conversation, but with the engine noise and speed of exchange, it reached him as a blur.

"He looks annoyed," mumbled Hyde with a smile.

Ignoring Hyde's gloating, Jock whispered a prayer. The sweeping line of Germans tramping across the fields came level, all armed and hunting their prey. Jock considered himself a fox riding the rump of a huntsman's mount.

The shouting ceased, and the officer inspected the line of prisoners with judgemental eyes. He nodded with condescending arrogance, waving the convoy forward.

Jock blew out the breath he held without knowing and watched as six vehicles crept past, their occupants' eyes all sparing an inquisitorial glance in the prisoners' direction.

"Does that not taste sweet?" asked Hyde as the last vehicle passed them.

"Aye, lad. Like nectar."

Chapter 16

"Morning, Jock," said Peters. "Sleep well?"

"Like the dead," declared Jock, arching his back and stretching his arms to the sky. "I recommend a couple of days oot of camp tae guarantee a good night's sleep."

"You seem better for it." Peters kicked at a pebble, struggling to hide a childlike grin.

"What?"

"You bloody did it, old chap!" exclaimed Peters. "The camp's buzzing. They all want to throw a party."

"May nawt be the best time," said an unenthusiastic Jock.

"Well, no, maybe not, but you're going to get a sore hand. Everyone wants to shake it. May be a Sunday, but you'll not get much rest." Peter slapped Jock on the back. "How did passing through the prison gate feel?"

"Ha, never has a prisoner been happier tae be back in prison."

"I thought one of those dogs might sniff you out."

"Did our doubles meet any difficulties?" Jock asked.

"Not with the dogs. Your uniform stinks too much. One threw up on parade, but at the back, out of view. Not sure Walker was happy though: covered the back of his trousers."

"We took one hell of a risk." Jock shook his head, his mind only now able to digest the last twenty-four hours. "They'd execute the entire camp if they found ye harbouring them."

"Don't exaggerate. A hut at most."

Jock grimaced, the black humour too close to reality. "We lost a good man. Wasnae hardly a man. Eighteen at most: same age as ma lad."

"Is that when Hyde took the bullet?"

"Aye, he's lucky tae be alive. We've got tae get that bullet oot!"

"Hmm," contemplated Peters. "I asked around, but no one's confident enough to try. Not without the right instrument, anyway. We made keys; how hard can it be to make what we need?"

"Bloody," stated Jock. "Ye won't make a blade from a stove. Needs a furnace."

"Ah, my failings as a clerk exposed again!"

"We'd better get him up for roll-call," mulled Jock. "He can sleep for the rest of the day. Wainthorpe said he tossed and turned throughoot the night. A fever, perhaps."

"A little broth may help."

"Aye, Grandma Mitchell always brewed a special broth tae make us better when I were a nipper," recalled Jock. "No idea what she put in. Mammy swore by the stuff."

"Did it work?"

"If Grandma Mitchell said ye were better, ye were better! Never more than a day in bed, a dose of broth, and back tae school or work, nae matter how much ye legs wobbled."

"Could have done with her in France! She would have got Jerry running."

Jock laughed and laughed, the stress of the last few days pouring out. "Stop, ye eejit! Yer making ma ribs hurt." He rubbed the bruise left by his scuffle with the SS guard.

"Come on!" said Peters, wrapping an arm around Jock's shoulder. "Let's give the hero a bit of Grandma Mitchell's love."

***

Sitting on the edge of Hyde's bed, Jock prodded the slumbering occupant. "Robbie, we've got ye some broth."

"Come on, sonny," added Peters, leaning against the head of the bunk. "We need you awake for parade."

"Is it true? We did it?" Hyde croaked, his eyelids edging open. "I dreamt wild dreams last night."

"We did," reassured Jock. "How ye feeling?"

"Not too bad." He betrayed the lie with a groan as he tried and failed to sit up.

"Get the lad another pillow!"

Three men leapt forward to offer theirs.

"Make yerself useful, Archie," said Jock. "Fluff them up and I'll help Robbie sit."

"There you go, son," said Peters, building a support for Hyde's back. "How's that?"

"Thanks. You don't have a fag? Haven't tasted one for a while."

Again, a multitude of willing hands reached forth with a gesture of appreciation.

Peters struck a match, the flame offered to Hyde's cigarette. "That'll get you on the road to recovery. Clears out the lungs."

"That's good," sighed Hyde, blowing out a plume of smoke. "Did someone mention food?"

"Glad ye've an appetite," commented Jock. "Who's got the bowl?"

"Wainthorpe! Get your arse over here with that broth!" yelled Peters.

"Been warming it on the stove," explained Wainthorpe, passing the bowl to Jock.

"Looks like ditchwater," observed Peters, as Jock held the bowl for Hyde to spoon himself.

"Tastes like ditchwater," quipped Hyde, slurping on the first spoonful. "And I should know; spent enough time up to my ankles in the stuff."

As the hut burst out laughing, Jock sensed all would be well with his friend, the old spark back. With a little more rest and food he would be strong enough for a makeshift operation.

"Hey, look who's here?" announced Hyde, making Jock and Peters turn to the door.

"Hello," said Piotr, standing with Jan in the doorframe, showing off his unmistakable smile. "Can ve come in?"

"We shall have our party!" cried Peters. "Come on in, chaps! The more the merrier."

Jock stood, greeting the Poles with a handshake, accepting with discomfort a hug and a kiss to the cheeks. "Good tae see ye both."

"It good to see you too, Yok," declared Piotr. "And you, Hyde. I vorry about you."

"Ha, takes more than a Jerry bullet to stop old Hydie." Hyde held out his good hand, clasping Piotr's. "We couldn't have succeeded without you and Jan."

"And Antek," added Jock.

"A hero to Poland!" proclaimed Jan, taking Hyde's hand. "Ve are now brooders!"

"Brothers! Never had a brother before," exclaimed Hyde, the excitement triggering a coughing fit.

"Slow down, laddie," said Jock. "One bowl of broth and a fag donnae make ye better, nae matter what Grandma Mitchell said."

"Eh?"

"Ne'er mind," said Jock, winking at Peters.

"Now we're all safe back in camp," began Hyde, his face taking on a serious appearance, "I guess I'd better tell you where I hid the gold."

The surrounding group leaned in closer.

"Now, hang on a minute," cautioned Jock. "While that bullet's still in ye, the Germans can connect us to the heist. Best wait until we get the blighter oot. Hey, lads?" Jock looked around for support.

A deafening silence answered.

"No, Jock," said Hyde. "Jan and Piotr deserve the truth. A good thief never cheats his partners when dividing up the loot."

"Ye're cheating naebody, lad. Just taking a precaution."

The clang of the summons alarm sent heads turning in shock.

"That's half hour early," said Peters. "What are they up to? On our day off too!"

"Let's keep calm," urged Jock. "We carry on as normal. Ye good tae get up, Robbie?"

"May need a hand or two."

"Everyone! Get oot on the parade ground!" instructed Jock. "They'll get suspicious if a hut's missing. Archie, give us a hand getting Robbie up and dressed."

Hyde, able to swing his legs off the bed, held out his good arm.

"I'd start with the other, unless ye want double the agony?" Jock guided the tunic sleeve up the limp arm.

"Stick your legs out straight!" ordered Peters, holding Hyde's trousers up. "Has anyone ever told you what knobbly knees you have?"

"All the lovers in my life," ribbed Hyde, blowing a kiss.

"Right, let's get ye standing," encouraged Jock, having bent Hyde's good arm into the remaining sleeve. "Can ye do it yerself?"

"Ain't my legs that they shot," said Hyde, rocking to launch himself. "But I may need your arm to pull on."

"Och, come here! Archie, ye push; I'll pull."

"Yes, told you I could do it," declared Hyde, on his feet, fighting the wave of dizziness and nausea. "Just need a moment. My blood's in the wrong place."

"Ye're lucky ye have any." Jock straightened Hyde's tunic and worked the buttons through their slots.

"Okay, let's try this." Hyde swayed, putting a foot forward. "Yes, I need to get moving, then I'll be fine."

"Well, get a move on!" urged Peters. "I can hear guards shouting for order."

"Put yer good arm round ma shoulder! I'll get ye tae the door."

They rested in the doorframe, inspecting the ordered rows forming on the parade ground. The Germans paced back and forth, hurling commands, growing angry at the lackadaisical mood of the prisoners.

"Here goes," said Hyde, striding down the steps unsupported.

Jock let him get a short way ahead, before following with Peters.

"Nothing to it," said Hyde, acquiring pace with each step. "That broth is working wonders."

"His walk's a bit of a giveaway," observed Peters. "Who doesn't swing both arms?"

Jock increased his pace, catching up with Hyde, shielding his damaged side from view. "Ye're doing grand."

"At least it weren't my good arm," whispered Hyde. "I give my two-finger salute with that one."

"Get in line and donnae bring attention tae yerself!"

The commandant took his usual position atop his soapbox stage, his hands tapping with impatience as the guards opened the gates for a small truck to enter.

"What's that aboot?" asked Jock, hidden in the back row. "Too small tae be transporting us oot."

"Red Cross delivery?" suggested Peters with glee.

"Maybe," said Jock. "Be nice tae get one, one day!"

"Achtung!" The order emerged from the front, the prisoners complying.

The commandant cleared his throat. "Gentlemen, I von't keep you long on your rest day.

"Ve have outbreak of typhus at camp IX. Our victories in east bring many Soviet prisoners: unclean animals. Ve cannot allow disease to spread. All camps vill be decontaminated. Ve vill combine today's headcount vith examination of each man and disinfection.

"Line up in single file before der truck and avait your instructions!"

The prisoners looked at each other bemused, awaiting someone else to lead.

"I'm surprised they're nae letting us all catch it and die," muttered Jock.

"They would if they could ensure we wouldn't infect them," said Peters.

"Schnell! Schnell!" yelled a guard, herding the first hut towards the truck.

The commandant watched for a moment, then signalled his departure.

"If typhus is about, let's hope he's already infected," remarked Peters, as the commandant reached the gate.

"Ye all right, Robbie?" asked Jock.

A haunted expression flashed on Hyde's face. "Yeah, I... Oh, nothing. Never mind."

Jock exchanged a worried glance with Peters.

A long, winding column formed with stubborn reluctance.

"How long's this going to take?" grumbled Peters.

"From the length of the queue, I would say all morning!" remarked Jock. "The priest won't be happy if I'm late for church. Bloody heathens!"

"Kleider aus! Clothes off!" A guard strolled down the line, repeating the order.

A hostile grumble rippled down the column amid the chilled morning air.

"Schnell!" cried the guard, his tone becoming angrier. "Clothes off!"

With reluctance, the prisoners disrobed.

All except Hyde. Without warning, he broke from the line, his determined steps transforming to an awkward run.

Jock's mouth dropped in shock, his eyes flashing between his friend and the watchtowers.

"Halt!" A surprised guard struggled for his pistol.

Hyde reached the first line of defences, a boundary of spiralled barbwire. Without breaking pace, he leapt over, his wounded side lending his flight a strange arch. One foot clipped a wire ribbon, sending him splaying on the other side. He scrambled to his feet; pain etched on his face. A burst of machine gun fire erupted from the watchtower, followed by a round from the guards within the camp. Hyde took one step more, stumbled and fell forward.

"Noooo!" screamed Jock, stuck to the spot amid a column of horrified eyes. He edged forward, desperate to run to Hyde's side, but found Peters's hand restraining his shoulder. "Why?" he sobbed.

The Germans, their numbers growing with reinforcements, squeezed the prisoners into a manageable scrum, their rifles aimed and threatening, as an angry murmur bubbled. Other guards scurried to the fence, towards the prostrate body of Hyde.

Jock stood still, his feet frozen, a helpless observer.

A ladder thrown across the wire allowed the guards to cross. They tested the danger from the unmoving Hyde with a kick to his stomach. Words were exchanged across the fence before a guard lifted Hyde and pushed him onto the wire for others to drag him across.

Jock turned away, retching at the demeaning spectacle.

"The barbaric swine!" cursed Peters, with far worse uttered elsewhere in the crowd.

As the Germans dragged the body past, Jock pushed forward, reaching out a hand. A rifle butt knocked him back, winding him. "Why? Robbie, why?"

A cruel wheeze escaped Hyde's mouth; his skin drained of colour, dappled in blood. Pain cried through his eyes, but a faint smile fought its way onto his face before his life ebbed away.

"Oh, Robbie, ye fool," cried Jock, trying to follow. "We could've found another way!"

Hands grabbed at Jock, pulling him away. He struggled before Peters's calming voice connected. "Let him go, Jock. Jerry won't hesitate to shoot you too!"

"He did it tae keep the secret," sobbed Jock. "He did it tae save us all!"

"I don't understand," said Peters.

"Jerry won't notice the old bullet in a body riddled with bullets. They'll throw him in a pit. He sacrificed himself. Nae way they'll know we did it now!"

"Jesus," whistled Peters. "I didn't think he had it in him."

"I'll tell everyone back home what ye did!" shouted Jock across the camp, hopeful that a spark of life might remain in his friend's limp body. "They'll remember ye!"

As the guards threw Hyde's body on a cart, the shocked prisoners turned away, unable to watch, their heads lowered in respect and despair.

"What about the gold?" asked Peters. "No one knows where it's stashed."

Jock sniffed, wiping away the tears he wished to remain private. "Aye, and so begins the legend of Robbie Hyde. Tae the wee scallywag goes the victory. He got away with it!"

The End

A Place More Dark
1945

Book Two

We are in the third circle, a place more dark.
Inferno, Dante Alighieri

Day One: Early Morning

The bleeding sunrise coloured the winter sky, as silence hung beneath a thin veil of mist. Across fields and streets lay thick snow, while chimneys coughed out their smoke, polluting the white landscape with a smudge of grey. Within cottages and houses, people stoked their hearths, invigorating the flames, tugging blankets tighter as the cold persisted. They cast a worried eye towards pitiful wood supplies, their minds drifting to that other scarcity: food.

In one such house, a young widow, her children asleep in the warmth of the solitary family bed, circled her knuckle on a window-pane, clearing the frost. She stooped, pressing her nose to the glass with one eye closed and reflected on the unfamiliar world. The high, red-brick fort walls dominated her view, as they had her entire life. But where once the doves perched, now sat piercing spotlights, their beams glinting off a barbed-wire crown. The breath of a gun-turret sentry crystallised in the freezing air, a strange beauty amid the beasts. Like the cold, the invader permeated everywhere and everything.

An unseen engine roared to life, breaking the silence. Shouting followed. The mother recoiled from the window, her eyes pausing on her babes undisturbed within the bed and then on the empty store cupboard. A single tear rolled from her tired eyes, and she returned to stoke the fire.

Richard 'Jock' Mitchell, on the other side of those red-brick walls and wire, stirred to the same disturbance. Awake for the last hour and struggling to keep warm under a thin blanket, he lifted himself onto his elbows, straining his ears. The grating squeal of rusty hinges fed into the commotion.

"Something's up," he remarked in his Ayrshire brogue, rubbing a stiff shoulder.

"Wake me in spring!" came the groan from the bunk above.

The violent clang of the camp alarm shattered all hope of a lie-in. Boots thudded up their hut's wooden steps. The door swung open. Silhouetted against the white background stood the unmistakable outline of a German soldier.

"Up! Up!" he yelled, banging his rifle against the wall. "Schnell! Vee go!"

"Och, shut the bleeding door!" muttered Jock, adding to a chorus of similar curses. "Ma toes cannae feel themselves."

Instead, the soldier yanked the blanket off the first bunk. "Vee go! Dress und sammelt alle eure Sachen."

Jock swung off his bed, tensing as his feet touched the cold floor. "What do ye mean, we go? Go where?"

Without answering, the soldier tramped down the hut, kicking at empty boots. "Schnell! Put on!"

"Eh," called out Arthur Hepworth, struggling with a boot, while craning his neck to peer out the door. "The gates are open. They're all in their winter best."

As the guard yelled in his direction, Jock considered him while rubbing his feet between his gloved hands. The lad Hepworth was right: even this pipsqueak bore the heavy burden of a warrior ready for action in his uniform. It looked comical on his skinny, teenage frame: another child roped in for duty by an exhausted country.

"Boots!" screamed the pipsqueak towards Jock.

"Ye call these boots?" replied Jock with a scowl, holding up his right boot to show off the flapping sole.

"And zeese!" cried the soldier, tugging on Jock's blanket and pointing at an old Red Cross parcel.

With feet housed in their boots, Jock stood, looking down at the German. At 42 and six foot one, Jock expected some respect. "Lower that voice. What ye trying to tell us, lad? Are we leaving this shithole?"

"Is the war over?" The question floated in from the hut's far end, triggering an excited murmur in its wake.

"Donnae get ye hopes up," chided Jock, calling on his long years of experiences as a prisoner of war. "You'll know the war's over when Fritz starts saying 'please'."

The overcrowded room descended into a noisy debate as the optimists and realists battled for supremacy.

"Silence!" Another silhouette appeared at the door, wearing the distinctive hat of a German officer. As the noise subsided, a barrage of vitriol flew out of his lips in his native tongue at the soldier. "Now," he continued in English, his composure regained, his displeasure sated. "Zee Reich has no intention of losing zis var, so forget thoughts of freedom. Vee are regrouping, preparing for zee final victorious thrust. You are moving to new camp."

"Where?" called out an anonymous voice.

"Vest," replied the officer. "You vill pack all belongings. Take vhat you can."

"West? Where, precisely? How far? Are we walking? What about food?"

The officer allowed the flurry of questions to die out. "You have vone-hour and zen vee march." With that, he spun on his heels and vanished out the door.

Archie Peters, Jock's friend and upper-bunk mate, landed with a practised grace. "Jeez! This is bad."

"Hmm," mulled Jock, tugging at the loose sleeve of his jacket. "I cannae see a stroll in this weather doing us good."

"The Wehrmacht diet lacks a little in nutrition and quantity," quipped Peters, tapping his prominent rib cage. "What you looking for?"

"Something to mend ma boot," grumbled Jock. "I'll nawt get far in these."

"Straw from the mattress? Swede peel?" suggested his friend. "Just to keep your feet warm."

"Aye, the same straw I wannae stuff in ma coat and the peel I'll be eating."

Tom Whatman, a young private whose skin retained the bronzed colour from his time in North Africa, appeared. "Do we travel light or loaded?"

"Good question," said Peters. "I don't think I have the strength to carry much."

Jock tapped the wood of the bunk. "We travel light and loaded."

"Eh?"

"Wear all you have but carry nothing. We'll take as much food and wood as possible."

"How?" asked Whatman.

"Ye ne'er made a sledge, laddie?" Jock's withered face cracked into a near-toothless grin. "Break these beds apart, use what we must tae build our sleighs, and the rest we load for burning."

Peters nodded in appreciation. "But what about rope?"

"Must I think of everything?" said Jock. "I'm using ma belt. Ye can use boiled leek, for all I care."

"What I wouldn't give for a leek," sighed Peters.

"What about strips from my mattress?" offered Whatman.

"Try a strip of curtain," suggested Jock. He looked up. "Or the cable from that lamp. Aye, let's rip out as much cable as we can. Fritz can pay for it."

"Won't the Germans object?"

"We're nawt coming back here, lad," said Jock. "Neither are the Germans. This is a retreat."

"What do they want us for?" pressed Whatman. "Why not just let us go?"

"Donnae try getting intae the mind of old Jerry," cautioned Jock. "They follow their own dark path. Now, less talking; more breaking." His size ten boot swung at the leg of his bed, folding the rickety construction inwards. "Pass the word. The winters are unforgiving. We cannae be unprepared."

"Jock's right," said Peters, stripping his top bunk clean, testing the joints with his open palm. "They've picked the worst time to take us on holiday."

"I'll get my bucket and spade," joked Whatman, wandering off to the next bunk.

Jock sighed and pulled his fingers down his sallow, stubbled jaw. A foreboding rumbled through his gut, exaggerated by hunger.

***

Jock adjusted his balaclava, the last item received via the Red Cross before the parcels stopped arriving the previous year, then placed a boot in the crisp snow. The footsteps of the morning's two German visitors remained cut deep among the crystals. Jock stepped to the side, preferring the virgin snow. It felt different to home. There, the crunch and texture stirred excitement; here, nothing but trepidation. His toes wriggled, testing the straw crammed in a sock, and pulled over another pair. Already his mind struggled to discern if the cold or moisture invaded his footwear.

"Room for another pot on your sledge, Jock?" asked Peters from behind a scarf.

"Aye." Jock wondered if he looked as ridiculous as his friend, adorned in a mishmash of all the garments he possessed. He tugged on his cable reins, sliding the sledge down the steps on to the snow. No more than the frame of his bed turned upside down and broken in half, it sat precariously under its load: the bundles of sticks, pots, cutlery and scraps of food, wrapped in his thin, straw mattress.

"I see Ted's hut had the same idea," commented Peters, casting an eye on the growing crowd of prisoners evacuating their dormitories and milling in the parade yard.

"But some haven't," sighed Jock. "Should have got word tae all. That lad's carrying a hoose!"

A bulging holdall hung from the shoulders of a young private lost in conversation with his mates.

"At least he looks fit," observed Peters. "Hasn't been here long."

"Hmm." Jock knelt, testing the bindings on his sledge. He glanced into the gutted hut. "I hate the place, but suspect we'll miss it."

"Germany's only a week or so's march. Not like our journey from France. Ouch, that left me with blisters. We'll soon be inside again. Can't be any worse than here!"

Before Jock could respond with a dose of pessimism, a black sedan pulled up in the outer enclosure; its red Nazi pennants frozen as though caught in a perpetual wind. Surrounded by his officers, the camp Commandant, Major Lange, saluted as a man in the familiar black uniform of the Schutzstaffel climbed out.

"Bloody SS," hissed Peters. "Been seeing too much of them."

"This'll be their doing," added Jock. "An exercise in humiliation and sadism."

"Eh, it's your girlfriend."

"Och, what ye talking aboot."

In the background, the commandant's wife rocked on her feet, struggling in the cold despite a fur coat. Before her, snuggled against the fur, stood their young daughter. The commandant motioned them forward, clasping his wife's hand, helping her into the car. He picked up the girl, swung her round and planted a kiss on her forehead.

For the first time that day, Jock smiled. "Oh, wee Birgit." As a father of two boys, a daughter remained an ambition. It was his loose connection to the commandant's girl, a thin strand of humanity in a world of barbarity. No words cemented their relationship, just shy smiles and timid waves through the window, from the commandant's cottage to the garden, where Jock laboured. He often wondered why she never betrayed Hyde and himself on their nefarious visit to the commandant's house all those years before. *Does she even know it was me?* Jock thought to himself. "Aye, it's best she's away from this place."

The commandant encouraged his daughter into the backseat and shuffled in behind her. The door slammed shut and, with a puff of smoke, the sedan moved off.

Back in the camp, chaos reigned, not just within the haggard ranks of the prisoners, but amid the once disciplined German guards. Their eyes roamed the grounds with a lost, childlike fear. Some shouted from habit, manhandling prisoners into a semblance of a column, others mingled within the melee of their captives.

"They look defeated," commented Levitt Quigley, a lad of 19 with tender skin defiant against the rigours of war.

"Morning, Babe," said Peters.

"A cornered beastie is at its most dangerous," said Jock, acknowledging the boy with a nod.

"Don't suppose we'll be getting any post now?" asked the lad, pulling some woollen socks over his hands.

"Not had any for months," remarked Peters. "Think of it as a good sign. Means we've broken Fritz's infrastructure."

"I'd prefer news from ma Jane and boys," said Jock, shuffling forward into the half-formed line.

"I've got a letter to go to my mum," added Quigley. "Wrote it ages ago. I'll end up hand-delivering it."

"Here's hoping. Hey, look! There's Konrad." Peters, hand over mouth, waggled a discreet thumb to his right.

Jock and Quigley turned their heads, spotting the German guard with his distinct stoop.

"Worth a word," said Jock, pushing through the crowd.

"Someone who may know what's going on," added Peters in his wake.

The guard spotted their approach, adding a further line of worry to his brow.

Jock pinched at his sleeve, preventing an escape. "Konrad, ma friend. Ye're dressed for war. Where ye taking us?" He surveyed their surroundings, ensuring no one watched them.

"Jock, I have no knowledge." Konrad adjusted his ill-fitting steel helmet. A grey moustache quivered under a slender nose. His neck jutted forward, shaped by years of bad posture at some industrious activity, while a scar tarnished his forehead, a reward from the last war. To define his age was impossible: perhaps over 50 or maybe aged by war. "Zee Russians are close. Zat ist all I'm told."

"Nae wonder yer lot are worried," said Jock. "Ye coming with us?"

"Ja," answered Konrad, his eyes flittering left and right. "Some go south; vee go vest."

"Why take us with you?" asked Babe Quigley, appearing at Jock's shoulder. "The Russians can look after us. Save you the hassle."

The German shrugged. "I must go. Zee var is lost but zee..." His fingers danced back and forth in search of the word. "... zee cruelty remains." He pushed himself out of the crowd of prisoners, almost tripping over a sledge.

"Didn't think I could like a German," said Peters.

"Konrad's all right," said Jock, having bonded with the guard on discovering his good English and love of Clematis. "Nawt all are Nazis."

"We still don't know what's going on," complained Quigley. "I hope we get moving soon. It's cold!"

Day One: Mid-Morning

The breeze stirred the fallen snow; dancing crystals glittered in the low morning light. A blackbird raided the berries off a bush, then sang in triumph, competing with the low rumble of vehicles winding down a road. In their wake, a rag-tag army of the beaten and worn trudged, their once regimented formation disintegrating despite the remonstrations of their guards.

Jock exhaled a stream of vapour from his nose and turned to see the city of Thorn in the distance. *Good riddance*, he thought, before shaking his head in memory at the size of the evacuation. So many prisoners. *Where have they all come from?* The mass divided into columns of 250, setting off on their trek in formation. *But to where?* Jock winced as the cold gnawed at his right foot. *Damn these boots!*

"You all right, Jock?" Peters glanced across, his beard already bearing an icicle.

"Aye. Hard to believe we're the ones winning this conflict."

"How many you reckon? Two... three thousand?"

"Lots more. I know they were cramming the huts full but..."

"You think we could overpower the guards?" cut in Peters, sneering at a German soldier trudging to their side. "Can't be more than a dozen or so of them."

"With guns and a meal inside them," cautioned Jock. "And more up front. They're nervy."

"Can't a man dream?"

"Only if he gets a good night's sleep! Och, I cannae feel ma toes."

The German yelled towards them with an angry wave. A motorbike and sidecar growled behind. The prisoners veered sidewards, letting them through, rewarded with a spray of sludge.

"How's your load?" asked Peters.

"The least of ma problems," answered Jock, feeling the tug of the cable reins between the sledge and his belt. "I hope wee Birgit's safe." It helped to distract his thoughts from his own predicament.

"Safe and warm," said Peters. "With papa readying our hotel for the night... I hope."

"Four-star accommodation?"

"But of course! Hot running water for the bath and four-poster beds with silk sheets."

"Bah, I'm staying in the bath! Donnae need nae silk sheets."

Neither laughed, their repartee a compulsion of tired minds and bodies.

Morning progressed. The world played out along the narrow strip of road. German families joined the exodus, their Polish excursion over. Children wailed; mothers calmed them, hiding their own tears. Old folk rode in carts pulled by emaciated nags, their life possessions crowded to their side. Soldiers pushed their way through, some against the flow, exploiting the advantage of their weapons and vehicles. Meanwhile, the prisoners, sombre and fearful, with the cold sapping their will, continued to place one foot before another.

"Keep up!" growled Jock, the column now single file and stretched out.

Bang! The distant sound of gunfire.

"The Russians!" Prisoners scrambled to the ditches, fearful of an indiscriminate barrage.

"Halt!" cried a guard, his own mind torn between diving in a ditch or shooting a prisoner. Life paused. The Russians failed to materialise, the prisoners went no further, and the guards refrained from shooting. After a moment, all regrouped on the road and they marched again.

A further hour passed. Up ahead, one of the German guards ushered the prisoners to the roadside.

"Esst! Eat!" He motioned with a hand to his mouth.

"Eat what?" mumbled Peters, finding a bank clear of snow, and slumping down.

"I've a can of condensed milk and some jam," said Jock, drooping next to him with his sleigh adjusted for his feet to rest on. He pulled a tobacco tin from his pocket, his gloved fingers slipping on the lid. "Och, cannae even get in, let alone roll a cigarette! Can ye take ma boot off? I cannae manage." He shoved the tin back in his coat.

"Sure, once I can feel my fingers." Peters stood, lifting Jock's leg between his gloves. The laces released with a light tug. "That was easier than I thought. Now, hold still...huh." The boot slid off.

"Och, ma sock. Wet! Nae wonder I cannae feel anything."

"Here, dry your feet and wrap them in this." Peters chucked a rag.

"Hut Six curtain? It dinnae keep us warm before. What makes ye think it'll work now?"

"Necessity, my dear Jock. Necessity."

"Aye, Archie. Ye may have a point there. What would I do withoot ye?"

A ruckus started along the bank. Prisoners scrambled to their feet, shouting as they darted into a writhing mass.

"What...!" Peters's eyes widened. "Food, Jock! Come on!" He dashed off, joining the scrum.

"Ma boot, man! I've only got one boot on." He slumped back with a bitter laugh.

Peters sauntered back a minute later, rubbing his shoulder, carrot fronds protruding from his mouth.

"A nice crunchy carrot?" asked Jock.

"Ha, you must be joking. Just a carrot top!" Peters sat back down, letting out a melodramatic sigh. "I've seen pigs at a trough behave better than that lot. Here, I got you some turnip peel."

"Thanks. I'll save the milk." Jock chewed on the sparse meal, wincing at the taste of mud and grit. "Pigs get treated better."

"Let's get that boot back on."

"Aye, I've got the blood circulating again." Jock lifted his leg as his friend pushed the boot.

A Yorkshire accent interrupted them. "You Jock Mitchell?"

Jock eyed two prisoners standing before him, as his fingers struggled to tie his boot. "Aye. Who wants tae know?"

"Ted Hennessey," said the taller of the pair. "RAF. This 'ere is Al Tupps."

The smaller man grinned, his eyes glowing with a strange intensity.

Jock climbed to his feet, extending his hand. "I dinnae see ye in camp. Where were ye held?"

"Stalag XXA," answered Hennessey. "Like you. Just a different compound. The place is vast."

"We're starting to appreciate that," said Peters, standing to join the conversation. "Conditions any better in your place?"

"Beatings, overcrowding, disease, lice and starvation," said Hennessey.

"And cold," added Tupps, his reedy voice suiting his weasel face.

"At least customer service was consistent," joked Peters. "Archibald Peters, West Kents. Pleased to meet you. Pilots?"

"Na," laughed Hennessey. "Rear gunner on a Lancaster. Shot down over Magdeburg. Al was a mid-gunner. Doesn't even remember where he went down."

"Many of you chaps captured?" asked Peters, always attracted to the glamour of the Air Force.

"Too many, but, yeah, we're the lucky ones." Hennessey sniffed. "The locals don't take kindly to those bombing their homes."

"I suppose not," said Peters.

"How ye know ma name?" asked Jock.

Hennessey and Tupps exchanged a smile.

"You're a legend," said the former. "You may not have known of our presence, but we knew of yours."

Jock cast his discerning eye at them.

"Gold!" whispered Tupps, those intense eyes almost bursting with enthusiasm.

"You gave it good to those scum," declared Hennessey. "You were the talk of the camp. Of course, took us a while to get the details. You know, names and the like. But here we are. We've found you."

"Ye've found me," echoed Jock without enthusiasm.

A silence followed, until Tupps could contain himself no more. "So, where is it?"

"What?"

"The gold!"

"I dinnae care!" Jock declared, reluctant to revisit the episode. It still pained him to think of Hyde's death, or the whole stupid plan to steal the Nazi gold. "Ma friend hid it and took the secret to the grave."

An inane smile remained on the pair's faces.

"But you must have an idea?" pressed Hennessey. "A rough area."

"Why do you want to know?" asked Peters.

Hennessey lent in with a furtive glance behind. "We're planning to escape and find it. There's no better time. The security is slack, and they won't care or even notice if a few prisoners are missing."

Jock laughed out loud. "Ye're crazy!"

"Crazy to want to get away from this? To avoid another year in a camp?"

"Crazy tae die in the snow on a fool's errand."

Hennessey shrugged. "You don't want to come? Fine. More gold for Tupps and me. At least give us a pointer to where you last saw your friend."

"And if you get away and find the gold," said Peters. "What then? You're in occupied territory."

"Ah, not for long. The Russians will soon be in control. We'll hide out until then, introduce ourselves to our comrades, and arrange passage back home... with loot in our baggage."

Jock and Peters exchanged a look of disbelief.

"I thought you had to be smart to be in the RAF?" said Peters. "Uncle Joe doesn't play cricket. Not really a sportsman at all."

Hennessey's smile faded. "Now, just one minute. Who you calling stupid?" He pushed his face towards Peters's. "You're the ones who stole the gold and lost it!"

"Steady, lad." Jock remained calm. "Let's nawt fight amongst ourselves. Ye do what ye want. Just leave us oot of it. Hyde was north-east of Thorn. Aboot a mile oot."

The smile returned. "Hyde? Your friend who squirrelled away the gold?"

"Aye."

"Any landmarks?"

"Naw, it were night. We stole a German troop truck and loaded the gold into it. That's all I can tell ye."

Hennessey turned to Tupps. "We'll have to depart soon, before we're too far away."

"You're making a mistake," warned Peters.

"I'll remind you of that as you open the door for me at the Ritz. Don't worry, I'll give you a good tip."

"Sure." Peters shook his head with a wry smile.

"Hoch! Hoch!" A German motioned with a furious hand, stomping down the line of prisoners. "Bewegung!"

"I guess lunch is at an end," remarked Peters, reattaching his sleigh's reins. "How's that boot?"

"As good as it's gonnae get," moaned Jock. He turned to Hennessey. "It's best tae stay with the pack, lad. We can look after each other."

"Thanks for the tip, but my mind's made up. And there's no time like the present. See you in Blighty!" With that, he lobbed a bag behind a tree, checked for the absence of a guard, and dashed up the bank, Tupps following.

"Good luck," muttered Jock, reharnessing his own sledge.

"That gold's a curse," said Peters, starting off down the road. "First Hyde and now Tweedledum and Dee."

"Where they get the energy from?" queried Jock, his tired legs straining with the trailing load.

"Ah, the pampered RAF! Fattened on the best swede and tatties the Stalag can provide." Peters winked at his friend.

"Halt! Achtung!" Angry voices sounded behind. "Halt!" A pause, then a burst of gunfire.

"Jesus!" cried Peters, ducking as he turned.

Two guards stood atop the bank, rifles to shoulders. Bang! Another round fired. Other Germans scurried towards them, yelling threats at the cowering prisoners on the road.

"Hennessey and Tupps?" said Jock, his brow drooping with foreboding.

The firing ceased. The guards exchanged triumphant words, before backing down the bank. One signalled towards Peters and Jock.

"You, come!" he barked.

Peters tapped himself with an uneasy finger.

"Ja, schnell. Come!"

"Bleeding idiots," cursed Jock through gritted teeth. "What they got us in tae?"

The guard clutched Jock's sleeve, yanking him to the bank's brow, despite his trailing sleigh. A colleague harangued Peters in the same direction. At 20 yards' distance, two lifeless bodies lay in the snow, the surrounding white turning a dark crimson.

"They dinnae get far," lamented Jock.

"Geh! Go!" said the guard next to Jock. "Bring Körper."

"Eh?"

"You bring here." He motioned with a hand. "Schnell!"

"Oh, Jeez," whined Peters, releasing his reins. "Why us?"

"Because of our friendly mugs," grumbled Jock, free of his sledge and battling through the deep snow. "Nae wonder they dinnae get far." He turned to see the rifles now levelled at them.

Hennessey and Tupps lay face down, bullet holes exposed through their coats.

"Shot in the back!" hissed Peters. "Bloody cowards."

"Come on, man. Let's get this over." Jock grabbed Hennessey by his boots and heaved.

"Jock!"

"Eh?"

Peters nodded at the dead man's boots. "He won't be needing them."

Jock grimaced. "Aye. Suppose nawt. And they're ma size."

"Fate, my friend." Peters tugged at the laces.

With a sharp yank, Jock pulled the boots off. "Here, tie the laces together. I'll get Ted moving before Fritz complains."

"There you go!" Peters wrapped the boots round Jock's neck. "That's one problem solved."

"Ta." Jock readjusted himself, his arms now behind, grasping the dead man's ankles. "I'll be taking yer socks too," he informed Hennessey as a courtesy.

"The bounty of war," said Peters, stripping Tupps of his gloves and scarf. He stuffed them in his pockets and grabbed the legs.

Tupps groaned.

"Jesus! He's alive." Peters dropped the legs, gaping at Jock.

Jock paused, turning his head, then looking back at the Germans. "He's alive!" he shouted.

"Schnell!" came the response, an arm waving them back.

"I'll carry him," said Peters. "We'll get help on the road." He pulled Tupps up by his arms, eliciting further groans that mixed with his own as he positioned the body over his back. "A weighty fella."

"Come on. Jerry is restless."

"I've not had my spinach," quipped Peters between huffs.

At the top of the bank, under the watchful eyes of the guards, Jock released Hennessey's body. It slid down the slope, resting at an unnatural angle at the bottom. Prisoners glanced across as they passed, their eyes venting anger, sympathy and fear.

"He's alive," repeated a breathless Peters, as he slipped Tupps from his shoulders before the waiting guards. "But he needs urgent medical attention."

The guards exchanged a word and ushered Peters back on to the road with a shove of their rifles. One turned, angled his gun at Tupps and pulled the trigger.

"You bastards!" cried Peters, one foot already sending him back to confront the soldier. A hand gripped his arm.

"Grab ye sleigh and get walking." Jock's even voice reached Peters's ear. "They have their trophies tae warn other prisoners nawt tae try escaping. Don't give them another! We win by surviving."

Peters let out a deep breath, grabbed the reins of his sleigh and yanked it with a bitter ferocity. "And I'll be there to see them lose!"

Day One: Evening

U nder the shelter of a tall pine forest, the day's light faded fast, sending the temperature plummeting. Congregating amid the trees, under the glow of a troop lorry's headlights, the prisoners waddled from side to side, hands rubbing their torsos as they tried to stay warm.

"Are we finally stopping?" asked Peters.

"Looks like it," said Jock.

A plume of steamy vapour lingered above the mass of bodies, adding an eerie atmosphere. Their aching muscles cried for a rest, but still they stomped up and down, fighting the cold. To their left, beyond the line of trees, a farmhouse nestled in an opening, trucks and cars filling the courtyard. A guard stood at the gate of a cowshed, inspecting the interior. He yelled a command, and his colleagues stirred to action.

"Is that our accommodation?" Tom Whatman joined his older companions, staring in dread.

"No hot bath then?" said Peters, as the prisoners trudged towards the shed.

"That's the commandant's car," observed Whatman. "Thought he'd be in Berlin by now."

With the snow cleared from the busy farmyard, the sledges grated on the frozen ground.

"At least we'll get the chance to sleep at last," offered Peters. "Though a four-poster would be preferable."

"Jock." Konrad appeared before them; his uniform hidden beneath an ill-fitting trench coat. "You made it."

"Nae thanks to yer countrymen," snapped Jock.

"Sorry, my friend. Madness rules der vaterland."

"I'm sorry," said Jock. "It's been a long day. Are we tae be treated like cattle?"

"Ja," answered the German, unable to hide his shame. "It is all zee locals can offer. For food, a broth."

"Tasty," remarked Peters, rubbing his stomach.

"Nae news on a destination?" Jock asked, as a queue took shape outside the cowshed.

Konrad shook his head. "Tomorrow vee march again."

"Breakfast at eight, my good man," joked Peters, as they neared the shed. "Er, one side has no wall!"

"Ja," confessed Konrad. "Just straw und broth."

"So, you said." Peters swung a boot at a pinecone.

"Is the commandant's family still with him?" asked Jock, glancing across to the farmhouse.

"Ja. He vants... er, everything normal. Ja?"

"Normal! He thinks this is normal?" Jock bent a leg, kneading the top of his boots.

"Ah, you got new boots, Jock," observed Konrad.

"Aye, bequeathed in a friend's will."

"Sorry?"

"Ne'ermind." Jock rummaged in his possessions, pulling out a mug. "Food's the priority."

"Ja, ja. I go." Konrad fumbled in his pocket, flicking a matchbox into Jock's hand.

"Danke, Konrad."

The German nodded, his lame smile conveying the burden of guilt, then wandered off. "Viel Glück."

"I'd have complaints as a cow sleeping in this carbuncle!" moaned Peters. "And the smell. No doubt rats. I hate rats."

"There's Arthur," said Whatman, waving to their former hut mate. "And Babe. Babe!"

The youngsters walked over, acknowledging their friends with a simple nod.

"You don't look so good," Peters remarked to Arthur Hepworth, wincing at a pungent aroma.

"My bleeding gut," complained the youth, trying to restrain a belch. "Had to stop every few hundred yards."

The others needed no further detail, recognising the symptoms of dysentery.

"Set up your mattress," instructed Jock, as they entered the long, crowded building. "Get some rest. I'm getting a fire going."

"He's not the only one struggling," whispered Peters. "Marching all day isn't what the doctor ordered."

"Hmm," concurred Jock. "We need to care for ourselves first to ensure we can look after them. It's only gonnae get worse."

Jock slung his mattress on the ground, kicking away a dried cowpat. To make a fire, he gathered straw and pinecones, stacking them at the open end of the shed. With the third match, the straw caught, shrivelling and contorting. He added more until flames consumed a cone, arranging the splintered fragments from his old bed around to build the fire. "That's doing nicely."

Peters held his palms into the rising smoke, absorbing the blissful warmth. "How far do you think we strolled today?"

Jock shrugged. "Ten? Twelve miles at best. We're nawt setting a great pace."

"Not sure I could manage more." Peters stared into the depths of the flames, contemplating their perilous situation. "It's harder than I thought."

"Go fill up a pan with snow," requested Jock. "We'll boil it. Arthur needs fluids. I'll manage the fire."

"Sure. I saw a patch back there."

Jock welcomed a further three prisoners around his fire. They shared a donation of wood, sparing time to warm themselves before unpacking. A gentle wind excited the flames, swaying them back and forth; the fire's light extenuating the hollow faces of the prisoners.

"Broth's ready," cried Babe Quigley. "Grab your mugs!"

"About time!" grumbled Peters on his return. "You coming, Arthur?"

The sick private found the energy to shake his head.

"Ye are coming, laddie!" stated Jock. "Help him up!"

"I can't," complained Hepworth with a quiver. "It won't stay down."

"Ye must try. We cannae bring ye any. Fritz won't allow it. Sip what ye can."

Quigley and Whatman supported the boy, the brief rest appearing only to have worsened his condition.

Exhaustion imprinted itself throughout the prisoners. There was no scramble for food now. They queued under the watchful eye of sentries, faces solemn and drawn. A scruffy German cook ladled his runny concoction into each prisoner's mug. They examined the content with disappointment before trudging back to the shed.

"The closest this got to meat was being stirred with a feather," moaned Peters, taking a further sip while feeding another piece of wood on the fire.

"At least it's warm," said Babe. "I had a nice chunk of potato."

"I'll bring my wife back to this establishment on your recommendation."

Babe gave Peters a quizzical frown, never certain if the older man was serious or not. "I spoke with an RAF prisoner today. Said they'd a smuggled radio in their compound."

The mention of the RAF caused Jock to look up, reminded of Hennessey and Tupps.

"The Russians are moving at a hell of a rate. Faster than our chaps."

"Any news of home?" asked Whatman.

"Nothing good. Have you heard of flying bombs?"

"Do plummeting bombs count?" quipped Peters.

"No," continued Babe, again unable to decipher his colleague. "They're taking off inside Germany and have no pilots. Causing terrible damage."

"Och, nae more talk of war," cried Jock. "Tell us aboot your life before the war."

"Sorry, Jock," said Babe. "Yes, of course. My father owned a greengrocery in Epping. Been helping since I was a babe."

"You're still a babe, Babe," chortled Peters.

"I'm old enough to manage the shop when pa's away," continued Quigley, affording Peters's joke a smile. "I'll take over one day. Give Dad a rest."

"Good for ye," said Jock. "Any hobbies?"

"Stamp collecting... oh, yes, I do some amateur dramatics."

"Give us your Hamlet!" urged Peters, winking at Jock.

"No, no. I've not had a lead role yet. I played the evil stepmother in the camp's panto last year."

The group smiled, recalling the chaotic production.

"And a sweetheart?"

The darkness hid Babe's blush. "No, not yet."

"I hear one of the ugly sisters had eyes for you," joked Peters.

Laughter spread round the campfire, as Babe looked to the floor, hiding his awkwardness.

"Sorry, lad," said Peters. "But a little humour lifts the spirits."

"It's fine."

A groan emerged from behind, dissipating the remaining smiles.

"How ye doing, lad?" asked Jock.

"Sorry, I need to go again," answered Hepworth through his contorting face.

"Nae problem. I'll help ye." Jock stood, assessing the rest of the group. "Ye lot get tae bed."

Day Two: Morning

As a robin sang from its high perch announcing dawn, Jock wondered if he'd slept at all. Returning from the makeshift lavatory with Hepworth last night, he'd found his companions packed together for warmth, still fully dressed and beneath their threadbare blankets. They chatted away, exhausted but unable to sleep. He recalled chiding them, demanding quiet and squeezing in besides, allowing Hepworth on the end, before closing his eyes. Then the cold returned to his feet and seeped through his mattress into his body. The darkness amplified the sounds from beyond: guards chatting, prisoners groaning, crying or vomiting and the creatures of the night with their hoots and barks. He'd squeezed his closed eyes still tighter, leaning into his neighbour for warmth, trying to will himself to sleep. Then the groaning invaded his calm, and Hepworth staggered outside again, leaving his left side exposed and shivering.

The prisoners arose slowly, without words. Drained faces exchanged glances, recognising themselves in the haunted faces looking back.

"He's asleep," whispered Jock, as he stepped over Hepworth.

Outside, the sound of rattling plates and mugs and the occasional car engine signalled others already at work.

"Is breakfast served in bed? Could do with a full English." Peters rubbed and arched his back, letting out a satisfied groan.

"I've forgotten what bacon tastes like," said Whatman, to the accompaniment of a yawn. "At least it hasn't snowed."

"Small mercies. Did I ever tell you about the time I…"

A wooden spoon drummed on a plate, summoning the prisoners.

"What time is it?" Hepworth stirred, his hand shielding his eyes from the morning light.

"Dawn. How ye doing?" asked Jock, crouching to examine his young ward.

A weak smile cracked on the boy's face. "I slept a little in the past few hours. Feel a little better for it."

"Good," said Jock, wondering if he too had managed a few brief hours. "Let's get ye up. We're summoned for breakfast, and I imagine we leave soon after."

"Really?" Despair filled Hepworth's eyes.

"I know." Jock patted his shoulder. "We'll look after ye."

"Don't hurry," sighed Whatman, returned from the breakfast queue. "There's no bacon, just dry biscuits."

"Hard, dry biscuits," added Babe, struggling to bite off a corner.

"Better for ye tum," stated Jock to Hepworth. "Come on, lad. Let's get ye fed."

Day Two: Afternoon

A snowflake hung in the air, cradled by a gentle breeze. As it drifted down, Jock stuck out his hand, allowing it to land on his glove. It lingered for but a second before melting. Another followed, then another, until a flurry turned into a blizzard. The wind grew in strength, rousing the flakes from their downward journey, agitating the view into a white blur.

"I can hardly see the road," yelled Peters over the roaring wind.

"Hang on tae ma coat-tails," urged Jock, ducking his head while shielding his eyes from the pelting snow with a hand.

Ahead, smudged charcoal shapes appeared and vanished. Jock followed in their wake, hopeful his imagination wasn't playing tricks on him.

Exposed on an open plain, the blizzard grew in ferocity, its biting wind penetrating to the bone. The snow settled, building in drifts, hindering each footstep, impeding the sledges.

Jock's boot kicked something. He prodded with a toecap, sensing a crisp, frozen surface atop a soft core. "Hold on!" he cried to the small column now formed behind. "I think it's a body!" He crouched, brushing away a layer of snow to expose the khaki outline of a prisoner. The vibrations of the shivering body ran up Jock's arm. "He's alive."

Peters felt his way around Jock, turning his back to the blizzard. "Let's get him up."

"Aye, come on, lad. Ye'll freeze down there."

As they raised him by his arms, the man whimpered, a crust of snow falling to the ground.

"What's yer name?"

No reply emerged from his chattering teeth.

"Put him on a sledge and pull him?" suggested Peters.

"It's warmth he needs," said Jock. "We all do!"

"Ain't getting a fire started in this." Peters rubbed his hands up and down the arms of the man. "There could be shelter within a few yards, but damned if I can see it."

"We keep moving," stated Jock. "Best way to keep warm. There is one unorthodox way. Means giving up our sledges."

"If we don't do something quickly, we'll all be like Jack Frost here!"

"Okay," shouted Jock, addressing the huddle of prisoners stamping on the spot. "Gather what ye can from yer sleighs. Don't overload yerself: food and blankets the priority. Swathe Jack here with those blankets!"

Lost in the white maelstrom, the prisoners wrapped their arms around each other, merging into a large, standing ball, three men deep, all facing inwards, with the newly named Jack Frost in the middle.

"That's my foot!" growled one as they tried to move.

"Wait for ma count," urged Jock. "On three. One, two, three."

Legs stretched in every direction, the ball's cohesion straining in the confusion.

"Och, naw. This ain't working."

"Which way we going? Forward and backwards look the same to me!"

"At least it's warmer."

"Speak for yourself! You're not on the outside."

"Shut up! Ye'll all get a turn." Jock, himself on the outer circle, bit his cracked lips. "That's it. Turn! We rotate and edge forward. Everyone keep stepping tae the side and I'll apply the pressure tae move us in the right direction."

"Sounds weird to me."

"Nae one will see ye, so get moving! Clockwise, ye numptie!"

The huddled mass, snow building on the backs of the outer layer, gradually turned, increasing in speed as they found a rhythm.

"It's working!"

"I'm dizzy."

"Where am I? What's happening?"

"Sounds like Jack's awake," said Peters. "What's your name, lad? We found you dozing in the snow. Trying to warm you up."

"Er, Lionel. Lionel Ratcliffe. I'm not dead?"

"Depends if being cuddled by smelly, half-starved men is your idea of heaven or hell."

"Archie! Ye're not dead, lad, but among friends. The snow's easing."

"I can see the road, and we're not on it!"

A strip of blue sky appeared, the snowflakes shrinking until just specks in the air.

"Ah, we appear tae have wandered on tae a field," said Jock, the huddle breaking apart.

"That's the last time we let you drive," quipped Peters, removing his cap and shaking it free of snow.

"Ye going to be all right, Lionel? Can ye walk?"

"I think so," said the boy. "I was so cold and tired. Sleep seemed so natural."

"Keep those blankets for the day and stick with us. Ye can sleep taenight. Ye're in the army: nae sleeping while on duty." Jock smiled. "Now, let's find that road before we get accused of trying tae escape."

Day Two: Evening

"We made it," remarked Peters, as they bedded down for the night in an abandoned theatre. "That tea is thawing me out. I don't even care how disgusting it tastes."

Jock sat on the stage edge, his legs dangling over. He watched prisoners sort through the abandoned stalls, emerging with cushioned seats and a contented smile. Tonight, their heads would rest in comfort. "What was that?"

"The tea," repeated Peters. "Disgusting but welcome."

"Oh, aye."

"Lionel's made a remarkable recovery. Thought we lost him."

Swinging his legs round until on the stage, Jock faced his friend. "He has. Good to see Arthur with us too. But it's only a matter of time until one of us freezes oot there. We also lost our sledges."

"There's stuff in here we could bind together." Peters stared at the decorated high ceiling and the old scenery, all gathering dust. "You're pretty down tonight."

"We were lucky taeday. It's nawt just the walking. We're fighting the Germans and nature. Perhaps this is their way of getting rid of us?"

"What, walk us until we drop dead? Jeez, that's grim. Wouldn't a bullet be easier?"

"That's against the Geneva Convention. Ye don't have tae pull a trigger if we perish in a snowstorm. It's just a regrettable loss."

"Semantics," said Peters, lounging on his side, his head resting on his hand. "That's murder, as far as I'm concerned."

"I'll tell ye what's murder," said Jock, scratching his neck. "These bloody lice! How do they survive the cold?" He unbuttoned his tunic, pulling it inside out and holding it up in the faint light. "Look at them!"

"It's the cosiest place."

"Hand me the matches. I'll give them 'cosy'!" Jock struck a match, holding the flame to his collar's hem. "Worse than midges. What am I saying? Nothing's worse than those wee critters. Have ye ever walked the Highlands in summer?"

The stomp of boots echoed through the stage, cutting their conversation dead. Two guards entered stage-right. They held their rifles as if brooms, sweeping at those getting comfortable as though leaf litter. With a shared snigger, the guards jabbed those at the stage edge, forcing them to jump into the orchestral pit below.

"Our audition's over," said Peters, gathering up his belongings. "Philistines don't recognise a true thespian when they see one. Gielgud will hear of this!" He slid off the stage.

"I won't be chased like a mouse," Jock declared, climbing to his feet.

The Germans paused under Jock's towering frame. From mischievous school bullies, their manner changed. They clasped their rifles, aiming at Jock, their faces taking on a determined seriousness, undermined by an edge of fear. A stream of shouted orders flowed from their mouths.

"I cannae understand a word ye saying," said Jock calmly. "Is there something I can help ye with?"

One guard turned red, his voice increasing in pitch, his pencil moustache wriggling like a worm under his bulbous nose. The other lowered his gun, uncertain how to proceed.

"Don't antagonise them, Jock," called up Peters.

"I'm doing what they want," replied Jock. "Just in ma own time." He collected his possessions, folding his blanket. With a barrage of orders continuing in his ear, Jock strolled back across the stage and down the steps at the side. "If ye didn't want us on the stage, ye should just have asked us tae move. Manners cost nowt." He winked at Peters, who stood watching with an exasperated face.

"You'll get yourself shot one day."

"Och, let Fritz wallow in his empty victory. It's important they learn tae treat us with respect."

"Hmm. If you say so. And where shall we reside tonight? I can offer a front-row seat or perhaps the royal box."

"The back row will suit me," said Jock. "Away from the stink of Fritz."

"Okay, but no kissing!"

"Och, get away with ye, man! How did they ever let ye in the army?"

Day Nine

Each day mirrored the last. Roused at daybreak, the prisoners first battled their stiff, frozen limbs and sores, then the despondency of marching on unsated stomachs. At day's end, they crowded in inadequate dwellings, sharing their coughs, sobs and woes, before a restless night of fighting the cold and their nightmares, with dawn reminding them they lived the nightmare. And on it went.

No longer did they walk through the virgin snow of quiet country lanes. Tyre tracks and footprints told of heavy traffic, of refugees moving westward, of troops transferring to and from the frontline, of other prisoners dragging weary feet. Walking on the ice and slush challenged every step, and with fading strength they covered fewer miles.

"What you eating?" asked Peters.

Jock stopped chewing and opened his mouth wide. "A twig."

"Oh, so you're not keeping a steak sandwich from me?"

"I wish. Tastes disgusting but fools ma tum intae thinking it's getting its fill."

"Good idea. Any tree you'd recommend? One can never understand these foreign menus."

Jock spat out a lump of hard pulp. "A Brit abroad can always rely on the oak. Its crisp exterior containing a surprisingly succulent maggot or two. Best served at fifteen degrees Fahrenheit."

"My doctor warned me off those rich foods. Said it made my gout worse."

"Aye, a diet of grouse, swan and twig can do that tae a man."

"Arthur's still suffering," remarked Peters, bringing the conversation back to a hard reality.

With a glance behind, Jock nodded his head. "Aye, they promised tae send the sick tae hospital, but a German's promise is nawt worth much. Half our lads need a few weeks under the care of a nurse."

"Count me in!"

"A split lip donnae count." Jock's pace slowed. "I'm gonnae lend a hand. Babe and Tom looked worn oot last night."

"Those maggots topped up your energy?"

"Something like that. Ye coming?"

"Sure."

They stopped, allowing other prisoners to trickle past, until the final stragglers appeared, the sick helped along under the support of their comrades.

"Jock. Archie. Everything all right?" Babe, weighed down with three bags, greeted them with a weary smile.

"Aye," replied Jock. "Thought ye might need a hand."

"Hello, Jock," said Hepworth. "I've managed a few steps unaided today."

"Wore himself out," added Whatman, his arm round Arthur's back in support.

Jock passed his bag to Peters and threaded his arm from the other side. "Have a rest, Tom. I'll walk with Arthur for a while."

"You sure?"

"Aye, anything tae get away from Archie."

"Oi! I heard that, Mitchell," said Peters. "You're stuck with me. And if you ever want to see your belongings again..."

The pair grinned.

"How much further today?" asked Hepworth, his feet barely lifting off the ground.

"Hard tae tell, lad," answered Jock. "I neither have the time nor a destination. That's how it was when I used tae walk the Highlands in the summer. Leave in the morning to nawhere in particular, explore and discover, then return home at dusk, tired but content. Strange how different this is."

"Home," repeated Hepworth. "That's the difference. You returned home."

"Aye, ye're right. It has a power, that word, does it nawt, lad?"

"I dream of mine every night. It's nothing grand. A terrace house with no running water, but my family's there."

"Ye got siblings?"

"Yes, a younger sister and a brother. He's three years older than me. Last I read, they'd sent him to Burma. It's warmer there."

"I suspect it is," said Jock.

"After the war, I want to travel to somewhere warmer. India, perhaps." Hepworth's eyes drifted upwards. "Have you read Kipling?"

"He's Jane's favourite. Well, Stevenson is, but a close second."

"Yes, *Treasure Island*. Another warm place." Hepworth sighed. "I used to retell myself those stories: from memory. But my mind's so foggy of late. I try to concentrate but can't."

Jock nodded. He suffered too. With so much time to think, why was it so hard to think?

"Sorry, Jock." Hepworth stopped, his apologetic, bloodshot eyes turning up to his companion. "I need to go again. Only the second time today. I'm getting better."

"Can ye manage yerself?"

"Yes, I've been practising." Hepworth tottered to the roadside.

A half-smile formed across Jock's lips. Humour was a good sign.

Day Nineteen

An elderly peasant woman, wrapped in her shawl, watched the prisoners from her garden while clinging to a precious bundle of twigs. Despite her own dire circumstances, pity filled her eyes. She hurried back to her run-down cottage, resting on the edge of a village.

"It's like something from medieval times," commented Peters, as they marched through. "Give me the quaint English village any day. They don't even have a pub!"

"They had everything taken away from them," remarked Jock.

At the heart of the village, the road opened into a square. The church dominated; its crumbling yellow plaster the last vestige of past grandeur. Three-storey terraced houses, in a similar state of disrepair, surrounded most of the square. A long-closed cafe harked back to better days; a dead horse, stripped of its meat, symbolic of the present. Chimneys trickled smoke, the only sign of life. Shut window hoardings and drawn curtains, a vain attempt by the residents to cut off the world.

"Ruhen Sie sich aus!"

"At last," sighed Jock, now familiar with the German phrase signifying a rest. "There's a water pump."

A tall statue of the Virgin Mary dominated the centre of the square, her head tilted to heaven, an arm stretched out. To her side rested an ornate cast-iron water pump, an icicle hanging from the spout.

"Frozen?" asked Peters, as he sank down on to the wall bordering the statue.

"Let's see." Jock cranked the pump's handle.

Nothing.

Jock slumped next to Peters. "The good lady's given up on us." He glanced up at the statue.

Prisoners dispersed throughout the square, occupying doorways, the church steps, and the statue's wall. Lighting their cigarettes, they rummaged through bags for what remained of their personal supplies, resting their weary feet and chatting. Curtains twitched, as nervous residents spied. Away from the prisoners, the guards congregated at the cafe, occupying the abandoned tables and chairs, their eyes scanning the plaza and their captives between conversations.

"God knows how many days we've marched and we've got nowhere," lamented Peters.

"At least Arthur's keeping up." Jock looked across to the church steps, where the young man sat, head buried between his knees.

"But more are ill now. I felt unwell this morning.

"We're trudging in the waste of others," said Jock. "The snow's nae longer white. There's nae other source of water. God knows what we're eating!" He cast a bitter eye towards the broken pump.

A door creaked open. Everyone turned as an elderly man appeared in the doorway of a townhouse. The Germans rose from their chairs, suspicious and nervy. As the man shuffled out, a walking stick supporting his bent frame, they relaxed, sharing a joke. He carried a steaming bucket.

"He's coming our way," remarked Jock, climbing to his feet. He touched the rim of his cap in greeting, receiving a toothless grin in reply.

With a swing of his walking stick, the old man clipped the icicle off the pump's spout, then tipped the contents of his bucket over the cast-iron. "Wkrótce ponownie zamarznie." He tapped the bottom of the pipe with his stick and worked the handle. A trickle of water flowed.

"A miracle!" cried Peters, jumping to his feet.

The man handed Jock the bucket, motioning to the pump. "Twoja kolej."

"Thank ye," said Jock, offering his hand in gratitude.

Instead, to Jock's surprise, the old man hugged him. Jock opened his mouth, then felt something pushed into his gut. He glanced down, seeing a bag. "Och, naw. Ye must need this for yerselves?"

The man stared into Jock's eyes, a tear forming. With a noble bow, he shuffled back to his house.

Peters already had his mouth round the pump's spout, working the handle. "It's bleeding cold but tastes good," he said, wiping a sleeve across his chin.

"First, let's fill the bucket," Jock said, nudging Peters aside. "Here, take hold of this. Another gift from our friend."

"What is it?" asked Peters, opening the bag and peeking in.

"Careful! Don't let Jerry see."

"Mmm. Smoked sausage and cheese."

"An old soldier," surmised Jock, casting a glance towards the man's house. "From a different era."

Boots clicked on cobbles, signalling the approach of Germans. Jock turned, finding himself confronted by a pair of guards.

"Zee vater may be poisoned," said one, enjoying Peters's look of horror. "Slavs cannot be trusted."

"Naw, it's fine," countered Jock, scooping a handful and dribbling it into his mouth. "A little metallic."

The German's eyes narrowed. "Zen bring zee bucket to us!"

Jock folded his arms. "I'll bring the bucket if ye get a horse and cart tae carry the sick."

"Ein cart und horse for bucket of vater?" The guard turned to his colleague and laughed.

"How aboot for a little smoked sausage and cheese?"

The laughing stopped, as the guards exchanged secretive whispers.

Peters's brow sank with disappointment.

"Ja." The guard looked over his shoulder at his colleagues, watching from the cafe. He turned back to Jock, circling a finger between the four of them. "Zis our secret, ja? You get cart und bring bucket, but sausage..." He lifted the finger to his lips.

"Ja, secret," said Jock, lifting the bucket. "Ye'll get the food on delivery of horse and cart."

"Jock!" hissed Peters from the side of his mouth.

"Rouse the men to come and drink," instructed Jock. "I know what I'm doing."

Day Twenty

"Let me try," urged Whatman. "We had horses back home." He gripped the reins, comforting the beast with a stroke of its mane. "Though in better shape."

"I'll get out," said Hepworth, his head appearing over the boarding of the cart. "I'd prefer to walk."

"Are ye sure?" asked Jock, helping him climb down.

"Thanks. Yeah, that bridge doesn't look too stable, and our nag's a little too skittish."

Jock inspected the bridge, a makeshift construct of bound boats, the nearby ancient predecessor a bombed ruin. Plates of broken ice drifted on the wide, muddy river, crashing against the bows. "Ye may be right. Anyone else want off?"

Four sickly faces answered through exhausted eyes.

"Walk on. Walk on. Come on, girl." Whatman cooed in the horse's ear, brushing its mane. A hoof scraped the ground, pondering the encouragement.

"Bewegung!" A guard appeared. "Du hältst uns auf." He waved those on foot on to the bridge.

"A little nervy," commented Peters, finding his footing on the pitching bridge.

To their rear, the distant rumble of shelling echoed over the landscape.

"Schneller!" screamed the guard, striking the horse's rump with his rifle butt.

The beast let out a shrill neigh, jerking forward on to the bridge. Whatman fell on his backside, his legs just missing the wheels.

"Jeez!" Peters staggered backwards towards the water's edge, arms flapping, trying to maintain balance. The cart's wheel crushed his sack of possessions as one boot slipped into the water.

"Gotcha!" Jock's hand shot out, grasping Peters by the arm and pulling.

Peters fell to his knees. "Thanks. That was close!"

"Looks cold," observed Jock, recovering himself with hands resting on his knees. "I wasn't planning on jumping in to save you."

The German guard walked past, a grin on his face.

"But you were going to push him in for me?" Peters's glare followed the guard.

"Oh, aye," answered Jock. "Now, get up. Arthur needs a hand."

Under the extra weight of the horse and cart, the bridge undulated wildly, requiring a wide gait for those in its wake.

"You all right, lad?" asked Jock of Arthur.

"Not so great," confessed the boy. "Can't tell if it's seasickness or weakness. I thought I'd feel better once over the dysentery, but I feel as weak as ever."

"Nearly there. What ye need is a good meal. We'll get you back on the cart on the other side."

Arthur froze, turned pale, and gagged. "Urrggh! There's nothing to come up anymore." His legs wobbled.

"Put yer arm round ma shoulder," said Jock.

"Thanks, Jock. I've a letter in my pocket for my parents."

"We all have one of those, lad. Ye can burn yers on the fire when ye get home."

"Thanks, Jock." Arthur understood the unspoken promise made.

As they stepped off the bridge, a celebratory mood greeted them. The guards assembled, toasting each other with spirits, laughing and joking.

"I'm glad someone's enjoying themselves," grumbled Jock.

Babe appeared, taking Arthur's other arm to help Jock. "This is Germany. I overheard the guards. We've crossed the Oder."

"They think they're safe from the Russians," said Jock.

"Are they?"

"I donnae know. The river will slow them down. Hopefully, the guards will lighten up on us."

Dramatic grey clouds scuttled across the horizon, the rumbling of distant artillery adding to the ominous atmosphere.

Day Twenty-Five

Commandant Lange appeared from nowhere, ducking through the small barn door. Despite the dark patches beneath his eyes, he was in a good mood, joking with his officers, engaging with the junior ranks. Jock, at the back of the barn, craned his neck, attempting to see if Birgit waited outside. It was too dark to tell and probably too late for her to be up.

"What's he want?" mumbled Peters, blowing his running nose on a sleeve.

"He's nawt having any of ma straw," said Jock, his legs buried under a mound of stalks. This, the best built and warmest barn they had yet stayed in.

"He's not even brought a pipe to rid us of the mice." Peters poked through the straw one more time, scarred by an earlier discovery of a nest of hibernating rodents.

"Don't think this is Hamelin. Not even sure where Hamelin is."

"Oh, blast," cursed Peters. "He's doing an inspection."

The shouting had already started, guards dashing to every corner of the barn, haranguing the resting prisoners to their feet.

"I was looking forward to a good night's sleep," moaned Peters. "Hey, look who it is?"

"Evening, Konrad," greeted Jock.

"I must shout," said the guard. "I apologise."

"Shout away," urged Peters, already climbing to his feet.

With a half-hearted attempt, the German let fly in his own tongue.

"You're getting quite good at this," said Peters, casually straightening his tunic. "Perhaps add a stamp of your boots or jab of the gun?"

"You must not joke," whispered Konrad, a finger massaging his temple. "Zee commandant may hear. Then vee are all in trouble."

"Just stand quietly," said Jock. "Let Konrad do his job."

"I thought being a nuisance to the Germans was our job?"

"Quiet!"

The commandant strolled through the barn, uninterested and distracted, followed by a gaggle of more zealous officers. With a lazy wave, he brought their attention to a prisoner for a minor infraction, a perceived lack of respect, or a sickly demeanour. An officer hung back, assessing further and conveying an order down the ranks, until a guard began shouting and pushing at the put-upon prisoner.

Sweat built on Konrad's brow as the commandant sauntered towards them. Lange brushed past Peters, pausing before Jock. His eyes worked up and down the Scot. He turned to his entourage, said a few words, and laughed. Each followed him by, assessing Jock and laughing. Jock stared forward, trying to show no emotion, fighting the inner urge to punch them all.

"What was that aboot?" he asked Konrad, with the commandant out of hearing range.

"He joke about your age. Said you are old enough to be German prison guard."

Jock frowned, surprised by the answer.

"Not a bad joke," commented Peters. "For a German."

"Aye, let's get some sleep. We donnae need any more comics in this war."

Day Thirty-Two

Jock rubbed his ankles. Walking on the cobbled roads of a town brought its own challenges. The acrid air, flavoured by factory smoke, caught the back of his throat. He coughed and spat, catching the eye of a German resident at the side of the road. Anger and hatred now greeted them, sympathy absent for those they blamed for their bombed-out houses and dead, the blue RAF tunic enough to trigger a curse or threat.

"They look as hungry as us," commented Peters.

"Aye," said Jock. "The sooner we're out of here, the better."

A stone whizzed overhead, missing the prisoners, landing harmlessly in a patch of weeds. Three children, no more than 12, darted away with a volley of bravado.

"Why you little brats!" cursed Peters, taking one step in their direction.

"Let it go!" urged Jock. "Ye clip their ears and Fritz will increase the stakes by a bullet."

"If they raised their kids better, we wouldn't have this war," fumed Peters.

"Ha, ye've never passed through the Gorbals in Glasgow. The scallywags will stone ye and steal yer shoes while ye're walking in them. But they make for grand soldiers."

"Yeah, well, I'm very picky about my stone-throwing hooligan. Prefer mine without the Nazi father."

A giant bite-like hole split a line of terrace housing. Rubble flooded onto the road, household wares littering amid the bricks. With no way round, the prisoners climbed the ruins, dislodging the debris, exposing the toy soldiers of a child.

At the next junction, a German guard stood corralling the prisoners down a side road.

"Early for a stop?" queried Jock.

Familiar sounds bounced off the tall townhouses hemming in the street.

"A train!" declared Peters.

The distinct odour of soot carried on steam drifted their way, and they emerged from the road on to a wide concourse, packed with soldiers and prisoners. Dark, grimy locomotives pointed east and west, venting and hissing amid the bustle, their rollingstock a mix of passenger cars and cattle trucks.

"No more walking!" exclaimed Peters with a smile.

"It's nawt gonnae be first class," cautioned Jock.

"Yeah, but no more walking!" repeated his friend.

Amid the noise of the station, the prisoners seeped in, building to a tight mass. Their guards sauntered around the edges, also optimistic their days of walking were over.

Babe Quigley wormed his way up to Jock and Peters. "Reminds me of Paddington on a bank holiday."

"I don't remember this smell," said Peters, his nose twitching. "Or the guns."

"Death and dung?" offered Jock.

"That will be it," agreed Peters, screwing up his face in disgust.

"Arthur seems better." Babe flashed a look behind, unable to find their friend in the crowd. "He'll be glad to stop walking. It'll give him a chance to fully recover."

The familiar, raucous commands of the guards erupted, signalling hundreds of heads to turn towards the carriages. Doors rolled open on rusty wheels, and rifle butts pressed into the outer ranks of the prisoners, herding them towards the cattle trucks.

"Here goes," said Peters. "Will someone serve tea and cake?"

Jock sniffed in appreciation of the joke. A memory of an afternoon surfaced: he dressed in his finest suit, Jane, his wife, uncomfortable but radiant in her lace dress. *Was it on the coast?* Porcelain cups steaming with tea rested on the table as the young waitress offered a selection from the cake trolley. Couples sat at adjoining tables, lost in trivial matters, but content. Jock sighed and shuffled forward.

A single plank, balanced at a sharp angle, led into the carriage. It bowed as a continuous line of prisoners climbed the gradient.

"The stink!" complained Peters, standing against the locked doors on the opposite side.

Jock stood next to him, finding a crack in the wood to look out. He rested his cheek on the board, drawing in the fresh air through his nostrils.

"Er, it's getting a little crowded in here," remarked Babe, finding himself nudged into Jock.

"We're full!" called out Peters in vain hope.

The prisoners continued to climb the ramp.

"Mind my toe!"

"Watch it!"

"I feel sick!"

The complaints built as more prisoners packed in, pressing shoulder to shoulder. At last, the wheels on the door grated shut, leaving the carriage in near darkness, thin rays of light through the cracks their only illumination.

"I think they've invented a new class of travel," said Peters, fighting to make space to turn.

"It's called cattle class," said Jock.

"I never treated my cows this bad," said a voice from the darkness.

"At least it's warm," offered Babe, snug between Jock and a stranger. "We'll soon be on our way."

"Aye." Jock peered through the crack, seeking an alternative view.

A muffled apology drifted from the darkness. "Oh, God! Oh, God!" The distinct sound of involuntary bowel movement halted all talk. A rancid odour saturated the already stagnant air, as each man took a step back, increasing the crush at the carriage's far end.

"We will be moving soon?" asked Babe in a whisper, his hand across mouth and nose.

The locomotive remained stationary, as the low-lying sun crept across the sky. Hours passed; the temperature inside rose with the tension.

"Let me out! I can't breathe!" The anonymous cry infected others. A push morphed into a surge.

"This is getting dangerous," warned Jock.

Peters cleared his throat.

"He careth for me, my father cares!

Oh, sweetest tho't to my spirit known."

His smooth baritone voice cut through the cacophony. Jock joined him.

"I have no fears for the coming years,

He ne'er forsakes me nor leaves His own."

Soon the whole carriage accompanied them with the hymn, the surge waning, the panic evaporating. A calm returned to the darkness.

Day Thirty-Three

The sudden jolt shocked Jock awake. He opened his eyes. Had he been sleeping? It seemed impossible pinned to the side of the carriage, breathing the stifling air. His legs cried out to collapse, letting him slump to the floor and rest, but there was no room. The carriage occupants were silent but for the odd groan. Jock's upper body rocked in time with his companions, the familiar rhythmic clack and clang of rolling-stock on rails confirming they were at last on the move. *How long has it been?* From the complete darkness, he could only surmise it was night.

A warm sensation ran down Jock's legs. He closed his eyes, ashamed and helpless, then pinched his trousers, pulling the urine-soaked fabric away from his skin. Not one man judged him, all fighting their own humiliation.

"You awake, Jock?" asked Babe.

"Aye. How long we been moving?"

"A couple of hours."

"Really?" Jock wracked his memory, trying to recall their departure, shaking his head in disbelief.

"I feel sick."

"Sorry to hear that, lad," said Jock, unsure what Babe expected from him.

"But hungry too."

Jock understood. His own mind and body conflicted. A sobbing prisoner expressed his feelings in the darkness, but Jock's despair stayed bottled up. "Hang in there." His tongue ran along his lips, already cracked from the cold, now dry with thirst.

"Why are they so cruel?" asked Babe.

Jock let the question hang unanswered. All the horrors witnessed resurfaced: the faces of the victims, the perpetrators, the innocent, and the guilty. His answer took shape. "Fear? Insecurity? Lack of faith? The Devil?"

"Yes, the Devil," echoed Babe. "With faith we can defeat him. Good will win out in the end."

"I hope so," said Jock, envious of the boy's optimism.

Silence returned. Jock closed his eyes, his head leaning on the wooden door. He wanted to shut out his thoughts, find tranquillity in a vacuum, but there was no escaping himself. At least when walking the sights provided some distraction. He tried inviting Jane and his boys in, picturing happier times, but every sketch featured pain, fear, and worry. His wife's face conjured the haunted women of Poland, the slave labourers, oppressed and vulnerable, while his boys appeared as himself, trapped and suffering. Only the clack and clang soothed him, its hypnotic rhythm drawing him in until, after another hour, sleep returned, bringing its own demons.

Day Thirty-Five: Mid-Morning

The carriage door rolled open, daylight flooding the interior. Each man winced, shielding their eyes with a hand, but welcoming the sweet, cold air wafting in.

Jock urged his stiff body round, his eyelids heavy. *Has it been two or three days locked inside?* His mind couldn't decide. The scrum around him eased as prisoners disembarked. With weary automation, he joined the shuffling column, hardly noticing the slumped bodies that remained aboard. How pleasant to be outside, away from the pungent reek and stale air. Peters and Babe followed him out, but he didn't care. Friendship meant nothing at that moment. The sights of the new town meant nothing. His spiritless body lumbered forward until a fresh aroma ignited something within. Food!

A steaming vat enticed the prisoners. First, they passed an open barrel of water, a guard offering them a full ladle. They gulped with desperation and relief, lingering in the hope of more, but forced on by the guards and their impatient comrades behind. Then a thin broth awaited.

Jock savoured the smooth water flowing down his throat, softening his palate, and held out his mug to receive soup, though still third in line. As his turn arrived, the hot liquid splashed over his hands, but it didn't matter. He blew once into his mug and then slurped with satisfaction. It burnt, but that didn't seem to matter either. The heat and nutrients unlocked his spirit. He felt human again.

"The best tasting soup I've ever had," remarked Peters.

"That it is," agreed Jock, looking down at the anaemic fluid. He took another gulp.

"Please tell me we're not going on another train," said Babe, some colour returning to his cheeks.

"I'll ask a guard," said Jock, seeking Konrad in the crowd.

With their German friend nowhere in sight, Jock approached an unfamiliar guard, hopeful that humanity existed within. "No more train?" asked Jock, pointing at the locomotive.

The guard assessed Jock, his nose curling in disgust at his aroma. "Nein."

"Have we arrived? New camp?"

"Nein. Tomorrow, more valk." The guard simulated walking with his fingers, disappointment on his own face.

Jock bit his lip. "How far?"

Before the guard finished his shrug, Jock turned and walked back to his friends.

Day Thirty-Five: Noon

No one talked. Moving one foot before the other took all their energy. The road was again their prison, with its endless dips, hills, bends, and parallel borders. There was no turning back, no chance of leaving.

A lone duck waddled across the frozen edge of a pond. Every prisoner thought the same thought, but all continued trudging on the road, lacking the strength or will to turn their fantasy into a realistic meal.

Patches of snow lined the fields of a ridge of hills running to the road's right. Below the brow, a scar cut through the frozen soil, leading to the scattered remains of a bomber. The broken segment of a wing displayed the American star. Even in the middle of nowhere, the war left its mark.

Jock chose not to consider the crew's fate. The burden of caring about others was too much. Everything was numb: his body and mind. His legs moved independently of thought, a relentless rhythm fuelled by fear. The train journey had destroyed something. Perhaps it was finding a greater darkness in the hearts of their captives, or the terror of those three days eating him from within. A trapped scream festered in his subconscious.

Arthur Hepworth shuffled by Jock's side, the horse and cart abandoned before they embarked the train. His pace slowed as the day progressed. Soon, he languished behind Jock, another consideration beyond the Scot's will.

"Jock." Konrad appeared at his shoulder.

Beyond a tired, acknowledging glance, Jock remained unresponsive.

"You look terrible. Are you sick?"

Jock tried to answer, but his dry mouth triggered a cough.

Konrad held out a flask. "Vater. Drink."

"Thanks," said Jock. He tipped the cannister into his mouth, appreciating the soothing liquid flowing down his throat. "It's exhaustion. Did ye see what we suffered in those carriages?"

"Sorry, Jock. I could not help you. Vee found two dead."

"I didn't know," said Jock, his foggy mind recalling no missing faces. "But it donnae surprise me. It almost killed me. I cannae do that again."

The German's hand touched Jock's arm. "I warn you about zee SS."

"The SS?"

"Ja, zee black car ahead." A hundred and fifty yards on, a car sat at the entrance to a farm track.

Jock shook his head. How had he not noticed it before?

"Zey hunt traitors und cowards. I hear three German soldiers shot vithout, how you say, pass? Drunk soldiers not alvays find papers, ja?"

Against the black outline of the car, a uniformed figure blended with his background, only a wisp of cigarette smoke exposing his presence.

"Aye," answered Jock. "Sounds like nae one's safe."

"I fear zem. Devil soldiers!"

Jock handed back the flask. "Thanks. I feel better for that. Er, best he donnae see us fraternising, eh?"

"Oh, ja." Konrad drifted away. "Look ahead. Avoid eye."

"Aye, be safe."

The drip, drip of adrenaline woke Jock's spirit. An anger and hatred stirred him. He straightened his cap, set his eyes on the horizon and lengthened his pace. Level with the car, he felt the man's eyes on him, burning and judging. A waft of tobacco reached him. From the corner of his eye, he noticed the faint glow of the cigarette tip under the white skull and cross bones emblem. He wanted to turn, glare, curse and so much more, but Konrad's advice was good. He continued walking, head straight ahead. Once past, Jock glanced at Konrad. The German nodded and smiled.

Day Thirty-Nine: Afternoon

"What do ye mean, he's dead?" cried Jock, his body shaking from cold and shock.

"I think his heart gave out," suggested Whatman. "He had this letter in his pocket."

"But... but he was only eighteen or nineteen!" Jock took the envelope, staring at the address and the name of Hepworth's parents. "Ye should've told me earlier!"

"It's a miracle he survived the train," said Whatman, trying to understand Hepworth's death himself. "No food or water after a bad dose of dysentery and so many days of walking. We tried to catch you up but... well, you know."

"Aye," said Jock, his promise to Hepworth to keep him safe echoing in his mind. "I'll write to his parents, pass on the letter, tell them he was loved by all." Jock's gaze drifted, lost and unfocussed, the shock and confusion still sinking in. With a shake of his head, he regained composure. "There was nowt ye could do. They as good as shot him!"

"I hear Forsyth didn't make it either. Baines and Donovan now have the shits. Evans is showing signs of scurvy and Price's asthma's plaguing him." Whatman's own pallor worsened during the telling.

"There won't be any of us left at this rate," said Jock, removing his balaclava to scratch at a sore. "Nae burial either, I suppose?"

Whatman shook his head. "Did you see the old married couple?"

"I did," admitted Jock, trying to erase the image of their statuesque bodies, huddled together and staring out from their last resting place by the road. "At least they were together."

Peters caught up.

"Heard about Arthur?" asked Whatman.

"I have, God bless his soul," responded Peters. "A few more may join him before day's end. But look!" He pointed to the crest of the hill.

The summits of two watchtowers appeared, followed by the familiar sight of barbed wire atop an imposing fence. As they crept up the hill, the roofs of huts hove into view.

"It's a camp!" gasped Whatman. "Thank God. I don't think I could manage another day of walking."

"We must be a good way intae Germany now," said Jock, his stride increasing by a fraction. "The question is, where are the Russians?"

Beyond the wire stood line on line of drab figures, their gaunt eyes following the wretched column.

"Looks crowded," remarked Peters. "Wonder how long they've been here."

"I just need a bunk." An unknown energy source propelled Whatman to increase his pace. "Any chance the odd chicken is hiding in there?"

"Just their shit." Peters stuck his little finger in his mouth and sucked.

"Still causing you problems?" asked Jock.

"Going a funny colour," said Peters, holding it up for examination.

"Frostbite?" suggested Jock, his own digits throbbing in sympathy. "Put ye glove back on, ye idiot!"

A guard yelled, prodding his rifle's muzzle at the passing men, bullying them up the track towards the camp.

"Do you still pray, Jock?" asked Whatman in a hushed tone.

"Aye." He remained silent for a moment. "But over-demand may have blocked the lines."

"That explains it," said the youngster with a wry smile. "I'll pray for Arthur this evening."

"He's in a better place," reflected Jock.

"Far away from the hell of the camp," agreed Whatman. "And the march!"

"This circle of torment," mused Jock.

The camp gates swung open, welcoming the new arrivals.

***

"Mmmm," crooned Babe Quigley. "There are chunks of meat!"

"It's true!" exclaimed a disbelieving Peters. "Chewy but never has a meal tasted so good."

Spoons dug in mess tins, shovelling the brown sludge to eager mouths.

"Slow down, lads," advised Jock. "Chew it properly. Yer stomachs won't thank ye otherwise."

They sat across two beds, their allocated hut home to the remnant of their column.

"Can anyone feel their feet yet?" asked Whatman.

"I can feel yours," said Peters. "Move over!"

"To where?" complained Whatman. "I've already got one cheek off the edge."

"I'm glad the walking's over," said Babe, "but we can't live crammed like this. There aren't even enough beds."

"We'll work something oot," assured Jock, trying to dislodge a grisly strand stuck between his teeth.

An icy wind stirred hair and uniforms. Heads turned to see who stood in the door.

"Evening chaps. Savouring the horse meat?"

"Blah!" Babe spat it back into his canteen.

"Mmm," countered Peters, taking another spoonful. "Never look a gift horse in the mouth." He awaited his audience's laughter.

"Shut up, Archie," said Jock, casting a sorry eye into his own canteen. "But best we finish it off. Remember: we win by surviving." He squeezed his eyes shut and closed his lips round the spoon.

"Sorry, chaps," said the newcomer, leaning in on their group. "Best you know. Not least, as it shows Jerry's desperate. I'm the camp doctor, Henry Cartwright. You look like you've had it tough."

"Evening, doc," said Jock, standing to offer his hand.

"Don't get up. You chaps have been on your feet all day."

"Aye, it's good tae rest. Have ye been here long?"

The doctor put a finger under Babe's chin, tipping his head up with a gentle push. "Just checking you out," he said with a smile. "Three years. Captured at Tobruk. How are your feet?" He turned from one man to the next.

"Grateful there's no more walking," said Peters. "Can you examine my finger?"

"Ah," Cartwright stood up straight, taking a backward step. "You've not been told?"

"Told what?"

The doctor cleared his throat. "You leave tomorrow. It's bed and board for the night only. Sorry, chaps."

"No!" cried Whatman, setting off a wave of outrage as word passed through the hut.

"They asked me to help get you ready," said the doctor, straining over the noise. "I'll check your finger if I have time, keep it warm and get the circulation going, but feet are the priority. Get your boots off! I'll examine you all."

"I'm not sure I can make it," sobbed Babe, looking his tender age.

"Ye can," said Jock, fighting back his own anger. "Ma pa always said when we hiked in the Trossachs, there's always another mountain in everyone. D'ye understand?"

Jock turned to Cartwright. "What aboot those with dysentery?"

"Difficult." The doctor chewed his tongue. "The worse off may be allowed to stay. Plenty of fluids. That's obvious. But a little charcoal can help: settle the tum. I can spare a little, but it's hard to create the heat when wood is in such short supply. You could also all do with some vitamin C. Your boy is showing early signs of jaundice and a few other faces. I have a couple of lemons. A squeeze in your tea for everyone; those with symptoms, suck on what's left."

"I can't believe it," grumbled Peters. "They've done this deliberately. Give us hope, then dash it. It's torture."

"Ye may be right," said Jock, "but let's use our time here tae prepare ourselves better. We know what's coming this time."

"You need that treated for starters," declared Cartwright, lifting Jock's bare foot in the air. "Those are nasty blisters. We don't want an infection." He plucked an iodine dispenser from his pocket and squeezed a drop onto a cloth.

Air whistled through Jock's teeth as cloth touched raw skin.

"You never said?" remarked Peters. "Just let me rattle on about my own blisters."

"Could'nae feel them, tae be honest. Too cold," confessed Jock, as the iodine seeped on to another wound, contorting his face. "Can sense them now! Thanks, doc."

"Sorry."

"They're made of stern stuff north of the border," said Peters. "No man dare wear a kilt without nerves of steel: too much exposed to danger."

Jock glanced sideways and down at Peters's feet. A sly grin spread across his face. "It's yer turn next, ye wee rascal."

Day Forty-One: Morning

"D'ye believe there's a mountain in ye taeday?" asked Jock as he caught up with Babe.

A tepid nod answered. "I slept well, despite Archie's feet in my face, and…," he shivered in disgust, "…the meal and juice have worked their wonders."

"Good."

"But…" Babe took a slow, long breath. "It was hard to start up again. Really hard. I thought it was over." A deep-seated pain etched itself across his features.

"I know, laddie. Nawbody should have tae go through this." Jock's hand rested on the boy's shoulder. "D'ye have an imagination?"

Babe spared Jock a quizzical glance. "Yes, I think so."

"I let maself drift off tae a peaceful burn – that's a stream tae ye lot," Jock added with a wink. "The heather is all aroond and I'm sitting with ma fishing rod, the grouse calling in the distance. Can ye picture that? Just sitting. Nae soul for miles. The only midge tempting a fish tae ma hook."

"Very nice, but I don't fish."

"Och, it donnae have tae be fishing. Find yer place. Let yer body worry aboot putting one foot before the other; use yer mind tae escape."

"I see. Yes, I like that," declared Babe, looking to the sky as his mind drifted. "I'm at the theatre, on stage. Not like the one in Germany. The Stratford, no less!"

"That's the idea."

"A standing ovation for my performance. Shouts of 'encore!' Vivien Leigh as my leading lady."

"Steady, lad. It's supposed tae calm ye, nawt get ye giddy."

A growl from a car behind disturbed the moment. They moved to the road's side.

"It's the commandant," said Jock with surprise. "Must have stayed near the camp and had a late start."

The car honked its horn, clearing the road of weary prisoners. It crawled past Jock, the face of Birgit, the commandant's daughter, at the window. He waved, and she gestured back with a smile of recognition. Its brakes then screeched, bringing it to a sudden halt.

"Something's afoot," said Jock, waiting for the scene to develop.

The commandant emerged from the car, momentarily ducking back with a curt word to those inside. Then he angrily slammed the door and marched over to a guard.

"Ouch," said Jock. "Someone's nawt been doing their job."

"It's nice we're not the ones being shouted at for a change," remarked Babe, as they continued past.

"Ha, wait 'til the big man has gone. He's kicked the cat and soon the cat will want to kick the mice."

Another growl interrupted the shouting. Jock turned, expecting more cars. "It's one of ours," said Jock, looking skyward. "Spitfire?"

"Hurrah!" cheered Babe, as restrained as his enthusiasm could manage. "Has he seen us?"

"Aye, he's following the line of the road." Jock shielded his eyes, trying to confirm the identity of the plane. "It's a Spitfire all right."

All along the road, the prisoners and Germans craned their necks, following the plane.

"It's getting lower," said Babe, his voice unsteady. "They do know we're prisoners?"

"They must!" said Jock, doubt creasing his face. "Intae the ditch, lad. Quick!"

As the Spitfire's cannons burst into life, Jock grabbed Babe by the arm and yanked him off the road. "Get down!"

Screams and shouts followed the pitted explosions as shells struck along the road. Branches toppled; men fell. The plane whooshed overhead and pulled up, banking right.

Jock raised his head from the ditch, spitting out snow. Flakes of material and straw rained down on him. "There goes ma bag!" He pushed up on one elbow, his feet struggling to grip. "Ye okay, Babe?"

"Damn, that was close," answered Babe. "A bullet whizzed by my ear. Why they do that? Bloody hell, we're on the same side!"

"Oh, hell, he's coming round again! Get down!"

The growling engine changed tone on its descent, adjusting its line with a tilt of the wings. Its cannons flashed.

Jock wrapped his arms round his head and whispered a prayer, wondering if either would make a difference.

"You bastard!" screamed Babe as the plane's shadow flickered by. He leapt to his feet, scrambling to the road with a raised fist.

"Are they gone, lad?" Jock rolled onto his back and exhaled a deep breath.

"Yeah. Bloody RAF!"

An eerie silence occupied a space between the screams.

Jock climbed to his feet, dazed and disorientated. Dead and wounded lay scattered along the road; body parts littered the dirt. The acrid smoke from vehicles and bodies consumed in flames irritated his nose. Nausea washed over him, before he vomited in the ditch. "Birgit!"

Jock stumbled towards the commandant's car, Babe instinctively following. "Birgit's inside!" Shell holes punctured the roof, while shattered glass lay strewn around.

As Jock gripped the rear door handle, he heard a groan. He turned, finding Commandant Lange crawling towards him, one hand outstretched, his lower legs missing. A smear of blood marked the two yards he had dragged himself.

"Hilfe…" A croak escaped the German's mouth.

"Ye're on yer own," snapped Jock.

"Helfen Sie Birgit und Gisela." The commandant inched closer with a push from his elbows.

The names caught Jock unaware. He saw a father and husband rather than a German soldier. "Donnae move," he said, kneeling down, clasping the commandant's hand. "We'll look after them. Birgit und Gisela gut." Jock raised a thumb.

Relief found a place amid the pain on the commandant's face. "Danke." His fingers tightened around Jock's hand in a near imperceptible gesture. With a rasp, his hand went limp, and he collapsed dead.

"Jock! Jock! She won't move."

Jock turned to find the sedan door open and Babe's torso leaning inside. Breathless sobbing emanated from inside. "Who won't move? Are they okay?"

Babe reappeared. "The driver and mother are dead."

"And the wee lass?"

"She's alive, unharmed, but won't leave her mother."

A shiver of relief ran down Jock. "Let me try." He bent into the car, greeted by the lifeless stare of the commandant's wife. A ray of sunlight from a shell hole lit the terrified face of the daughter, blood speckled over her. "Birgit," said Jock, as softly as he could. "How ye doing?" He offered his hand. "Why nawt come with me. Get oot of this place."

The sobbing eased as recognition filtered through. She sniffed and glanced at her mother, recoiling in grief.

"Och, I know. She's at peace now. Come on, lass. I'm Richard. Ma friends call me Jock." He smiled.

"Papa?" whimpered the girl.

"How's it going?" Babe asked.

"Move her father's damn body!" said Jock through the corner of this mouth.

"Yeah, already done. I'm going to help the wounded. You going to be okay?"

"Aye, thanks, laddie. I'll be with ye shortly." Jock felt into his inner pocket, withdrawing a battered photo. "This is ma wife and bonnie boys," he said, showing it to Birgit. "They're a wee bit older now."

"Papa?" she asked again.

Jock lowered his eyes and shook his head. "Sorry, lass."

Instead of tears, Birgit took Jock's hand.

He smiled in encouragement. "That's it." He clasped her under the armpits, lifting her over the mother. "Ah, ye've grown some!" Her arms tightened around his neck, her warm skin pushing against his ear, her traumatised body shaking. "It's gonnae be okay." A memory surfaced of carrying his sons to bed after a tiring day. "It's all gonnae be okay."

Out of the car, Jock lowered her to the ground. "Let's have a look at ye. Make sure ye're all right." He held her by the shoulders, brushing the hair from her face, scrubbing the flecks of her mother's blood away with his tattered sleeve.

Her lost eyes watched him as her fragile body shook.

"Nae cuts. That's good." Jock straightened, surveying the horrors. "This is nae place for a wee lass." He guided her to the back of the car. "Sit down." Leading by example, Jock rested his back against the wheel, looking away from the road. "That's cold." He stripped off his tunic, laying it down as a blanket, motioning the girl to sit.

Birgit remained standing, tilted her head, and then shook it.

"But…"

She picked up Jock's tunic and offered it back to him. "Bleiben Sie warm. Wir haben unsere eigene Decke."

"What ye telling me, lass?" Jock raised himself, sliding his arm back into a sleeve, following her gaze. "There's something in the boot? Let's have a look." Twisting the handle, the boot popped open. A woollen blanket lay neatly folded on top. "This will do nicely." He handed it to the girl, sparing a glance at what remained. "Bugger me!" Jock's face widened in disbelief. A wicker basket filled with bottles, jars and cans of food and drink occupied most of the cavity. "Sorry," he said, lifting some pickled eggs to examine. "Nawt everyone is going withoot." He replaced the jar and slammed the boot. "That's right. Take a seat. I need tae help others."

The girl withdrew a small book from her coat pocket. "Es wird mich davon ablenken."

"Ye're in shock, lass. Don't go anywhere." Jock backed away with a smile and an encouraging wave. "I'll be right back."

A nightmare greeted Jock as he looked down the road. Exhausted prisoners knelt by their comrades tending wounds, others staggered in bewilderment. Captives and their captors lay still, victims of death's indiscriminate scythe.

Jock found a small group of hunched bodies shielding the fallen.

"Jock!"

"Konrad?"

The German, crouching over a prisoner, rose to his feet. "Zis is terrible."

"Aye, can I help?"

"A leg vound," explained Konrad. "Vone of zee lucky vones."

"How many were hit?"

The guard shrugged. "Zee line is too stretched out to know. Is zat...?" His voice trailed off on spotting the commandant's car.

"Aye. Dead. Only the daughter survived. She's sitting by the car."

Silence followed as the German attempted to comprehend what the commandant's death meant.

"Let's find others in need of help," suggested Jock. "Ye got any bandages?"

Konrad shook himself out of his stupor. "Ja, ja." He tapped his belt.

They found a prisoner halfway down the ditch, his attempt to evade the attack halted by a shell through one side of his abdomen.

"Jesus, the pain!" He grimaced, clasping Jock by his shoulder.

"We'll compact the wound," said Jock, letting Konrad cut back the layers of clothing. "What's yer name?"

"Dominic. Dominic Campbell. Cameron Highlanders."

"Dia maille riut. Richard Mitchell. West Kents."

"You speak Gaelic. Tapadh leat. That's far from home."

"Aye, it's where the work is. Ma family's with me. Ye got kids?" Jock glanced at Konrad, whose eyes expressed concern.

"F... five," answered Dominic, grinding his teeth in pain.

"A handful."

"Aye."

A gun fired in the distance. Campbell's eyes worked desperately, trying to find the source.

"Stay calm," urged Konrad. "I put on..." He looked to Jock for help.

"The compact. Brace yerself. This will hurt."

"Arrgghhh!"

The cry distracted from another gunshot, this one closer.

"Ye're doing well," reassured Jock, ignoring the blood colouring the bandages.

"Zur Aufmerksamkeit des Soldaten!" A shadow fell across Campbell. The unmistakable black-clad figure of a Waffen-SS officer stood above.

Konrad jumped to his feet, almost stumbling backwards in shock. "Heil Hitler."

A brief exchange took place between the Germans, the icy tone of the officer obvious to Jock. Konrad jogged away, gesturing and shouting at the dispersed prisoners, leaving the officer assessing Jock.

"Back to zee road! Leave your friend."

"But he needs help," stressed Jock, looking into Campbell's eyes.

"To the road, now!" said the officer, unclipping his holster. "You vill be ready to march in fünf minuten." He held up five fingers.

Jock raised himself, his eyes flitting from Campbell to the officer. "Aye, I'll be ready. Just make certain the medics pick him up."

"Schnell!" snapped the officer, as he pulled out his gun, levelled it at Campbell and shot.

"Ye bastard!" yelled Jock, charging the officer. He grabbed him by the waist, sending them both to the ground, the gun flying into the air. Both climbed back to their feet, facing each other.

"Bravo!" said the officer, with a nonchalant brush of his uniform. "You stay vith your friend."

Realisation dawned on Jock. This was an unfair fight. His layers of clothes hid his skeletal frame, but his gaunt cheeks and sunken eyes exposed all. A gloved fist met his chin, sending him back to the ground.

The SS officer smiled and bent to retrieve his gun. "Erbärmlich!" He took a step forward, standing over Jock. "You have signed zee death varrant of all who vitness your act of rebellion." He raised his gun. "Ouch!"

"Lass ihn in Ruhe!"

The officer looked in astonishment at Birgit, her foot ready to swing at his ankle again. With a wave of a hand, he struck her across the face.

Birgit stumbled back with a scream.

"That's the commandant's daughter!" cried Jock. "Ye'll nawt lay a finger on her."

"To strike an officer of zee Vaffen-SS is instant death sentence." He turned the pistol on the girl.

BANG!

Jock looked away, then felt the weight of the officer fall on his legs. "What the...?"

"Are you all right, Jock?" Konrad held out one hand, his smoking rifle in his other.

"Ye shot him!" A hysterical laughter escaped Jock's mouth.

"I had to. He vould shoot girl... and you."

Jock slapped the guard on his back. "Danke, Konrad. Are ye okay, lass?" With one hand resting on his knee, he held the other out to the girl. "And danke, Birgit. Ye both saved ma life."

Prisoners gathered around as Birgit hugged Jock, a further stream of tears burning her cheeks.

"What the hell have you done, Jock!" cried Peters, arriving at the scene, his trouser leg covered in another man's blood.

"I dinnae do nowt," growled Jock. "This scum was shooting prisoners."

"And about to shoot the girl," added Babe, appearing in the crowd. "I couldn't believe what I was watching."

"And who shot the scum?" asked Peters. His question answered by all the heads turning to Konrad. "Good on you, Konrad."

The guard looked sheepishly to the floor. "But vhat now?"

"An excellent question," said Jock, scratching his chin.

***

"Why me? Why does it have to be bleeding me?" Babe emerged from behind the sedan, his chin lost in the delicate hairs of a fur coat. His legs wobbled, struggling to balance in the black, high-heeled pumps. One hand grasped the scarlet pillbox hat with its decorative feather, the other a handbag.

"Hey! Even the shoes fit our Cinderella," quipped Peters, stopping mid-goose-step, as he assumed the role of his own costume change. "At least the blood doesn't show on black." He pulled the swastika on his sleeve and spat at it.

Jock closed the car bonnet, rubbing the grease from his hands on his trousers. The engine looked fine. He directed his gaze across the road to where Konrad engaged in an intense conversation with two of his fellow guards. Chaos still reigned down the road. If their plan was to work, then first the German had to win over his colleagues before others arrived and reasserted control.

"Well?" asked Jock, as Konrad strode back to the car.

"Zey have no love for zee SS und saw vhat he tried to do to zee girl," said the guard, his eyes stuck on Babe. "Vee are good."

Jock blew out his cheeks.

"It is our best chance," said Konrad. "I cannot stay. Zee SS vill find zee truth. Vee are all in danger."

"Aye, but what aboot Birgit? It's bad enough she's lost her parents, but this...!"

The girl sat curled up in a ball, hiding from the world.

"I vill speak vith her. For nine, she is grown-up. But vee must act fast. Please put on zee jacket and hat."

"I donnae like this one bit," grumbled Jock as Peters rehearsed a Nazi salute to his side.

"Please Jock," pressed Konrad. "Vee now know zee route." He waved the commandant's itinerary and map discovered in the sedan's glove box. "It can vork."

"Och, fine!" Jock snatched a pile of clothes from the car roof.

"I think I out-rank you, Herr Major," commented Peters, tapping his SS insignia, as Jock reappeared in the commander's uniform. "Not sure about the trousers."

Jock sneered. "I'm sticking with ma own. Nawt much is left of his."

"Das ist gut," said Konrad, his own transformation to the driver a simpler affair.

"And Birgit?"

"Zere vere tears, but she understands."

Her light sobbing got lost beneath Babe's whining. "Why can't I be the SS officer?"

"My beard didn't match the fur," countered Peters. "And your legs go perfectly with that dress."

"Enough!" snapped Jock. "This is nae time for ye jokes." He placed a reassuring hand on Babe's shoulder. "A family group is less suspicious, and this is the stage ye dreamt of."

"Er, no it isn't. I was playing opposite Vivien Leigh, not as her!"

Whatman appeared, his role unchanged as an emaciated British prisoner. "I've removed the contents of the hamper, replaced with your uniforms and bags," he whispered to Jock. "All have something in their pocket."

"Good lad," said Jock. "How they feeling aboot this?"

"Everyone's behind you. I'm sure some would prefer to be smuggled in the boot, but… Well, you're the right age for the commandant, Babe's the only one who doesn't shave yet, and Archie has taken to his role as an SS officer rather well. Oh, by the way, I've left you a couple of tins. Not sure what. My German's not good."

"Thanks. Now, listen carefully," said Jock, his eyes locking on Whatman's. "We're gonnae stay ahead of ye, tae steer clear of anyone who might actually recognise the commandant. It's a long way tae Hanover, but we'll steal food from our hosts and leave it for ye tae find."

"How will we know where to look?"

"I'm getting tae that part, lad. I'll leave a sign. On a wall, hut or something obvious. Next tae the road." Jock stopped to think. "A large 'V'."

"For victory!"

"Aye. It may be subtle: twigs, dirt. On the way out of the stop-over location. So, keep yer eyes open. I donnae know how long we'll keep the deception going."

"There's a truck coming up the road!" called out Peters. "Hopefully help for the wounded. Time to go."

Jock offered his hand to Whatman. "Good luck. Exploit those guards in on the secret. There's a bullet waiting for them if their superiors find out."

"See you in Hanover."

***

Jock sat in the middle of the back seat of the sedan, Babe to one side, Birgit the other. The young girl curled herself up, facing the window and reticent, her thumb in her mouth. Peters occupied the front passenger seat, fiddling with his uniform's array of insignia.

"Perhaps a prayer is in order?" suggested Konrad as he turned the engine key. "Gott im Himmel!" The motor spluttered, then died.

"Give it some choke," urged Peters.

"I have!" Konrad turned the key again.

The men held their breath as the ignition whirled, only to fail again.

"Now what?" whimpered Babe. "I'm not walking in this!"

Jock leaned across the youngster, one hand grasping the window frame. "Give us a push, lads!" he shouted.

The prisoners awaiting their departure massed behind the car.

"Try again," said Jock to Konrad. "Easy on the choke or you'll flood the engine."

The car rocked forward as the prisoners shoved.

"Now!" cried Peters.

As momentum built and the sedan rolled under the steam of the prisoners, Konrad turned his key with a whispered prayer. "Ja, ja!" he cried in excitement as the engine growled into life.

They jumped forward and Jock turned to wave in gratitude to those left behind, their cheer carrying to his ears.

"Thank the Lord!" said Babe, looking to the heavens.

"Jeez, that's cold," complained Peters as the wind rushed through the glassless windscreen, building with their speed.

Jock glanced to the roadside, where the lined bodies of the dead lay, other prisoners beginning their march westwards. He closed his eyes.

Day Forty-One: Afternoon

Jock woke to the sound of Peters's snoring. For a moment, he considered he might still be dreaming: the comfortable seat, his rested feet and contented appetite, the absence of threat. None felt real. He looked down at his commandant's coat, across at Birgit staring out the window, the bitter wind all the while stinging his face. Reality reintroduced itself.

"How long have I been asleep?"

Konrad turned and smiled. "An hour. You look besser… er, better."

"Aye, well…" Jock shuffled upright, embarrassed to have let his guard down. "Where are we?"

Babe mumbled in his sleep, turning to find warmth in his coat.

"Near Eberswalde," said Konrad. "Tonight's rendezvous for zee prisoners."

Jock nodded. "You're good with maps."

"Nein. A guard at zee checkpoint told me."

"What!" Jock's eyes bulged in disbelief.

"W… what's going on?" Peters woke as though from a drunken stupor. "I was having a pleasant dream."

Babe rubbed his eyes, his bottom lip protruding in displeasure at the rude awakening.

"We got stopped at a checkpoint and Konrad didn't wake us!" explained Jock, shuffling forward to the edge of his seat.

"Ist gut, Jock," said Konrad, his eyes on the road. "Asleep, zee guards do not question you. And you do not speak. No?"

"Aye, I suppose so," admitted Jock grudgingly.

"They weren't suspicious of anything?" asked Peters, licking his cracked lips.

Konrad shrugged. "They not see a Vaffen-SS officer asleep before. A myth says zey do not need sleep."

"This one does!" Peters straightened his collar.

"But we're okay?" pressed Babe.

"Ja, zey not vant to vake SS officer. Vee got through vithout close... how you say? Inspektion."

"Er, inspection."

Konrad chuckled. "Ja. Language same!"

"Where did ye learn English?" asked Jock, leaning back again, sparing a smile for Birgit, who followed the strange conversation with curiosity.

"School and at vork," answered Konrad. "I vas a clockmaker. Special clocks. Have you heard of Cohen's of Dresden?" The driver turned to his front seat passenger.

"No," admitted Peters.

"I start as apprentice at zwölf... twelve. Herr Cohen taught me himself. A kind old man."

"Jewish?" enquired Jock.

"Ja," said Konrad with a deep sigh. "I not know vhat happened to him or his family. His business vas taken from him. I should have helped him more. A big regret."

"Make it up after the war," suggested Babe. "Things will soon get back to normal."

"You have been avay from zee vorld for a long time," said Konrad.

Babe looked to Jock in confusion, only to receive a shrug.

"I stay in London in 1931," continued Konrad. "Help distant cousin of Herr Cohen. Golders Green. You know?"

"I got my wedding ring there," chirped in Peters.

"My landlady, a German-Jew, she help teach me English."

"She did a fine job," said Peters. "I understand you better than I do Jock."

Jock's hand flicked forward, catching his friend on the back of his head.

"Ouch! There's no respect for the SS these days!"

"You should not make light of zem," cautioned Konrad. "I see many horrible things zey do. Devil soldiers."

"Aye," agreed Jock. "They're evil bastards, but the Brits like to pop balloons with humour."

"I do not understand," said Konrad.

"Ne'er mind. Ask Birgit if she's all right."

Jock watched the pair's exchange, understanding only the odd word.

"She is cold, hungry and misses her parents," translated Konrad. "As vone vould expect. And..." Konrad hesitated.

"And what?"

"She does not like Archie. It is zee uniform." The guard shrugged an apology.

Peters looked crestfallen. "Hey, that's not fair. Kids love me." He smiled for Birgit only to receive a scowl.

"The uniform maketh the man," offered Babe. "Every cast needs a baddy."

"Oh, shut up! I hope you explained I'm a good guy?"

"You are zee enemy. Your people drop bombs on our cities." Konrad drove with a haughty, defensive air. "Zee SS bring misery to us vithin. She has reason to dislike you."

An angry flush coloured Peters's face. "Your lot started it! I've spent five years suffering under you bastards. You didn't have to invade bloody Poland." He grabbed Konrad's collar, causing the car to veer.

Birgit screamed.

"Enough!" cried Jock. "We need each other. Innocents suffer on both sides."

"Ja, ja. I am sorry." Konrad, the car under his control again, held up a hand in apology. "Zee var is terrible for all. I vish for zee end soon."

Peters released his grip, folded his arms, and turned to glare out the side window in silence.

"Gott im Himmel!" cried Konrad as the engine spluttered to a stop, steam rising from the bonnet.

"Now what?" asked Babe.

"Wasn't me," mumbled Peters.

The car rolled to a standstill, its occupants looking at one another with alarm.

Konrad hit the steering wheel. "Kaputt!"

"We've broken down?" asked Jock, already knowing the answer.

"Ja."

A plume of steam drifted through the car's interior, cooled and transformed into delicate ice crystals. Only Birgit, distracted from her tears, thought it beautiful.

"What if we can't fix it?" whimpered Babe.

"Let's find out what's wrong first," urged Jock, motioning for the lad to get out of the car with a nod of his head.

The four men stood around the open bonnet.

"Kaputt," repeated Peters, one foot resting on the bumper, his strop forgotten.

"The radiator pipe's split," observed Jock, his head buried in the engine.

"Can you fix it?" asked Babe, wandering to the verge to urinate.

A family of refugees on a horse and trap crept past, their eyes noting the odd scene with fear and confusion.

"Naw, if we top it up, the water will just leak out in nae time." Jock pursed his lips in thought.

Konrad looked around in concern. "A kommandant should not vork as mechanic."

"Can you fix it?" challenged Peters, as he warmed his hands over the hot engine. "No, didn't think so."

A growl and cough announced a vehicle heading towards them. Babe yanked down his dress and closed the fur coat. "A motorbike and sidecar!"

"Jock, get back," urged Konrad, pushing the Scot to one side. "I vill be mechanic and do zee talking. You look important."

"I can do that," said Jock, clasping his hands behind his back and watching the bike with a discerning air as it slowed.

The bike pulled to a halt, its rider and passenger masked in goggles and scarfs under their German helmets. The rider dismounted, pulling his scarf down to his chin. "Heil Hitler!"

Konrad straightened from his examination of the engine and saluted in reply. "Heil Hitler!"

A fraction of a second passed, almost indiscernible, but a hesitation. "Heil Hitler," said Jock, pointing an arm to the sky, Peters echoing with a little more aplomb.

The rider lifted his goggles, his frown exaggerated by the rings of dirt. "Gibt es ein problem, kommandant?" He awaited Jock's reply.

"Ein Rohr ist geplatzt," announced Konrad, with a melodramatic flourish of his hands. He stepped forward to face his countryman, a hand guiding him away for a discreet discussion.

The goggles of the sidecar passenger remained locked on the others.

"Are they suspicious?" whispered Peters, one hand covering his mouth, the other clasping his holster.

Jock turned his back to the Germans. "Stay calm, lad. Konrad's brighter than yer average Kraut. Our watcher seems most interested in Babe."

The young prisoner struck his most feminine pose, a hand adjusting his hair, his lips puckered.

"I'm half convinced myself," murmured Peters with a sly grin.

"Ich kann Ihnen mit Ihrer Pfeife helfen."

Jock spun round to find the rider and Konrad before him.

"Das ist gut. Ja, kommandant?" said Konrad, his eyes urging a reply.

"Ja. Danke." Jock lifted his chin, delivering his line with a curt authority.

"Das könnte eine Weile dauern," said the rider. "Ich kann meinen Kollegen hier lassen, um das Problem zu beheben und den Oberst zu seinem Zielort zu fahren."

"Ja, ja," said Jock, waving a dismissive hand, before realising the German addressed Peters.

Peters stared down the road, oblivious, while Konrad's face twitched in alarm.

"Ha, ha," laughed Konrad, his nervous energy pouring forth a long-winded response in his own tongue.

Jock folded his arms, attempting a contemptuous manner, while the indecipherable words washed through him. He noticed the rider's eyebrow arch, suspicion creeping in as Konrad's monologue stirred a reaction. His mouth dried; his pulse beat faster. *What were they thinking trying to play Germans to a German audience?* Jock's fingers touched his own holster, easing the clip off, his eyes trying to signal to Peters.

"Mutter, Vater, ich habe Angst. Wird Onkel Otto uns beschützen?" Birgit climbed out of the car; her big, imploring eyes directed at Jock.

The German rider smiled, uttering a phrase Jock took as a clear compliment. *A father should respond to such praise*, thought Jock, his mind scrambling through his limited German vocabulary.

"Mein kleines baby!!" cried Babe in his best falsetto voice, taking centre stage. He opened his arms and gathered up Birgit, his eyes looking to heaven.

Jock decided on a simple. "Ja, ja." He nodded his head and ruffled Birgit's hair.

It prompted a conversation between the rider and his passenger; a smile exchanged, their suspicion fading.

Sensing the lighter mood, Konrad ushered everyone back into the car, sharing a commentary for the watching Germans. He lent into Jock, whispering in his ear, "I say, a family should be together." With a check behind and a smile for the soldiers, he added, "Even Uncle Otto."

"Does he know that?" Jock helped Birgit back into the car and offered a courteous hand to assist Babe.

An oblivious Peters continued playing his part, aloof and uninterested, prowling back and forth.

"I have said his hearing is kaputt," said Konrad with a wink. "Bomb damage, ja." He shut the door behind Jock and smiled at the soldiers. "So eine liebevolle Familie."

The passenger climbed out of the sidecar, rolling his sleeves up as he ambled over to his colleague. They stood over the car engine, pointing and prodding.

"Back in zee motor!" urged Konrad, alarming Peters from behind.

"Are they fixing it?" Peters asked in a whisper.

"Ja, zey have tools vith zeir bike." Konrad spared them a quick glance. "Stay in zee motor and no vords. I vill help and get rid of zem."

"Good man." Peters paused. "Er, sorry about earlier."

***

Birgit leaned across Jock, waving to the two Germans as their bike revved, spurting a plume of smoke from the exhaust.

The driver's door to the sedan opened. Konrad climbed in, slumping in his seat. "Mein Gott!"

"Are we good?" asked Jock, not daring to look at their good Samaritans.

Konrad waited until the motorbike pulled away. "Ja... I hope. Zee Auto is fixed." The engine started, supporting his declaration.

"They weren't suspicious?" asked Babe.

"Ha," laughed Konrad. "Two starved and silent officers, one with zee wrong trousers and an unusual-looking woman. Ja, zey vere suspicious but also afraid." He indicated the SS uniform on Peters, with a tip of his head. "I told zem you recover from... er, how you say, sickness of stomach?"

"Dysentery?"

"Ja."

"What do you mean 'unusual'?" asked Babe.

The three men spared the lad a disbelieving glance.

"Zee girl save day, no?" Konrad smiled at Brigit, who leaned into her mother's fur coat for warmth.

"Aye, from the mouths of babes," said Jock. "Will they report us?"

"I think not. Zee country is in chaos. Zey vant avay from zee Russen: nothing more."

Peters sniffed. "Afraid of a taste of their own medicine? If you think we're treated poorly, you should see what your lot do to the Russian prisoners. Poor sods!"

Konrad's shoulders slumped a little. "It is true. I am sorry. Die Menschheit hat sich verirrt."

"I'm sure you're right, whatever you said," remarked Peters. "Now, let's get moving before Babe gets asked for a dance by one of your countrymen."

Day Forty-One: Evening

"I don't know," said Babe, studying the bustling town from the car window. "That's an awful lot of Germans."

"And the flags," added Peters. "Says, 'Nazis only' to me."

Their car, parked in the high street of a small provincial town, sat across from a large hotel, its nineteenth century grandeur tarnished by an array of draped swastika banners.

Konrad shifted himself round, holding up the map. He tapped it with his finger. "Zis is vhere Kommandant Lange and his family stay. Look, Hotel Kaufmann."

"There are a lot of soldiers entering," observed Peters.

"Ja," said Konrad with a sigh. "It is for military only. Officers."

"Oh, great. Talk about walking into the lions' den!"

"Let's just find a quiet barn. Eh, Jock?" said Babe.

Jock sat in quiet contemplation. A sleeping Birgit rested on his shoulder, rising and falling to the rhythm of her breathing; her tears finally ceased. "We promised the lads food," he said at last. "Won't find any in an isolated barn. Naw, we need a good night's sleep. If we stay in our rooms, we'll be fine."

"I can't go in there like this," exclaimed Babe, opening up his fur coat to expose his dress.

"Jock's right," sighed Peters. "We can pilfer food from the kitchens. Just enough to fuel the lads for a day. We'll be long gone before anyone notices. Wherever we go, there'll be lots of Germans. This is Germany, after all."

"I do all talking," stated Konrad. "Book rooms and order food."

"Aye," agreed Jock. "Sent to our rooms. We eat, we sleep, we go."

"Yes, but what about me?" persisted Babe.

"Let's get this done," said Jock, ignoring the youngster. "This scrapheap of a car is drawing attention." He opened the car door, shooing away a small group of children gaping at the bullet holes. "I'll carry Birgit."

The girl opened her sleepy eyes as Jock scooped her up, emitting a light moan. Clasped in the Scot's arms, her head drooped onto his shoulder, and sleep reclaimed her. A passing woman smiled, uttering a comment. Jock smiled back, recognising the universal language of parents.

"Come," said Konrad. "Before all rooms are gone."

Peters opened the rear door next to Babe. "Your audience awaits. It's showtime!"

"Oh, shut up!" snapped Babe, emerging with a face like thunder.

"You look like a bull on the charge," commented Peters. "Only a Spaniard would find you attractive at the moment."

Babe opened his mouth for an angry rebuke, only to find the impatient eyes of Jock and Konrad locked on him. "Oh, all right." He lifted his chin, sucked in his cheeks, and crossed the road with a debonair swagger.

"By Jove," declared Peters. "I think he's got it."

Within the hotel lobby, with its rich, velvety red wallpaper and crystal chandeliers, German officers lounged on leather armchairs under a cloud of cigarette smoke. Their eyes followed Babe as he entered.

"A shortage of ladies," Peters said under his breath. The only other woman in sight was an old maid serving drinks. "Make sure you lock your door tonight."

As they passed a column, Babe guided a heel to the top of Peters's boot, extracting a muffled yelp. "A lady must use all the weapons at her disposal," said Babe with a triumphant grin.

"Quit messing aboot!" hissed Jock, as Peters leaned against the column, rubbing his foot.

After a few minutes, Konrad returned from reception, dangling two keys between his fingers. "On floor two," he whispered. "Rooms next door. Ist gut. Lift kaputt. We use stairs."

"Oh, great. More walking," grumbled Peters.

Jock placed Birgit into a chair, rousing her from sleep. "Ye're too heavy tae carry, lass."

Aware of her new surroundings, Birgit rubbed her eyes and studied the lobby. "Wo sind wir?" she asked in a sorrowful tone.

Jock looked to Konrad.

"I will tell her all," said the German, offering his hand to the girl. "Komm mit. Wir übernachten heute in einem hotel."

"We'll wash her dress while she sleeps," said Jock as they climbed the stairs. "Get rid of her mother's blood."

"Good idea," said Babe, examining his own attire. "Perhaps we can borrow some needle and thread, and I can repair the holes."

"I'm just sleeping," said Peters with a yawn, following behind.

***

"Mmm, egg," crooned Peters. "Okay, powdered egg, but it's still egg." He shovelled another fork-full into his mouth.

"And butter," mumbled Babe, his cheeks bulging from toast.

Jock sat on the windowsill, surveying the street below. "How ye paying for this?"

"Ah, zee military and ration books." Konrad opened his tunic, pulling out a bundle of tatty booklets. "I rescue vhen vee…" He looked across at the sleeping Birgit, tucked under the covers of the double bed.

"When we hid the bodies," said Jock, returning to the view from the window.

"Ja. Zey not need now."

"That's a fine sunset," said Jock, enjoying the colourful sky from the warmth of their room. "Either that or somewhere is taking a hell of a pummelling."

"Pummelling?" queried Konrad.

"Ne'er mind. Finish yer dinner. We need to be up early."

"How early?" asked Peters, fearing the answer.

"Before everyone else. I don't want us seen when we raid the kitchen."

"That's early!" Peters slumped sidewards, his head pressing into the soft bed. "Can we steal a mattress, too?"

"Go tae yer room, ye numptie. And nae snoring. These walls are paper thin."

***

A drummer marched down the middle of the French high street, his vibrant uniform unbefitting a war zone. Even within his dream, Jock thought of this as odd. He hid in the ruin of a patisserie, the walls crumbling around shelves stocked with unblemished delicacies. Teased by the aroma of the cakes, Jock willed his legs to move, but they disobeyed, confused by the call of the eclairs and the battle erupting around. The drummer beat his instrument, braving the bullets and shells, putting Jock to shame. He should be out there fighting. Once more, the drum beat, now louder. Thump! Thump! Thump! Jock sprang upright, the dream collapsing as he recognised the hotel room through the darkness.

"There's someone at the door," he whispered, nudging Babe and grabbing his gun.

"What time is it?" mumbled Babe.

"I donnae know," answered Jock as he tip-toed to the door. He placed an ear to the wood, listening in the darkness. "Ja." It was all he could think to say.

"Jock," came the hushed reply. "It's us, you fool. Open up!"

Jock edged the door open, his gun held in his clammy fingers. "What?"

Peters and Konrad pushed in, dressed and booted. "It's gone four," whispered Peters. "We should be going."

"As late as that?" said Jock, scratching his hair. "I could have slept forever."

"Yeah, well, lucky for you. Konrad talks in his sleep, so I've been up a while."

The German responded to Peters's glare with a sheepish grin.

"Where's Birgit?" asked Peters.

"Oh, she's in there somewhere," said Jock, patting the jumbled blanket, as he sank on to the bed. With a flick of his wrist, he clipped Babe's exposed leg. "Get up, lad. It's time we left."

The youngster emerged with arms stretched, his mouth wide in a yawn. "Really?"

"You slept with make-up on?" asked Peters with a smirk. "Your lipstick's smudged."

"Bah," said Babe, wiping a hand across his face. "Don't start again!"

"Come on, lass. Time tae get up." Jock rocked the lump beneath the blanket.

"Mama," called Birgit, her head emerging. On seeing Jock, she burst into tears, sleep her only escape from the nightmare.

"Don't cry," urged Jock. "Say something, Konrad."

The old guard appeared by Jock, straightened and delivered a short sentence. The crying ceased, replaced by a wobbling bottom lip.

"What did you say?" asked Babe, struggling to balance his artificial breasts under his dress.

"Oh, zat zer Führer demands, as a good German girl, she stop."

"Does he do lullabies too?" asked Peters.

"Less talking, more dressing," demanded Jock, pushing his toes into his boots. "Is Birgit's dress dry?"

"Yes, though still stained," answered Babe, plucking the dress off the chair's back.

"It'll have tae do." Jock tightened his belt, catching his reflection in the mirror. Unable to stomach his emaciated self or the commandant's ghost, he turned away. "Archie, get the car started. Babe, ye get Birgit dressed and fix yer face, then head tae the car. Konrad and I will visit the kitchen. We may need a quick getaway."

"Shouldn't I go with you?" asked Peters. "No one will question me in uniform. And Konnie's better with the car."

"Naw, we may have tae bluff our way oot. And yer German's atrocious."

"Teacher's pet," said Peters, sticking his tongue out at Konrad.

"I not understand."

"Few understand our Archie," said Jock. "Now, hurry, before our neighbours wake."

The trio sneaked through the corridor, down the stairs, and into the lobby.

"Guten Morgen, meine Herren. Früh aufgestanden?"

Jock cursed under his breath. A member of the hotel staff, busy unlocking window shutters, addressed them. Only when the man turned did he expose a missing arm, his empty sleeve pinned to his chest.

"Guten Morgen. Ja, der Krieg erwartet uns." Konrad pushed to the fore.

"Keep on walking!" whispered Jock to Peters. "Konrad's got this."

"We're not the only early birds." Peters nodded to the bar, where two officers chatted over a hot drink.

A sudden thud from above sent the pair spinning in alarm. Babe and Birgit appeared, the girl wide awake and enjoying her descent by hopping from stair to stair.

"Go!" hissed Jock, shoving Peters toward the door.

As Peters vanished outside, Konrad concluded his conversation, while Babe and Birgit stepped off the final stair. Jock ruffled the girl's hair, as any father might. "Keep her quiet!" he said to Babe through gritted teeth.

With that, Birgit spotted the bar and in a loud voice said, "Kann ich einen Milchshake haben? Erdbeer."

"What did she say?"

"She wants a milkshake," answered Konrad. "Err, strawberry flavour."

"Oh, dear God," muttered Jock and leaned toward Babe. "Get her in the car quick. Promise her a milkshake for later." He turned to Konrad. "Where's the kitchen?"

"Follow me, Jock," said Konrad, while Babe led Birgit away. "I tell man ve leave a note for cook. A thank you for meal last night."

Jock raised his eyebrows in surprise. "Aye, the powered egg was a triumph."

They pushed through a pair of swing doors into the dining area, staff already milling about, setting tables. Curious eyes followed them; Konrad tried to disarm with a hearty greeting. There was a strange normality to the place. Jock pictured it full: couples conversing across the tables, a band playing on stage, waiters rushing back and forth with the orders. *Will it ever be like that again?* The clatter of pans shook Jock from his daydream. They had reached the kitchen doors.

"We got up too late," grumbled Jock. "Too many people aboot."

"I... er, lenke sie ab, you steal, ja?" Konrad looked to see if Jock understood.

"Lenk sie ab? Distract?" Jock pointed behind the German, and as he turned, pushed him.

Konrad chuckled on recognising Jock's charade. "Ja, ja. I distract."

Humid air struck them as they entered the kitchen, the smell of boiling vats intriguing their senses. A man with a mop stopped and inspected them with suspicious eyes, while from within the steam, another with a ladle appeared, his large, bushy beard hanging down to a prominent belly. Neither looked happy to see them.

Konrad threw his hands up in the air, a flurry of ingratiating words addressed to the pair. A cigarette packet appeared, and with a helping hand, he guided the two together.

Jock hung back, leaning on a sideboard. He laughed when they laughed, sparing a nonchalant inspection of the kitchen as he awaited his moment. Nervous glances came his way, but ceased as Konrad absorbed their attention. Jock unbuttoned his tunic, fanning his face, and then they turned their backs. Sneaking along the shelves, he tipped a bag and jar against his stomach, gathering them under his jacket. Two carrots on a sideboard dropped into a pocket, a leek up his sleeve. A string of sausages lay on the side awaiting boiling. *Will they miss a couple?* His fingers walked along the surface, his gaze directed upwards.

"Geht zurück an die Arbeit, ihr faulen Schmarotzer!" An angry voice shouted as the doors flapped open.

Jock withdrew his hand, gathering his tunic together. The new arrival spotted him, the tone changing to respectful. His seniority within the kitchen was obvious, but all Jock could do was smile as meaningless words drifted his way. Jock's hand moved to his holster; the leek slid down, poking out from his sleeve. He up-righted his arm, pretending to scratch an ear, the vegetable slipping back. Konrad then appeared, clasping the man by the hand, shaking it vigorously. Somewhat taken aback by the show of gratitude, the man shrugged, allowing Konrad to continue with his praise. The other two men, rebuked back to work, watched with amusement.

Without stopping his flow, Konrad motioned Jock to leave with a light hand to his shoulder, exiting the kitchen backwards as the platitudes continued. The sprung doors waved back and forth until sealed.

"Vee go quick," Konrad urged. "Zee chef is no fool, zhough he thinks vee are."

Jock gripped his abdomen, holding their loot tight. "What did ye say tae him?"

"I ask for recipe for his scrambled eggs. You have not eaten such a fine meal for very long time, I say."

"Well, that part's true, lad. But the competition was nawt great."

They found a side door, emerging into a grim alleyway along the hotel's side. A rat sniffed at them before scurrying behind some discarded crates. The alley led to the high street, where their car awaited. The doors swung open and Peters slid across to the passenger seat.

"You get something good?" asked Babe as Jock dropped on the back seat, spilling his load.

"Not much, but something," he answered, leaning his head back and letting out a deep breath. "Get us oot of here!"

As the car jerked and pulled away, Birgit held up the jar and giggled.

"What's so funny?" asked Jock.

"You bring us mustard, Jock, but no roast beef." Konrad laughed.

"Och, that's nae good to us. What aboot the bag?"

Konrad turned his head. "Ah, dried fruit. You do vell."

"Yes, there's enough to share," said Babe, trying to peer into the bag.

As Jock pulled the leek from his sleeve, Birgit giggled again. "She seems in a better mood taeday."

"We're now friends," said Peters, winking at the girl.

"Really? And how did ye manage that?"

"Oh, just a few magic tricks taught to me by my uncle Eric."

"He's quite good," remarked Babe. "We could have done with you at the Christmas show."

"Children's parties only," declared Peters. "And if you bring me a real SS officer, I'll show you how to make that leek disappear."

"Cover yer ears, lass. I would'nae let ye near ma kids, Archie!"

"We do good, ja?" said Konrad, as the prisoners laughed.

"We live tae fight another day," answered Jock, with a hand gripping the German's shoulder. "But, aye, we did good. Now, keep yer eyes open for a good place tae leave this bag. Somewhere the lads can find it, but Jerry won't notice. I guess we'll keep the mustard."

"It'll come in useful when forced to eat our boot soles," said Peters.

Laughter erupted again as the car rattled over the cobbles to the edge of town. Birgit tugged on Babe's coat. "Milchshake?"

Day Forty-Six: Evening

After a day of stop-starting, the road emptied as twilight descended. The refugees, with their bewildered expressions, had vanished, the darkness too dangerous. Overhead, the first rumble of night-time bombers signalled the despair and suffering about to befall the cities on their route.

Konrad squinted: the headlights off, the grey road merging with the grey fields. As the rear wheels drifted on a patch of ice, he compensated, jerking the steering wheel sharp left, keeping the vehicle travelling forward. The others had welcomed the first sign of melting snow during the day, but he understood the dangers it brought with plunging temperatures after sundown. What he was less certain of was their location. He scanned the map covering the top half of the steering wheel, scratching his chin as it flapped in the wind.

"Can we stop or not?" pressed Peters, not for the first time.

"I think so," answered the German, still to admit they had missed the official stop-over location.

"We should sleep in the car," urged Babe, tired of the leers from soldiers on previous nights.

"It's too cold, lad." Jock peered into the darkness in search of the enemy. "If a patrol came upon us, how would ye explain it away? Naw, we behave as our uniforms require."

"There's a farmhouse!" declared Peters, making out the familiar sight of chimney smoke. "We requisition a room. Hell, why not the whole farmhouse? That's what your lot would do?"

"Ja." Konrad nodded, accepting the criticism.

"And if they see through us, do we shoot them?" Babe squeezed Birgit closer, his transformation to mother hen almost complete.

"Nawt unless they threaten us," said Jock. "We'll cross that bridge when we have tae. There are limits tae what these uniforms require us tae do."

"And what do we say if spoken to?" pressed the reluctant Babe.

"Konrad? Ye got a phrase for any situation?"

"Err, danke für Ihre Gastfreundschaft."

"Jeez," exclaimed Peters. "You got us admiring their holes?"

Konrad frowned. "It means, thank you for your hospitality. Danke für Ihre Gastfreundschaft."

"Oh, the 'shaft' bit threw me."

"Shut up and try saying it!" instructed Jock, mouthing the words to himself.

"Leave talking to me," sighed Konrad, turning up the farm track.

Three storeys tall, the farmhouse's white timber beams, ordered around tight-packed red bricks and small windows, glowed in the fading light. The familiar smell of livestock triggered nostalgia for Jock. While a steep, thatched chalet roof, despite a covering of snow, promised warmth.

Konrad climbed out of the car and ducked into the arched recess under which a door nestled out of the wind. The others watched nervously from the car.

"What if they don't have room?" asked Babe.

Jock ignored him.

"Or food?"

The door opened a crack, with the face of an elderly woman appearing. Konrad bowed his head, removing his cap.

"What are they saying?" asked Peters, shuffling to the edge of his seat.

"I donnae know!" exclaimed Jock. "Ma German teacher's been busy."

"She looks a stern one," continued Peters, unperturbed by Jock's sarcasm. "Reminds me of my great aunt Isobel. Even my pa feared her. Did I tell you…"

"It's good. Konrad's waving us in." Jock opened his car door and stood tall, straightening his uniform.

"Perhaps another time," whispered Peters over the roof of the car.

The farmhouse door swung open. The woman stood to the side, arms folded under a humourless face, her white hair bunched in a tidy ball.

"Frau Dünge lives here vith her husband," said Konrad in Jock's ear as he returned to the car. "Vee are not zee first to requisition her house. She is not happy."

"I can tell," whispered Jock.

As Birgit appeared, the old lady's eyes followed her, losing a little anger.

"Vone of her sons is dead, zee ozher avay in zee army. She has granddaughter but never seen her." Konrad's haggard features dropped in sympathy.

"So, no love for the British then?"

Konrad answered with a tired nod, a finger to the lips urging silence.

Their host's face returned to its grim setting as Jock approached. He removed his hat and bowed, as Konrad had before him.

"Frau Dung, danke for Ihre Gasfriendshaft," said Jock, confident with his pronunciation, failing to notice Konrad's eyes glance to the sky.

A quick-fire reply came as a string of indecipherable words, the woman's toothless mouth moving up and down under her intense eyes. Jock smiled.

Peters then stepped up, his smile causing the old lady's grimace to intensify. "Dank for Gastfreundshaft." Peters's attempt compelled Konrad to whisper a prayer.

Unease and confusion worked their way across the old lady's brow.

"Er kommt aus Estland," explained Konrad, unable to engage eyes as he lied.

With her chin set firm, the old lady shuffled down the hall, motioning for her guests to follow.

Jock looked behind, checking Babe and Birgit were in tow. To his surprise, he caught them in what appeared to be a conversation. "Ye speak German?" he asked in a whisper as they came level, hand in hand.

"Oh, only a little," replied Babe, a little too loud.

"Shh!"

"Sorry," whispered Babe. "Birgit speaks a little English too, so we chat. She's a clever girl."

"Aye, always has been." Jock stroked the girl's hair, reciprocated with a smile.

They followed the old lady into the kitchen, savouring the warmth of a raging fire. The husband sat at a table, a pipe in his mouth. He watched them in silence, unmoving except for his bottom lip working the pipe.

Birgit's face brightened in sight of the flames, her social confidence expressing itself through her own greeting and inclination to make herself at home.

The gruff voice of the wife softened as she and the girl exchanged pleasantries, converging at the stove, where sweet aromas emerged.

"What's going on?" asked Jock under his breath.

"Vee vill eat und zen be shown to our beds," answered Konrad.

The old lady called over to Babe; his feeble smile a confession to his limited German.

"Zee ladies are expected to look after zeir men together," explained Konrad, urging Babe to join the others round the stove.

Babe mumbled under his breath, before transforming into his demure character and sauntering over.

"He makes a fine lady," remarked Konrad, "but not so good an Estonian."

"Estonian?" Jock frowned.

"Ja, it is vhat I tell our host to explain your poor German."

"Jeez," said Peters. "How big a hole are we digging for this lie? And if she speaks Estonian?"

Konrad shrugged. "Let us sit and be polite guests."

"The sooner we're in bed, the better," whispered Jock, pulling out a chair and bowing to the reticent farmer.

The three sat opposite the old man, awkward grins confronting his languid stare. Konrad attempted to engage in conversation, receiving monosyllabic replies or a near imperceptible nod. Soon silence descended across the table, the void filled by Birgit's excitable chatter drifting across the room.

"Mahlzeit!" Frau Dünge placed a large casserole dish in the middle of the table, as Babe passed round chunks of heavy rye bread and Birgit poured a syrupy ale.

"Mmmm." Peters's eyes widened as he drew in the rich aroma through his nose.

The old lady raised the lid, exposing the stewing outline of a whole rabbit.

Jock and Peters exchanged the look of schoolboys locked in a sweet-shop.

"Das sieht wunderbar aus, finden Sie nicht, kommandant?" said Konrad, looking at Jock with expectant eyes.

"Err, ja. Wunderbar," said Jock on cue.

The rabbit fell apart as Frau Dünge served, ladling the thick sauce over every portion. Peters gripped his cutlery tight, fighting the urge to tuck in, while Babe closed his eyes, wallowing in the smells tickling his senses. The old lady said a brief prayer, and the etiquette was complete.

The prisoners ate in haste, unable to conceal the habits picked up in captivity. Jock came up for air, clutching his ale glass, biting off a chunk of bread, ready to mix it all in his crammed mouth. He discovered Frau Dünge's stern eyes on him, her jaw moving with decorum on a lesser morsel.

"Wunderbar," mumbled Jock in appreciation, before he noticed his host's plate. He compared it with his own. Each guest had a generous helping, in contrast to the measly portions on Frau Dünge and her husband's plates. Jock stopped chewing and gulped. He lifted his plate, scraping a rabbit leg on to the old lady's, sending Peters a gentle kick under the table.

"Ouch!"

"Nein, nein," objected Frau Dünge, the rest of her protestations meaningless to Jock.

Peters caught on, bidding his contribution a forlorn farewell, stirring further objections as it plopped on the old lady's plate. Babe followed suit, his donation for the husband, who offered no response other than a satisfied belch. As Konrad added his offering to Herr Dünge's plate, he calmed the wife, expressing their gratitude but desire not to deprive their hosts of a fair share.

"Nehmen Sie bitte auch etwas von mir." Birgit lifted her plate, ready to contribute.

"Nein!" The chorus erupted from both host and guests.

Birgit withdrew her plate, confused.

"Die Kleine braucht eine gute Mahlzeit im Bauch," said Frau Dünge, her stern features melting to a smile. She picked up the rabbit's leg shared by Jock and bit into it; her host's pride restored with the compromise for Birgit.

Smiles multiplied around the table, skipping Herr Dünge, his face buried in his food. Soon, Birgit beamed with the others, no less confused, but happy.

Day Forty-Seven: Early Morning

"Sleep well?" asked Babe, as the dawn light broke into the room.

"It was the most comfortable restless night I've had for years," replied Jock with a yawn and stretch.

A stale odour dominated the room, unoccupied as it had remained for a year. But despite dust and spiderwebs, it felt luxurious to the prisoners.

"Took ages for my gut to settle," confessed Babe.

"Aye, our tums are nawt accustomed to such rich food and ale. I'm just glad I wasn't sick."

Birgit, already out of bed, sat on the windowsill, looking out. As a 'family', Frau Dünge insisted they stay together, a small bed available at the foot of the double bed.

"Guten Morgen," said Babe, adjusting a stocking that had rolled up in the night.

The girl turned and smiled, her cheeks marked red from tears.

"Hey, what's the matter?" Babe climbed out of bed, still in the dress.

"Ich vermisse Mama und Papa."

"Of course ye do," said Jock, understanding enough to get the sentiment. "Seeing us in her parents' clothes dinnae help."

"There's no chance of finding what remains of her family now," said Babe, putting a comforting arm around the girl. "What are we going to do with her?"

Jock scratched his scruffy hair. "Good question. The plan was to protect her from danger. But if she remains with us…"

"I know. Every encounter's a risk. They'll shoot us all if we're found out."

"We'll leave her here," declared Jock, climbing to his feet. "Aye, Frau Dünge's a good woman and will care for her."

"B… But… ," stuttered Babe, sparing a protective glance at Birgit. "The Red Army's on its way or, if it's not them, then our boys. Germany's a battlefield."

Jock buttoned his jacket. "And we're nawt get her oot of this god-forsaken country. It's best she has a roof over her head and food in her stomach. She can help the Dünge's on their farm. They're her own kind. What must be going through the wee lass's head in our company?"

The question went unanswered. Babe joined Birgit staring out the window, a sullen expression on both their faces.

There was a gentle rap at the door.

"Come in!"

Konrad's head appeared. "Guten Morgen. Ve should not stay long. Are you ready?"

"No," answered Jock. He leaned over a bowl of water and splashed his face. "Brrrr. That's cold!"

"Jock thinks we should leave Birgit here," spluttered Babe, the mention of her name stirring the girl.

"Ja, good idea," said Konrad, to Babe's disappointment. "I vill speak vith Frau Dünge."

"It's the safest place we've seen so far," said Jock, drying his hands on a towel. "And the old lady comes alive in her company."

"And if Birgit doesn't want to stay?" challenged Babe.

"It's nawt her choice," snapped Jock. "I'm fond of her too, but we can't keep her safe and she's a burden tae us. We're prisoners of war, nawt tourists!"

"But..."

"Enough! Konrad, tell Birgit to remain here while we go downstairs. Where's Peters?"

"Collecting vood," answered the German.

"Really? Okay. Babe, sort yer hair out: back intae character. And stop sulking!"

Downstairs, they found Peters hunched over the fire, stacking his harvest of wood in neat piles. Frau Dünge stood over the stove, stirring a pot.

"Morn... er, Morgen," said Peters, brushing his hands clean.

"Where's the master of the house?" muttered Jock in Konrad's ear.

"Milking his cows."

"Good." Jock straightened his collar. "Guten Morgen, Frau Dünge."

The suspicious and dour woman of the previous day greeted them with warmth.

"She asks how you sleep," said Konrad out of the corner of his mouth.

"Gut, danke," answered Jock.

"She asks about Birgit," translated Konrad.

"Well, ye know what tae say."

"But vhy vould two loving parents vant to leave zeir child?"

Jock paused on the last step. "Er."

"It is because we love her that we want to leave her with someone we trust, away from the bombs," interjected Babe. "It is too dangerous where we're going."

"Aye," said Jock, his eyes assessing Babe. "What the lad said."

"Leave to me." Konrad wandered over to the old lady, while the others congregated in the far corner.

"Do the SS usually collect wood for peasants?" asked Jock through narrowed eyes.

"Thank God I'm not really SS," replied Peters, levity in his voice. "And seemed the decent thing to do after she fed me a boiled egg."

"An egg!" Babe's eyes glowed. "A real egg!"

"Only the early bird gets the egg," said Peters with a smirk.

"And ye changed yer tune!" Jock turned to Babe.

"I was being selfish," said Quigley. "You were right. We're driving into the lion's mouth. Birgit's safer here."

"Eh? What's this?" Peters looked between his companions.

"We're leaving Birgit with Frau Dünge," explained Jock. "Konrad's speaking tae her now."

"Oh."

"I've never seen a crestfallen SS officer before," remarked Babe. "Looks weird."

"Yeah, well, no," said a tongue-tied Peters. "It's just, you know, she may not have liked me at first, but we connected. I'm fond of her. After five years in the camp, it's been special reconnecting with..."

"An innocent?" offered Babe.

"Yes, I guess so. Someone not involved in or responsible for this bloody war."

"Aye," added Jock. "Ye start tae believe in 'normal' again. I cannae..."

Frau Dünge's voice rose in pitch and volume, causing the prisoners to turn in alarm. The farmer's wife dashed over, her mouth spouting a torrent of incomprehensible words. Babe tensed as she gripped his shoulders, tears flowing. Konrad appeared behind, his mouth working hard to convey a silent message. Something got through and Babe nodded in response to the old lady's outpouring. As Babe found himself consumed in a tight hug, Konrad grinned, giving the thumbs-up and passing a prop for the next part of the lad's performance. Babe took the hankie, pulling away from Frau Dünge's grip, burying his nose into the rag and blowing hard.

Avoiding the physical embrace, Jock smiled awkwardly as the old lady turned her emotional monologue on him. An animated Konrad fidgeted behind, one arm stretched out, the hand dipping down, his head egging Jock towards Babe. As the unorthodox charade filtered through to Jock, he sidled to Babe's side, placing a stiff arm around him. Frau Dünge clasped her hands together, enjoying the moment, continuing her gushing discourse.

Jock and Babe pretended to listen, nodding and smiling, until, with a last flurry of excitable gabbling, Frau Dünge returned to her stove.

Konrad whispered, "She is honoured to care for Birgit and understands your pain at leaving her."

"Yeah, we got that," said Peters, grinning at Jock and Babe still in their awkward embrace. "You can let go now."

"Bah, let's get oot of here!" mumbled the Scot, pulling his arm away. "It won't take long before Birgit tells the truth. She deserves that much."

"I'll say goodbye to Birgit," said Babe.

"Naw, ye won't." The words stuck in Jock's throat. "We donnae want a scene."

"Perhaps after the war?" offered Peters. "When the world is at peace."

"I know," admitted Babe, a tear welling.

Konrad nodded. "Gut. I vill inform Frau Dünge and thank her."

***

"Quiet, man!" growled Jock after Peters slammed the car door. "I want us away before Birgit notices."

"Sorry."

"Gosh, I hope the Dünges can afford to be this generous!" Babe's head emerged from a large sack. "There's apples, bread, biscuits, pickles…" He angled the bag gifted by Frau Dünge towards Jock in the seat next to him.

"We keep enough for one meal," said the Scot. "The rest we hide by the roadside for Whatman and co."

The car's engine roared into life. Konrad took a deep breath, checking with his passengers that all were ready to depart.

"Let's get going!" said Jock, refusing to look back as the car crept along the rough farm track.

"There's Herr Dünge," commented Peters, spotting the farmer tottering along the road in their direction. "A chatty chap."

"Lucky for us," said Jock. "I didn't fancy having tae play the reticent officer tae a curious farmer."

"I hope he's kind to Birgit," said Babe.

"I vill give our thanks," proposed Konrad, bringing the car to a standstill and winding down his window.

The farmer rested on a crook, as Konrad conveyed their gratitude for his hospitality. His eyes flittered between the four men, his head nodding.

"Auf Wiedersehen," said Konrad, to end the one-side conversation, rolling up his window as the old man opened his mouth.

"Good luck." Herr Dünge shuffled towards his house.

As the car pulled away, the four passengers looked at one another.

"Did he say, 'good luck'?"

"He did!"

"It's not the same in German?"

"Nein," said Konrad. "Zat vould be 'viel Glück'."

"He knew we were British!" declared Jock.

"Bloody hell!" cursed Peters. "The sly old fox. Do you think he knew all along?"

"More to the point," cried Babe, "will he tell the authorities? Is Birgit safe? We should go back!"

"Calm down, lad," said Jock. "Ye donnae play yer hand with the words 'good luck' if ye plan to betray someone. We've chosen well. They've nae love for the Nazis or this war. He's an old soldier of the Great War. Did ye see the photo on the mantlepiece? He may not like the British, but he respects a soldier."

"Do you think Frau Dünge saw through us too?" asked Peters.

Konrad turned the car on to the main road. "She believed you vere parents to zee girl. But she will learn zee truth soon."

"I hope she's not angry when she discovers we lied and fooled her," said Babe.

"Donnae worry, lad," said Jock. "The wee lass will keep her happy. We need tae focus on getting through our next night. Perhaps we'll have tae risk a night in the car? Let's find a place tae stash the food.

Where the farm track meets the road should do. Thought I saw a rotting tree trunk."

"It won't go too far, but the lads can ration it out," said Babe.

"Err, vee must also stop at army depot," said Konrad, tapping the car's dashboard. "Vee need fuel."

"What about the spare can?"

"Used."

"Bugger!" Peters stared with disbelief at the driver. "It's one thing to lock ourselves in a hotel room surrounded by Hitler's goons, but in broad daylight! Can't we just steal some? Syphon it from another vehicle."

"Syphon?"

"With what?" cut in Jock. "And if we get caught?"

"We just requisition it from some sap."

Jock thought the matter over. "What do ye think, Konrad? The less attention we bring tae ourselves, the better."

The German swung round. "Vee get it vhere vee can. If vee run out, zen vee get noticed."

"Aye," agreed Jock. "How far can we get before then?"

Konrad shrugged. "Fifteen kilometres? Maybe tventy."

Peters slumped his head forward in despair.

Day Forty-Seven: Late Morning

The sedan crept along the pitted road, hindered by the debris of war and the familiar obstacles of refugees, soldiers, and prisoners of war.

"Fifteen kilometres may have been generous," said Babe, his chin resting solemnly on a hand as eyes followed those they passed.

"If only we could give some of our lads a ride," said Peters. "They look exhausted."

"Aye," said Jock with an absent disregard.

"Wonder where they're from?" asked Peters. "They're well ahead of our boys. Think that one's the Sherwood Foresters." He motioned towards a haggard figure. "Every Stalag must be on the move."

"Aye," repeated Jock, his mind drifting to thoughts of home.

A line of artillery trucks rumbled past, forcing those on foot to the road's side. Konrad tutted, manoeuvring their car onto a grass verge behind a few bedraggled prisoners. A guard rested twenty yards on, lighting a cigarette, and checking around for his straggling wards.

"Poor sods," muttered Peters, as the prisoners in front surveyed the stationary car with unease. "Never thought I would consider myself lucky, but sitting here sure beats being them. What we got left from Frau Dünge?"

Babe looked inside his hat. "A couple of apples and a small loaf. Do you think we left too much in that tree stump? The boys will be happy to find anything we leave for them. Won't miss something they didn't know about."

"What you talking about?" Peters shook his head. "I'm proposing we slip those sorry souls that loaf."

"But what will we eat?" whined Babe, clutching the hat to his breast.

"That rabbit stew of last night not enough?" Peters's face darkened. "Another feast perhaps awaiting us tonight, courtesy of these uniforms? How quickly you've forgotten what it's like out there!"

The raised voice stirred Jock. "What's that?"

"This young scally's gained a taste for the high life and doesn't want to give it up!"

"No, no," protested Babe, flushing red. "It's just a misunderstanding. I'm happy to go without."

"Go without what?" asked Jock, still only half engaged.

"Food! Those chaps need it more than us." Peters held a demanding hand out before Babe.

The deep rumble of the passing trucks buried Jock's response. Only his eyes, melancholic and absent, conveyed his feelings. Surrendering Birgit hurt more than he could confess. He had already abandoned his boys. Left them to fight a war; a war spent behind barbed wire. *Why do I have this guilt?* None was his fault.

"Thank you!" snapped Peters, as Babe passed him the hat containing their food. The last truck rocked past, and he turned to Konrad. "Get going! Slowly, mind you."

The sedan crept forward under the watchful eye of the prisoners at the side of the road. They waited patiently, ready to resume their trudge westward. Their weary eyes held enough strength to convey hatred and fear at the sight of the SS uniform. As Peters wound down his window, they took an involuntary step backwards. The sight of the red lady's hat, with its delicate veil piece, caused confusion.

"Happy St Swithin's day chaps," called out Peters. "Grab the food and not a word!"

The men just stood there, bemused and unmoving, watching the car move past.

"Come on, you lemons!" Peters lent out the window, urging the men to follow. "Haven't you ever seen a gift horse in disguise before? Think of me as Robin Hood, you poor peasants. Quick, before Fritz notices!"

Convinced this was no Trojan gift horse, the prisoners got in step with the car, plucking the loaf from the hat.

"Who are you?" asked one, examining the faces looking back from within the car.

"Best you don't know," answered Peters. "We got fed up with walking. Enjoy your meal and see you in Blighty."

As the man opened his mouth to ask another question, Peters wound the window up and urged Konrad to speed up.

"That was weird," remarked Jock. "Ye didn't think aboot talking tae them in English?"

"I couldn't have been more English," countered Peters with a smirk. "Ever heard an SS officer call someone a 'lemon'?"

"True. Ye're a strange people."

Babe craned his neck backwards, as the prisoners faded into the distance. "They really enjoyed that. You can see a spring in their step." His stomach gurgled its own view.

***

They drove through a small town, its medieval walls and castle a pleasant distraction. The war had yet to visit its tranquil streets.

"A fuel depot!" declared Konrad, as they left the gatehouse arching over the road. It was little more than a parking lot for fuel trucks, with a queue of thirsty vehicles.

"That's a lot of German soldiers," observed Peters.

"It is good. You stay in car," said Konrad, parking the sedan. "I do all. Vee go soon."

"I hope so," said Jock, lowering his head, unable to look at the milieu beyond the window.

"Relax," urged Konrad, slamming the door shut in his wake.

"That's easy for him to say," said Babe. "I think one just winked at me!"

Peters laughed. "You shouldn't encourage them, you alluring Siren."

"Oh, shut up!"

Jock blew out a breath, his fingers tapping the seat.

"You all right?" asked Babe. "Rarely seen you so stressed. That's my job."

Jock gave a half-hearted smile. "Aye. Do ye ever wonder if our luck's about tae run oot?"

"All the time!"

Peter's rapped the side window with a knuckle. "The lad's got us a Jerry can. Hey, do you think Jerry calls them Jerry cans?"

With the container gripped in both hands, knocking between his legs, Konrad shuffled closer.

Babe rolled down his window. "That was quick. Do you need a hand?"

"Nein!" exclaimed Konrad, shooing the young Brit back with a wave of his hand. He leaned against the window, lowering the can with a huff. "Stay inside and silent. Zis is to take with us. I get another for engine."

"Any news on the war?" called across Peters.

"Later!" hissed Konrad. "Others ask about car. Zee bullet holes und Windschutzscheibe." He flapped a hand at the missing windscreen, then brought it to his lips. "So, silent, ja?"

"Ja, ja," said Peters. "Just get a move on!"

Babe wound the side window up and looked to Jock. "I wonder how Birgit's getting on."

"Lots of work tae do on a farm," said Jock, equally reluctant to stay silent. "Keeping busy is the best way tae be. Nae time for sad thoughts. That's the problem with prison: too much time."

Peters closed his eyes, relaxing as best he could. A thud signalled the spare Jerry can dropping in the boot. One eyelid crept open, noted Konrad brushing his palms, then closed again as the German wandered off.

"Everyone seems so normal," commented Babe, the depot bustling with soldiers and vehicles coming and going. "Only the uniforms are different."

"And their cause," remarked Peters, his state of relaxation no obstacle to his cantankerous nature.

"Normal men get lost tae abnormal causes," said Jock. "There's at least one good man among them."

"And here he comes," said Babe, rubbing his sweaty palms. "Thank God. We'll soon be out of here."

Konrad struggled with the second Jerry can, his face now red from the effort. With a funnel in one hand, he attempted to lift and angle the container towards the petrol tank.

"It's a two-man job," said Peters. "Or it's more than a single-Konrad job."

"We have our orders," stressed Jock. "He'll ask for help if needed."

"He's getting there." Babe gave a thumbs-up, missed by its intended recipient. "Though a fair bit's going over Konrad."

"Remind me not to smoke in his company." An instinctive hand searched for a cigarette packet in his top pocket before Peters remembered they were long gone. "Just when I could do with one!"

After a few more minutes, Konrad stepped back from the car, swinging the empty can with a triumphant air.

"About time!" grumbled Peters. "I wonder how much ended up in the car?"

"Why must you complain so," said Babe, folding his arms.

"Because I'm good at it."

"There's an art tae being a curmudgeon," said Jock. "Our boy here's the Da Vinci. Ye've heard of his masterpiece: the Moaner Lisa."

Babe groaned. "That's a court ma…"

"Now where's he going?" huffed Peters, interrupting Babe as Konrad walked off again. "Let's just go!"

"Returning the can? Filling in a form?" suggested Jock. "Aye, the Germans like order. Best he does all by the book."

"Haven't seen much order in this world since they invaded Poland!"

"You know what I mean." Jock flicked Peters's earlobe. "Now, stop complaining!" He winked at Babe. "And here comes our wee man."

"Looks pale?" observed Babe.

"That'll be the fumes," said Peters.

"I'm not sure…"

A breathless Konrad leaned over the glassless windscreen. "Sorry, I have no choice." As he paused for breath, his passengers straightened in alarm. "A… A general orders ve take him vith us. I not able to say 'no.'"

"A general?"

"Ja. Say nothing. General Meier. Salute and…" Konrad glanced over his shoulder. "He comes!"

The next moment, Konrad opened the passenger door, stepping back with his arm raised in salute. A reek of alcohol first entered the car, followed by a red-cheeked man, his ample belly fighting against his tunic's buttons.

"Mach Platz, mein Liebling." The general's eyes glowed at the sight of Babe in his lush, red dress.

Babe shuffled across the seat in alarm, making room for their guest, who sidled up to his neighbour.

A broad grin broke out on the general's face. He slapped Konrad's shoulder. "Komm! Ich darf nicht zu spät zur Dinnerparty kommen."

The driver started the car, sharing a nervous glance at Peters.

As the general continued with a loud bombardment of words, he withdrew a hipflask from an inner pocket. His face edged towards Babe's, his tone apologetic as he thrust his arm across, offering the flask to Jock. "Trink, mein Freund!"

Jock licked his lips. It had been some years since he'd last enjoyed a tipple. The attempt to make a still in the camp had ended in failure, the product too bitter, the consequences on weak stomachs too severe. Jock took the flask and raised it. "Prost!"

The jovial face of the General encouraged him. "Prost. Auf das Vaterland!"

Babe cringed as the alcohol-soaked breath tickled his cheek, the general's hand now resting over his.

As the car escaped the depot, Jock let the warming schnapps trickle down his throat. "Oh, och, good stuff!"

Three alarmed faces swung round, anticipating exposure, only to find the general in full flow again, oblivious to Jock's slip.

"Gut. Ja, sehr gut," said Jock, realisation of his mistake etched in his eyes. He offered the hipflask back.

The general waved it away, pointing to Peters, without stopping his verbal flow.

"Danke," acknowledged Peters as he sampled the fiery liquid, blowing out the chilled fumes as it hit his digestive system.

Still the general talked, laughing, seeking recognition for a joke, triggering faux-laughter in response. Konrad prompted reactions with his own. "Ja, ja, mein General." "Nein. Gott im Himmel!" Only when the hipflask was empty did the general cease, disappointment replacing his bonhomie as the final drip hung from the upturned flask. With a last flurry of words, he pinched Babe's cheek, pulled his hat over his face and went to sleep, the car remaining in uncomfortable silence until the hat vibrated to the general's snoring.

"What are we going to do?" hissed Peters. "Why did you give him a ride?"

Konrad glared back. "I no choice! He is a general."

"Where does he want tae go?" asked Jock in a whisper, shuffling to the edge of his seat.

"Near Wolfsburg," answered Konrad, one eye checking on the slumbering general.

"How far's that?"

"Forty kilometres." Konrad tapped on the scrappy map laying on his lap.

"Forty kilometres!" echoed Peters, a little too loudly.

The general mumbled, stirred by the noise, then his rhythmic snoring returned, his head flopping on to Babe's shoulder.

"Don't move!" urged Peters of Babe, receiving a withering glare in return.

"That's too far," sighed Jock, as the general's belly rose and fell. "He'll see through us when he's sobered up."

"Keep him drunk?" proposed Peters, grimacing as the schnapps wreaked vengeance within. "Maybe he'll sleep all the way." He struggled to control a belch. "God, I feel sick. Pull over!"

As the car braked, Peters swung his door open, leaned out, and vomited.

"Are you all right?" asked Babe.

Peters climbed out, bent over with his hands pressed on his knees. "Should never have taken that bleeding German poison!" He spat residual bile to the ground. "You not suffering, Jock?"

No reply came.

"Jock?" Peters sucked in a deep breath, stood upright and peered in the car.

General Meier glared back, wide awake. "Was ist los?"

Konrad laughed nervously. "Hatten Sie einen schönen Traum, mein general?"

The general dismissed the driver with a wave of his drawn revolver. "Halt die Klappe! Ich will, dass der Betrüger antwortet."

Peters stood still, his mouth agape in bemused uncertainty as the revolver pointed in his direction.

"Vhy is an Englishman in SS uniform?" asked the general, demonstrating a good grasp of English. He turned to Jock, converting back to German with a further question.

"Er, ja," said Jock, his eyes flitting between the gun and the general's face.

"Enough!" cried the General, the gun angling on to Jock. "Vhat is going on? Have you kidnapped zis poor lady and her driver? I should shoot you here and now as spies. Put your hands up!"

"We're nawt spies!" said Jock, raising his arms. "Just prisoners who found some uniforms to keep us warm."

"Ha, vee shoot escaped prisoners too."

"You lot would shoot your own grandmother if she smiled at a gypsy!" Peters fought the urge to vomit again.

The general nodded. "Zere is too much brutality, it is true, but you are prisoners again. Vee vill vait here until I hand you over to a passing convoy." He leaned towards Babe. "Deine Tortur ist vorbei, mein Liebling. Wir werden heute Abend ein Glas Champagner auf deinen Mut erheben." His free hand squeezed Babe's leg.

"Get your hand off me!" screamed Babe, grabbing the general's skull between his hands and shoving it against the door. As the general shook his stunned head, Babe's fist followed, striking the German's nose. The Englishman pulled the door handle, angled his foot up and kicked the general out of the car.

"Get in!" shouted Jock to Peters, as Babe scrambled to close his door.

Konrad put his foot down on the accelerator with Peters half in. The wheels span, then gained traction, sending the car speeding off.

"I've got ye," said Jock, gripping tight to Peters's arms. "Climb in, man!"

"I'm in! I'm in!" declared Peters, straightening up in his seat. "Jeez, that was close."

They turned to see the general sitting on his rear in the middle of the road, his hands gesticulating wildly in frustration and anger.

"That was some right hook for a dame," laughed Peters. "Some fella's going to have his hands full with you!" Before Babe could retort, Peters turned a pale green and threw up over his shoes.

"Serves you right," said Babe, scrambling in his footwell in search of something.

"Well done, lad," said Jock. "What ye lost?"

"A shoe," answered Babe, frowning in frustration. "It looked quite expensive."

"Must have gone oot with our friend," said Jock, ignoring Peters's groans. "Donnae worry aboot it. We'll have tae change back intae our old uniforms anyhow."

"Eh?"

"Jock is right," chipped in Konrad. "I vill miss zee car."

Peters turned to him, wiping a sleeve across his mouth. "What you talking about?"

"Soon half the German army will be hunting for us and this car," explained Jock. "We can't afford tae use it and these uniforms will have tae go too. On the bright side, paranoia will infect them, with every officer suspected of being a Brit in disguise."

"Hoo-bloody-ray!" grumbled Peters. "More walking."

"I would still like to find that shoe," huffed Babe. "They go so well with the dress."

Day Forty-Seven: Afternoon

On the brown, withered grass along the roadside sat the four men, the snow having retreated in the last day. They reclined in the afternoon sun, resting on their bags.

"Did I really smell this bad?" remarked Peters, sniffing at his British army coat. "Why did nobody tell me?"

"Could'nae smell ye over ma own odour," said Jock, reacclimatising to his own uniform.

"I don't remember it itching so much," complained Babe, scratching his arm.

Konrad, unchanged in his uniform, sucked on a finger, burnt as they set fire to the car and their borrowed German uniforms down a quiet side road. No one would pay much attention to it. What was one more burnt-out wreck in this war?

"So, then, what now?" asked Peters, some colour seeping back into his cheeks.

"We walk slowly westwards," said Jock. "There's nae shortage of prisoners on the road. We'll merge intae the next column. With Konrad in tow, nae one will question it."

"Won't they be looking for us?" asked Babe, fighting a new itch on his leg.

"They'll looking for Brits in German uniforms. But the sooner we're consumed within the other prisoners, the better. A drunk general won't even remember what we look like."

"And food?" Peters belched. "Not that I could stomach anything."

"Again," said Jock, "the sooner we merge, the better. It's back tae the bare minimum now, but hopefully we're not too far from our final destination. What's it called again?"

Konrad removed a stalk of grass from his mouth. "Fallingbostel. About a veek's valking. Perhaps less. Perhaps more."

"Well, come on," urged Jock, climbing to his feet. "The sooner we get walking, the sooner we get there."

"Argghhh!" cried Peters with dramatic flair as he eased himself up. "We could have got another few hours out of that car."

"Quit moaning! Come on, Babe." Jock offered a hand to the youngster, heaving him up.

"Thanks. Every moment in that car was terrifying," confessed Babe. "But returning to this life is worse."

"Aye, lad. I know."

A songbird, recognising the first signs of spring, whistled from a treetop. Konrad imitated as best he could, then raised himself up with the aid of his rifle.

"Do we need to surrender to you again?" asked Peters.

"Ja, ja," said the German with a grin. "For you, Tommy, zee var is over."

"Bah, the last time one of your lot said that to me, it couldn't have been further from the truth." Peters set off down the road with a sneer.

Konrad shrugged at Jock.

"Donnae worry, lad. He only laughs at his own jokes."

***

At their ambling pace, they made slow progress, their only companions on the road refugees. After an hour's walking, a small German army convoy approached from the opposite direction. They moved to the roadside; Konrad showing off his rediscovered authority with a languid motion of his rifle and a command. The vehicles passed, unseeing or caring for the small group of straggling prisoners.

"We're nobodies again," said a relieved Babe.

"That's for the best," said Jock.

"Do you think they're looking for us yet?"

"I suspect so. That's if the general admits tae it. Bit embarrassing, eh? Taken on a ride by escaped prisoners."

"And being kicked out of the car by a woman," chuckled Babe.

"Few men, or women, can say they've kicked a general." Jock slapped Babe on the back.

This didn't feel like the march they started all those weeks ago. They had somehow won a victory: delivered a young girl to safety, humiliated a general and survived. Each step was proof they would make it, not march to the Nazi tune.

"What will you do when we get to Fallingbostel?" asked Babe of Konrad.

The German quickened his pace to fall into step. "It is question I ask myself."

Jock pursed his lips. "Aye, it's a problem. Ye cannae melt in like us. Yer unit's many days away."

"Ja, and I shoot SS officer."

"There's that too," said Babe. "Gosh, I hadn't thought about it. The end of the war can't be too far off. You could hand yourself in: a month or two in prison."

Konrad slowly shook his head.

"That's nawt how things work here, lad," said Jock. "Their justice, if ye can call it that, starts and ends with a bullet."

"Jock is right. I must vanish. Zere is chaos. I can hide. Maybe give myself up to your army." Doubt remained in Konrad's eyes.

"Why don't we try to get through to our own line?" suggested Babe. "We can then put in a good word for Konrad."

"We're nawt going intae a battle zone, lad. I've nawt walked this far tae get shot. We donnae even know how far away it is."

"I suppose not."

"Naw, we stick with the plan. Let's catch up with Archie. He may have stopped sulking by now."

***

The wind built, bringing a biting air from the east. Jock lifted his coat collar, angling his body behind a tree for shelter. Its stinging lash undermined his earlier mood. Above, Allied bombers in their hundreds dotted the blue canvas, their growling drone mixing with the whistling gusts of wind. Jock watched them with awe and fear. This was not the war he had left behind in 1940.

"Which poor bugger are they visiting?" remarked Peters, sheltering behind his own tree.

"And not a Messerschmitt in sight," added Babe, as a rare puff from an exploding air defence shell fell short of the unstoppable formation.

"It means you have von," said Konrad, his expression neutral.

"Aye," agreed Jock. "But no one's surrendered yet."

A distant shout caught their attention. They listened hard, trying to block out the noise from above. There it was again.

"A cheer?" suggested Babe. He stepped forward, out of the trees and onto a bank above the road. "There are men coming our way."

The others joined Babe, straining to see.

"Prisoners? Some are waving hats to the sky."

"Aye, prisoners," said Jock, smiling to himself.

A few minutes later, the head of the column reached them. They remained on their vantage point, inspecting the procession.

"Jeez, they did well to lift their hats," muttered Peters. "I've seen skeletons with more meat on them." He acknowledged a curious gaze from a passing prisoner with a nod of his head.

Two German guards paused for a brief exchange with Konrad.

"What did they say?" asked Jock as they moved on.

"Zey moan und zey ask vhere vee come from. I say vee fall behind another column due to..." Konrad tapped his tummy.

"And where are they going?"

"Zey do not know, but zis road leads to Fallingbostel."

"Good," declared Jock, slapping his thigh. "Then we had better join them." He stood, swung his bag over his shoulder, and scurried down the bank. "Don't be shy!" He motioned for the others to join him.

"Afternoon," said a man from the column, as Jock gained his rhythm on to the road before him. "You chaps get lost?"

"Not quite," replied Jock. "Let's say we took an unorthodox route."

"Where did you start out from?"

"Central Poland. Stalag XXA. Ye?"

The man whistled. "That's a long way. You look... Er, Stalag IIIC. East of Berlin. It's been hell."

"Aye, a few more days and we'll arrive at the destination."

"Where? Someone tell you that?"

"Fallingbostel," answered Jock. "We came across a map."

"That'll perk up the men. Er, Charles Pertwee, East Surrey Regiment." The man held out a hand.

"Pleased tae meet ye. Richard Mitchell, West Kents. I go by Jock." He shook Pertwee's hand, then looked behind to ensure the others were following, finding them engaged as he was in making new acquaintances. "How long ye been under the care of our friends?"

"Oh, you mean the Germans. Why, three long years. Got out at Dunkirk. Thought that was my time served, but then we got sent to North Africa. It was fine when it was only the Italians, but once the Germans got involved... Well, here I am. I don't know what I hate more: the heat or this bleeding cold. Still finding sand in my clothes! Where did you go after Dunkirk?"

"Poland," came the terse response.

"Wow!" exclaimed Pertwee. "I've not met anyone left behind before. That's a long time to be a prisoner."

"Aye."

A distant thundering vibrated through the air. Instinctively, Jock and Pertwee looked to the sky to find it cloudless. Still the rumble continued, rising and falling in volume, until after several minutes it faded away. Neither man spoke, continuing their walk in solemn silence. After a few more minutes, the familiar drone of the bombers returned, this time flying northwards to home, their bomb bays empty.

Day Fifty

The moon shone through the bomb-damaged church roof, lighting the exhausted faces. A malaise hung over the prisoners, huddled together on the cold stone floor. Even the warm gruel served on arrival failed to raise spirits.

Jock sat with his back against a wood column, lost in thought amid the austere Lutheran sanctuary. The groans, coughs and cries, familiar from earlier days, punctuated the air: nightmares and suffering venting in the night. Closing his eyes failed to shut it out. How quickly the internal torment had returned. The car, with its speed, privacy and modernity, allowed hope to build, but now they had fallen back into this hellish abyss. He knew the march was almost over. Even peace must be near. But the thought of one more day's walking, of that soul-destroying cold, the grime, the hunger, the smell, the fear. And the lack of sleep! If only he could vanish down slumber's well; forget everything and feel nothing. Just for a few hours!

Morning arrived. A sunbeam coloured the white ceiling with an orange tint. Jock remained against his column, staring into nothing.

"You with us, Jock?" Peters stood, waving his hand before the Scot's eyes.

Jock shook his head. "Eh? Oh, aye. Sorry. Away with the fairies."

"I think I prefer a barn. At least they have straw."

"Aye, you would think a church would soothe the soul, but..." Jock left his feelings unspoken.

"Tough night, eh?"

"Help me up! Ma bum's numb and ma legs donnae want to move." He groaned as his friend pulled his arm. "Ma bag! Where's ma bag?"

"Relax. Your neighbour's borrowed it for a pillow." Peters waggled a foot to his side.

"It's got ma gun in it!" whispered Jock. The object was one of the few items kept from his time as a commandant. He whipped the bag from under the sleeping man's head.

"Hey!"

"That's ma bag!" growled back Jock, receiving a sluggish shrug in reply. He rummaged through the bag for the gun, its distinct outline obvious. "Must have a head like granite."

"Or he was too tired to care."

"Aye," said Jock, his anger subsiding.

***

A dusting of snow lay on the road as they set off, contradicting the early signs of spring germinating from the soil. Clumps of violet crocuses and daffodils reminded all that nature's beauty persevered amid humanity's folly.

Jock walked alone, his mood unfit for company. Behind, he heard the chatter of Babe and Peters, the latter's sardonic manner at odds with the youngster's simplistic outlook on life. Konrad strolled a short way ahead, detached and lonely among strangers.

As he often did when consumed by a black mood, Jock thought of home, of Jane and the boys, his garden and better days. His hand touched his chest, connecting with the photo and letter languishing in an inner pocket. *Will my words ever do justice to my feelings?* He was no wordsmith, but did it matter? If Jane ever read the letter, he would be dead. *Of course it matters*, he chided himself. Five years without an embrace; a lifetime of marriage without telling her how he felt. He would rewrite it tonight. In death, she would learn what he couldn't say in life.

"BANG-phut-BANG-phut-phut-phut-BANG!"

Jock jumped out of his skin.

"Bloody hell!" cried Peters.

Amid the woods surrounding the road, a small cutting presented itself. Within, two SS Waffen soldiers gripped smoking MP-40 sub-machine guns, an officer supervising from behind. Before them lay the bodies of a dozen men, clothed in identical grey linen.

"They bloody shot them!" cursed a disbelieving Peters.

In the following silence, a groan emanated from the pile of bodies. The SS officer stepped forward, unholstered his Luger pistol and fired into the mass. His head turned, eyes falling on the frozen prisoners watching from the road.

"This ain't good," said Peters.

"Start walking," urged Jock.

"Halt!" The command arrived before their first step touched the ground.

"Hier her!" The officer waved them over in an almost friendly manner, while the submachine guns rotated to face them.

"Why is it always us?" whimpered Babe.

"The bastards!" muttered Peters. "They were defenceless. It's murder!"

"Quiet!" ordered Jock. "Just do as we're told." Yet the same thoughts swirled round his mind. A fury replaced the maudlin funk.

This was the reason he had waved goodbye to Jane and the boys: to defeat this barbarity.

A group of six prisoners trudged into the wood, eyes glazed with fear.

The SS officer greeted them with a smile. He indicated a large hole with his gun, before pointing to the bodies. "Kindly move."

Jock fought the urge to retch. *What type of monster behaves with courtesy after such a crime?* He dropped his bag and caught the eye of Peters; a silent message conveyed. But Jock shook his head in reply. He gripped the still warm ankles of the first body, waited until Peters grasped the wrists, then swung and released it into the pit. It only occurred to him as he lifted the second how light and skinny all the dead were. His own emaciated body was as nothing to the loose-skinned, skeletal corpses they now discarded. *What deeper level of hell have they been through?*

The SS chatted among themselves, lighting cigarettes and laughing. Jock kept one eye on them, his jaw quivering with rage. A prisoner dropped a body before the pit, turned and vomited, triggering a ripple of laughter from the watching Germans.

Peters leaned closer to Jock. "What's to stop them shooting us? We witnessed their crime."

"Aye. We need a diversion. Do ye understand me?"

Peters winked and sidled up to Babe, whispering in his ear, all the while lifting another body for its unceremonious disposal.

At the sickening crack of the body hitting the pit's depths, Babe placed the back of his hand to his forehead and let out a dramatic wail, collapsing to the floor. Laughter broke out between the Germans. The officer flicked his cigarette to the floor, unholstered his gun again, and strolled over to the prostrate Babe. He stood over him, turning to share a witticism with his colleagues, and then angled his gun down.

"BANG!"

Prisoners yelped, dropping the bodies in transit to the pit, gaping across to the motionless Babe on the ground. Before their cries faded, Babe opened one eye in time to see the silhouetted figure of the SS officer fall towards him. He rolled to his left, letting the German thump to the ground under the shocked gaze of the other two soldiers.

"BANG! BANG!"

It was over in a blink. Jock and Peters gripped tight to their smoking Lugers as the two soldiers gaped in surprise and fell to their knees. "BANG!" Another round fired. They slumped forward, their faces crashing against the frozen earth, dead. "BANG! BANG! BANG!" Jock and Peters continued to fire, tears flooding down their cheeks.

"Jock. Archie." A gentle, judgeless call sounded behind.

Jock turned to find Konrad.

"Enough, Jock," urged the German. "Vee don't vant to attract attention."

As Babe sat up, brushing the dirt from his knees, the other prisoners followed in bewilderment.

"It's okay, lads," reassured Babe, now on his feet. "He's a friend."

Peters dropped his pistol. "I... I've never shot anyone before."

"They were monsters," said Jock, regaining his composure. "It was them or us."

"I know," said Konrad, wandering closer to examine the scene. "Zey must join zese poor souls and zen vee must cover. Ja?" He laid a comforting hand on Peters's back.

"Ja," agreed Jock. He glanced at the pit. "Who were they? What had they done tae deserve this?"

"Jews? Slave vorkers?" Konrad lifted the feet of the officer and dragged him towards the pit. "Vee must be quick, before others come."

"But what had they done? Ye donnae kill someone for nowt, for being themselves."

There was no answer to the unanswerable.

A few prisoners wandered by on the road, lacking the desire or nerve to see what had taken place. They didn't care most of the dead had dug their own grave. They just cared about making it to day's end.

"That'll do," said Jock, throwing down his spade. "Let's get out of here. Nae word tae anyone: about the guns or their work. Understood?" He locked eyes with the unfamiliar prisoners, receiving a sharp nod from all. "Good."

"I can't stop shaking," confessed Peters in a whisper.

"Aye, me neither. Nae man should have tae witness that. Where's Babe?" He turned to find the lad kneeling by the grave, deep in prayer. "Let's join him, eh?"

"I'd like that."

***

"That's good of ye, but I'm nawt hungry."

"But Jock, you must eat," pressed Konrad, offering the bread roll again. "I stole from Wilhelm. A most, er, pompös corporal." He smiled in encouragement. "Save for later, ja?"

"Okay," said Jock, taking the roll. "Thanks." He pushed a finger through the crust. It was fresh enough to last a day. He slid it into his outer pocket. "Nae news among yer lot aboot this morning?"

"No. It vill be a long time before zee car is found, and zen vill zey think to look..." Konrad motioned as though digging, shrugging his eyebrows.

"We didn't bury them too deep," remarked Jock.

Konrad shrugged. "Only zeir own kind care."

"And that's four SS deaths yer implicated in. Even yer colleagues won't turn a blind eye tae that if they find oot."

"I know. But who vill tell?"

"A man under torture." Jock let the words sink in.

Konrad slumped his head forward and blew out his cheeks. "You must vin zis war quickly."

"Aye, that would be best for all." Jock's mind wandered off for a moment. He scanned the German. "I have an idea. Do ye trust me?"

"Jock, ve have faced death together. I trust you."

Day Fifty: Evening

"Ye're wearing two pairs, for heaven's sake, man! Spring is here." Jock stood over his fellow prisoner, hands on either hip.

"It snowed last night," challenged the prisoner, annoyed at the intrusion into his space in the barn.

"We're days from our destination and the war will be over long before next winter. Come on, lad. Less weight too."

The man folded his arms in defiance.

Jock tapped his foot in thought. "What about a tin of something in exchange?"

"What you got? I fancy some meat."

"Sure. I donnae have it yet, but I can get it. Deal?" Jock spat on his palm and offered it to the man.

"Deal!"

They shook hands and Jock wandered back to his own corner of the barn, stepping over the trailing legs of those already bedded down for the night.

"What are you up to?" asked Peters, as Jock lowered himself next to him. "Prowling round, chatting to strangers."

"Keeping maself busy. How ye doing?"

"The shaking's stopped, but the image's stuck in my mind."

Jock dipped into his pocket, withdrawing the bread roll. He broke a piece off. "Here, eat this even if ye're nawt hungry."

"Thanks."

Popping a chunk into his own mouth, Jock chewed without enthusiasm. "Do ye know of anyone carrying dog tags for a fallen friend?"

Peters turned. "Come on, out with it. What you up to?"

"We're recruiting Konrad tae the British army."

"What! Are you serious? We're stuck in enemy territory. Our shade of khaki ain't in fashion round here and our lot will shoot him for talking funny."

Jock smiled, glad to hear Peters's humour return. "His shade of German ain't popular either. If they don't get him for desertion, there's the small matter of helping us and then shooting his own. Unless the war finishes in the next couple of days, his options are near zero."

"Near zero," echoed Peters, rolling his eyes. "Whatever you've got planned, I don't like it."

Jock leaned in. "We hide him amongst ourselves, in whichever ghastly camp we find ourselves in. One anonymous face among hundreds. The Germans won't look for him there and we'll protect him from our own."

"Jock! Oh, Jock," exclaimed Peters. "Why would anyone choose to put themselves through the hell we find ourselves in? It may be his turn to dress up, but really!"

"If there was one thing I've learned taeday, it's there are others even worse off than us and people willing tae do unspeakable things. Konrad's a friend. I donnae wish tae see him treated as a traitor by those monsters who've betrayed humanity."

"And if he's caught in a British uniform or if they choose to eradicate us all? I've seen enough to think that's possible. The men talk about it. You know? Hitler getting rid of us, his burdensome millstone, for good. But..." Peters closed his eyes, drawing in a deep breath, as the image returned to his mind. "They just laughed and carried on as if it were normal, making us clear up their slaughter. What's stopping them from doing the same to us?"

Jock gripped his friend's arm, the haunting image from the woods burning in his mind too. "I know. I know. We have tae hope they need us. After all, why march us so far just tae shoot us?"

"I hope you're right." Peters sniffed, wiping his nose on his sleeve. "Of course I'll help, but only because it's you, Jock." He cleared his throat. "And if you tell me where the gold's hidden."

"Och, ye eejit."

Peters started laughing, but then turned away. A tear rolled down his cheek; his jaw shook. He curled up in his blanket and sobbed.

Day Fifty-Four

Charles Pertwee waited by the road, doffing his hat. "Jock, old chap. A glorious morning."

"Aye," answered Jock, keen to avoid distractions as he sought Konrad.

"A little birdie tells me you own a gun." Pertwee leaned in with the air of a spiv.

Jock cursed under his breath. "Who told ye that?"

"Oh, news travels round. Is it true?"

"Aye." Jock gripped his bag tight.

"And you shot some SS?"

"Bleeding hell!" Jock borrowed Peters's colourful phrase. "Ma boot's going tae be kicking some backsides. Does the whole column know?"

Pertwee shrugged. "I imagine so." He patted Jock on the back. "You're a hero, old chap. I've witnessed terrible things on this slog. What I could have done with a gun!"

"Well, it ain't for sale."

"No, no. You keep it. Just good you're with us. Err..." Pertwee scratched his hair. "The boys are curious, though."

"Aboot what?"

"Well, why you've not escaped. I mean, when we found you, you were alone with one guard – a sorry specimen for the master race. With a gun you could…" Pertwee raised his brows, allowing the inference to go unspoken.

"Konrad's a friend," said Jock.

"Really?"

"Aye, a good friend. Are we going tae have a problem with that?"

"My dear chap, not at all." A wry smile formed. "But you've yet to explain your disposition not to escape. It would calm uneasy thoughts circulating among the boys. Not with me, you understand, but some of the more volatile minds need further details. It's a matter of trust, I guess."

Jock nodded his head. "It's a long story." He recognised Pertwee from the bureaucrats littered throughout the army: able to extract and coerce with their sugary words. *They usually let ye down too*, thought Jock. He then told the story of the Spitfire, the commandant and his wife's death, Konrad's life-saving intervention, the decision to help Birgit and all that followed. "By the time we ditched the general, we were too far intae Germany that escape was impossible. There was also our obligation to Konrad. By all accounts, the war's almost over, so getting closer tae our troops makes sense."

"I suppose so," said Pertwee, shaking his head in wonder. "And you stole food for those left behind?"

"Oh, aye. Not an enormous amount and only for a few days, but I hope it helped."

"I wish we had a guardian angel looking after us," said Pertwee. "Imagine knowing there is something positive awaiting you at day's end on this slog."

"What will ye tell others?" asked Jock. "They donnae need the details."

"I'll tell them they can trust you."

"Thanks. Ye donnae know someone with a can of meat?"

"Not among the brethren," answered Pertwee. "Why?"

Jock explained his plan for helping Konrad. "It's only going tae work if I have stuff tae trade with."

"I see," said Pertwee, scratching his chin with a finger. "You don't make life easy for yourself. It may be the boys won't like a Jerry in their midst."

"Then they can complain tae ma face."

"He seems a decent chap. Honourable and all that." Pertwee stopped abruptly. "You know what? I think there's a stone in my shoe. Carry on without me. I'll find the bugger and see you later."

"Err, okay." Jock strode on, unsure what to make of Pertwee.

***

"Here are the trousers." The man dropped them at Jock's feet.

"Thank ye." Jock looked up from his canteen of soup. "I've nawt got yer can of meat yet."

"Forget it. You were right. The weather's improving and I'll get far too hot wearing both pairs." With a nod, he walked off.

Peters, with his mouth full of bread, mumbled something.

"Eh?"

"That's a result," Peters repeated after swallowing. He tapped his chest. "Argh. Indigestion! Didn't chew it properly."

"Aye, a change of heart. Good. Didn't fancy asking Konrad tae steal some cans."

"You Jock?" Another unfamiliar prisoner stood before them.

"Aye."

"I hear you're on the lookout for clothes. These puttees any good?" He draped them over his arm.

Peters rubbed the material between his fingers. "Looks good."

"Thank ye," said Jock, smiling at Peters as he accepted the gift.

"Anything to help a friend," said the man before strolling off.

"Word must have got round," said Jock, placing the puttees over the trousers.

"And looks like more are on their way," declared Peters at the approach of two further prisoners.

A lad not yet out of his teens dangled a dog tag in front of Jock. "It's just a loan, right? I kept it to give to Pete's ma."

"Sorry, lad?" Jock climbed to his feet, recognising the conversation's solemn edge.

"I 'eard you wanted dog tags for your friend – the Kraut," said the boy. "These 'ere are Pete Clancy's. 'E were my mate but died of typhoid back at camp."

"This is a cap," said the other man. "Belonged to Ernie Black. Dysentery got him. Kept it as a keepsake, to remember him by."

"Aye," acknowledged Jock, accepting the items in a hand. "They sound like bonnie lads. If we get through this, ye'll get them back. I promise."

"Is it true you kicked a German general out of a stolen car?" asked the youngster.

Jock smiled. "It was a friend, not much older than ye. Gave him the heave-hoo with his right boot."

"More a slipper," interjected Peters, unwilling to miss out on the notoriety. "You should have seen his face. It was a picture: flapping in the middle of the road on his arse."

They laughed.

"And you shot some SS?" asked the older of the two.

"Hmmm." Jock turned his face away, reluctant to discuss the matter, as Peters's grin dissolved. "The unpleasant side of justice."

"Pete and Ernie would like that, and that they're helping now."

"Aye, they are," agreed Jock. "We owe them." Jock's thumb touched the embossed numbers of the dog tag; a pitiful legacy to a life cut too short.

"Your man came good," remarked Peters after they were alone again.

"Pertwee? Aye, seems I misjudged him," said Jock. "Not sure I like everyone knowing our business though. Only takes one tae escape a punishment by snitching on us."

"We seem to be heroes, but that's the last thing I am." The melancholic hue colouring Peters since the shooting returned.

"We're survivors, like the rest of them," said Jock, a concerned eye on his friend. "What's important is we almost have enough tae fit oot Konrad."

"Does he know yet?"

"Well, naw, but I wanted all in place before sharing the details."

"Bleeding hell, Jock. What if he says no? He may not want to play Pete Clancy!"

"Och, ye're suffering the blues. He'll be fine."

Day Fifty-Five

"Nein, nein, nein!" Konrad squeezed his stubbled cheeks between finger and thumb, exaggerating his weary features. "Is zis idea to save me? Ich glaub' mein Schwein pfeift!" His eyes fell on Jock with a helpless desperation.

They ventured further into the woods, away from onlookers and the grisly sight of two bodies hanging from a roadside beech tree. Two further nooses swung unoccupied, their earlier victims of Nazi retribution rotted and now broken amid the tangled bracken below.

"It's a good plan," stressed Jock, grateful for this break from a hard day's walking. "Look what the lads collected for ye." He lifted the bundle of clothes.

"Ja. Choice is shot by my own kind, or throat cut by yours!"

"Nae one will touch ye, I promise. Ye said ye trusted me." Jock gripped the German's shoulder. "Look, it's yer choice, but ye'll be among friends."

"And if zee SS decide to shoot all prisoners?"

Jock gulped. "Will they? Is that what they plan? Come on! What ye heard?"

"Just rumour. But you saw vhat zey are like."

"Aye." Jock's eyes flickered as he considered the dilemma. "So, they shoot ye as a prisoner rather than a traitor. Or the Allies arrive before then and free us all."

"Zen zey shoot me."

"For heaven's sake, man! We donnae do that."

"Zee radio says you do."

"That's nonsense, as is everything Herr Hitler and his cronies say. Their lies got ye intae this mess." Jock stuffed the clothes back into his sack. "I donnae know how much longer we've got, but think about it."

Raised voices interrupted them, stirring two crows from their perch.

"That was a brief break," commented Jock, tilting his head in a struggle to decipher.

Konrad checked his watch, scraping off a smudge of dirt on its cracked face. "Vee move vhen ordered…"

"Shh!" urged Jock, a finger to his lips. He recognised something amid the shouting. One word grew in volume until it dominated.

"Jock! Jock! JOCK!" Pertwee appeared red-faced and gasping for breath.

"Steady, lad," calmed Jock. "What's happening?"

"It's one… it's one of yours, Jock," spluttered out Pertwee. "Tried hanging himself." He pointed behind while drawing in another breath. "We cut him down, but you'd better come."

"Peters!" cried Jock instinctively. "Well, come on, man. Show me!"

They hurried through the trees until emerging by the road. The beech tree loomed over them, its two guests still festering on their ropes. Only one free noose swung in the wind now. Beneath, a crowd of prisoners swarmed, agitated and helpless.

"Peters!" cried Jock as he pushed through the crowd.

A body lay motionless. Two prisoners knelt over it, administering care.

"Peters, ye damn fool!" exclaimed Jock. "What have ye done?"

The man with his back to Jock turned his head. "Jock! I haven't done anything. It's Babe!" Peters backed away, exposing the prone body of the youngster.

"Babe?" repeated Jock in shock. "I thought... I..."

"He's alive," reassured Peters. "We got to him in time."

"I dinnae think he was... ye know?" Jock knelt, stroking Babe's soft hair.

"Suicidal?" said Peters.

"Aye. Why, lad? Why?"

"It's a wonder we're not all at it," said Peters, dabbing a wet cloth to Babe's lips. "What, with all we've been through."

A groan escaped from Babe's mouth; his eyes crept open.

"Ye're back with us, lad," said Jock. "Ye made a mistake, but it's all right now."

"I'm sorry, Jock," whispered Babe, grimacing with each gulp. "I saw the noose and, well, it looked so easy. A chance to get away from all this."

"I know. I know. Ye gave us a fright."

"You're not getting out of that shilling you owe me," said Peters, his frightened, moist eyes betraying his true feelings.

Babe answered with a fragile smile.

"Can ye sit up, lad?" Jock slid a hand behind the boy's head. "We don't want the wrong Jerry to find ye like this." He looked around. Konrad watched from the back of the crowd. "That's it. Can ye move yer neck?"

Babe slowly turned his head one way and then the other. "It's sore, but nothing's broken. Oh, what was I thinking?"

"You weren't," said Peters. "The war buries your soul until you can't sense or act rational. Then the demons take you by the hand."

"It did feel like someone was leading me," remarked Babe as he gingerly climbed to his feet. "A darkness: a void. It's hard to explain." He spotted all the other faces watching him. "Oh, I..." His legs wobbled.

"It's okay, lad," said Jock, gripping his arm. "Nae one's judging ye. We help our own kind."

"I know, but I feel so stupid."

"Aye, well, maybe it was stupid and maybe it wasn't. We're all trying tae escape from hell. Nae one knows yet which is the correct direction. How aboot ye try ma way for a while longer: get tae this camp and wait oot the end of the war?"

"I will," replied Babe. "I promise."

Day Fifty-Six: Early Afternoon

"A camp!" called out Peters, pointing to the south. "It's a big one."

Behind familiar barbed-wire fences and watchtowers sat row on row of huts.

Babe twisted his torso round to look, his neck locked tight. "Something smells odd?"

"There's a fire burning," remarked Jock. "A few fires from the amount of smoke."

"Somewhere warm," said Peters, with a dreamy smile. "I can picture the dormitory with a roasting log fire at either end, a stool to place your feet on as you toast crumpets, and a giant kettle of boiling water to pour into a tin bath."

"It ain't public school," said Jock. "And anyway, we appear tae be continuing west."

"What is that smell?" Babe screwed his face up, regretting it as his neck muscles tightened.

"I guess we'll never know," said Peters. "How you doing? You appear unaffected, apart from the..." Peters pointed to his own neck.

"I'd rather not talk about it," said Babe, colouring red.

"Fine. As long as you're all right. We'll be checking in on you quite a bit from now on. Eh, Jock?"

Jock noticed Babe's discomfort. "Let the lad be. He knows we've got his back."

They walked in silence, winding north on the road, away from the camp. A skylark hovered in the air, its distinctive song a further reminder of spring's advance. To the west, a bank of clouds hinted at a change in the weather. The debris of chaos littered the side of the road: abandoned vehicles peppered with bullet holes, discarded belongings deemed too heavy by refugees, and the dead. Flies, invigorated by a feast, buzzed over a horse, while a small, hungry dog tugged at its leg, struggling to tear away the remaining flesh.

Konrad waited by a derelict cottage, acknowledging them with a discreet smile. Falling into step beside them, he pulled out a pack of cigarettes, offering them round.

"You're a lifesaver," said Peters, drawing in a lung full of smoke.

"Any idea where we are?" asked Jock.

Konrad rummaged in his inner pocket, retrieving the car's map. He folded it out, crumpled it back on itself and focussed down on their locality. "About here." His finger tapped on a small village.

"What's that say?"

"Bergen. Zee camp we pass is Belsen."

It meant nothing to Jock, but he nodded. "How far left?"

"Tomorrow, Jock," declared Konrad. "Vee arrive tomorrow."

Day Fifty-Six: Night

Jock laid back, cupping his hands behind his head. Above, the stars appeared, unaffected by the madness of humanity. Despite the familiar noise and chill, Jock felt at peace. Tomorrow it would be over. No more walking; no more camping in the open or in bomb-damaged churches. It didn't matter that their future still lay in doubt. They would finish this perverse challenge. His mind drifted to Tom What-man and the others from Stalag XXA still out there. *How many more days do they have on the road? How have they fared?* Jock fought the wave of guilt at leaving them, only for another to wash over him when Birgit's face appeared. *It was the right thing to do.* She had probably already forgotten them.

The crunch of footsteps broke his thoughts. Peters stood before him, chewing on a bone.

"Was there ever any meat on it?" asked Jock, as his friend sat down next to him.

"I suspect the fella had his fair share in life," said Peters. "But it was all gone by the time it reached me."

The darkness swallowed Jock's smile. "What news?"

Peters adjusted himself, shuffling off a root protruding from the ground. "All that racket earlier was an army unit setting up camp next to us. We'll be well guarded tonight."

"Which way they heading?"

"Hard to tell. Didn't get too close."

"A shooting star!"

"Eh?"

"I just saw a shooting star," said Jock, his gaze lost amid the heavens. "Supposed tae make a wish."

"And? I hope you included me."

"Aye."

"You're not going to tell me what you wished for, are you?"

"Naw."

"Typical Scot!" teased Peters. "Too tight to share."

"Ha, ye ungrateful Sassenach! Get yer own shooting star."

"May the haggis nibble on your sporran as you sleep," retorted the Englishman.

How strange that Peters should discover his old self in the wake of Babe's brush with death, thought Jock, as he glanced across at the youngster sleeping in a hollow between two trees. It was as if the boy's gesture had represented and appeased Peters's own pain.

"He looks at peace," remarked Peters, noticing Jock's attention drifting.

"Aye, but what's going on inside?" Jock adjusted himself onto his elbows and looked hard at his friend. "Ye'd never do anything so stupid?"

"No way," replied Peters. "I'm not letting a German bullet take me and I won't do their job for them either."

"Good." Jock let the moment fade into silence. His head reclined back to the ground, his eyes closing.

Day Fifty-Seven: Morning

By dawn, clouds rolled in, bringing a misty drizzle. Droplets built on hanging leaves, then fell, disturbing the soil or a slumbering prisoner.

Jock groaned, swatting the first droplet as though a fly, then stirred with the realisation he was getting wet. He eased himself against a trunk and turned his collar up, leaned his head back, and opened his mouth. The stubborn rain refused to find his tongue, dotting his legs and arms instead.

"What time is it?" mumbled Peters.

"Daytime," answered Jock.

"Strange. Could have sworn it was night-time." Peters yawned, rubbed his eyes with his fists, then examined his bare wrist. "My watch must be wrong."

"Our last day of walking," said Jock, his voice hesitant.

"I bloody well hope so." Peters uprighted himself, pulling his blanket over his knees, tucking one end under his chin. "We've been lucky."

Jock nodded. "We're the luckiest misfortunates alive in this world."

"It's not over, you know? We're still prisoners; still at the mercy of the merciless."

"Hmm, but I can smell home now."

"I can smell something," responded Peters. "But it ain't home." His nose twitched like a rabbit.

"Cabbage for breakfast?" suggested Jock, his shoulders sinking. "It's definitely not over."

They joined the queue, canteens at the ready, their tastebuds lacking the eagerness of their stomachs. With daylight, the military vehicles declared themselves, snaking around the edge of the wood, sheltered from prying aircraft. The soldiers sat hunched around campfires, as worn and fatigued as the prisoners; only an extra pound or two and their uniform distinguished them. No longer did they exude a conqueror's confidence.

"I wonder if they're eating the same as us?" asked Peters, examining the greenish sludge in his canteen.

"One can but hope," said Jock. "Nae army could fight on this stuff." His tummy rumbled, dissatisfied, as his first sip disappeared down his throat.

Amid shouted orders, a laugh floated on the air. Jock and Peters exchanged a glance.

"I recognise that laugh," said Peters.

"Aye. I cannae quite place it."

A frown formed on both foreheads; their eyes searching for the source. Campfire smoke mixed with the drizzle, creating a mist over the adjacent fields. In the haze, a rotund figure stood with hands on hips, the familiar bulging shape of gabardine jodhpur trousers clear to see.

"General Meier!" exclaimed Jock and Peters in unison.

"He's coming this way! What if he recognises us?" Peters tucked his chin into his neck, tipping his hat forward.

"He's nawt looking for prisoners," said Jock, unconvinced by his own argument. "Where's Babe?"

They swung round, scanning the woods.

"Can't see him!" Panic rose in Peters's voice. "Where... Oh, there he is: third in queue."

"Where the general's heading!" stated Jock.

"What do we do?"

"Nowt," answered Jock, feeling his heart beating faster. "There's nothing we can do."

General Meier strolled up to the steaming vat, his attaché in train. He tapped the container with his swagger stick, exchanging words with the cook. That familiar laugh sounded again. All the prisoners in the queue faced towards him; all except the third placed. The confidence devoid among his soldiers remained in the general. He surveyed the defeated faces, nodding his head.

"Oh, God! He's inspecting the line!" gasped Peters, as the general gripped his hands behind his own back and began conversing with the prisoners.

Jock and Peters watched in horror as the German and youngster came face to face.

"He's taking too long!" complained Peters. "He's recognised him! It's over."

"Shut up!" growled Jock. "He's moving on."

The general strolled down the queue, assessing the vanquished; the quick glance back at the face he couldn't place, unnoticed by almost all.

"He's suspicious," whined Peters, hovering behind a tree.

"Unless Babe curtsied, he won't recognise him," said Jock, still not convincing himself with his logic.

"Oh, Jeez!" exclaimed Peters. "He's buggering off. Thank God!"

Jock released the breath he hadn't realised he was holding, as the general wandered away towards his own men.

"It may still dawn on him," cautioned Peters, as Babe hurried over to them.

"Guess who I just saw?" asked the youngster, his canteen unfilled.

"Aye, we observed," said Jock. "What did he say tae ye?"

"Oh, some nonsense about them winning the war and how grateful we should be for the care we receive. I should have kicked him harder out of the car."

"Do you think he recognised you?" pressed Peters, one eye still following the general.

"I don't think he looked at my face in the car; just my chest and legs."

"Hmm, let's hope so."

"Psst." The noise came from the trees.

The three turned to find Konrad beckoning from behind a tree.

"Konrad! What is it?" asked Jock in a hushed voice.

"Zee clothes: give me zee clothes." Konrad's eyes were wide in fear.

"Ye've changed yer mind?" asked Jock.

"Ja, ja," answered Konrad, his cheek twitched. "General Meier is here."

"We know," said Babe. "Not for long though, I hope."

Konrad laughed bitterly. "After vee deliver you to camp, vee join his battalion! I vill be recognised or sent to front. For sure."

"Are ye certain aboot coming in with us?"

The guard's body sagged in despair. "I have no choice."

"I'll get ma bag," said Jock, heading off deeper into the wood.

"Won't the other guards spot you?" asked Peters. "I mean, you've been eating and sleeping with them for the last week."

"Ja, my friend, but I have plan."

"You've been in Jock's company too long," joked Peters, as the Scot reappeared with the bundle of uniform.

"Here ye go," said Jock, handing the clothes and dog tag over. "Ye new name's Peter Clancy."

The German sniffed at the bundle. "Peter Clancy. Ja, a good name."

Day Fifty-Seven: Afternoon

The column progressed with its usual sullen reluctance and slow pace, despite the promise their march neared its end. Every face carried the strain of captivity, their legs the fatigue of starvation and abuse. None considered how far they had covered, 500 miles from Poland or 200 from North Germany. The day ahead was their challenge. Past achievements meant little. Survival never dwelt on the past, nor on false hope. The next meal; the next step. No other details concerned these prisoners of war.

Jock crouched by the roadside. The morning's breakfast had gone right through him. He cleaned himself with a leaf, examining the steaming mess for signs of blood. Relieved at its absence, Jock pulled up his pants and trousers. He rubbed his gut, hoping time would settle it. Others continued past, unperturbed. Shame existed but hid itself amid each man's grievances, behind the numb space created to survive. Jock grabbed his bag and rejoined the march.

Babe and Peters had not got too far ahead, their promise to dawdle fulfilled.

"All okay?" asked Peters.

"Aye," lied Jock, his stomach tender and gurgling.

"Kendrick's coughing blood," remarked Babe, failing to notice Jock's irritated scowl.

"Let's focus on getting taeday over with," said Jock, unwilling to dwell on ailments. "Is that Konrad?"

Up ahead, a figure in the distinct uniform of a German prison guard ambled behind a cluster of prisoners.

"I hope so," said Peters. "We told him to stay close."

"It is," added Babe. "He has a distinct stoop and gait."

"Not too distinct, I hope," said Jock, grimacing as his gut spasmed. "Let's try to catch up."

"Acceleration's never been much good for this old beast," said Peters, struggling with the effort of changing pace. "Oil probably needs changing."

"That explains the noises you make at night," teased Babe.

"Hey, I'm the one with the jokes. Your only job is bemusement."

Babe grinned. "Must be rubbing off on me."

"About bloody time. Jock notices if I repeat them. Jock? You okay?"

The Scot belched, gripping his abdomen. "Sorry!" He dashed to the verge, his belt undone and trousers already round his ankles.

"Come on, lad," said Peters to Babe, as he picked up Jock's bag. "Let's leave him be. I'll tell you some of my oldest jokes."

"We'll go slow," promised Babe with a concerned glance back at the preoccupied, squatting figure.

"Damn tum!" cursed Jock to himself. He felt a moment's relief at having answered the immediate call of nature, but knew the cramps would return. What he craved was to curl up in a silent, empty place, as he did when a child: let the world carry on without him until the pain vanished. He looked around him for suitable foliage to clean himself.

"Valk! Schnell!"

Jock gazed up at a German guard, distinct with a red, bulbous nose and well-manicured pencil moustache. "Aye, let me make maself decent first." He leaned back, clasping a clump of grass.

"Sofort!" The guard seized Jock's collar, heaving him to his feet.

Their eyes locked for a second. A dozen curses simmered beneath the surface, but Jock restrained himself. "I'm moving, lavvy heid." As Jock bent to lift his trousers, a rifle butt shoved against the base of his spine. He staggered forward, his trousers falling back down, tangling with his boots. Over he went, his face and hands striking the gritty surface.

"Valk!" repeated the guard, this time with gleeful pleasure.

Jock took a deep breath. Blood dribbled down his face, into his mouth. His tongue ran along his lips, tasting the warm fluid. He spat it out, and turned his head, keeping his tormentor in sight, levering himself upright with one hand, tugging his trousers up with the other. His palm and face stung, but he ignored the pain. Soon, he stood looking down at the guard, a defiant air possessing his features.

"Lucky I don't have ma gun," Jock mumbled to himself, as he took a step along the road, hands gripping his trousers at the waist. "Nae gommy should humiliate another like that." He brushed his hands together, dislodging the gravel from his cuts. A fury lengthened his stride; an energy his body could ill afford. He would show this brute how a proper soldier behaved. His stoop vanished; his head lifted high. With his belt tightened, his arms swung to the rhythm of the parade ground. Soon, he passed a staggering prisoner, receiving a bewildered expression, then another and another, until he passed Peters and Babe, the guard fading in the distance.

"Jock! What happened? What are you doing?" called out Peters, his face sharing the disbelief on Babe's. "Slow down!"

No answer came as Jock ploughed on.

"He'll kill himself!" exclaimed Babe.

"So will we, catching him up," said Peters. "But what the hell!"

The pair broke into a jog, soon coming level with Jock, his eyes glaring forward, intense but lost.

"Stop!" cried Peters.

Jock whipped his head sideways in shock, his face draining of colour as his legs wobbled to a near standstill. The adrenaline had all gone. His body demanded payment, but Jock had nothing to give.

"We've got you," assured Peters, as he and Babe eased Jock's arms round their shoulders, ignoring the familiar odour. "Let us take the weight for a while. There's no hurry."

"Sorry, lads," whispered Jock, now limp within their grasp.

"I'm just happy you weigh next to nothing," quipped Peters. "You going to tell us what happened? Your face is a mess."

With effort, Jock rotated his head, checking to see if the guard was in sight. "I had a need tae punch Fritz but, as that option wasnae available, I went a little crazy."

"You can say that again," said Babe. "And the face?"

"A disagreement with the road. It came off worse!"

"Ha," laughed Peters. "That sounds more like our Jock. Here, have some water." He splashed a little on to the wound, eliciting the expected grimace from Jock. "That'll cure your insanity."

"Thanks," said Jock, before the can touched his lips and he gulped down two mouthfuls. "That's better. I'll nawt need yer help nae more. But thank ye." He extricated himself, his legs still wobbling.

"You sure?"

"Aye, just need tae get ma rhythm."

"I'll keep your bag until you've found it," said Peters, a sceptical eye on his friend. "And walk next to you should you need a lamppost."

"I'm nae dog!" Jock's shame surfaced in anger.

"We're just trying to help," said Babe.

"Sorry," said Jock, one hand gripping Peters's shoulder for support. "What's that?"

A column of thick black smoke rose beyond the brow of a gentle incline, its acrid taste bitter on the tongue. Anxiety twisted Jock's already tender gut.

"No one's stopping," observed Babe of those on the road before them.

The summit revealed a decimated, armoured column, vehicles engulfed in flames littering the road and ditches. Charred bodies hung from the gutted chassis.

"Poor sods," commented Peters, pulling his scarf up to cover his nose. "I hope none of our chaps got caught up."

"There's Konrad," said Jock. A solitary guard sat on the verge ahead of the first vehicle.

"Wouldn't want to linger around that scene if I could help it," said Babe, shivering in disgust.

A faint smile emerged on Jock's weary face. "I think I know what he's up to."

Konrad climbed to his feet as they shuffled their way towards him.

"Vhat happened, Jock?" he asked with concern.

"One of yers objected tae me shitting!"

The German frowned, only half comprehending. "Er, who?"

"Thin moustache. Big nose." Jock mimed to aid his description.

Konrad nodded. "Lehmann. His vife leave him for another man."

"Good," said Jock. "Ye waiting for us?"

"Ja. Vee are vone kilometre from camp."

"And the smoke and vehicles are the perfect stage for yer transition?" concluded Jock.

"Ja. You agree?"

"Oh, aye." Jock made a shallow bow, beckoning for Konrad to lead the way.

They wound their way through the carnage, stepping over smoking debris and bodies. Under the intense heat of a burning troop carrier, Konrad whipped his hat off, slinging it into the fire. He plucked a British cap from his pocket, slipping it on his head, receiving a nod from Jock when angled correctly. Then he unbuttoned his tunic, revealing the uniform of a British private.

"Weren't you hot?" asked Babe, shielding his face with a hand from the leaping flames.

"Oh, ja," replied Konrad, throwing his old guard's jacket into the nearest fire. He stopped to slide his trousers down, leaning on Babe. "How do I look?"

"Like an average Tommy," declared Jock, squinting as the smoke aggravated his eyes.

"Who always pushes to the front of the food queue," added Peters, trying to laugh, but coughing instead.

"Och, ye look fine."

"Gut," said Konrad, dropping his old trousers in a burning engine.

"Goodbye Konrad Müller; hello Peter Clancy," announced Babe, shaking the German by the hand.

"I didn't know Müller was your surname," said Peters between coughs.

"It's not," answered Konrad with a smile, showing off his dog tag. "It's Clancy."

"A little practice on pronunciation, perhaps." Peters slapped Konrad on his back. "Now, let's escape this hellish inferno!"

***

"It's big," said Jock as the Fallingbostel camp appeared in sight.

"Huge, more like," said Peters.

Konrad halted, an ashen pallor colouring his face.

"Don't stop, Clancy!" urged Peters. "You're supposed to stay amid us, not stand out like a swot on his first day of school."

Shaking his head with incomprehension, Konrad rejoined the group. "It looks monstrous. I never thought…" Words failed him.

"I know. Feels different when it's your home," said Babe, trying to count the rows of huts without success.

"We've walked all this way tae find ourselves back where we began," commented Jock.

"Eh?"

"Hell!" Jock spat to the ground.

"Perhaps there will be more room," suggested Babe. "Looks big enough."

"A bed and regular food will suit me," added Peters.

The straggling column of prisoners slowly formed into a more cohesive unit, readying itself for as dignified an entrance through the daunting gates of the camp as it could manage. Konrad found himself at the heart, out of view from the discerning eyes of his fellow guards.

From their watchtowers, sentries observed the column of prisoners. Their machine guns rotated to welcome the new inmates. Three tall fences, stretching as far as the eye could see, made up the perimeter. On either side of a central courtyard, behind further rings of wire, stood the huts: row on row of them. Crowds of prisoners loitered amid the muddy outdoors, hands in pockets, despondent faces tucked behind collars out of the wind. Their eyes followed the slow march of their comrades.

"Not so much room," complained Babe. "There's thousands."

The camp gates opened. A unit of guards trotted out in formation, lining up on either side of the road.

"A welcome party," said Peters. "Tea and scones await!"

"Don't mention food!" growled Jock, his digestion still in turmoil. "What can we expect, Konrad?"

The German shrugged. "Er, zey take record. Names and numbers."

"Then food?" asked a hopeful Peters, receiving a glare from Jock.

"I've just had a thought," piped in Babe, almost apologetic.

"Go on," said Peters. "Though I find them overrated."

Babe ignored his friend. "How are we going to explain our early arrival? It's not like we can pretend to have come from Stalag IIIC."

A deep frown creased Jock's brow. "Ah."

Silence followed.

Day Seventy-One

"Sorry, Jock. Time's up." A short, ginger-haired man bent over Jock.

Jock sighed, fighting the weight of melancholy. He slid off the bunk, angling his head to avoid hitting the low base of the middle bed. "Warm oot?"

"Warm rain," said the man, laughing at his joke, as he ducked his head to occupy the cosy indent made by Jock.

Two weeks had passed since their arrival at the camp, but it felt an eternity. Chaos and order existed side by side, the former perhaps the reason no one had questioned their early arrival. Over 400 prisoners occupied the hut. Jock counted 150 beds. More prisoners arrived at the camp every few days.

Jock turned and twisted, avoiding beds and men, stepping over those sleeping on the floor. He made for the door as rain pattered on the roof, mixing with the snoring and rumble of conversations. It was a wonder anyone could sleep.

A cluster of men waited at the entrance, weighing up whether the rain was better than the claustrophobic confines of the huts.

"Excuse me, lads," said Jock, his mind already set. Outside, on the step of the hut, he closed his eyes, letting the relative peace filter through, appreciating his freedom from the oppressive hut. A large puddle awaited unwary feet at the bottom of the step. Jock stretched his long, thin legs, landing in the mud with a squelch. Dark clouds hung overhead, but patches of blue in the distance promised a drier afternoon. He tipped his head back, allowing the raindrops to hit his tongue.

Others strolled around the yard, preferring the mud to the company of their fellow captives. Jock spotted Regimental Sergeant Major Earle, busying himself as usual. He was the reason for the order: the shifts on the bunks, the daily parades and exercises. Jock ducked his head, trying to avoid Earle's eye. He couldn't face him. In Earle, Jock recognised his old self, with the vigour and purpose, looking out for others and fighting the war through an undefeated spirit. That spirit had long gone, drained by five years and 500 miles. On days like these, when the black dog visited, Jock didn't want reminding.

"Jock!"

Spotted, Jock stuffed his hands in his pocket and ran through the puddles toward the latrine. Any prisoner would understand a snub for nature's emergency.

A foul stench hit Jock as he approached the latrines, the rain doing little to temper the smell. It triggered a memory. That of his first days in camp, as his gut plagued him, sending him running here every few hours. At least there was no queue today. Taking a deep breath, he pushed open the door, a new level of foulness grabbing him. A long length of wood with regular holes lined one side: almost all occupied. A sickly sound mixed with the stink. There was no privacy and no plumbing, the holes leading straight into a single cesspit behind the hut, covered with thin boarding. Jock dreaded the day his number came up to clean it out. Finding a free space, he lowered his trousers and sat. The man next to him groaned, his head slumped forward between his knees. Jock recognised himself from just a fortnight past.

"Fresh air!" Jock burst out the door, gasping for breath. He checked around to ensure Earle hadn't spotted him and shuffled off toward the fence. It was a popular spot. Like standing outside a bakery with no money: if you couldn't taste freedom, then at least you could smell it.

"Hey, Jock!"

Jock's stomach lurched before he recognised Babe. "Morning, lad. Thought ye might be the general," he said, referring to Earle's nickname. "Enjoying the rain?"

"There's another column arriving," said Babe, pointing beyond the wire. "Too far away to recognise anyone. It can't be too long before our boys turn up. They were only supposed to be a few days behind us."

"More men! Just what this camp needs!" Peters appeared behind them, a moustache-less Konrad in tow. "Thought I'd find you here."

"I hear zey plan to move some out," whispered Konrad, self-conscious of his accent.

"Another march!" exclaimed a despondent Babe.

"Just RAF men."

"Those guards being indiscreet in your company again?" Peters smiled.

"If I vere guard, I not say such things among prisoners. You do not know who speaks your language. Ja?"

They laughed.

"I think that's them!" cried Babe, drawing their attention back to the column of prisoners.

"Who?" asked Konrad.

"Our lot! Whatman, Charlie, Cheddar."

"Cheddar?"

"A nickname," explained Babe for the German's benefit. "You know, like Babe or Jock. His real name's Cheeseman."

Konrad shook his head. "Vee Tommys are a strange lot."

"You need a nickname," suggested Peters. "How about Willie? After the Kaiser."

"Vhy vould I vish to have name of Kaiser?"

"Or Paddy," continued Peters, undeterred. "Clancy's an Irish name, after all."

"No, there's several Paddys already," said Babe. "How about…"

"Pete Clancy is nickname enough," said Jock, trying to rein in the boyish excitement stirred by the anticipation of seeing old friends again. "Let's go welcome them. They'll be thankful tae see a friendly face in this tip."

"Oh, there's Worm!" announced Babe, clapping his hands, as he followed the others through the slalom of puddles. "Bookworm," he said to Konrad. "A keen reader. Don't think I know his real name."

***

Two hundred bewildered faces stared out at those watching them, their clothes soaked, their cheeks withered and grubby. Jock recognised the look. There was no relief. They had walked 500 miles, only to find themselves lost.

"Tom! Tom!" called out Babe, waving an arm.

Whatman acknowledged with a faint smile, his eyes heavy and unenthused.

"They don't look so good," observed Peters. "I hardly recognise some."

"But they made it," said Jock, struggling to keep his emotions in check. "I've had nightmares."

"Really?"

"Aye. They didn't find the food we left them. Starved bodies in the ditches. Frozen faces in the snow."

"Jeez, I didn't know," said Peters, surprised at Jock's admission.

"Guilt, I suppose," said Jock, his unfocussed eyes lost in the distance.

"Bloody hell, Jock," said Peters. "You... we did what we had to do. Don't you remember? Birgit, Konrad, the SS officer?"

"Archie's right," added Babe. "We saved Birgit. Did all we could to help our mates."

"Here they come," said Jock.

A group of new arrivals shuffled towards them. Babe rushed forward, greeting all with a handshake and pat on the shoulder.

"We made it," said Whatman, offering his hand to Peters. "How long you been here?"

Peters shrugged, clasping the hand with both of his. "Time means little here. How was it for you?"

"Hellish." He addressed the word at Jock, took a step forward and flung his arms around the Scot. "But you got us through." He stepped back, wiping a tear from his eye. "We went through a terrible stretch. Another visit from our own air force: who named it friendly fire?" He snorted in derision. "They didn't feed us for two days after that. A punishment! But your food stashes got us through. We couldn't believe how much there was at one."

Jock and Peters exchanged a confused look.

"Where?"

"No idea," answered Whatman. "Just past a farmhouse. Had the Tudor-like walls."

"A long track leading up tae it, lined with poplars?" quizzed Jock.

"I think so. An old couple and their granddaughter watched us pass. How did you get that urn of milk? It tasted fresh."

"We didn't," said Peters, sharing a broad grin with Babe and Jock.

"You can thank our friends," added Babe.

"Milk, ye say," said Jock, shaking his head in wonder, as he placed an arm round Whatman's shoulder. "Come on, lad. Let's show ye around and introduce ye tae people. Have ye met Clancy, Pete Clancy? He has one of those faces where ye think ye've met him before."

Whatman shook the hand offered by Konrad. "Er, I see what you mean. Nice to meet you, Pete."

"Vhato, old boy," responded Konrad.

His friends burst into laughter, as Whatman frowned in confusion.

"You're getting there," said Peters, giving Konrad the thumbs-up. "Just a little work required on those double-u's. Try this one: Toodle-pip old chap."

"We've got some explaining to do," said Jock, the spark of hope returning. "It's quite the story."

Epilogue: 16th April 1945

An inexplicable buzz spread across the camp. Rumours, persisting for days, coincided with more considerate behaviour from the Germans, building hope. But most rumours came to nothing. Then the rumble of tanks confirmed the news. The prisoners rushed from their huts, crowding before the nearest fence, welcoming their liberators.

"I can't believe it!" sobbed Babe, wrestling for a view of the troops. "They're British. They're our boys!"

"And Fritz ain't putting up a fight," said Peters.

The German guards marched through the camp gates, disarmed and with hands on their heads.

"That's not all of them," observed Jock, fighting his own sense of giddiness.

"Zee cruel will be hiding or run away, ja?" said Konrad, uncertain of his own fate.

"Aye, hiding from justice."

"I'd like to get my hands on them," said Peters, waving as the liberators waved back.

"They're the Hussars. The Eighth Hussars." The words spread through the crowd of prisoners. Ration packets flew over the fence, gifts from the soldiers, causing a mad scramble among the prisoners for the food.

"Bet they've not seen anything like this before," said Peters, motioning to the emaciated crowd around him. "I remember looking that healthy once."

"What's the first meal you'll eat when home?" asked Babe, looking with disappointment at the dry biscuit claimed from the scramble. "A lamb cutlet with roast potatoes. That's what I'll have."

"Fish and chips!" declared Peters.

"Bangers and mash!" cried Whatman. "You Jock?"

"Anything Jane makes me. It'll taste sweet, whatever it is. Perhaps a wee dram, too."

"Oh, yes. Make mine a pint of Butler's bitter: smoothest thing there is." Peters licked his lips.

"How about you?" Babe turned to Konrad.

The German's eyes sunk to the ground. "I not know vhen I see home again."

"We'll get you back to Blighty," declared Babe. "You can start afresh."

"Zey vould velcome a German?"

Babe's inability to face Konrad answered the question.

"Donnae worry," said Jock, breaking the awkward silence. "We'll speak with the army. They'll need friends here when the war's won." He looked around at the cheerful faces of the prisoners pressing around him. One sour mouth at the back caught his attention. A knot creased his brow. Despite a ragged British uniform, the face appeared out of place: too round and nourished. Then there was the pencil moustache beneath a bulbous nose. "Jings! That's a Jerry. The gommy who did this." Jock tapped the scab lingering on his cheekbone.

"Where?" Peters craned his next.

"Lehmann?" queried Konrad in alarm.

"Aye, I'm sure of it," said Jock. "He's trying tae avoid capture by hiding in here. But I can see ye, ye diddy." His eyes locked on the guard, whose jaw dropped in panic. "Let's go say hello!"

As the group confronted the frozen German, his eyes didn't follow Jock, but another in the party. He raised a shaking arm, pointing at Konrad, his face colouring in anger. "Verräter!" he cried. A hand whipped inside his coat.

"Gun!" shouted Peters, stopping in his tracks. "Don't do anything stupid, Fritz. Your war's over."

Lehmann shook with rage, screaming until all around watched. "Du verrätst das Vaterland mit dem Feind! Ich werde dich töten." He levelled the gun at Konrad. "Striben!"

"Run, man!" yelled Jock, pushing Konrad out of the way as the pistol fired. The bullet whizzed past his ear, ricocheting off a fence post.

Konrad sprinted towards the huts, his face turning in horror as Lehmann followed, firing off another round. Splinters flew off the wall, showering Konrad as he ducked.

"After them!" urged Jock, now leading an angry mob of prisoners. "Archie, go round. We'll trap them. Don't get too close!"

"At least I'll die a free man!" shouted Peters as he disappeared round a small shed.

The chase led Jock between the packed huts until they emerged by the latrines. Lehmann stood in the open space, his head swinging back and forth in panic as prisoners encircled him.

"Bleibt zurück!" screamed the guard, waving the gun in a circle, forcing his pursuers back.

Konrad clung to the edge of the latrine hut, gasping for breath. "He promises to kill me, Jock!"

"Tell him we'll tear him tae pieces if he does," shouted Jock, holding his ground.

Before Konrad finished the translation, Lehmann yelled back in defiance.

"He is insane!" cried Konrad. "He says, I must die as a traitor."

"I'll get my pistol," suggested Peters, one hand on Jock's shoulder.

"It'll take too long," said Jock. "What we need..."

Lehmann made a dash for Konrad, firing as his compatriot ducked round the corner. Behind the latrines, Konrad leapt across the hoarding covering the cesspit. It bowed under his weight but held. He stepped on to the final board. Crack! Like a trapdoor, the board split and opened as Konrad plummeted.

"Hilfe!" Konrad's fingers clung to the lip of the cesspit; his feet submerged in the detritus.

At the far end, a grinning Lehmann angled his gun down at his prey. "Du wirst sterben wie der Hund, der du bist!"

Jock appeared behind him. "Hang on, Konrad!"

Lehmann waved Jock back with a waggle of the pistol.

"Och, think, man. What'll this achieve?"

The grin on the German's face morphed into terror. Beneath his feet, the board sagged, cracked, then fell apart. A scream escaped Lehmann's mouth, followed by a loud plop and silence.

"Hurry, Jock!" urged Konrad.

"I'm coming!" shouted the Scotsman, as he edged round the edge of the cesspit. "Hang on!"

Lehmann resurfaced, gagging for breath, arms scrambling for something to hold. "Hilfe! Bitte helfen Sie mir!" Relief flooded his face as his toes touched the bottom, the slurry lapping to his chin. The gun remained floating on the surface. Lehmann grabbed it, lifting it with a squelch, aimed at Konrad, and pulled the trigger. A click followed but no bang. With a desperate curse, Lehmann examined the gunge-filled barrel, and threw the useless gun at his compatriot, only to miss.

"For you Fritz, the war is over!" Peters appeared, holding back the clamouring prisoners, eager for a view. "The Schwein's found his natural habitat, I see. Need a hand, Jock?"

"Aye. This one's a little heavy for me." He winked at Konrad as he offered him a hand.

"Mein Gott! Thank you, Jock." Konrad grabbed his hand and then took Peters'. "And you, Archie. Zee smell is, how you say, whiffy."

"Hey, spot on!" laughed Peters.

"Let's get you cleaned up," said Jock, guiding Konrad away from the latrines.

The crowd of prisoners followed in their wake, chatting with excitement about the incident and their imminent release.

"Verlass mich nicht!" cried Lehmann, but no one remained to listen to his screams.

"Morning chaps." An officer stepped out in front of the prisoners. "Lieutenant Childs, Eighth Hussars. What have you been up to?" His eyes dropped to inspect the rich, brown stain on Konrad's trousers.

"Nothing," answered Jock with a schoolboy grin.

"Looks like you've had a rough time. Glad to see you've made it through."

"Aye," said Jock, ignoring a muffled scream bouncing off the walls.

"What was that?" asked the officer.

"The man cleaning out the latrines. His shift ends soon." Jock's answer set off a wave of sniggering from those behind. "We're thrilled tae see ye."

Lieutenant Childs motioned them on. "We'll get you fed and watered and then we move on. Fritz has not given up yet. Stubborn chap. You're lucky to be out of it."

"Oh, aye," said Jock, rolling his eyes. "Luck seems tae follow us aboot."

THE END

For All The Treasures Buried Far
1948

Book Three

The Bride of Abydos

By Lord Byron (George Gordon)

Now thou art mine, for ever mine,
With life to keep, and scarce with life resign;
Now thou art mine, that sacred oath,
Though sworn by one, hath bound us both.
Yes, fondly, wisely hast thou done;
That vow hath saved more heads than one:
But blench not thou thy simplest tress
Claims more from me than tenderness;
I would not wrong the slenderest hair
That clusters round thy forehead fair,
For all the treasures buried far
Within the caves of Istakar.

Introduction

Richard 'Jock' Mitchell spent his last days in a nursing home on the south coast of England, departing us in 1984 at 82 years old. With his beloved Jane having passed away a couple of years earlier, it was only in his final years that he spoke of his time spent in Stalag XXA, confessing to his part in the incredible theft of the gold from the Nazis and of having to leave its secret to the Polish countryside when the Germans marched him and his fellow prisoners westwards in the terrible winter of 1945. I had the privilege of bringing those tales to the public eye, celebrating the heroics of the brave and oft-forgotten prisoners of war, but I always suspected a new struggle, as great as any which went before, awaited Jock on his return home: adjusting to freedom after five years of mistreatment and incarceration, while carrying the scars from all he had witnessed and suffered.

In 2024, my phone rang. Jock's daughter, Jean, greeted me, now a mother and grandmother herself. Imagine my excitement when she told me of the discovery of a handwritten manuscript in Jock's own hand while clearing her attic. She thought I might be interested, as it appeared to cover an incident after the war. We met at a tearoom in a converted post office, and I marvelled at page after page of text in Jock's spidery handwriting. It was not always easy to interpret, written as it was by a tired old man on the edge of dementia, his pen slipping as he perhaps nodded off to sleep, but with the words intriguing me, I read on to discover one last incredible adventure.

With Jean's permission, I have worked over the last year to edit and polish Jock's manuscript, telling this story in his own words. It is a fitting conclusion to those turbulent years that scarred his life, but I hope also a tribute to all those involved.

Nathaniel M. Wrey, 2025

Chapter 1

I remember resting on my spade, admiring the vegetable patch, the early spring sunshine warming my face. Jean, my wee bairn, crawled over a blanket spread on the grass, and new life sprouted through the soil to the tune of a robin, watching me with impatience. It was paradise, and yet... I pressed down on the spade, turning the soil. The robin hopped forward, searching for worms, as Jean's giggle carried across the garden. A butterfly frolicked in the light wind; Jean's chubby arms reached out in vain to grasp the delicate traveller. Something was wrong. A sensation washed through me. I paused my labours again, trying to interpret the feeling. How does one explain such things? If I said the cake I ate tasted odd, with an unexpected flavour buried amid the sweetness, then you may understand. Familiarity and strangeness clashed.

Jane, my wife, emerged from the house with a mug of tea, her apron covered in the debris of her baking. She smiled at Jean, who crawled to the edge of her blanket, somehow fearful of venturing further onto the grass. The smile Jane offered me cleared my confusion: a plaintive regret mixed with pleasure, as though she remained unconvinced the man before her was the man she had married.

I was no longer that man. Happiness had returned, but mixed with guilt, regret and a hundred other bewildering feelings. How could I enjoy life when so many had suffered? When I understood the torments of hell. Sweetness now contained a sour, poisoned edge. When Jane extended her arm to offer me the tea, an inexplicable anger welled from within. I grabbed the mug and threw it to the ground, eliciting a gasp from my dear, confused wife. If I told you I watched all this from within, shocked and helpless, knowing I was wrong and a fool, you may well dismiss my claim, but this is the truth. I was not in control. Part of me would not accept happiness and contentment, rebelling with petulance. Once the red mist descended, it took control.

I don't remember storming off or Jean's tears, just the burnt umber view through the beer glass at my local pub. It was an escape of sorts. Oh, the irony! Five years of captivity under the brutal German yoke in distant Poland, and each night in that ramshackle prison I dreamt of a garden's tranquillity, of the embrace of my family, of finding happiness again. Each day I buried my feelings, focussing on survival. Yet there I was, three years since my release, a survivor, but not for the first time fleeing my idyll for sanctuary in another prison, the realm of king fluid. I can't explain it, but it explains what happened next.

With the automatic compunction of a drunk, I staggered home with the arrogant notion all would be fine. My belligerence exhausted through arguments around the bar, I found some appreciation in the peace as I swayed down the road, a canopy of trees, thickened by fresh growth, a stage for the evening chorus of birdsong. It wasn't my beloved Scotland, but it was a fine second best.

As the sun edged towards the horizon, I made out a black car parked on the verge in the fading light. Nothing compelled me to consider it had anything to do with me, even if no other house but mine was nearby. I walked past, more intent on carrying myself with dignity than questioning its presence. A man sat behind the wheel of what I recognised as an Austin 12, hidden behind his newspaper, cigarette smoke curling over the top. With a touch of my cap, I acknowledged him, receiving only a disinterested glance in response. The lights of the house, visible through a hedge, caught my attention, and I paid the man no further heed. Smoke wafted from the chimney, stirring a pleasing thought that I might spend what remained of the evening in front of the fire. I kicked my boots against the doorstep, dislodging a crust of mud, and pushed the front door open, an unfamiliar aroma greeting me.

"Evening, squire." A stranger dressed all in black greeted me from the hallway, his arms folded, a shoulder resting on the doorframe of the sitting room, his neck craned to inspect me.

"Good evening," I replied, somewhat taken aback.

"You Jock Mitchell?" he enquired with an earthy London accent, reminding me of Hyde.

"Who are ye? Jane?"

"In here, Jock!" answered Jane with no hint of concern. "We have visitors."

"Aye, I can see," I said, a sceptical eye locked on the stranger as I brushed past into the sitting room.

"Ah, there ye are," said Jane, her tone carrying a hint of castigation. "This is Mr Trenton-Harper." She motioned to a man smoking a pipe, the source of the new aroma, occupying what I considered my chair. "And his colleague, Mr Walker."

The man at the door straightened, nodding in my direction.

"They're here tae see ye, Richard," continued Jane, use of my formal name a clear sign of her residual anger. "All the way from London."

Trenton-Harper rose to his feet, removed the pipe from his mouth, and extended a hand toward me. "How do you do, Mr Mitchell. Please excuse our intrusion." His clipped accent complemented a sharp suit and superior air.

I shook his hand, aware his eyes assessed my gaunt frame.

"And how can I help ye?"

"Straight to the point. I like that. May I?" He motioned at the chair with his pipe.

"Aye." My face kept its wary scrutiny as he sat back down.

"Forgive me, Mrs Mitchell," he said with the utmost civility. "You've treated us as royalty, but may I request a moment alone with your husband? This is government business, after all."

The chilly evening air on my walk had sobered me a little. His last sentence completed the job. "Government?" I echoed with alarm as Jane climbed to her feet.

"Of course. I'll check in on Jean," she whispered, smiling at Mr Walker as she edged past.

I confess to placing thoughts of my poor Jean, asleep upstairs, behind those causing my heart to race. "What's the government want with me?"

The senior man smiled, instructing his colleague with a curt nod to close the door. "It's your country that needs you. His Majesty's government is not without admiration for your service during the war."

"I was locked up!"

"For the most part," continued Trenton-Harper. "A terrible business, that debacle in 1940. Left you chaps high and dry. Few suffered worse, and none are more deserving of our gratitude for their sacrifice."

I learned then that Mr Trenton-Harper had a way with words. He knew how to soften a dried-out veteran of the camps. "Can I get ye a wee dram?" This offer was more for my needs than a courtesy to a guest.

"I say, most welcome," answered Trenton-Harper, rubbing his hands together. "Your wife's tea was lovely, but it didn't quite warm the hard-to-reach spots, eh, Jock? May I call you Jock?"

"Aye." I poured his whisky, awaiting his given name, but he never offered it. "Yer man want one?"

"Best not," said Trenton-Harper, winking toward Walker as he sipped the spirit. "One requires a bodyguard to remain alert."

Such disclosures only fuelled my confusion and anxiety. I gulped my measure in one go. "Who in the government do ye work for?"

"Oh, you won't have heard of us, dear boy. We organised all the clandestine stuff during that disagreeable scuffle with Herr Hitler. Now the war's over, well… The world is still not as safe as we would have hoped. Our inbox is as full as ever, with Comrade Stalin playing by his own rules."

"Stalin? Aren't the Soviet Union our allies?" A fragmented image of emaciated Russians, crowded together in the filth of Stalag XXA, flickered in my mind.

"Hmm," mulled Trenton-Harper. "Communism has never been a friend of this country, and Stalin now has his tendrils across Eastern Europe. He's causing us grief in Berlin at present. Disrupting our lines in and out of the city. Wants us out of there! If we lose Berlin, then what next? Perhaps all of Germany? Your man Stalin is no better than Hitler, and with a victorious, battle-hardened army behind him."

"We're going tae war again?" I gasped, my already fragile stomach quivering in shock.

"I hope not," said an indignant Trenton-Harper, stretching to empty his pipe on the hearth with a sharp tap, before slumping back and tucking the pipe in his top pocket. "Uncle Joe won't want a visit from the Yanks with their atomic bomb. No, he's just pushing buttons at present. Seeing what he can get away with. It's a new sort of game. A facade of mutual respect covering mutual loathing."

"And what's this tae do with me?" I offered him a top up from the whisky bottle.

"Ha, yes." Trenton-Harper shuffled to the edge of his chair, sniffing the single malt with satisfaction. "There will be no war, but there are battles to win: discreet battles no one will ever hear of. We have just the battle for you."

"Nae, ma army days are over! And I ne'er fought in a battle." Not even another swig of whisky dampened my dread. "My life's here with Jane, the boys and Jean. The little one's nae more than nine months old." They were strange words to utter after my earlier behaviour, but I meant them.

"Of course, of course," said Trenton-Harper with a sympathetic pout. "We'll have you back in no time. You see, Jock, you're the only man who can help us."

"Really?" My foreboding increased.

"Do you remember giving Hitler a bloody nose in '41?"

I closed my eyes in resignation, knowing where Trenton-Harper headed. "Och, this is aboot Hyde's gold, isn't it? How d'ye know aboot that?"

"Intelligence is my business, Jock. You did an incredible thing in stealing that gold. Imagine if Hitler had turned it into munitions. More bombs on Blighty; more families wiped out." The rotter had the nerve to glance up at the ceiling, where the footsteps of Jane sounded, making his inference with raised eyebrows.

"I'll tell ye what I've told everyone aboot that gold: I donnae know where it is. Hyde did away with it and took the secret tae the grave. What ye want it for, anyway?"

"The same reason you snatched it from Hitler, old boy," answered Trenton-Harper. "Poland is under Stalin's grip now. It gets tighter with each passing year. We don't want Uncle Joe to have a sweetie fund."

"But it's Soviet gold." I'm no defender of tyrants, but I spoke the truth. "The Nazis stole it from them."

Trenton-Harper lost his agreeable grin. "Ownership is no argument when talking about the communists. They strip all of their private property. Locusts do less harm. Look, Jock, I'm not here to talk to you about ethical nuances or politics, but to tell you your king and country are calling you to service again. If I could tell you more, I would. But it's essential we get our hands on the gold before the Soviets. You're the last man alive to see it and talk to Hyde."

"Are ye saying I have nae choice?"

"I'm saying you'll get paid well and you'll enjoy the continued gratitude of His Majesty's government and not its enmity."

Why I snapped at Jane's offer of a mug of tea and not at this fait accompli, I'll never know. But my manner remained calm. Perhaps the promise of danger pacified my guilt? That Freud chap would no doubt have had something to say on the matter. "So, ye want me tae go tae Poland? Is it nawt under the grip of Stalin? They won't let me in. What did Mr Churchill call it?"

"The Iron Curtain," replied Trenton-Harper, the grin back beneath his pencil moustache. "Don't worry about that. Remember, a world of mutual respect still exists."

"I'm nawt a young man nae more," I protested. "Five years as a POW ages a man." Oh, how it had aged me! This was not the time to tell him of the stiff joints, aching back, or my damn stomach. My taste buds yearned for rich sensations, but all my gut could hold was the plain and drab. That's what a period of starvation does to you.

Why I tortured it with alcohol was a mystery. I poured myself another whisky.

"You'll be little more than a sightseer," reassured Trenton-Harper, reclining in my chair with a satisfied sniff. "We won't have long, will require luck, but we must take this chance while we still can. Before they draw that Iron Curtain tight shut. Walker and Crouch will accompany you. Do any lifting, so to speak. I'll be with you too, handling the locals and riffraff."

I correctly assumed Crouch to be the surly man in the car. My thoughts already questioned his credentials as a travel companion.

"Now," began Trenton-Harper, withdrawing a small notepad from his inner pocket. "Let's talk money." He scribbled in his pad, ripped out a page and passed it to me. "This is your proposed payment. Satisfactory?"

I whistled.

"That's for ten days away," he clarified. "Any longer and we'll see you right."

It felt churlish to whistle again, but the urge was there. "That's mighty generous." A niggling thought scuppered my elation. "Ma job? They may nawt give me time off and the house... well, it comes with the job."

Trenton-Harper frowned. "I see. Hmm. We don't want to make a fuss and bring attention to you. Perhaps the passing of a dearly beloved relative? They won't begrudge you a funeral back in Ayrshire, eh?"

"I suppose nawt." I was about to express my doubts when Trenton-Harper cut in.

"You'll get a letter. I'll write it myself. Your dear papa has passed after a brief illness. Mama urges you to return home posthaste, for she longs for her boy at this difficult time. The estate will require sometime to settle. Yes, that should do it."

"But ma father's long dead? I havenae spoken tae ma mother for years."

"Pah!" Trenton-Harper brushed away what I considered strong points with a wave of his hand. "As long as your employers don't know that."

I shrugged.

"Excellent." The government man climbed to his feet. "Well, Jock, this is going to be some adventure." He plucked a business card from a pocket and handed it to me. "You've no phone, so I'll need you to make a trip to a phone box and call this number after Wednesday. Use the code word 'hide and seek' and a charming lass will provide you with a date and point of departure. Good walking boots and a change of clothes. Nothing too cumbersome." He extended his hand.

There have been a few times in my life when saying 'no' would have done me wonders, but the word eluded me again. I simply shook his hand and watched as he departed with the reticent Walker.

"Mum's the word," said Trenton-Harper, turning at the front door, tapping his nose. With that perky grin, he pulled the door shut, leaving me bewildered in my home.

"They've gone?" It was Jane standing on the stairs.

"Aye." The roar of the Austin's engine starting drifted through the window.

"And? What did they want?"

"I'm tae go away for a wee while. Nowt tae worry aboot." I felt Jane's eyes on me as I returned to the sitting room, collapsing in my chair, still warm from its previous occupant. Again, a cruel disregard surfaced in me. I knew her mouth parted, a further question poised, but I closed my eyes, my manner aloof. She remained silent, and I listened to her weary footsteps as she vanished into the kitchen. With an afternoon of beer and an evening of whisky, I was soon asleep, back in the company of haunting images from my war.

Chapter 2

We spoke no more of the visitors. As the week progressed, I continued as normal, managing the flower beds and lawns across the estate, tending the fresh growth on the vegetable patch. Daffodils and tulips brightened the overcast days, bringing me manageable happiness. I took to buying a newspaper, finding a quiet corner with my bread and cheese and following the events in Europe I had once ignored. Berlin appeared daily, echoing Trenton-Harper's concerns, a pawn in a terrifying new game. For one side, a foothold for influence in Eastern Europe; for the other, a capitalist infection waiting to spread. Since March, tensions had risen, the Soviets imposing and easing restrictions on road and railway traffic, while harassing incoming flights, one fatal collision the price for this brinkmanship. The world, meanwhile, held its breath.

On Thursday, I ambled to the nearest phone box, waiting outside with my cigarette while Mrs Turnball finished her call to a daughter in Sidcup. A toothless grin thanked my patience as she emerged, clutching her handbag.

"Twins!" she announced, and I congratulated her with a blind presumption it deserved such a response.

As she sauntered down the road, I rummaged in my pocket for coins, removed my cap, and squeezed into the red kiosk. Only, as I stood there, facing the phone, a coin held between finger and thumb over the slot, did I question myself. What was I committing myself to? Was it right to leave Jane and the kids? Who the hell was Trenton-Harper, anyway? That stranger, born of the war, surfaced again in the recesses of my mind. A nihilistic compulsion to escape and find true peace eased my digits apart, and the coin descended with a clunk. What I appreciate now was what I sought was death and its eternal peace, and this adventure offered it. My finger rotated the dial.

"Hello, how may I help you?"

I held the business card up to my eyes. "Hello, operator. Please put me through tae Whitehall 4820." My breath wavered as the clicking of exchanges fed through the receiver.

At last, a young female voice answered. "Good morning, Whitehall 4820."

Silence followed as I froze.

"Hello?"

"Sorry. Err, hide and seek." How silly I felt uttering such a thing, awaiting a perplexed reply or the line to go dead.

"Ah, good morning, Mr Mitchell. I've been expecting you."

I gulped. "Ye have?"

"Are you alone?"

Like a fool, and nerves my only defence, I looked around the tiny phone box to check. "Aye."

"You are to join the 11.34am bus from Victoria Station for the continent on Sunday, 25th April. Respectable dress. Don't be late! Expect to receive a package at your home containing a passport and visa, a map and other materials. Do not share or show to anyone. Is that clear?"

"Very clear." My mind calculated how many days until that Sunday. Just ten! "What aboot money? I donnae even know what currency Poland has."

"Mr Trenton-Harper will take care of you. Is there anything else?"

"Er, nae, I donnae think so." My generation trusted in authority, despite my experiences in France, and that polished voice, with its matter-of-fact manner, conveyed authority.

"Then good day, Mr Mitchell." The phone went dead.

I studied the receiver as though it had more answers, before a tap on the glass broke my stare.

"I'm back!" It was Mrs Turnball, wobbling with excitement. "I just must tell Mabel the news."

"Of course." I held the door for her and placed my cap back on my head, wondering who Mabel was. As Mrs Turnball's breathless voice leaked from the kiosk, and talk of babies confirmed my earlier assumption, I thought of Jean. Guilt stirred within. She needed her father. A memory of the war flashed to the forefront of my mind - as they often do - of little Birgit, the camp commandant's daughter. I remembered the pain of leaving her at the farm and a vague recollection of saying after Jean's birth I'd never abandon her. But something lay deeper within me; some compelling open wound. I know now it was young Robbie Hyde, that incorrigible rascal in Stalag XXA. He sacrificed his life to save us, to save me. I played his death over and over in my head. Could I have stopped him from dashing for the wire? Every bang or crash reminded me of the erupting machine guns; every drop of blood his bullet-riddled body carried across the yard. I walked back down the road to the estate, tugged from all sides by guilt but determined my duty lay in Poland.

Chapter 3

As promised, a parcel arrived a few days later, on the weekend. Jane answered the door to the postman, and as was the way in a quiet country community, both were intrigued by its contents.

"Are ye expecting something?" asked Jane as she wandered into the garden, Jean clasped in her arms, the parcel protruding in a free hand. "Mr Jeffries says there's a government postmark."

It is impossible to say if my huff answered her question, but I snatched the package and disappeared into the shed. Jane's patient explanation to Jean of her father's rudeness reached me as a piecemeal muffle. I cleared a shelf, making a mental note to spray the young cabbage for caterpillars as I moved a box of Derris powder. With a small pair of pruning shears, I sliced the parcel open, shaking the contents out. The passport caught my eye first. I had never owned one before, despite my time abroad. It was an anticlimax as I flicked through the empty pages. That is until the last page, when a photo of my younger self stared back. My confusion at the photo's source was as nothing to that stirred by the name on the passport: a James Macleod. As I said, this was my first passport, and, in my ignorance, I convinced myself all was normal, this Macleod an official. Then the visa plunged me back into puzzlement: it too made out in James Macleod's name. I re-examined the passport, studying it in more detail, realising this Macleod was the man photographed, and I had a new name and a new profession: teacher. A sickening cramp afflicted my stomach. I was to be a spy! Every soldier knows the fate of a spy if caught.

Under an old tea crate, I hid a bottle of homemade elderberry wine for emergencies. I broke it open, swigging a mouthful or two.

Reinforced, I held up the next document. It meant nothing to me. Just dates against strange, foreign names. Even the heading, while in English, was an enigma: Hornchurch St Agnes Tour. Only when I examined the map did things fit together. Between the cities I recognised - Vienna, Berlin, Prague, Warsaw - a line connected those strange, foreign names, including one I'd hoped to forget: Thorn.

I took another swig of elderberry wine, trying to bury the memories bubbling to the surface, pushing the map away.

"Jock!" Jane's call broke my maudlin stupor.

I shuffled the papers together, stuffing them back in the envelope, only then noticing the outline of a letter announcing the death of my father and 'signed' by my mother, but in a hand most definitely not hers. Lifting the wine bottle, I toasted his memory and slid all under the crate. "Coming!"

Jane awaited me on the path, a floral headscarf covering her hair, the pram before her with a dozing Jean within. "I'm going shopping. What do ye want me tae try for with our meat rations?"

"Pork chops," I answered without delay. "Ye look lovely." The words emerged with the same spontaneity as my petulant rudeness. Perhaps it was fear? I still had the letter I wrote her on the march across Europe, undelivered and unopened. Then, with death as a companion, I found the words to express my love. It felt like I was to hitch a ride with death once more.

A subtle frown creased Jane's brow before she smiled. "Yes, some pork will be nice. See ye later."

"I leave next Sunday," I spluttered out, feeling the time was right. "I'll be gone aboot two weeks. It's good money, and ye donnae have tae worry."

She didn't answer, just studied me with placid eyes, before nodding and releasing the brake on the pram, wheeling it down the path.

"I'll miss ye." I may have whispered those words. I can't remember, but she didn't hear me or turn her head.

Chapter 4

The weather had turned for the worse, with rain hammering against the window and the cold invading the house. A thoughtful mood possessed me since the parcel's arrival. I sat at the kitchen table while Jane undertook a stock-take of the larder. A fountain pen rested against my lips as I pondered the half-finished letter before me. I had already delivered the one to my employers, playing the mournful son, receiving reluctant permission for an unpaid absence.

"Ye'll be needing waterproofs," said Jane, as she stretched from a stool to the upper shelf, grabbing an anonymous jar.

"Aye," I replied.

"And food for the journey."

"A little." A week ago, I might have snapped at this series of questions, but a serenity replaced the anger.

"Are they putting ye up?"

"Aye. It's all organised." Of course, I knew no such thing, but why worry Jane.

A thought came to me, and I scribbled a further sentence on the letter, blowing the ink dry. My tongue pushed against my cheeks, seeking further inspiration.

"Tom's popping in."

I acknowledged the reference to my youngest boy, now a man, with a smile, and worked my pen again to tie up this precious correspondence with some idle mention of families and their importance. With a last flourish, I signed my name, leaning back to read the completed letter in the window's light.

"Can ye take a letter tae the post office for me, luv?" I folded it and slipped it into an envelope.

Jane's head appeared around the larder door. "Post office? Nawt the letterbox?"

"Aye, it's an overseas letter," I explained, scratching an address on the front. "An old war friend."

"Still in the service?"

"Something like that." I licked the envelope and sealed it as Jane appeared on my shoulder.

"That's a German name and address. A friend, ye say?" There was no judgement in her voice, just a wife's curiosity.

"Aye, Konrad and I share a love of clematis."

"That wind and rain's doing yers nae good." Jane peeked into the crib, where Jean gurgled. "Are ye sure ye won't take a blanket?"

I stared out the window, the view distorted by the heavy rain. "Nae, I must travel light." A growl mixed with the downpour, and a dark shape appeared in the driveway. "I think Tom's arrived. The eejit came on his motorbike!"

A mother's panic consumed Jane. "He'll catch his death!" she cried, scrambling round to ready herself and the house.

As I opened the front door, a sodden figure sprinted in, his head covered by a leather helmet and goggles.

"Hello, Dad!"

I clipped him across the back of his skull. "Trying tae kill yerself?"

He lifted his goggles and smiled. "It wasn't raining when I left the hall. But glad to be indoors."

Jane appeared. "Oh, my wee bairn. Thomas, look at ye! Let's get ye oot of those wet clothes." She started unbuttoning the trench coat.

"Don't fuss, woman," I admonished in a gruff tone. "Let the boy look after himself."

"Nonsense," she countered, spraying the lobby with water as she yanked the jacket off Tom's arm. "He's drenched through. Could hardly take his gloves off."

"Nae one helps ye in the army," I mumbled, escaping back to the warmth of the kitchen.

I stood above the cot, Jean's eyes widening at the sight of her father. "Ye're a beautiful one, aren't ye?" My finger stroked her round cheek. Her inquisitive features morphed to concern. I recognised the sign. "Come here, sweetheart." I lifted and rested her against my shoulder, patting her back, eliciting a small belch. "That's better, eh?"

A farce played out in the lobby as Jane disrobed our boy, a squelch and curse following each action.

"Ye'll take care of yer mam, won't ye?" I instructed Jean, her velvet skin pressed against my rough neck. "I donnae know if I'm doing the right thing. A little gold makes men go funny, and 150 bars of gold turns them crazy. That's right: 150 bars – or nears aboot. Had it in the back of a truck. Sat on it!" I held Jean out before me with my arms locked. "Robbie would have loved ye. Nae one loved him when he was a bairn, but he turned oot all right."

"Who ye talking tae?" asked Jane, appearing with an armful of Tom's garments, she herself a soggy picture.

"Just our Jean," I answered, placing my girl back in her crib.

"I told you he was a big softy," declared Tom, dressed only in his long johns, his accent already corrupted by the south. "Mum tells me you're going away."

"Aye." I intended my curt reply to end the conversation.

"Anywhere nice?" Tom had already made himself at home, cutting a chunk of bread from the loaf. "I hear it's all a bit hush-hush."

I imparted a withering glare toward Jane. "Nae, just collecting something."

"Don't tell me they've found Bormann, and they need a Mitchell to bring him to justice?" A mischievous grin broke as his cheeks filled with his sandwich.

My face remained stern. "Nae, just a few boring bits and bobs. Now, tell yer mother aboot yer course. She's dying tae hear all aboot it."

Chapter 5

I rose before dawn on that fateful Sunday. A mist layered the ground, bringing a chill to the air. I had slept in the spare room, hoping to slip from the house unnoticed, but Jane greeted me as I descended the stairs. She nodded with approval at my choice of a tweed jacket, straightening the collar with a fussy inspection.

"I've porridge warming on the Aga," she indicated, rummaging in a drawer for a spoon. "Ye're tae fill that stomach." It was an order, rather than advice.

I looked at the mantel clock and nodded. In truth, I had slept little that night and was up with plenty of time to spare before my train to London. "Jean sleep well?"

"Aye," answered Jane, ladling the oatmeal into a bowl.

"Ye get Tom or Dick tae help with any heavy lifting," I instructed, blowing on my porridge. "The rose has come off its frame. I'll secure it when I get back. Too many blooms."

"It's a good year for them." This was the language of a long marriage. "Here's some food for the journey."

"Bless ye." I chuckled within, thinking there was enough to feed the entire coach from the bulging bag.

"I'll take Jean tae the service this morning. The Macleods keep asking after her."

The name triggered a flush of anxiety. "Aye, give them ma best." I pushed the half-finished bowl away and stood. "I must be going." With my sailor's holdall on my shoulder, my food parcel stuffed within, I kissed Jane on the cheek, sparing a glance back as I strolled down the front path. Jane stood in the doorway, a tear running down her cheek. Was it shed for the departing stranger, I wondered, or the man she hoped would return?

***

Steam mixed with the lingering mist as I boarded the train from Tunbridge Wells to London. Due to the early hour and it being the day of rest, I had the third-class carriage to myself; the guard appeared surprised to find me as he walked through. We exchanged pleasantries as he checked my ticket and then I attempted to catch up on sleep. The rhythmic rattle and clank of the rolling stock induced a hypnotic peace, but as my conscious mind stepped aside for my subconscious, that same cadence drew up darker memories of less savoury travel in Germany. A claustrophobic terror jolted me awake. To my surprise, a family, dressed in their Sunday best, occupied a bank of seats across the aisle. I acknowledged them with a smile, only to receive a quizzical look in return, leaving me to wonder what drama I had played out while lost to my nightmares. The Kent countryside offered a distraction for what remained of my journey, as the blue sky promised a fine day of weather.

As we arrived at Charing Cross, I pulled my fob watch from its pocket, concluding I had time aplenty to walk up to Victoria. The city, though calmed by the Lord's Day, still bustled with the necessities of urban life. Porters scurried from platform to taxi rank, road sweepers tidied horse dung and litter, delivery drivers heaved boxes from their trucks or carts, while Bobbies on their beat observed all with their casual curiosity. From Trafalgar Square, I walked through St James Park, a sanctuary from the bomb damage scarring the city. The Household Cavalry, out for a morning exercise, trotted past on their pristine steads. How young they looked, I thought: a new generation already in place. From the park, I cut through to Victoria Street via Cockpit Steps. Outside the shell of St Andrew's Church, its spire no more, its crumbled walls a martyr to a direct hit, a preacher stood on his soapbox, a Bible cast to the sky as he warned passers-by of their sins. I stood for a moment listening with a small group of children, wondering what sins they had accrued, then made my way to the coach station.

Stepping through the art-déco frontage, order and chaos, so familiar to an old soldier, reigned at the station. People criss-crossed, scrambling between notice boards and vehicles. Stacks of luggage littered the ground, porters collecting and transferring on their trolleys with admirable dexterity, while coaches came and went, their fumes lending an acrid flavour to the air.

I slung my holdall to the floor, glancing at the large clock hanging from the iron rafters. Half an hour to spare. A line of cream boards, darkened by grime, hung over each bay, identifying the regular routes. People queued under each, a cigarette, book or child in hand, awaiting the order to board. It was only then I appreciated my destination was somewhat vague.

"Excuse me." I tried to catch the eye of a porter, but he hurried past, head down, a deadline to meet. An arrow pointed me to the central ticket and information desk, but sight of the lengthy queue dissuaded me from joining.

On the bottom step of a green coach just arrived from Weston-super-Mare sat its driver, chomping on a thick sandwich.

"Sorry tae bother ye," I said. "I'm looking for the 11.34. Do ye know which terminus it goes from?"

He looked up, his jaw working hard on the crust. "You Scottish?"

"Aye."

"I thought yous was. I'm pretty good with accents. 'Ave to be in my line of work. I once recognised a lad from the Isle of Man. Now, where was 'e 'eading to?" He pondered with a scratch of his ear.

"The 11.34?" I repeated.

"What's its destination?" He took another bite of his sandwich.

"Er, the continent. Central Europe... I think."

"Gosh, rather you than me, mate. Done my time over there and I'm not going back." He clicked his fingers and smiled. "Felixstowe. Yes, that's it."

"What's 'it'?" I queried, regretting my choice of guide.

"Your man from Man," he chuckled. "Fink they call themselves a Manx. 'E was 'olidaying in Felixstowe. Before the war, you understand."

"I see," I said with a frustrated huff. "Well, thank ye for yer time." I turned to leave.

"Bay ten."

"Sorry?" I spun round again.

"Your coach to the continent, mate," clarified the driver, pulling himself to his feet with the door rail and brushing crumbs off his jacket. "Bay ten. Suspect it's a chartered service. Most are for the continent. 'Ope it's got comfy seats: long way. You'd better 'urry."

I glanced at the clock again. 11.24. "Thank ye. Most appreciated." I turned right, then left, unsure which way bay ten lay.

"That way." His thumb jerked to my left. "Bright red coach. A Leyland Tiger…"

All I could offer was a sharp doff of my hat as I dashed off, leaving the man conveying some irrelevant fact in my wake. I pushed through the crowd, apologising and side-stepping, until I spied, standing before a bright red coach, Trenton-Harper, his hands anchored to his hips, a pipe lodged between his lips, one foot tapping with impatience.

"Sorry I cut things fine," I gasped through a breathless approach.

"You certainly have," he said, lifting his hand to show off his wristwatch. "But you made it, and that's the important thing. Let's get your bag in the hold and introduce you to our travelling companions. They're all aboard awaiting you."

"I have ma papers on me." My hand patted the bulge of my jacket, the passport and visa stored inside.

"Good man. Give your bag to Walker. He'll secure it for you."

In my rush, I had failed to notice the bodyguard leaning against the coach with one boot raised, flat against its gloss paintwork, a cigarette hanging from the corner of his mouth. Under the lights of the station, I noticed a scar beneath his chin and his cauliflower ears, giving him a less salubrious appearance than in the shadowy half-light of my hallway. He took my bag with a knowing grin.

"Thank ye," I said, before turning back to Trenton-Harper. "I have questions. Lots of questions. What does Hornchurch St Agnes Tour mean?"

Trenton-Harper's hand touched my back, guiding me to the coach door. "We'll have plenty of time for that on the journey, old chap. Let's get you on board and introduced." He rapped on the closed door, which opened with a hiss.

To my surprise, Crouch occupied the driver's seat, the uncommunicative man I passed in the car outside my house. His manner was no better on this occasion, assessing me with a half-interested glance.

"You remember Crouch," said Trenton-Harper as he climbed the steps first.

"I do," I replied, a worried frown having gripped my brow at the terrible din within the coach.

"And these," began Trenton-Harper as my head came level with the seating, "are the good ladies of the St Agnes School orchestra."

My jaw dropped. From row three to the back of the coach, teenage girls, dressed in light-blue uniforms and cream hats, occupied most seats. The noise was deafening as they giggled and conversed with excitable volume, paying me no attention. I don't believe even the approaching Germans at Albert in France on the day of my capture caused me this much fear.

"From Hornchurch, in the east of the city," clarified Trenton-Harper with a smirk. He clapped his hands. "Ladies! Ladies! Your attention, please."

It took a while for the noise to subside; Trenton-Harper was standing in the aisle, his raised hands conducting a gradual silence. "They think I'm Board of Education," he conveyed to me through the side of his mouth.

"Thank you," he said with silence at last achieved. "I want to introduce you to your final chaperone, Mr Macleod. A teacher of English. He has a little experience in Poland, one country you'll be playing in. So, feel free to ask him questions." He looked at his watch. "Ladies, it is 11.34 and time we were off. How about a song to celebrate our departure?"

With that, he slid into one of the empty seats behind the driver, urging me to take the adjacent one. I sank down, expecting my long legs to struggle for room, but I was most grateful to discover raised seats, suiting my needs most favourably.

Walker appeared on the steps, the door closed, and Crouch started the engine. While I remained disorientated amid my unexpected companions, a voice broke into song and the previous cacophony morphed into a beautiful choral rendition of A Tree in the Meadow, as the girls of St Agnes School sang as one.

Trenton-Harper nudged me. "Rather good, eh?"

"We're going behind the Iron Curtain with a party of schoolgirls?" It was impossible to hide my incredulity.

"That's right. A cultural exchange party, as we like to put it. Miss Henshaw behind is their music teacher. The young chap with the beard..." Trenton-Harper tilted his head across the aisle. "That's the deputy head, Davies. I know! So young. But that's what war does to the workforce. They'll look after the girls. Crouch and Walker will take it in turns to drive, and you and I, well, we are the local experts."

"Experts?" I spluttered, as the bus jerked forward and we pulled out onto the streets of London. "I spent five years locked up in a prisoner of war camp. Expert! I donnae even speak the language. Do ye?"

Trenton-Harper dismissed my concerns with a wave of his hand. "Pah! Every British gentleman can make himself understood with a firm tone and steely look."

I rolled my eyes in disbelief. "And where precisely are we going?"

He lent in, his voice restrained. "To distract attention from our principal aim, we are on a tri-nation tour. We go into Czechoslovakia via the American zone, then up into Poland, collect our prize, then across to the Soviet-German zone and out again. The girls have a concert booked in a town in each country. Including three days in Toruń. Think that will be long enough?"

"Toruń?"

"Oh, it's what you'll know as Thorn. The Poles spring-cleaned their Germanic past and have renamed it. Don't blame them. Did you know Copernicus was born there?"

"Sightseeing wasnae top of ma interests when I visited," I muttered. "Three days is nawt long tae find a needle in a haystack."

"I'm not a negative man, Mr Macleod," said Trenton-Harper. "And, what's more, I've undertaken some groundwork. I have my contacts: the old partisans. They're vulnerable under the communists but hanging on. Now, let's enjoy the girls' singing. They really are rather good."

Chapter 6

We drove south to Dover, the adults introducing ourselves through idle chatter, before joining a ferry to Dunkirk, enjoying the chance to stretch our legs. The rolling channel stifled the excitement of the girls; my anxiety at stepping foot back on the continent was subsumed by nursing those with delicate stomachs. Somehow, my own had no ill effect, and I found an empty bench to tuck into Jane's picnic.

I had seen little of Trenton-Harper on the boat; he favoured the company of the mysterious Crouch. But as I shelled a hard-boiled egg, he sidled up to me.

"A poignant return to Dunkirk." A hand kept his trilby on his head, the sea breeze ruffling the exposed hair as he stared at the distant shoreline of France.

"Ye were there?" I asked, biting the top off my egg.

"No, but its name carries such weight since 1940. How do you feel about it?"

I shrugged. "Just another port. I disembarked there but never made it back."

"You were part of the retreat, old chap, but not the rescue," remarked the government man, turning his head to watch my reaction. "That might turn a man bitter."

"Nawt me." The truth lay buried under the conversational etiquette. I had yet to process my feelings. How does a man judge what might have been, with what transpired? Would my life have been different had I got out? "The Lord's plans are nawt for me tae question."

"That's the spirit," declared Trenton-Harper, rising to his feet and stretching his arms and back. "Enjoy your meal, old boy. I'll see you back on the coach."

As I watched him vanish down the stairs to the deck below, a faint voice surprised me from behind.

"Does Poland have a king?"

I turned to discover one of the St Agnes girls, her pallor an off-green. "Hello, what's yer name?" I asked, hiding my food to avoid triggering an unwelcome reaction.

"Bridget," she answered, occupying the seat next to me. "I play the cello."

"I'm looking forward tae hearing ye play, Bridget. Now, ye asked aboot Poland. They have nae king. Nawt for a few centuries. I donnae know much aboot their government."

"Do they have a navy?"

"Er, I... I donnae know. They had a tough war and may nawt have got round tae building one yet."

"Mr Trenton-Harper said you knew about Poland?" She accompanied her question with a frown.

"I spent the war there," I explained, a hint of shame in my voice.

"You don't look like a soldier. Did you shoot anyone?"

"I was a prisoner. The Germans captured me in France, and I spent most of the war in Poland at a camp."

"Oh, so not a proper soldier? My daddy has a medal."

"Has he?" I responded through a shallow smile, reaching into my picnic for a spring onion. With a crack, I bit off the end, offering another to the girl.

Her hand went to her mouth, her skin turning a darker green. "Excuse me!" She dashed to the side and vomited.

I was not proud of my behaviour, but it was a fine spring onion, dispensing its own vengeful justice on me for the rest of the day.

***

From Dunkirk, we drove east, through Belgium and into the British-occupied zone of Germany. I expected to find the British army manning the border, but Belgian soldiers greeted us in their distinguished red berets.

"The Belgians manage a sub-zone for us," explained Trenton-Harper with his erudite manner, as he climbed off the coach to negotiate our entry, leaving a coach full of giggling schoolgirls waving at the soldiers.

I watched him from my seat, observing the suspicious and tense soldiers melt under his charm. A senior officer wandered over, engaging with Trenton-Harper as though old friends. They shook hands, and we were on our way again.

We headed south towards Cologne and the Rhine. The teenage bonhomie of my travelling companions faded through a mix of boredom and respect for the sheer destruction in view. They were no strangers to bombed-out buildings, but it is impossible to put into words the scale of devastation confronting them in Germany. Everywhere we passed through work gangs, made up of men and women of all ages, laboured amid the ruins, passing and ordering stones and bricks, repairing roads and constructing a ramshackle future. It was admirable and shocking.

Holes pockmarked the once envied, but since neglected, motorways. Military roadblocks were everywhere; jeeps parked across the road flagged us down, allowing Trenton-Harper to turn on his charm, before smiles and waves sent us on our way.

Excitement stirred as we neared Cologne, its towering cathedral spires holding us in awe. All around, skeletal buildings told of the fierce fighting, but the cathedral, despite carrying its own wounds, emitted majesty and hope. And we had time to admire it; for the bridge across the river, destroyed by the Germans themselves in 1945, remained unpassable. Instead, a Bailey bridge was our only route across. More substantial than a wartime construct, it still appeared fragile, and after an hour's queuing, we crawled across, destabilising those prone to seasickness again.

We stopped every few hours to stretch our legs but drove through the night, Crouch snoring in the seat across the aisle, Walker on driving duties.

"What are their stories?" I asked Trenton-Harper, the pair of us unable to sleep as the coach bounced over the uneven and rutted roads.

"Walker and Crouch? Eastenders: both of them," he explained. "One played his part at Anzio, the other on the beaches at Normandy."

"They donnae talk much," I observed.

"Not much time spent in polite society," confessed my employer. "You know the sort. Not too dissimilar to that Hyde of yours, eh? A little time in the glasshouse. But just what I need in my line of work."

"Oh, I see," I said, recalling some of the lurid tales of Hyde's life of crime. "Are they trustworthy?"

This triggered a guffaw from Trenton-Harper, waking Miss Henshaw behind. "There is no such thing as trustworthy in my business. But they're paid well. Ah, I think we're at the American zone."

In the darkness, powerful floodlights stung the eyes as we approached a checkpoint.

"Better armed and better fed, eh?" chuckled Trenton-Harper as our coach came under the scrutiny of the US soldiers and he readied himself to alight.

These guards, in their steel helmets and with Garand rifles, were immune to his charms, boarding the coach in their thundering boots, waking all, shining their torches at faces, rummaging through the luggage rack. The girls, rubbing eyes or adjusting their attire, grumbled at the disturbance, too weary for adolescent excitement, stirring Miss Henshaw to complain in an elevated warble. A GI paused, blinked, then ignored her. I sat rolling a cigarette, unperturbed, a veteran of military inspections.

Half an hour later, Trenton-Harper returned and slumped in his seat with a heavy sigh. "Splendid chaps, the Yanks, but a little on the brash side. Won't let the girls stretch their legs. Though glad they were on our side in the war."

"Is there a problem?" I asked as we remained stationary.

"No, no," reassured Trenton-Harper, checking his fringe and moustache in the window's reflection. "A few phone calls to make. Paperwork hadn't arrived, so a little confusion, but they'll soon clear it up." He glanced at his watch. "Don't want to get too far behind on our schedule."

I closed my eyes, grateful for some time out of the potholes, and, despite the continuous murmur of stroppy teenagers, I fell asleep, waking an hour later as the engine roared back to life.

With nothing but my reflection to view in the window, my memory of the next section of the journey is vague. I drifted in and out of sleep, my body craving rest, the bouncing coach fighting my efforts. We passed north of Frankfurt, to Schweinfurt, around Bayreuth and then to Weiden, just west of the Czechoslovak border, as the sun rose announcing a new morning.

My backside was numb, my legs and back ached, and my stomach growled its regular demands, but I had no complaints. Compared with my last trip across Germany, this had been luxurious. Before us lay the Iron Curtain, my dread mounting as to what awaited us beyond.

Chapter 7

With its long, intimidating name, I had always considered Czechoslovakia an exotic and mysterious country: a place visited in storybooks but too distant for a humble man such as I to visit. This was a view shared by my countrymen, explaining our general indifference when Chamberlain betrayed its good people at Munich in 1938. The war exposed both Chamberlain's naivety and my ignorance. In those chaotic days of 1940, I had heard of and seen the bravery of the exiled Czech infantry fighting beside us against the overwhelming German forces, and even when incarcerated, word filtered through of the exploits of their fighter pilots during the Battle of Britain. Yet, as we approached their border, a mysterious blanket once more enveloped the nation, and the elaborate defences on both the American and Czech sides deepened my foreboding.

"They're called Czech Hedgehogs," declared Mr Davies, polishing his round utility glasses and chuckling, as we crawled between the first line of American anti-tank obstacles and towards the formidable wall of barbed wire.

"Looks more like a prison camp," I muttered, unaware I clenched my fists around the seat's rim until pins and needles prompted their release. "Will they treat us well?" I shook my hands, pumping the blood back to the extremities.

"Everyone treats a well-presented group of young ladies right," declared Trenton-Harper, adjusting his own tie. "But things have not gone well for democracy in Czechoslovakia since war's end. Our timing could have been better. It's goodbye republic and Benes and hello the communists and Soviets. We can but hope they haven't forgotten their table manners."

As he whittled on about the Soviets and their Machiavellian ways, my mind drifted off, thinking of Jane and the family. The happiness I pushed away when home now burnt as a beacon calling me back. My guilt demanded payment, following me wherever I went, adapting to continue my torment. I fought it, finding sanctuary in a black void, and then I remembered why I had volunteered to join this half-baked scheme.

The Americans were as thorough as before with their checks, much to Trenton-Harper's annoyance, finally allowing us through into a stretch of no-man's-land, which led us to the next bank of unwelcoming barbed wire and machine guns, belonging to the Czechs.

This time, as the soldiers boarded the coach, they directed their guns at us, shouting incomprehensible words and motioning for us to get off.

"A Soviet tank," remarked Trenton-Harper as he stepped off to a welcome party of barking Alsatian dogs, pulling on their leads. "I had rather hoped for flowers and schnapps."

I followed him off, my eyes on the goliath, and its gun turret angled in our direction. We appeared to be an object of much curiosity. The border guards, wide-eyed youngsters, studied us, their numbers growing as the girls alighted. For a moment, nature won out over politics; shy smiles exchanged, compliments aired, and gun barrels lowered, before a senior officer growled an order at the top of his voice. The guns rose, the smiles vanished, and they herded us against a wall.

"Who is leader?" asked the officer in broken English.

Trenton-Harper stepped to the fore with his diplomatic grin, holding out a bundle of papers. "Mister Trenton-Harper MBE at your service." His offered hand remained unshaken; the papers were snatched from his grip. "Delighted to be visiting your country at the behest of His Majesty's government and your own, to build our cultural bonds through a mutual love of music. Do you have a particular favourite? Hadyn? Bach? Mozart? Dvorak?"

Only the last name triggered a reaction. I wouldn't describe it as a smile, that appeared beyond the poor fellow, but his eyes sparkled to life. "Anon, Dvorak. I like."

"The New World Symphony is my favourite," announced Trenton-Harper, patting his chest above the heart and humming a short section. An arm encircled his shoulder, and the officer guided him into a hut as though a long-lost comrade.

We remained standing, helpless, as the guards unloaded the instruments and bags from our transport, taking great delight as they rummaged through the girls' clothing.

"Mr Davies!" piped out Miss Henshaw. "Do something!"

The deputy head shrugged. "I find the man with the gun possesses the strongest argument, whatever his point of view."

His sound philosophy failed to placate the music teacher, whose jaw set firm. She stepped forward, ready to act herself.

"Och, ye donnae want tae do something foolish," I remarked, striding to block her path. "This is nawt some Walter Scott novel. The war created monsters of men."

"Well, really!" she complained. "And cowards of some, too, it appears."

I bit my tongue, confronted by the yelling complaints of the guards, unhappy at our disturbance. Encouraged by a snarling hound and raised rifle, Miss Henshaw complied as I guided her back to the wall. "We'll be moving on shortly and will ne'er have tae see them again."

Rather than answer, she directed her energy to the girls, encouraging an elegant poise in keeping with a proper British lady.

Trenton-Harper emerged twenty minutes later, his breath reeking of alcohol, shooing us lost souls back onto the coach. "The people of Czecho... Czechoshhloovakia welcome ush to their fine country," he declared with a drunk's finesse.

Once back in our seats, he collapsed forward, groaning.

"What's the matter?" I enquired with alarm.

"They're barbarians!" he whimpered. "Bloody barbarians!"

"What did they do tae ye?"

"Pumped me full of herbal schnapps. Don't light a match near me! I'll burst into flames. And then..." He released a despairing sigh. "Then, as they checked our papers, he played me Dvorak on the gramophone. I hate Dvorak!"

I tried not to laugh, but all that pent-up anxiety needed its release. "Ha, England expects that every man will do his duty."

His withering look only made me laugh harder.

And so, we were behind the Iron Curtain, heading east. The beautiful, wooded rolling hills soon destroyed my preconceptions of a soulless wasteland. Colourful villages lined our route, a mixture of wood-slated cottages with red or white framework and large houses from the imperial era, their painted facades and grandeur faded since the war but still impressive. On the occasional hilltop, a castle stood, glorious and dominant, its fierce military heritage tamed by neat and practical wooden roofs atop its towers. Those working in the fields wished us well, returning waves from the girls. It was different, but normal.

While engrossed with the view, Miss Henshaw shocked me as her head popped between the dozing Trenton-Harper and myself.

"The girls tell me we are being followed," she disclosed, looking at us over her glasses, nudging Trenton-Harper awake. "You don't suppose we left something behind at the border?"

"All crew accounted for," declared Trenton-Harper, rotating to face the music teacher with a playful, tipsy salute. "I suspect they are keen we don't get lost." As he turned back, he signalled to Walker, back in the seat opposite us.

The bodyguard shuffled from his seat, swaggering down the aisle to the back row. "Room for a little 'un?" he asked of the girls, squeezing in as they made space.

"What do ye really think?" I whispered to Trenton-Harper over the growling engine.

"They don't trust us, old boy. As simple as that. I'm hoping that by Poland they'll think of us as harmless."

Miss Henshaw's head popped through again. "Really, Mr Trenton-Harper. Your man now has Mildred on his knee. This just won't do!"

"Oh, my," chuckled Trenton-Harper, glancing back to where Walker frolicked with the schoolgirl. "A little light fun and no harm in it."

"She's 14!" exclaimed Henshaw.

"Ye donnae have a daughter?" I asked Trenton-Harper, my tone even.

"Not to my knowledge," he answered with a frown.

"Fathers donnae like others getting over-friendly with their wee bairns. So, get yer man oot of there and tell him tae leave the lasses alone!" I knew how to add malice to an order.

"I see," he said in surprise, his face turning red. "Walker!" He clicked his fingers, summoning his man back. "What did you see?"

"Yeah, we 'ave company," answered Walker. "Two men in a black car."

"Very good," said Trenton-Harper. "But less fraternising, if you don't mind. There's a good chap."

I heard Miss Henshaw fidgeting behind, no doubt like me, somewhat underwhelmed by Trenton-Harper's chastisement.

As we entered our first Czech city, Pilsen, Trenton-Harper declared we had permission to stop and stretch our legs, see the sights, and top up the engine with fuel, a privilege in that age of shortages. On the outskirts, tall industrial chimneys pumped out smoke, while I noticed the first scars from bomb damage. However, the city centre was a delight. Elegant four-storey houses, in a range of vibrant colours, with delicate, embossed decorations, lined each road, untouched by war. We disembarked in the large central square, rotating in awe as we marvelled at the churches with their dome-tipped towers, the burning orange roof tiles and baroque fountains. Had we stayed longer, we may have noticed the signs of decay, but, after twenty-four hours on the coach, no one cared.

Our presence drew attention. Locals stared, whispered between themselves, and inspected our transport. None approached us; a hint of fear or suspicion emanated from their faces.

"Flanagan and Allen are still with us," remarked Walker to his boss.

It took me a while to comprehend the reference to the two popular British comedians and singers until I followed Trenton-Harper's gaze. Our security tails, their car parked nearby, loitered on the edge of the square in conversation with a policeman, their eyes tracking our every movement.

"Extraordinary!" Davies, sidled up to me. "A young man has just asked if we can take him to England. At least, that's what I think he said."

"And what did ye say?" I asked, trying to spot this bold want-away amidst the crowd.

"Well, I said 'no', of course. He should buy a ticket for a coach service like everyone else."

"Hmm. I think they've suspended all services until further notice." My sarcasm got the blank look it deserved.

After a quick tour of a church, where locals dared approach seeking cigarettes and dollars, and a trip to the lavatory, we re-embarked on the coach, bidding a fond farewell to Pilsen.

With our tails back in their car and in our wake, the girls took to waving and blowing kisses through the back window, earning a sharp rebuke from Miss Henshaw.

Meanwhile, the landscape had changed. The hills flattened to a wide-open plain, trees replaced with fields, while strange eruptions of sandstone massifs with bold cliffs protruded, putting me in mind of Conan Doyle's *Lost World*.

However, it was Soviets I spied from the window rather than fanciful extinct beasts. Amid the military vehicles and soldiers bearing the Czech colours mingled those with the sickle and hammer, watchful and in control.

On we went, turning north to avoid Prague, until, after two more hours, the plain gave way to foothills and then forested mountains.

Trenton-Harper spread a map out on his lap, a finger gliding across the surface. He tapped a point. "Jablonec nad Nisou. Our first stop."

"Is it famous?" I asked, marvelling at the winding forest roads as our altitude increased.

"Not in the slightest," he answered, folding the map up. "But they have a theatre, will accommodate us, and we're not too far from the Polish border."

Chapter 8

And so, we arrived in this small mountain city in the middle of Europe, weary and in need of a bath. A reception party stood awaiting us at the town square, a local brass band murdering our national anthem at a slow tempo.

I struck a poor example of British vigour as I hobbled off the coach, stiff and crooked, after over twenty-four hours aboard. A portly man in a sombre suit greeted me with a flurry of incomprehensible words. He grasped my hand in his and shook for what felt an age. I smiled and quoted Rabbie Burns, for want of anything better to say. Meanwhile, girls in traditional embroidered dresses brought around a tray of shot glasses, their fiery contents enough to loosen the stiffest muscle. As the St Agnes girls dashed forward to claim their own sample, Miss Henshaw clucked in helpless outrage, unwilling to upset our hosts.

Trenton-Harper leaned towards me. "Mr Svoboda is the mayor," he explained, his eyes falling on our hand-shaker. "A communist, I suspect. Runs the local glass factories."

"Seems a friendly sort," I said, feeling the schnapps burn my empty stomach as I took in our surroundings. Steep cobbled roads linked the three-stepped levels of the city centre, each opening into a square surrounded by those familiar grand, ornate buildings. We stood outside a modern town hall, its tall brick clock tower lacking the grace of its older surroundings but with its own charm. The streets seemed in flux, their facades crumbling and in need of repair, the signs all new and building work everywhere.

"This was a predominantly German city," explained Davies, his head part-buried in a Czech guidebook. "Part of the Sudetenland. The ethnic Czech residents fled in-land in '38, then returned to kick most of the Germans out in '45. All looks so peaceful now."

To their credit, our hosts allowed us time to rest and refresh. We found ourselves at the local school, camp beds left over from the war set up in its hall, a simple curtain dividing us men from the girls and Miss Henshaw. A washroom was available, but, exhausted after our drive, we all crashed out on our beds, roused a few hours later by Mayor Svoboda, eager for us to ready ourselves for the show.

I showered, standing under the refreshing water for far too long, then undid the good work by re-dressing in my travel attire. People paid little attention to such things in those days; hardship and its odour were accepted with silent politeness. Our host, Mayor Svoboda, had his own unique fragrance of tobacco, soot, and sweat.

With visible pride, he and his small entourage led us down another steep hill, the girls lugging their instruments, past a splendid post office and to their theatre, which took my breath away: as grand as anything I've seen in London. Constructed in the art nouveau style in 1907 from enormous granite blocks with elaborate sculptural decoration - or so I read later - it was a thing of majesty. Mounted atop the facade, on either side of the entrance, sat bronze chariots, each pulled by two lions. I could see some girls hesitate, no doubt overawed, as a large crowd greeted us, the flags of Czechoslovakia, the USSR and Great Britain fluttering in their hands. In this mood of friendship, I wondered about our watchers, Flanagan and Allen, vanished from sight since our arrival in Jablonec.

The interior was as impressive, if not more so. Beautiful, locally made chandeliers hung from the auditorium ceiling, lighting the stucco walls with their paintings and gilding work. One girl burst into tears, overwhelmed at the prospect of playing in such a venue. I joined the others in turning in wonder, mouths ajar and eyes wide. Another round of schnapps awaited us adults before they led us up the stairs, the handrails adorned with an exquisite, pressed plant relief in sheet brass. Somehow, this journey behind the Iron Curtain felt less ominous when in the company of this cultural magnificence.

The girls and Miss Henshaw disappeared backstage to prepare, while Mayor Svoboda led us to our seats, the theatre filling with locals. It's strange, but I have little recollection of how we communicated with our hosts. They talked a lot, and we smiled and nodded. Trenton-Harper always seemed engaged in discussion, laughing, and back-slapping. Yet, we knew as little Czech as they knew English.

After the coach journey, sitting still was no simple task, but to my relief, the Jablonec school orchestra soon took to the stage, taking my mind off the discomfort. I recognised not one composition played but enjoyed it. It was a confident performance, showing a sophistication beyond their years, the lead violinist most accomplished and only 14. More accustomed to a brass band in a park, I clapped early and with vigour in appreciation of this high art, earning a frown from Trenton-Harper.

Despite my somewhat deceitful presence in their company, I felt a loyalty and attachment to St Agnes School, sharing some of their nerves as the girls set up on stage, preparing to showcase British musical prowess. Miss Henshaw fussed among them as they tuned their instruments, adjusting collars and dresses, before taking her place at the conductor's lectern. Anxiety coloured the start; notes half-formed, strings pressed too hard. But with the first movement completed, their confidence grew, and the audience nodded its appreciation as they tackled a simplified arrangement of Bach's Brandenburg Concerto with admirable aplomb. This time, Trenton-Harper joined me in clapping with a patriotic gusto as the girls stood and bowed at the end of their performance, Mayor Svoboda sending fulsome praise in our direction, or so his smile implied.

"Quite brilliant," whispered Trenton-Harper, leaning into me. "And no bloody Dvorak in sight!"

"It was," I agreed, fighting off a yawn. "I'm looking forward tae a good night's sleep."

"Of course," he said, rubbing his hands. "I hope the reception doesn't go on too late."

"Reception?"

"Did I not tell you?" He was already shaking hands with the Czech dignitaries as we climbed to our feet. "Receptions really: a short one for the girls and then one for us bigwigs. Don't forget to line your stomach!"

"Must I go? I'm nawt a bigwig."

"My good man, you are essential. We must cultivate a perfect sense of innocence." He continued to grin for the benefit of the dispersing audience, talking to me with the rigidity of a ventriloquist. "Those girls have laid our smokescreen, and we must continue the illusion: you the dedicated English teacher and I the dour Education Board official. They must learn to ignore us as insignificant nobodies, so that we might disappear and reappear with the ease of a magician."

My body complained, but I held my tongue, recognising we needed every advantage if we were to pull this off.

The girls rushed from the changing room, bursting with renewed energy, Miss Henshaw battling in vain to temper their exuberance. I congratulated every one of them, listening to the trivial performance dramas they felt compelled to tell me about, perhaps as a surrogate for their parents. Even Miss Henshaw glowed in their success, feigning a modest refusal for all the praise, as she wandered around seeking it.

A generous buffet awaited us all in the auditorium, the girls descending like vultures on the table of open sandwiches. I sniffed around the foreign fare, wary of what this unfamiliar food might do to my stomach, but conscious most suffered from shortages. A large local woman, mistaking my hesitancy for politeness, grabbed my elbow.

"Eat! Eat! Dobré jídlo" She led me forward, filling my plate with a range of sandwiches, pickles and cheeses.

"Thank ye," I said through an uneasy smile.

"A pivo!" she cried, herding me further along to a barrel. "Beer."

"Ah." I nodded my head in understanding, my smile more natural as she filled a tall glass with the amber fluid. "Ist gut," I said as I sampled the brew, hoping my choice of German wouldn't offend.

"Ja, sehr gut." She slapped me on my back and laughed.

"Mr Macleod."

I turned to find two St Agnes girls looking up at me.

"Er, Bridget," I said, recognising the girl from the ferry. "Is everything all right?"

"Cynthia's father was in a prison camp, too."

I assumed Cynthia stood before me. "Is that so?" I bent down until the girls' height. "Did ye miss him?"

A near indiscernible, shy nod answered me.

"He was captured in Singapore," continued Bridget on her friend's behalf. "The Japanese were very cruel."

"Aye." I had tried to avoid reading about the suffering of my fellow prisoners, but news of the barbarity meted out in the Far East was hard to avoid. "And how is yer father now?"

"Not well," said Cynthia, her eyes lowered to the floor.

"I'm sorry tae hear that."

"He's always grumpy and screams in the night," added Bridget, prompting Cynthia to lower her head still further. "My mum says Mrs Rowley said he's no longer the man she married."

I straightened, the air in my lungs intoxicated with a bubbling fear. Two large gulps of beer failed to ease the dread, a flush of light-headedness washing through me. "Yer daddy loves ye very much," I said, placing my quivering hand on Cynthia's shoulder. "He is the same man ye mother married, but he has tae find himself again. Do ye understand?"

Cynthia nodded without looking up.

"I want ye tae tell him ye love him, even when he's silly and grumpy. He may nawt deserve it, but it will give him a beacon tae follow, so he can escape and find himself again."

"Is that what your family did for you?" Cynthia looked up, her eyes moist with tears.

"I'm still lost maself," I replied with all honesty. "But I can see that beacon."

With no warning, she flung her arms round me, sobbing into my jacket, Bridget following with a show of support. I comforted both in a loose embrace.

"Mr Macleod!" Miss Henshaw appeared before me.

"The lasses are upset and missing home," I explained, tightening the hug. "As am I."

"Well, that's as may be, but there is a time and place for such behaviour, and this is not it." She glared at me over those spectacles. "What must our hosts be thinking?"

I released the girls, offering my handkerchief for the tears. "That we're human, just like them, and nawt the enemy."

"Bridget, Cynthia: straighten your clothes and hair!" Miss Henshaw brushed her hands down their dresses, tugging at the hem. "Get yourselves a squash, and no more tears."

Despite the disappointed glower Miss Henshaw cast my way as she hurried the girls away, I admired her protective and dedicated qualities towards her wards. The noxious panic had evaporated from my lungs; the hug was as therapeutic for me as for them.

In need of fresh air and a cigarette, I pushed open a side exit, grateful to feel the fresh mountain breeze. The sun had already dipped behind the mountains, bringing darkness to the empty streets. I checked my watch, surprised to find it so quiet at only six o'clock. As I lit my cigarette, the theatre door opened.

"Ah, great minds." It was Walker, followed by Crouch.

"Nice food and beer," said the former, "but all that 'obnobbing! Don't even like that music. Give me the music 'all any day."

I smiled out of politeness. "I thought the girls did us proud. It must be wonderful tae play an instrument so well."

"I'm more an opera man, myself," offered Crouch, surprising me by talking and his cultural appreciation.

The conversation tailed off, and we looked out into the darkness, puffing on our cigarettes, listening to the hubbub seeping from the theatre.

"So," began Walker, breaking the peace, "how much gold is there?"

I flicked my cigarette away. "Aboot 150 bars."

A familiar whistle greeted my answer. "That's a lot of money: millions! But you don't know where it is?"

"Nae. I waved goodbye tae the truck in the night. Ne'er saw it again."

Crouch spat and cleared his throat. "Boss says you met up with Hyde the next morning, so he couldn't have got far?"

"I suppose nawt."

"And the Germans searched high and low for you and the gold, finding nothing?" Crouch's pebble eyes flickered in thought.

"Aye."

"What you getting at, Crouchy?" pressed Walker.

"A truck's impossible to hide if you don't know the place, and one man, a wounded man, can't unload 150 bars of gold on his own. Someone must have helped him."

Such a thought had never crossed my mind, but it made perfect sense. Well, almost. "But he dinnae know anyone ootside the prison camp."

"You sure about that?" questioned Crouch. "Didn't you steal it with the help of the Poles?"

"Aye, but..." I scratched my head, recalling those tenuous friendships formed with locals on the work parties under the glare of the Nazis. "I just donnae think Hyde was the sociable type. We had nae time or the freedom tae..." I shrugged, my mind still ordering my thoughts. "He was a resourceful lad. Maybe he planned something withoot telling me."

"That sounds like ou..." Walker shook his head. "I mean, that sounds likely. Yeah, your boy had it all planned."

"So, think hard, Macleod," said Crouch. "It will make our lives a lot easier."

"Och, I dinnae know names. There was Antek. A fine lad, but he's dead. After all this time, I cannae even picture their faces." The war seared my memory, stuff I was trying to forget, but one sorry, downtrodden face among hundreds was impossible to recall. I had other concerns. "What if we find the gold? What then? They searched the coach at every checkpoint."

"Don't you worry about that," said Crouch in his gruff tone. "Just find it!"

"Yeah, Percy has that all sorted," added Walker.

"Percy?" I queried.

"Percival Trenton-Harper," clarified Walker with his best imitation of his boss's accent. "Smart man."

"Ye've worked with him before?" This odd, incompatible partnership intrigued me.

Crouch ignored the question, turning to stub out his cigarette on the granite of the theatre.

"We do all sorts for Percy," said Walker, adding a private snigger. "It's our unique skill set. That's what he tells us."

"Enough!" snapped Crouch, demonstrating his position in the hierarchy. "We don't want our absence noticed." With a tip of his head, he motioned for Walker to get back inside. He followed behind, turning to look me in the eye. "You think hard about what Hyde got up to and who he knew! I'm not leaving without the gold."

Menace flavoured those words, and I glanced to the heavens, cursing the bewitching power of the precious metal.

After an hour, the girls and Miss Henshaw departed, as did the children from the local school, leaving us 'bigwigs,' as Trenton-Harper put it. Mayor Svoboda regaled us with a speech, standing halfway up the stairs; a young female translated for our benefit. Trenton-Harper followed, his silver tongue praising our hosts, the city and the bond that is music. I focussed on the rather fine beer.

"I understand you English teacher?" The translator approached me at the end of the ceremonious activities. "'There is a tide in the affairs of men, which taken at the flood, leads on to fortune.'"

"Er, aye." It was impossible to hide my bemusement.

"Shakespeare," she clarified. "Julius Caesar."

"Och, aye. Shakespeare. Of course," I bluffed. "Yer accent caught me oot, lass. More of a Burns man."

It was her turn to look bemused.

"Rabbie Burns! Do they nawt teach ye the Bard of Ayrshire?" I shook my head in mock disgust. "'The best-laid schemes o' mice an' men, gang aft a-gley, and leave us nought but grief and pain, for promised joy.'"

"I not hear of this Burns," she answered through pained confusion. "Is not Shakespeare taught at your school?"

"Oh, aye. We like a bit of Shakespeare, but the laddie's overrated. Ne'er had to fight off a midge in his life!" I supped deeply of my beer, the alcohol loosening my tongue. "Now, Rabbie, he were a true poet. 'Some hae meat and canna eat, and some wad eat that want it. But we hae meat and we can eat, and sae the Lord be thankit.'" I raised my glass and laughed. The poor lass retreated.

By loitering at the beer keg, I aimed to build diplomatic bridges through my appreciation of their fine elixir; the locals sharing my enthusiasm for its consumption.

"Ah, Macleod. There you are."

I turned to find Mr Davies approaching with a companion in tow.

"There's someone I'd like you to meet," he declared. "I've just met my first Russian. This is Ivan."

I struggled not to empty a mouthful of beer down his front as the man offered me his hand. "Flanagan!" I spluttered. Or maybe it was Allen, but before me stood one of our tails.

"You are liking beer?" asked the Russian, ignoring my odd behaviour.

I shook his hand. "Aye."

"Ivan's been telling me about the local glass-making industry," explained Davies, oblivious to my unease. "Highest quality and world famous."

"Really?" I said, studying the Russian's face, sunken eyes set amid his broad Slavic cheekbones.

"Da, how you English say, tip-top." Ivan laughed.

"I'm Scottish."

"A Scottish English teacher," added Davies with his own peculiar titter.

"And what do ye do?" I asked, finding little humour in my nationality.

"Scottish English teacher," repeated Ivan before his face drained of levity. "I find enemies of revolution to punish."

Davies continued to laugh, the real world a stranger to his ivory tower in Hornchurch.

"But we here to celebrate music, da?" Ivan's joviality returned. He grabbed a shot of schnapps and cried, "Za zda-ró-vye!" Then swallowed it whole. "Blah! Russian vodka better."

"Ah, James. I see you've met Mr Kuznetsov." Trenton-Harper joined us, acknowledging the Russian with a polite bow. "Interesting fact for you: Ivan Kuznetsov is the Russian equivalent of John Smith."

The Russian shrugged. "Da, da. Very common name."

"And has he informed you," continued Trenton-Harper, "that he'll be joining us on the coach for the next leg of the journey? A cultural liaison, so to speak. I've said it won't be necessary, but he insists."

I almost fell over backwards in shock. "On the bus?"

Kuznetsov smirked. "For such important guests, ve make sure you not get lost. This vorld new and you long vay from home."

"I say," cheered Davies. "Wonderful news. You can teach me some Russian."

"Konečno, ty imperialističeskaja svin'ja." Ivan gripped Davies's shoulder, and they both laughed.

Trenton-Harper lifted his watch. "Goodness, is that the time? We've got a long journey ahead of us tomorrow and need our sleep. We'll see you tomorrow at twelve noon, Ivan. Don't be late. We wouldn't want you to miss the bus."

"I thought we left at 11 o'clock?" I whispered to Trenton-Harper as we strolled away.

"That we do, old chap," answered Trenton-Harper. "That we do."

Chapter 9

I tossed and turned throughout the night, my stomach a martyr to the drink, with Crouch's snoring enough to stir the dead. A hangover accompanied the morning light, and I waddled to the showers with a splitting headache. Once all had dressed, our hosts cleared the camp beds, replacing them with rows of long tables and benches, from which we ate a simple breakfast of rye bread and cheese. I picked at mine, trying to avoid the girls' affability, every cheery greeting stinging like a burst of light.

After breakfast, I found a quiet spot outside, rolling cigarettes in the company of birdsong. I passed an hour undisturbed, leaning against a large fir tree, letting the fresh air reinvigorate my sorry head. The tranquillity lulled me to sleep, only for distant voices to rouse me a short while later.

I scanned my surroundings, hunting the source, spotting two bodies in the shadows between buildings about 100 feet away. The odd English word carried, the others lost in the wind. I strained my eyes, making out Walker with one arm stretched forward, leaning on the structure before him, a smaller figure beneath, their back to the wall.

"The bawbag!" I growled, jumping to my feet, recognising the school uniform of a St Agnes girl on that mysterious figure. With my long legs, I strode forward, fists locked and ready to land a blow.

"Get away from her!" I cried, startling Walker, who stepped back. "What do ye think ye..." I turned the corner, able to see between the two buildings.

"Keep your bloody voice down!" It was Trenton-Harper, standing just to the side of the pair.

I looked around, checking no one else was in sight, and ducked down the alley. "What's going on?" I hissed. "Ye had better nawt have..." Again, I failed to complete my sentence, my eyes drawn to the girl. "Who the hell are ye?"

"This is Monika," announced Trenton-Harper with a heavy sigh. "She'll be joining us from here on in."

"Er, how do ye do," I said, touching my cap, flummoxed at the unfamiliar face.

"Doesn't speak a word of English," continued Trenton-Harper. "How's your German?"

"What's going on?" I demanded.

"Long story," said Trenton-Harper with a disinterested sniff. "Gist is, father's a German physicist now working for the Americans, mother's a Czech and dead. We don't want the Soviets exploiting the situation, so we're reuniting a family. Now, we've got her this far and don't need your big boots messing things up. So, play along like a good chap."

My jaw dropped. "Nawt only are we smuggling gold oot, but a refugee too, and with a Soviet agent in tow. Why donnae we knock off Stalin while we're here? Ye've had this planned all along!"

"It's 'need to know', old boy. That's how we run things, and you didn't need to know. Are you going to be a problem, because you're upsetting the girl?"

I turned to Monika, whose wide brown eyes flitted between us in fear. "And what aboot her papers?" My tone calmed for her benefit.

Trenton-Harper tapped a pocket. "A passport for one Monika Smith."

"Och, ye spies are so imaginative. And what's the story for the others? Won't they be a wee bit surprised tae discover a new classmate speaking only German?"

"Just find us the gold," said Trenton-Harper, a grin back on his face. "Leave the rest to me."

I rolled my eyes. "This I have tae see!"

***

There is a photograph in existence, perhaps in the school archives, of the St Agnes girls standing before their coach in the grounds of Jablonec school, Mayor Svoboda occupying the centre, Mr Davies and Miss Henshaw either side and an awkward yours truly towering behind. Trenton-Harper is in there somewhere, hiding his face with a movement timed to perfection. If you look closely, you will find one stone-faced girl among the beaming smiles of her classmates: that is Monika.

To the Czechs, she was just another English schoolgirl. Did they have a moment of doubt, questioning how twenty-two girls became twenty-three, before dismissing such ridiculous thoughts and placing her at the back of the orchestra, behind a cello? I don't know. But Trenton-Harper earned his money when he hoodwinked those from his own country.

"A little surprise for you all," he announced before they gathered for their photo. "I'd like to introduce you to Monika." Walker manhandled the reluctant girl forward into Trenton-Harper's grip.

"Monika is a local girl who will join us for the rest of the trip as an exchange student."

The news stirred excitable chatter among the girls, all eager to befriend this exotic newcomer. Mr Davies raised an eyebrow in surprise, while Miss Henshaw's mouth opened, ready to complain, only to find Trenton-Harper had more to say.

"The Nazis killed both her parents, so Monika is alone in this world. She doesn't speak our language, but I know you will make her part of the St Agnes family, giving her the love she misses as an orphan. Do practice your German with her and teach her some English, but…" He lowered his voice. "Don't mention the war or her parents. Not the done thing, eh?"

Miss Henshaw closed her mouth, a matriarchal sympathy replacing her outrage, as the girls surged forward, surrounding the terrified Monika and bombarding her with questions she had no chance of understanding. Trenton-Harper emerged from the crush, winking in my direction.

***

There was a mixed mood at 11 o'clock as we prepared to depart. It had been an intense last twenty-four hours, but wonderful. Genuine sorrow existed as we bid farewell to our hosts, whom we now considered our friends. We toasted to friendship with a last round of schnapps, Miss Henshaw urging a reciprocal visit to the United Kingdom, which, to my knowledge, never happened. I failed to escape a hug from Mayor Svoboda, but left him with another quote from

Rabbie, seeding what I hoped was a lasting appreciation for the bard in Czechoslovakia.

Miss Henshaw insisted Monika sit beside her on the coach, thus settling the fight among the girls for the honour and surprising us by engaging with the newcomer in a flurry of German, much to Trenton-Harper's discomfort and my amusement. As Crouch started the engine, the girls gravitated to one side of the coach, waving to the crowd through the window.

"Where's Mr Davies?" cried one.

"We can't leave without him!"

Trenton-Harper glanced at his watch. "Where's he got to?" he grumbled. "Walker, find him! There's a good chap."

"Here he comes!" someone shouted before Walker had time to leave his seat. "He has someone with him."

I craned my neck, spotting Davies receiving a fond farewell as he pushed through the crowd of Czechs.

"Damn," cursed Trenton-Harper. "It's that bloody Russian!"

"Language!" chided Miss Henshaw, trying herself to spot who followed in Davies's wake.

"Sorry, I'm late," said a breathless Davies as he climbed the coach stairs. "I had the good fortune to bump into Mr Kuznetsov on my morning constitutional. There was some miscommunication on timings, and we had to rush back to his apartment to collect his things, or he'd have missed our departure." He emitted an odd, high-pitched laugh, pushing his glasses back up his nose. "I don't think there's another bus along for a while."

"That was a bit of luck," said Trenton-Harper through gritted teeth, as Kuznetsov followed Davies aboard, a small suitcase in hand.

"Good day," said the Russian, removing his black fiddler cap, bowing his head left and right.

Miss Henshaw leaned forward. "Who is he?"

"Ladies," began Trenton-Harper, climbing to his feet. "Can I introduce you to Mr Kuznetsov, a cultural liaison from the USSR. We will have the pleasure of his company on our journey to Toruń." He brushed past me, into the aisle. "Now, I think it would be of benefit if Mr Davies sat with Mr Kuznetsov amid the girls. He won't find much culture among us old fogeys." This got the laugh Trenton-Harper sought. He waved at two girls occupying a seat towards the rear. "Margaret, Edith. You move forward and let the men take your place. That's right, come on!"

With reluctance, the girls moved forward.

"Jolly good idea," declared Davies, as he led the Russian in the opposite direction.

Trenton-Harper retook his seat, leaning his head back into the orbit of Miss Henshaw's hearing. "The Soviets shot Monika's beloved pet dog, so best keep her clear of our new guest." With that gross lie delivered, he folded his arms, ignoring the whimper from the music teacher. "Come on, Crouch! Let's get moving."

And so, we departed Jablonec nad Nisou, heading east, higher into the mountains, soon reminded of the discomfort of coach travel on the crumbling roads. Spectacular views greeted us on the winding route, but a tired malaise soon returned as our traveller aches and sores resurfaced. We crossed the border at Harrachov, Trenton-Harper's mood lightened by Kuznetsov smoothing our passage with a show of Soviet authority. Poland lay before us.

Chapter 10

Yes, Poland lay before us, but a few years hence, it was German territory. The Allied post-war settlement pushed Poland westward, up to the banks of the Oder. As such, the landscape carried the scars of a defeated nation, a new Polish population, wearing their own war scars, moving in with their brooms.

Our first stop was the city of Wroclaw. Unlike its Czech counterparts, there was little left from the pre-war period. Construction competed with destruction. Between the ruins and bulldozers, new buildings arose, growing within fragile scaffolding, shirtless labourers scurrying back and forth in the sun.

We alighted, stretching our limbs, then collapsed on the grass verge, enjoying the warming sun.

Kuznetsov remained standing, hands on hips. "You see progress under Soviet leadership?" he asked of his disinterested audience, pointing out the complete buildings. "Vorkers create future before us. In summer vorld visit city for great event for peace. Last year, no city exist. Da, Soviet progress."

"I've always had the utmost respect for the Poles," responded Trenton-Harper, fiddling with his pipe. "Hard workers and hard fighters. Forever trying to get rid of an occupier, though. Rotten luck, don't you think?"

"Da, but now liberated from foreign and class oppressors."

"Well, that's a bit of luck," declared Trenton-Harper, blowing out a waft of smoke. "I hope you chaps have told them."

"I must find phone," announced the Russian. "Arthur, you join me?"

Davies sat up. "A walk will do me good. Anyone else?"

Before others could answer, Miss Henshaw spoke. "The girls will not be wandering around a building site."

"Quite right," responded Davies, pulling himself up with the aid of Kuznetsov. "Which way?"

Without hesitation, Kuznetsov pointed north. "You not go vithout us." He smiled at Trenton-Harper.

"Heaven forbid, old boy."

We watched them trudge along the dusty road, locked in conversation.

"They appear inseparable," I remarked. "Do ye think Davies has any idea who his friend is?"

"Not a dickie-bird. Nothing between the ears of that one," answered Trenton-Harper. "But our Soviet parasite knows exactly who Davies is: a stooge and his hostage. Won't let him off the leash in case we scarper."

"Is it wise tae antagonise him?" I bit into the bread roll gifted to us for the journey by our Czech friends.

"Antagonise? Don't know what you mean, old boy." Trenton-Harper caught the attention of Crouch, beckoning him over. "But we must use these moments alone to our advantage.

"Ah, Crouch. What's our next city? Show us the map."

"Poznan," answered Crouch, fighting the wind as he spread the map on the ground. "About four hours away if the roads are any good."

"Hmm," pondered Trenton-Harper. "I have a contact to meet there. He'll make things easier for us when we get to Toruń." His head rotated to look at me.

"What?" I was beginning to dislike the man.

"I'll need to disappear for a while. Can't let our babysitter get suspicious." Trenton-Harper jabbed his pipe at my chest. "You must occupy Kuznetsov. Let him think he has another stooge, but you'll hold the leash."

"Och, nae. I'm a gardener, nawt a spy. What aboot Walker or Crouch?"

Trenton-Harper frowned. "And why would coach drivers take an interest in a passenger? No, absolutely not. Has to be you. Teachers are a bolshie, idealistic bunch. Far more plausible."

I was about to put a stop to this nonsense when a shadow fell across the map. It was Miss Henshaw.

"Monika tells me she left her dog with her grandmother. Alive and well."

Trenton-Harper took his time folding up the map. I could almost hear the cogs working on his next lie. He climbed to his feet, his face sombre.

"I had hoped to save you from the detail," he said, releasing a long, exaggerated breath. "The Soviets did unspeakable things to women in their conquered territory."

"Unspeakable?" questioned Miss Henshaw, folding her arms.

"Like with Jacob's daughter, Dinah, in Genesis," explained Trenton-Harper, forcing a gasp from Miss Henshaw. "Trauma will often make a person build an alternative memory. What poor Monika witnessed or suffered on that day, I don't know. But perhaps best we let her believe her dog's alive and... Well, need I say more?"

The blood drained from the music teacher's face. "Oh, my poor babe." She fled back to the sanctuary of her wards.

"Ye're a bastard!" I snarled.

"Guilty as charged," responded Trenton-Harper with that annoying grin.

***

Davies and Kuznetsov returned half an hour later, dropped off by a black sedan driven by 'Allen'.

"Enjoy yer walk?" I asked the deputy head as he wiped his forehead with a handkerchief.

"A most peculiar affair," he answered. "We ended up at a police station. They were jolly nice but, well, they asked a lot of questions."

"Aboot what?"

"Oh, the usual things: where I was born, my family, my school, where I trained. But it was all rather intense and..." He scratched his chin.

"Ivan had already asked you all those questions on the coach." It was a classic technique for sniffing out a lie.

"That's right. Is it a Russian thing?"

I sniffed in amusement. "Ye could say that. Be careful, yer new friend is nae ordinary policeman."

"I'm starting to realise that." Davies blew his nose. "There was screaming. They pretended it came from outside, but I'm not so sure. I've been a little naive. My first time away from England, you know?"

"Donnae worry," I reassured him. "Friendliness is nae crime, though often used by the wicked tae open doors too."

"What should I do?" pressed Davies with imploring eyes. "I can't just ignore him for the rest of the journey."

I cursed Trenton-Harper under my breath as I uttered my answer. "Ye sit up front for a bit. I'll share the seat with Ivan. Otherwise, just act yer friendly self."

"That's awfully good of you." Davies grabbed my unsuspecting hand and shook it. "You know these foreigners so much better than I."

Putting the innocent fool within Trenton-Harper's grasp felt just as dangerous, but he was a grown man and I no nursemaid.

I clocked Trenton-Harper's smug grin as Davies claimed my old place on the coach with an apologetic explanation. Kuznetsov gave nothing away when I appeared by his side.

"Ah, the Scot," he said. "Ramsay MacDonald."

That I had not been expecting. "Er, what aboot him?"

"Another Scot, nyet?"

"Aye, there are a fair few of us. Prime ministers and bottle-washers." Amid the girls, it was necessary to raise my voice.

"And yet you teach in English school, in English language?"

This I had been expecting. "There's nae work at home."

The Russian tutted, leaving the lure in the water, awaiting me to bite.

"What?" I bit.

"Your people oppressed by English imperial masters. Is this not so?"

I decided he would have to work for his conversion. "We fought shoulder tae shoulder in the war: as brothers."

"Da, that is so. Ve all brothers in war. Vhere you soldier?"

"The Germans captured me in France and held me in Poland." The truth was the best camouflage for my deception as James Macleod. "Five years."

"A prisoner." Kuznetsov spoke the word with deliberate caution, as though uncomfortable in his mouth.

"I met some Russians in the camp. They were nawt treated well. I often wonder what happened tae them. What aboot ye?"

"My brother, Mikel, he prisoner." For the first time, Kuznetsov's eyes lost their zealous fervour. He turned to look out the window.

"Is he home now?"

He turned back with a cold, emotionless glaze. "He gone. Ve not celebrate failure like you. He betray revolution."

"Mr Macleod is a hero." Bridget, occupying the seat in front, appeared kneeling before us with her prim demeanour. "He deserves a medal, like my father."

"Thank ye, Bridget," I said, regretting further my behaviour on the ferry.

"Your brother too," she added, tilting her head in sympathy in Kuznetsov's direction.

"For medal he die in fight, not give up. That Soviet vay."

"Well, that's just silly," articulated Bridget with almost the same words that floated in my head. "We're humans, not lemmings. Mr Macleod wouldn't be here to help, would he? Don't you miss your brother?"

Kuznetsov's face quivered, I feared from rage, though perhaps from loss.

"Bridget Archer!" Miss Henshaw's piercing voice reached us. "Sit properly and leave the adults alone!"

The girl huffed, her bottom lip protruding in protest. "I thought you wanted us to engage," she mumbled to herself, slinking back to face forward.

"We have different ways," I said to the Russian, receiving a curt nod in answer, and we continued on our journey in silence.

I failed to pay attention to the landscape, my eyes closed, listening to the trivial and obscure conversations of the girls. They talked of music, of home, of boys, of dancing, of friendships. This was the future I wished for my Jean. Not war, dictators and suffering.

An hour later, with my mind content in absent thoughts, a faint bang alarmed us all. The coach veered right, rocking and shuddering, triggering screams. I heard Crouch curse before he gained control, bringing the vehicle to a stop, its nose off the road at a sharp angle.

"It's a flat tyre," yelled Trenton-Harper, straightening his fringe with a flamboyant sweep of his hand, trying to bring order. "Nothing to worry about." He waited for the girls to calm down. "A good time for a break and stretch of our legs, eh? We can watch Mr Crouch and Walker fix the tyre."

"Our first one," I remarked, amid the grumbling complaints as we alighted. "That's nawt bad on these roads."

The mountains had vanished, the land less dramatic and flat, with deciduous trees stretching out on either side of the road.

"There's a man," I heard a girl call out.

Indeed, there was. An elderly man sat on a tree stump, his bicycle resting against another tree. He watched us with mild curiosity, a bread roll occupying his mouth.

"Hello." I removed my cap, waving a greeting, while a group of the girls hovered behind me, a sudden attack of shyness afflicting them. It was hard to tell if he acknowledged us, perhaps a tip of his head or a word uttered amid his chewing.

"Argh, this is going to take a while," growled Crouch behind us, as he kicked the shredded tyre with his boot.

His companion, Walker, circled the bus, checking the other tyres with his own size tens. "Just the one. I'll get the spare."

"Who's our friend?" asked Trenton-Harper, wandering over.

"He peasant," remarked Kuznetsov, inspecting the man with typical scrutiny and suspicion.

Trenton-Harper sniffed, reluctant to engage with the Soviet. "Perhaps you can ask him where we are?"

The conversation took place within our earshot but meant little to me. A sharp tone from Kuznetsov stirred the old man to his feet, his eyes remaining languid. I noticed his legs bowed inward, reminding me of the waifs from the poorer parts of London and Glasgow.

"I only wanted to know where we were," complained Trenton-Harper. "Not have a bloody recital of *War and Peace*!"

After a few minutes, an exasperated Kuznetsov finished with a flurry of "nyets", which even I understood, but the Pole appeared intent on ignoring.

"A stupid peasant!" declared Kuznetsov, returning to us. "I tell him you play music, now…" He shrugged his shoulders, lifting his hands in frustration.

The old man rummaged in a box tied to his bicycle, pulling out a squeezebox. He smiled, feeding his hands through the straps, pulling the bellows apart. A slow drone threatened dissonance, only for a melody to emerge as his fingers danced between the keys and he worked the bellows back and forth.

A circle formed around him, the girls an appreciative audience, ignorant of the huffing and cursing from Crouch and Walker in the background. From a melancholy start, the song burst into life, the old man singing in a low baritone voice.

"I'll get my violin," cried Mildred, dashing back to the coach.

Others followed, stopped by Miss Henshaw's call. "We only need one, thank you!"

On sight of the string instrument, the old man nodded with enthusiasm, urging Mildred forward. The other girls clapped to a rhythm, creating quite the atmosphere. Even I tapped my foot.

Mildred found the key, accompanying the tune, but it somehow fell flat, unable to complement the energy from the squeezebox. The old man slowed the pace, encouraging his pupil to find her place, but a creative divide remained.

Then, to everyone's surprise, Monika stepped forward, her hands outstretched. Mildred continued playing, confused by the interruption.

"Let Monika borrow your violin," instructed Miss Henshaw. "I think she wants to play."

With reluctance, Mildred handed it across, stepping back into the watching crowd, her folded arms suggesting resentment. But she soon joined us all in wide-eyed wonder as Monika worked the bow with a practised fury, delivering a vibrant duet with the old man. We clapped and stamped our feet, some girls dancing, thriving off the energy, exhausting ourselves and cheering wildly as they finished on a crescendo. What a sight for any passer-by, but we were alone.

"So, he doesn't know where we are?" asked Trenton-Harper, somehow immune to the music.

"On road to Poznan," confirmed Kuznetsov, his face as unmoved as his counterpart's.

Not for the first time, Monika found herself swamped by her new classmates, this time enjoying the camaraderie. Music again a bridge across the language divide.

Miss Henshaw clapped in her unique style, hands at right angles held to the side of her head, one patting the other with vigour. "Sehr gut, mein Engel."

As for the old man, he took the acclaim without fuss, packing away his instrument in its box, reclaiming his spot back on the tree stump.

"Dziękuję," I said, exhausting the Polish vocabulary I learned during the war, and offered him a cigarette.

He took it, sniffed the tobacco, and nodded. I can't tell you his name, for he never uttered it.

Crouch and Walker shuffled across, covered in sweat and grease, bemoaning their experience, begrudging us ours.

"We're done," said Walker, wiping a sleeve across his brow. "It were a bugger. Could have done with some help."

"Stop complaining," snapped Trenton-Harper. "Get yourselves cleaned up! What must the ladies be thinking?"

Back on the road, I found Kuznetsov once more in a talkative frame of mind.

"He soldier in 1914 imperial var," he remarked.

"The old man?" I asked, knowing the answer. "With those legs! What else did he say?"

"Nothing." The Russian snorted. "I ask if he fight in 1919 var. He say 'nyet,' but I not trust these people."

I did not know of this war, so let the matter rest, and sought to change the subject. "He was a fine musician."

"Hmm, as is girl." Kuznetsov jabbed a finger in Monika's direction. "How she learn music of this land?"

"Well..."

"She talk in German," continued Kuznetsov, his eyes narrowing in thought. "Who she?"

"Ah," I answered, scrambling to construct a plausible story. "She's a Swiss lass. Well, British father, Swiss mother, but was stuck in the cantons during the war. They've sent her tae Hornchurch tae improve her English. More talented in the music department, if I'm honest."

"Sviss, you say?"

The lines on his brow convinced me I had more work to do. "Aye, popular girl. I think the father's a diplomat. Travelled a fair bit. Must have developed a good ear for folk music. Have ye ever been tae a ceilidh?"

"I not know this vord."

"Och, ye poor lad. It's a party with music and dancing. Oh, and a wee drop of whisky. Ye've heard of whisky?"

"Da, da. My people like to sing, dance and drink!" He slapped my shoulder, laughing, then withdrew a flask from his inner pocket. "Drink!" he instructed.

I laughed too, relieved my inner Trenton-Harper had spun such a convincing web of deceit, and sniffed the open flask. The vapours already burnt, but I sipped it all the same. "Slainte Mhath."

Chapter 11

A light drizzle greeted us as we arrived in Poznan a few hours later, though I doubt even the sun would have brightened its appearance. The site of a pivotal battle, as the Germans tried in vain to hold their line against the unstoppable Soviets, the city was a monument to the power of modern artillery: any wall left standing bore the scar of a shell impact. As in Wroclaw, new buildings rose amid the ruins, but the scale of destruction was immense. Within the heart of the old city, Greco-style columns hung before a gutted interior, hinting at its lost beauty, while the once impressive medieval town hall tottered as a sorry carcass.

We parked by the river, its banks free from buildings and overgrown with grass. A collapsed bridge stirred up the flow, boys sitting on its tilting, near-submerged framework with their fishing rods.

"Do ye need tae report in?" I asked Kuznetsov, as I undertook a regular stretching routine in the shadow of our coach, much to the amusement of the locals.

He shook his head, more intent on inspecting the building work across the river.

"I might take a walk along the river," I suggested. "Join me. It'll do yer legs good."

"Nyet." He wandered over to the river's edge, reclining on the grass.

Urged on by Trenton-Harper, I tried again. "Do they have such a thing as a pub?"

"Pub?" questioned Kuznetsov.

"Aye, an inn, a drinking house. I fancy a quick beer. Is Polish beer any good?"

"Blah." He dismissed my suggestion with a flick of his wrist. "How you say, the piss of horse."

How does one reply to that? I retreated under the glare of Trenton-Harper, who whispered in Walker's ear.

"I'll go for a walk with you." It was Davies, keeping his distance from Kuznetsov. "Be nice to find a pub with a garden."

I was in a hole, struggling to think of an excuse to avoid my suggestion, when I noticed Walker amble towards the riverbank. A group of the girls loitered on the grass, throwing pebbles and daisies into the water, as though a lazy Sunday afternoon by the Thames. The bodyguard paused, glanced backward, and then, his head still turned, moved quickly onward, bumping the rear of a girl. She staggered forward to the edge of the bank, swaying on the lip, a four-yard drop below her into the river. Walker cried an apology, reaching out a hand in support but, as their fingers connected, the only help he seemed to offer was to speed her fall backwards. With terror in her eyes, she crashed into the water. The splash triggered a chorus of screams as her friends rushed to the edge.

The world slowed as it does in moments of great drama. Images of flailing arms amid the choppy water, of the current pulling the girl from the side, and of others exchanging panicked looks with cries for help and of despair, arrived in my mind all at once.

"I can't swim!" yelled Walker, directing his confession at Kuznetsov, imploring for his help with open hands. He turned to the school party. "Keep back from the edge, girls. We don't want to lose another."

I stepped forward only to find Crouch's hand placed on my chest. "What the…"

"Stay!" he commanded.

It was then I realised this was no accident but a Plan B: a contemptible plot of distraction. I fired a glance to my right, seeking Trenton-Harper. He had already utilised this crisis to vanish for his secret rendezvous.

Splash!

I swung around. The water erupted, penetrated by a diving body. Moments later, Davies's head popped up, spitting out a mouthful of water. He flapped his arms, rotating his head, trying to locate the girl. Only when he spotted her and attempted to swim across the current was it clear he too was in trouble. The fool had jumped in wearing his boots and woollen jacket.

Meanwhile, Kuznetsov remained watching, reclined on one elbow, a cigarette held between two fingers. He showed no concern and no pleasure. I mention the latter as I have witnessed the voyeurs of suffering, but our Russian appeared devoid of emotion, a mere observer.

I could take no more. "Oot of ma way!" I shoved Crouch to the ground, hopping forward while I dislodged one boot and then the other. Before I reached the grass, I flung my tweed jacket backwards and soon I flew forwards.

Splash!

I don't remember the cold or the darkness as I submerged, but I remember a second of indecision. Davies already lay within reach and rescue, his head just above the surface.

"Can ye hang on?" I shouted.

"Save Edith!" he spluttered.

I knew then Davies was worth saving but would have to wait his turn. All I could offer was advice. "Try tae get yer boots off!"

With the churning water, it was impossible to spot the drifting Edith, so I turned to the bank, using the frantic pointing of the growing crowd to guide me. I felt the tug of the current and prayed the strength to overcome it lay within me. Strange things cross your mind in those moments. A memory of my last swim popped up, a spontaneous affair among my unit in France, 1940, as we rested after a morning of digging defences. I cannot remember the river, just the relief and laughter as its cooling waters refreshed our tired muscles. The recollection charged me with a youthful spirit, and I cut through the water, Edith in sight but her energy fading. Her head vanished beneath the surface, one hand breaking through, fighting for life.

"Donnae struggle!" I cried, hoping my voice carried. "Float on yer back."

She resurfaced, gasping for breath, and then disappeared again.

Still a few strokes away, I dived under, blind in that murky water, banking on lady luck. And that mistress - whom I still can't decide whether she deserted me or saw me through the war – came to my rescue. My hand bumped against the soft torso of Edith. Instinctively, I gripped her blouse, tugging it towards me, gathering her in my arms, as I kicked for the surface. I rolled onto my back, opened my eyes and drew in a deep breath, my precious load limp on top of me.

That rediscovered youthful spirit soon faded, unable to ignore five years of starvation and inactivity, and sapped by the cold. I used the current, only kicking to angle my body toward the collapsed bridge and the point where the snapped road, at a forty-five-degree angle, vanished under lapping waves. Two Polish boys, their fishing rods discarded, climbed along the iron framework, hands at the ready to catch me. Soon they were out of my vision as I drifted backwards, trying to gauge the distance to the bridge. I gambled, stretching an arm behind my head, listening to the boys' shouts and wondering if they carried helpful advice. Something yanked my arm, and I twisted around in the water until sideways against the bridge. Two youthful faces stared down at me.

"Take the girl!" I urged, fighting the surging water, knowing they wouldn't understand.

But they had sense enough to do the right thing. I had found a hold on a rusting girder, allowing me to use my other hand to push Edith towards them, while they pulled on her arms. She offered no help, her body still lifeless. The boys struggled just to hold her above water, lacking the strength to lift her out.

"Out of the way!" Walker's face appeared. Having slid down the bridge's road, he loomed above the boys. Reaching past one, he gripped Edith's wrist, pulling her up, while the boys assisted with some pushing.

"Donnae forget me," I called through chattering teeth, as Walker struggled back up the slope with the girl over his shoulder.

They didn't forget. Two adult Poles appeared moments later and, with plenty of groans and cursing, lifted me to safety.

Back on dry land, I sank to my knees, exhausted and frozen, thanking my own rescuers. But there was still Davies to rescue, while Edith's life remained in the balance.

"James, you did it!"

I looked up, still not used to my borrowed name. A sodden Davies shivered, his boots missing, a soppy beam on his face. "Ye made it," I gasped.

"Thanks to you," he said, offering me a hand to get to my feet. "I wasn't thinking. Too focussed on drowning. Once I followed your advice, I swam to the side, and Walker pulled me up. I owe you both my life."

"Hmm." I was in no mood to beatify Walker. "Where's the lass?"

A crowd of people surrounded Edith, her body spread on the grass. The girls of St Agnes sobbed, unable to look, comforting each other by the coach.

I heard Miss Henshaw's quivering voice as I barged through the bodies. "I'll try one more time." She slapped Edith's face, hoping to stir her back to life. The girl's ghostly features failed to rouse, and the music teacher collapsed with a wail.

A sickening despair absorbed me, and I collapsed back onto my knees.

"I assist." Kuznetsov's level voice cut through the air, as the crowd parted for him. He knelt by Edith's side, pumping down on her chest with his locked hands. After several thrusts, he stopped, putting his mouth to hers and blowing. He repeated the process three times until Edith spluttered to life, coughing up a lungful of water and breathing. Kuznetsov rolled her onto her side, stood and ambled off with an indifferent air.

As Miss Henshaw smothered Edith with tender care, I staggered after the Russian.

"Ye're a miracle worker," I declared. "But why dinnae ye help her in the water? Cannae ye swim?"

He drew on a cigarette. "I svim, da, but girl not my..." He waggled his cigarette, seeking the word. "Not my problem. You teacher: your problem, da."

"But ye then saved her life?" I pressed, confused by his motives and behaviour.

"Pah, a simple technique." Kuznetsov tilted his head back and blew a lungful of smoke upwards, as though relaxing at day's end. "Useful vhen question prisoner. Dead suspect not answer."

I frowned, not understanding him.

He saw my confusion and laughed. "Ha, maybe one day I question you."

Five minutes later, Trenton-Harper strolled back down the road, a spring in his step and that grin on his face. "I say, what's been going on here? Looks like there's been some drama. Is everyone all right?"

I fought the urge to push him into the river. The girls had suffered enough and didn't deserve further drama.

"There was an accident," announced Miss Henshaw. "Poor Edith fell in the river; almost drowned. Mr Macleod and Kuznetsov saved her."

"Oh dear," answered Trenton-Harper, concern etched across his face. "And how is she now?"

"Recovering on the coach, but very upset." Miss Henshaw shivered in recollection. "As are we all. She should see a doctor, but Mr Kuznetsov says it won't be necessary."

"I'm not sure we would find a doctor," remarked Trenton-Harper, shaking his head. "This place has little more than builders and soldiers." His eyes then fell on me. "You should get out of those wet clothes, old chap. Don't want you catching your death. Same for old Ivan, I suppose."

"He's nawt wet," I said, my voice as frosty as I could make it. "Left the swimming to me!"

"I see," replied Trenton-Harper, digesting the news. "Oh, well. All's well that ends well. I had a most satisfactory walk. Now, if you'll excuse me, I need a word with our drivers about the next leg."

With that, he hurried away, summoning Walker and Crouch with a sharp command, leaving me to steam in anger.

"I'm not sure it's wise to continue our tour," remarked Miss Henshaw, close to tears.

"Aye, this is nawt the place for yer girls," I agreed. Something I had always known. "But we donnae have a choice. Yer man there won't allow it and neither will our hosts."

"The show must go on," she sighed, her fragile smile disintegrating as she burst into tears and threw her arms round me. "Thank you for rescuing Edith."

"Er, donnae mention it." I said, presuming this was an appropriate time and place for a hug. "Perhaps I should change ma clothes."

She stepped back, drying her eyes, adjusting her hair. "Of course. You're a good man, Mr Macleod."

I found my spare trousers and a jumper in my holdall, hiding behind a bush to change. As warmth returned to my body, my anger grew. I recognised the same blind rage that consumes me in the peace of my Kentish garden. There, I had no excuse or target, the outlet for the intolerable bubble of pressure, an escape to the pub; here I had cause and knew the guilty. My fury stumbled at the sight of Trenton-Harper surrounded by the girls, but Crouch had the misfortune of passing me. Though stocky, my height gave me the advantage over our driver as I grabbed him by his collar.

"Ye've got a nerve," I growled. "How dare ye put that girl's life in danger!"

Crouch's eyes remained docile, as though assault was an everyday occurrence. "Let me go, you Scottish prick." Even his voice remained calm, though not without threat.

I clung tight. "Ye think I'm helping ye find the gold after that, ye English diddy."

"Look about," he urged. "Do you see all the men dotted around in those grey trench coats?"

It's strange how you only see things when looking for them. Along the riverbank, eight men, adorned in identical coats, blended in with the other onlookers. "Aye, one of them helped me oot the river."

"They're the secret police. Working for our Russian friend. Been watching us since our arrival. Had you got Kuznetsov out of the way, some would have followed you and the girls could have distracted the others. But we had to resort to something dramatic to focus their attention. Didn't realise Kuznetsov was such an unfeeling bastard. He was supposed to dive in and save her before she drifted from the edge."

I released his collar, pushing him away. "Donnae use the girls again! Ye want tae risk someone's life, risk yer own."

"The best way we keep these girls safe is completing our mission," said Crouch, straightening his jacket. "You've no idea how dangerous these people are. They're rounding up anyone who poses a threat to the government. We give the game away and it's a bullet, if we're lucky. Then what will happen to the girls?"

"Shouldnae have got them involved in the first place, should ye?"

"We're just soldiers following orders, not the generals." With that, Crouch stormed off, muttering under his breath.

Again, I counted our watchers, noting the casual glances in our direction, and wondered what sort of victory the war had achieved for this poor country. The coach fell victim to my wrath, a dent appearing to raise eyebrows later: bruised knuckles my price.

We re-embarked on the coach in a sullen mood. Edith sat with Miss Henshaw, wrapped in a blanket, the teacher monitoring her every move. Colour had returned to the girl's cheeks, but the trauma haunted her eyes.

Chapter 12

As we headed north to Toruń, the coach remained silent. Only Kuznetsov appeared unaffected, but I soon made it clear I was in no mood to chat. Even the countryside darkened my disposition, reminding me of those torturous days in the winter of '45, traipsing through the snow in the company of death.

Four hours later, the towers and spires of Toruń declared themselves on the horizon. The bombers and gunners had spared the city. I felt the tingling oxygen of apprehension enter my lungs. As the girls found their voices again, I retreated, battling my inner demons as the memories returned. I knew the city and its people bore no responsibility for my suffering, but they housed my scars.

The river Vistula glistened in the late afternoon sun as we arrived at the medieval city hall, with its famous clock tower. A young boy, a lookout, sat by the door, and on sight of our coach, vanished inside. As we tramped off our boneshaker, surveying the cobbled square, a delegation emerged from the city hall. They were no less welcoming than our Czech hosts, though spared us the brass band. A group of schoolchildren presented our girls with garlands of flowers, triggering a smile from poor Edith. But I won't bore you with further details of toasts, handshakes, and diplomacy, not even the laughter at the shoeless Davies.

It was what happened next that I must convey. With three days in the city, our hosts were eager for us to rest, showing us to our accommodation without delay. The thought of a bed and sleep appealed to us all, even if sunset was hours off. Kuznetsov had already slunk away to do whatever it was he did. We drove a short distance, and, as luck would have it, an ideal location awaited, with rooms fitted out with beds. The girls appeared excited to have their own dormitory within such interesting surroundings, while Trenton-Harper nodded his head as he assessed the location. Horror seized me. We were back at the fort - the vast, red-stoned bastion that housed thousands of prisoners of war, including myself: Stalag XXA!

What a strange feeling to arrive freely at this prison 'home' – a home of five years. This was no cottage with a welcome mat, a warming hearth, and a family to greet me. Each day I spent in that hell, I dreamt of escaping it, and my return fostered similar emotions. A knot of anxiety set up home in the pit of my stomach. The sights, the sounds, the smells - they all triggered haunting memories, building to a crescendo of panic.

"Come on, Mr Macleod," said Bridget, looking back at me unmoved from my coach seat. "We're going to explore."

I couldn't move. My legs refused to work. I answered Bridget with a weak smile.

"Is everything all right?" she asked, walking back down the aisle toward me. "You don't look well."

My mouth was dry, my hands clammy, while my heart raced. I struggled to answer.

"I'll get an adult." Bridget hurried off the coach, leaving me as the sole occupant.

Her choice of an adult left a lot to be desired. Walker's head appeared, urged on by Bridget behind. He stood for a moment, assessing me, then turned to the girl. "Best leave us, luv."

"I've seen that look before," he said, sitting across the aisle, Bridget departing with a concerned look backward. "Good pal of mine at Monte Cassino. Bravest guy I knew, but something just tripped. Wouldn't move; couldn't move. Tried shouting, slapping him. Nothing worked. Of course, there were a battle going on. We had our orders. So, we left Bill. Came back an hour later. No sign of him, just a shell crater and his broken helmet."

"Is that supposed tae make me feel better?" I snapped, anger breaking my funk. "Yer friend getting blown up?"

"Oh, no," continued Walker. "Bill was fine. The medics had found him and taken him to hospital. Git was living the high life with the nurses. No one told us for forty-eight hours!"

Our eyes locked. His mouth quivered, then spread into a smile. Laughter followed, and I could not help but join in.

"So, what set you off?" he asked, offering me a cigarette.

How I had wanted to punch his lights out for that outrage at the river, but only another damaged veteran could have talked me out of my fugue. "Thanks. This is where they held me prisoner."

He nodded. "That's rough. Bet you saw some horrid things?"

"Aye. Ne'er reacted like this before, though." I waggled my feet, taking back control, sucking in a lungful of smoke and releasing it in a steady puff.

"There ain't no shells and no nurses, so how about you get off your arse?"

I chuckled, recognising a soldier's humour. "Aye, thanks. I heard Monte Cassino was a bad one."

"I have a cold sweat every time I see a hilltop building," confessed Walker.

Bridget awaited us as we climbed off the coach. "You better, Mr Macleod?"

"Aye, thanks for yer help, Bridget. Ye're a good lass." My legs shook a little, but I could walk unassisted.

"Been at Kuznetsov's vodka," said Walker, winking at the girl.

"Och, just show me tae ma bed!"

To my relief, they housed us within the stone section of the fort, once home to my former captors, with some evident post-war improvements. The thought of returning to my old hut would have finished me. I prodded my bed, content that the mattress was firm and clean, and collapsed onto it in my clothes and boots.

"I would hurry and get to sleep," urged Walker, kicking his boots off in the bed next to mine. "Crouchy's already in dreamland."

A snort and grunt punctuated our driver's heavy breathing.

"He deserves it," I answered, tucking my hands under my head, feeling more beneficent toward the man. "I donnae know how he dinnae get lost."

"Old Crouchy's a blimming homing pigeon. Can find his way into anywhere and outta anywhere" said Walker. "Including getting out of trouble."

"Unfortunately, Mr Crouch has an unhealthy habit of finding his way into trouble, too," chipped in Trenton-Harper from across the room, his eyes closed, arms crossed over his chest. "Now, a little less noise please, gentlemen."

"Quite," added Davies, tucked under his blankets in the next bed, a new pair of boots by his bed, gifted from the city.

I'm not one to push worries aside; they fester. So, I lay staring at the ceiling, trying to understand my reaction on the coach, my behaviour towards Jane, what I was doing back in Stalag XXA and what I was going to do about Trenton-Harper. His behaviour still rankled. I played out a scene in my head: leaping from my bed, placing my boot against his bed, kicking it and him to the ground. With my foot on his throat, I'd demand contrition, and it would pour forth through tears: Edith's brush with death avenged.

But something strange happened in that moment. I turned my head, noticing the brickwork contained a legacy from past occupants. Names and symbols told a tale, etched by bored and lonely hands. These were my oppressors; monsters who starved, beat and humiliated me, killing my friends. Yet a scratched love heart, a sweetheart's name, a memorial to a friend, portrayed humanity. I thought of Walker: willing to push a girl in the river, but with empathy enough to help me out of my crippling despair. What complex creatures we are.

Those strands keeping me awake wove together until in a tangible, visible form. It was an abstract sensation, but my guilt floated on its own plane. It solved nothing, but a clarity formed. My guilt at surviving fed into everything, leaking out as anger and violence. At that moment, I hated myself. Quick to anger, morose and thuggish, I had within me a monster. The same as those guards or Walker. Violence solved much in war, but my war was over. Poor, innocent Jane suffered most. So, I resolved to change, a starting point to bury my anger with Trenton-Harper, see this harebrained scheme through and return to Jane a better man.

Sleep arrived with time, though a fitful affair. The ghosts from the camp visited: emaciated spirits with sunken eyes and charcoal monsters with bayonet claws. Jane appeared, a benign figure watching, calling me home. Those spectres still visit me to this day, but from that epiphanic day, I've been able to view them with a detached understanding: companions on my journey to peace, rather than inflictors of punishment for my sins.

Schoolchildren arrived to wake and collect us for a welcome reception at the city hall. In a sweet touch, each held a hand, walking us through the cobbled streets. My guide chatted away in Polish, proud of their responsibilities, and I nodded for each sentence, rewarding the effort, oblivious to the subject, though had I heard reference to Marxism and Leninism?

We gathered in an inner courtyard, where tall, slender niches tucked amid the brickwork created an illusion of more space. A three-piece folk band played a whimsical tune in the corner as we passed down a long line of dignitaries, shaking their hands. As with our Czech friends, the Poles showed us nothing but generosity and kindness.

"Ah, beer!" I licked my lips as they brought around large flagons of brown liquid. A mighty gulp had already travelled down my gullet before I realised my mistake.

"Kvass," a young maid explained as I fought back a shocked grimace.

I tried again, sipping the kvass, allowing my brain a warning. It had a sweet-sour taste, and I was to learn later, made from fermented rye bread with minimal alcohol. "Yum." I raised my glass, a diplomatic grin wavering.

Kuznetsov appeared, his sidekick, Allen, in tow. Their presence sucked the carefree atmosphere from the air, the hosts on edge, weary of their words and behaviour.

I moved to the opposite end of the courtyard, finding Trenton-Harper in conversation with a young Polish gentleman.

"I was a very keen scout in my youth," stated Trenton-Harper, nibbling on a gherkin. "Do you chaps have something similar?"

The Pole reacted with a blank stare, and I wondered what Trenton-Harper was up to. For a man with the ability to charm for his country, it seemed an odd topic for conversation. However, not ten minutes later, as I scoured the buffet for something without pickles, I heard him repeat the phrase and question to another Pole, and then again, with a third.

"What are ye up tae?" I asked, getting Trenton-Harper on his own.

"Up to?" he replied with an innocent frown.

"Asking our hosts aboot scouts? I'm nawt seeking any more surprises."

"Hmm, not having much luck, to be honest," he said, lowering his voice. "Trying to contact a local agent. Most haven't a clue what I'm saying, let alone giving me the correct answer."

"Which is?"

"Oh, I suppose you can help," he said with a grudging pout. "Make friends, mention scouting and ask if they have something similar. If they answer, 'We had the Polish Scouts,' then that's your man."

"Or woman," I added.

He blinked in surprise. "Damn! I'm an idiot. Assumed they must be male, but their ladies had no shortage of balls in the war." He inspected the courtyard for suitable targets. "They'll be in their early twenties, maybe younger."

"How do yer know?" I asked.

"The Polish Scouts were a resistance group in the war. Just kids shooting Nazis rather than tying knots, because that's how desperate things were. Germans didn't hesitate to shoot back."

I didn't need a lesson on the barbarity of the war. "And can we trust them?"

"This one." Trenton-Harper nodded, drawing on his pipe. "I hope." His words disrupted the smoke trickling from his nostrils. "My contact in Poznan gave a glowing reference."

Mention of his clandestine jaunt in the south tested my newfound philosophy. My hackles rose as I fought the surging anger.

"You all right?" he asked, concern leaking through his brow. "Look a little peaky, old chap."

I opened my nostrils, filling my lungs. "Aye, just missing the Czech beer." My craving for violent repost passed.

"You take that side of the courtyard. I'll take this," suggested Trenton-Harper, scratching his nose, as though aware it had escaped a nosebleed.

I hurried away, keen to distance myself from yet another member of the gathering, finding myself before the band. A small group of St Agnes girls hovered, watching the performers, while giggling among themselves.

"Ye enjoying yerselves?" I asked, building myself up for engagement with the locals.

"They've invited us to paddle on the river tomorrow, followed by a campfire in the woods," announced Margaret. "Did you know they have bears and wild boars?"

"I dinnae know that," I confessed. "Perhaps one for Edith tae sit oot." This caused tittering, which I frowned upon. "Is she feeling better?"

"She's fine," said a girl whose name I forget. "Telling everyone she died, but she's a fibber."

I didn't correct her; this world of schoolgirl rivalry and envy unfamiliar to me.

A tall Polish woman approached, her age difficult to judge with the baggage of war. She paused to appreciate the music, offering a genial nod in our direction.

"Hello," I said, unwilling to make a fool of myself by trying it in Polish.

"You like?" she asked, shaming me with her passable English, her hand sweeping towards the band.

"Oh, very good. Dobry. Dobry." I threw in one of my Polish words to foster goodwill.

We shared an awkward silence, falling back on inane smiles, until I conjured a moment of inspiration. "Dobry," I repeated.

"You play?" she asked, her fingers twiddling on an imaginary instrument.

"Nawt since I was a wee lad in the Boy Scouts." It sounds lame as I recount those words now, and no less so back then. "Do you have something similar in Poland?"

She narrowed her eyes, contorting her face as though eating a lemon. "I not understand."

"Scouts," I repeated. "Do ye have Scouts?"

"I not know this vord."

"Och, donnae worry aboot it," I said, apologising through an inept shrug.

We allowed the music to fill the silence after the failure of our international exchange until the band stopped for a well-earned rest. The St Agnes girls dispersed in search of friends and food, while my Polish acquaintance drifted away in the hope of better company. I caught Trenton-Harper's eye, his glowering brow conveying his continued frustration.

"Ve have Polish scouts."

The voice caught me off-guard. I turned to find a young woman; her short, cropped hair, tunic and trousers, and stern mouth lending her a masculine appearance. She also clasped a fiddle. "Err…" I had not planned for this part. "Yer with the band."

"Tak." I had hoped for a bit more, but she remained po-faced and unmoved.

"Let me introduce ye tae Trenton-Harper," I said, trying to catch his attention with a vigorous wave. "He's the man ye need tae speak tae."

She hissed an unfathomable word at me, which in hindsight I concede may have been the Polish word for 'idiot'. What did they expect from a mere gardener?

"Aye, I understand." With a calmness more in keeping with our secretive rendezvous, I ambled across to Trenton-Harper, uttering some nonsense in his ear about scouts.

"The game is afoot, my dear Macleod," he replied, waggling his pipe in my direction, failing to convince as Sherlock Holmes.

He led us back, ignoring the fiddle player, standing disinterested by a table of biscuits and cakes. I didn't know what to do, loitering by his side, looking anywhere but at our contact.

After a while she wandered over, examining the biscuit selection, reciprocating the disinterest.

"I hear you were with the scouts," said Trenton-Harper, addressing the brick wall.

"Tak, the Polish scouts," replied our contact to the jam-filled folded pastries on the table.

I turned my back on them, alert to Kuznetsov or any other potential intrusion. Not for the first time, Trenton-Harper surprised me, continuing the conversation in scrappy Polish. I interpreted the odd word, but what they spoke of, I couldn't say. By the time I turned back, she had gone, leaving Trenton-Harper sniffing at a biscuit.

"Was that it?" I pressed.

"First contact, old chap," he answered, biting down on the pastry, his eyes revolving as he contemplated the flavour. "She has photographs of local partisans and those used for slave labour. Those who came through the war. Someone will slip them to us tonight in our dorm. You can see if any look familiar."

"And then what?"

"You and I go and have a chat. Find out if they remember Hyde and his habits."

Trenton-Harper was not an easy man to test my new pacified resolve on. "And how do we do that without bloody raising suspicion?"

"This foreign food has a way of unsettling a British gentleman's refined constitution, don't you find? I think you and I are due a number nine." He concluded his plan with a chomp of another biscuit.

A number nine. Now, that was a phrase I hadn't heard for a few years.

***

Back at the fort, we men sat around talking in our room, enjoying our freedom away from the responsibility of diplomatic niceties and female sensibilities.

"What I wouldn't give for a decent cup of tea," said Davies, trimming his moustache with a small pair of scissors.

"What was that shit?" threw in Walker. "Tasted better dishwater. Don't they have beer?"

"It was for the kids," I said, the thought of a beer also on my mind.

"Did you see that meteor on our walk?" Davies wandered to the window, pulled the curtains apart and pushed his face to the glass, craning his neck upwards. "I think the Lyrid meteor shower is this time of year. Sky is clear. I may stay up to watch them. Anyone else interested?"

I noticed a worried glance between Trenton-Harper and Crouch.

"A good night's sleep would be best for all of us," said Trenton-Harper. "Don't you think, old boy?"

"Never been a big sleeper," answered Davies. "Anyway, I caught a few hours earlier."

"I see." Trenton-Harper put his hands together, two index fingers tapping his lips in thought. "Well then, a strong coffee is what the doctor ordered. I brought some, suspecting the local brew of inferior quality."

"No tea, I suppose?" asked Davies.

"Crouch," said Trenton-Harper, ignoring Davies. "Put a pot on the stove. There's a good chap."

"Coffee makes things sharper at night," offered Walker, and I knew then they were up to something.

Davies continued to regale us with astronomical tales, fuelled by his engaged audience. I struggled to stay awake, hanging on with a gut-feeling Davies would need saving.

After twenty minutes, Crouch carried in two steaming mugs of coffee. He handed one to his boss, the other to Davies.

"Not really a coffee drinker," confessed Davies, eyeing his mug with distaste.

"That's because you've never drunk proper coffee," declared Trenton-Harper, wafting the aroma up his nose. "Mmmm."

"A drop of the strong stuff helps." Walker withdrew a hip flask, took a sip and offered it to Davies.

"Oh, no. I mustn't," said a sheepish Davies. "Not while the girls are under my supervision."

"My teacher used to drink in class," said Crouch as he brought round further mugs of coffee for Walker and me.

I snatched the flask from Walker's hand. "I'll have some."

"Well, gentlemen," began Trenton-Harper, raising his mug in the air. "It's been some journey so far, but we go no further east. We're at the rainbow's end. From now on, Blighty gets closer. Cheers!" He blew on his coffee and took a sip.

"Cheers!" Davies lifted his mug. "You have a fine way with words, Mr Trenton-Harper. Rainbow's end – yes, I like that. What treasure will we find here?"

Gentle laughter rippled through my colleagues.

"What treasure indeed," said Trenton-Harper, taking another sip. "Oh yes, that is a fine brew, Mr Crouch."

"My, what a rich flavour," admitted Davies, sampling his own beverage. "Bitter but not unpleasant." He sipped again, nodding in appreciation.

"Good man," said Trenton-Harper. "Coffee is the future. The only thing Italians do well, eh, Walker?"

"I met a few Italian ladies who did a lot of things well." Walker's ribaldry fell flat with all but Crouch, Davies hiding within his coffee mug.

"You must forgive Mr Walker his primitive ways," said Trenton-Harper to the deputy head. "Abandoned as a baby and raised by the baboons at London Zoo."

I blinked in shock at the cruelty of Trenton-Harper's words, but they tickled their target, Walker snorting with amusement, mimicking the apes by plucking a non-existent tick from his hair and eating it.

"Gosh," said Davies, shuffling on his bed. "I'm feeling rather tired. You were right, Mr Trenton-Harper. A good night's sleep is required. Oh, dear, so sleepy." He rubbed his eyes and dropped his head onto the pillow. Within half a minute, sleep overwhelmed him.

"About time!" said Walker. "Who cares about stars and bloody planets?"

"Ye've drugged him?" I accused with a resigned sigh, the tactic too unsubtle to rile me.

"You're not drinking your coffee," remarked Trenton-Harper.

All three pairs of eyes focussed on me, awaiting my reaction.

"If I thought it would give me a good night's sleep, I would." I sipped my coffee, yawning with exaggeration. "But I suspect Mr Davies is yer only victim."

"Very good," said Trenton-Harper, leaning back on his bed. "Don't want our man here caught up in tonight's encounter. For his own safety, you understand?"

"Ye're all heart."

"Keep that coffee flowing, Crouch," instructed Trenton-Harper. "It's going to be a long night."

Despite the demands of my body, sleep was no longer the sanctuary of my pre-war years, my tired mind afflicted by fractured, disturbing nightmares. So, staying awake appealed, and the coffee helped. I must have dropped off a few times as the hours passed, the silence and rhythmic breathing of Davies lulling me under, but when Crouch, on watch at the window, signalled someone approaching, I was wide awake.

Trenton-Harper remained dignified on his bed, his smile at the ready, while Walker and Crouch positioned themselves on either side of the door, poised for trouble.

Footsteps crunched on the dirt path before the door to our room creaked open. A foot appeared, then a hand.

Walker gripped the upper appendage, dragging the individual in, while Crouch slammed the door.

"Baden Powell!" cried the man, terror on his face.

"Let the chap go," ordered Trenton-Harper. "That's the code word." He climbed off his bed, studying our visitor. "Did anyone follow you?"

The man shook his head, cowering under the intimidating presence of Walker and Crouch.

Our driver pried the curtains apart, inspecting the courtyard, then nodded at his boss.

"Good. You speak English?" Trenton-Harper prowled around him, compounding his fear.

"Yes, my name Tomasz."

"Excellent. You have something for us?"

"Tak, tak." Tomasz rummaged in a pocket, withdrawing a battered envelope. "Photos. Some not so good."

"Give the man a drink from that flask of yours," instructed Trenton-Harper, taking the package and flapping it at Walker. He turned to me. "Make yourself useful, Macleod, and tell us if you recognise anyone." The envelope flew across the room, landing on my bed.

I swung my feet off the mattress, easing the photos out. "Ye know all their names?" I asked Tomasz. As he nodded, I waved him over. "Take a seat."

Cold, haggard faces stared out at me from the top few photos, the chemicals already degrading on the images. "Where are these from?"

Tomasz leaned in. "Germans leave behind."

That explained the haunted eyes, I thought, slipping them to the back. A family photo from before the war spoke of better times. I squinted, considering each face. "This one looks familiar." I tapped the teenage son.

"Ah, tak. That Wojeich Filipek. Only mother lives from photo."

"Just the mother, eh?" I repeated with a nod.

"Would Robbie have known him?" Walker strolled across, peering over my shoulder.

"I donnae know. Nawt even sure I do." I slid the photo to the back. "Now, her I remember." A soft-skinned beauty posed for her picture with an enigmatic faraway look. "Ne'er spoke tae her, but she brightened a hard day with her smile."

Walker wolf-whistled, triggering a stirring groan from Davies.

"Is he okay?" asked Tomasz, fidgeting with discomfort.

"Ignore him, lad," I said as Davies returned to a deep state of peace. "Sleeping off his drink."

That got a sniff of approval from Walker. "You got a name for her?" he demanded.

"Natalia..." Our guest pursed his lips in thought. "Natalia Grabowska! Tak. Grabowksa. Natalia liked by all boys."

"Now we're getting somewhere," said Walker, taking it upon himself to massage my shoulders in triumph as though I had just won the last round in a boxing ring. "Our Hyde would have noticed her."

"We all noticed her," I replied, "but she dinnae speak English and Hyde dinnae speak Polish."

Walker removed his hands in disgust.

"Keep checking the photos," urged Trenton-Harper. "We at least have one name to start with. She may know something."

I dismissed the next few photos, cracked images of unassuming faces, and was about to slip the next to the back, when something caught my eye. Not the sombre central figure but an interested by-stander loitering in the background, an out of focus face but distinct gait. I tapped the image with a finger. "I know his name. A friend of Antek. Now what was it?"

Trenton-Harper shuffled to the edge of his bed, willing me on, while Tomasz studied the face.

"Och, it were an unusual name. Gee…? Nae, Ris…? Help me oot, Tomasz!"

He flapped his hands, drawing inspiration. "Err, Grzegorz? Jacek? Janusz? Ryszard?"

"That's it!" I shouted. "Ryszard." My pronunciation may have differed from his. "Had a clubfoot, but a hard worker. Ye had tae be tae survive."

"I know of this Ryszard," said Tomasz. "Not name of family, but I know. He help partisans. Lives in Koniczynka" He pointed up.

"North of Toruń?"

"Tak."

"But he'll have worked with Hyde?" pressed Trenton-Harper, grabbing his map.

"Oh, aye," I answered. "Though donnae recall them talking."

Trenton-Harper had slid from his bed, onto his knees, spreading the map on the floor. "Now, you've told us you left Hyde north-east of the city. Is this Kon…, oh, whatever it's called, within easy reach?"

I leaned forward, studying the names, trying to get my bearings. "We stole the g…" I stopped myself under Trenton-Harper's withering stare. "We stole the truck here, Lubicz: on the river."

"Did you cross the river?"

"Nae."

"And what about the railway?" Trenton-Harper ran his finger along the straight line on the map, running north-east from Toruń.

"Er, nae, I donnae think so."

"Oh, come on! Did you or didn't you? Think, man!"

A plume of anger rose to the surface, ready to erupt.

"Have a drink." Walker thrust his flask under my nose. "Helps the brain cells."

I took his advice, the fiery liquid dampening my fury. "It was night; we had Germans on our tail, a dead man on board and a wounded driver. It's hard tae recall every detail." I took a deep breath. "But I donnae recall a railway."

"That will have to do," stated Trenton-Harper. "We can assume you swung westwards at some point, heading back to Toruń, but no further than the railway." A pencil appeared between his fingers. He reached down, drawing a circle on the map. "So, let us work on the basis that you parted ways with Hyde somewhere within here." He looked me in the eye. "You agree?"

"Aye."

"Excellent." Trenton-Harper was running at full steam. He ringed the village of Koniczynka and drew a line between the circles. "Our friend, whatever his name is, lives less than a mile away. It's just a theory but hear me out. Hyde drives on without a plan, goes through..." He tapped his second circle with his pencil, looking to Tomasz.

"Koniczynka."

"Yes, then by chance finds..."

"Ryszard." Tomasz had got the hang of it.

"Yes, who, for whatever reason, was out after curfew. He sees the army truck and panics, thinking he's in big trouble, but is delighted to learn Hyde is behind the wheel. Grateful he's not for the firing squad and alarmed at Hyde's condition, he offers to assist him, squirrelling away the…" Trenton-Harper waved away mention of the gold. "Well, what do you think?"

It all sounded far-fetched to me, so I shrugged.

"Vhat you steal?" asked Tomasz.

"Oh, just some secret documents, old boy."

"I told it gold." Our Polish friend brought a smile to my face.

Trenton-Harper laughed a little too hard to be convincing. "Goodness. What fanciful tales get told in wartime. No, just boring papers. Could be embarrassing to the Soviets."

Quite by coincidence, Davies chose that moment to utter some incomprehensible words, startling us all. I like to think it was some subconscious critique of Trenton-Harper's character.

"So, gentlemen," continued Trenton-Harper. "Our plan for tomorrow is clear. We steal out of here on the bus. Will you meet us somewhere, Tomasz?"

I cut in. "I've not looked at all the photos yet."

"Well, get on with it, Mr Macleod!"

Tomasz pressed a finger on the map. "I or friend meet you here."

"Very well," said Trenton-Harper, adding a cross with his pencil. "A time is difficult to pin down, but we will aim to be there by noon, maybe earlier, with the girls occupied and out of our hair."

By then, I had finished looking through the photos. Did I recognise anyone else? Maybe, but I wasn't telling Trenton-Harper that.

Tomasz slipped away into the darkness, Crouch twitching at the curtains again to ensure his exit went unnoticed. I was ready for sleep by that late hour, spying Davies with envy, but my colleagues appeared energised by the apparent headway on our mission. They spoke in hushed tones, excluding me, plotting for tomorrow. I strained my ears, trying to piece together fragmented words, but my heart wasn't in it, and I soon drifted off.

Chapter 13

"What a strange dream," declared Davies as we met over a washbowl. "A strange night. Got a splitting headache this morning."

I splashed cold water over my face, laying out my shaving equipment. "Really?"

"One of those paralysed dramas," he began, while covering his face in lather. "People surrounded me. You were there. Everyone was talking, but I couldn't speak or move."

"What were they saying?" I asked, my face now a white lather too.

"No idea. So frustrating. I could hear you all, but didn't understand a word. Have you had a dream like that? I tried screaming out, letting you know, but nothing emerged. Do you think it has meaning?"

I pinched my nose, pulling my razor down to my lip. "Och, aye, lad. It's a warning. Trust nae one."

"You think so?" He paused, shaking his razor in the murky water. "Not how I interpreted it. I thought perhaps it spoke of insecurity. An inability to place myself at the centre of things. I was always a shy child."

"Maybe," I said. "But mine is better advice. Are ye well enough tae join the girls taeday?"

"Of course," he answered, grimacing as he nicked his chin, a droplet of blood falling into the bowl. "Suspect swimming in the river has given me a minor chill. I'll soon be as right as rain."

"Good man. Best tae get intae the countryside. This place has a poisonous atmosphere. Too many ghosts." Anywhere away from Trenton-Harper was safer for him.

"Did they really hold you here as a prisoner?" asked Davies.

"Aye. The worst time of my life but with the best friends. Ye learn who ye can trust when yer life depends on it."

Walker entered the washroom, topless with a towel draped over his shoulder, a cigarette stuck in his mouth. "Percy's throwing up," he announced. "You don't look so good, Jim. Must have been the sewage served at the reception."

It took a while for me to realise I was 'Jim' and then another second or two to remember my agreement with Trenton-Harper to throw a number nine, old army slang for throwing a sickie. I did not require such a pretence. My stomach, abused by coffee and spirits, had already protested that morning, leaving me cramped and bent in the outside toilet. Most days it protested, but life had no time or sympathy for complaints. "Och, aye." I patted my tummy. "Delhi belly."

"Oh, I wish you had said," remarked Davies. "I've been going on about my silly headache."

"It's fine, lad. Just need a day of rest and access tae the Devil's pit. The toilet!" I clarified, responding to Davies's frown. "A prison latrine's the closest thing tae hell on Earth."

"Nah, that's an army canteen," said Walker, the joke only appreciated by myself.

"Do you have a book to read?" Davies wiped a towel across his face, removing the residue of his shave. "Keep the boredom away. I have a copy of Pilgrim's Progress."

"I…" The thought of hours in the company of Bunyan's prose did not appeal

"You can help me and Crouchy fix the engine," cut in Walker. "Something ain't right."

I saw Davies about to object, and answered in a blink. "I'd like that. Fresh air and a problem tae solve. Nae heavy lifting, mind ye!"

"Never seen a Scot do any yet," said Walker.

"The monkey donnae need tae see the organ grinder." Again, we old soldiers left the young deputy head bemused with our hardened banter.

***

We found Crouch with the coach bonnet open, assessing it with the superficial concern of a garage mechanic about to quote an extortionate cost for repairs. While Trenton-Harper, his rosy disposition at odds with Walker's diagnosis, held court with a local official, a palm to his forehead, a melodramatic assertion of his illusory malaise.

I tried to sneak past, unwilling to listen to another tall tale, but Trenton-Harper saw me from the corner of his eye, encouraging me over.

"Ah, Macleod. There you are," he said. "Just been explaining to Mr Adamik about our affliction. Damn stomach bug!"

"Aye." I tried to appear stricken, my natural war-exhausted demeanour more convincing than Trenton-Harper's.

"And then the coach!" continued Trenton-Harper with a forlorn appeal to the heavens. "It doesn't rain, it pours. The good news is the girls can trek to the river. They'll be glad to stretch their legs after all that sitting."

Mr Adamik followed the monologue with nods and smiles, leaving me undecided whether or not he understood.

"So disappointed not to join the girls," lamented Trenton-Harper. "But the important thing is they have a good time." He then spoke in Polish, convincing me Adamik was no linguist. They conversed, leaving me to adopt the polite ignorance of a non-speaker.

As they shook hands, Trenton-Harper turned to me. "Mr Adamik has kindly offered to organise a doctor to pay us a visit, but I stressed it was unnecessary. Peace and rest are what we need, eh?"

"Aye." My apathy doubled as lethargy.

So, back to bed we went, missing breakfast and confined as we played out our latest deceit. Noise from the real world invaded: Crouch and Walker cursing and banging, the girls working up their excitement. Davies popped in and out of our room, readying himself for the day.

"Feeling any better?" he asked, not for the first time.

Trenton-Harper brushed any lingering crumbs from his mouth left by the pastries Walker had smuggled in. "Getting there, old boy. You heading off soon?"

"I hope so," replied Davies. "You know how hard it is to organise those girls."

"Not even Monty had it so bad," chuckled Trenton-Harper, his portrayal of a sickened traveller only deserving of the amateur stage.

A rap at the door turned our heads.

"Is everyone decent?" came an unmistakable voice.

"Come in, Miss Henshaw," called Trenton-Harper. "We are as decent as the good Lord made us."

"I'm glad to hear it." She sniffed the stagnant air with a discerning nose as she entered. "All the girls send their love."

"How sweet," declared Trenton-Harper. "Do say we'll miss them terribly but look forward to hearing all about their adventures."

"I'm rather hoping we don't have any of those," chipped in Mr Davies. "A nice, quiet day with no drama will be just fine."

"Absolutely," concurred Trenton-Harper, struggling to hide his impatience. "Don't let us sick dogs keep you. The world awaits!"

Miss Henshaw remained stationary.

"Is there something wrong?" I asked.

"Oh, no," she said. "Well, it's Edith. I don't think she's up to the walk, and definitely not for paddling on the river. Would it be too much to leave her in your capable hands?"

Trenton-Harper shot upright. "Goodness! I'm not sure that will be appropriate. A young lady left in the company of men – sick men at that."

"I know, I know," fretted Miss Henshaw. "But what choice do we have? I must stay with the girls. Perhaps we could ask the Poles to provide a chaperone to stay here with her?"

"Ah, yes, well…" It was the first time I had heard Trenton-Harper lost for words.

"We'll look after her, Miss Henshaw," I promised. "Best she's nawt in the company of strangers." I was aware of the burning glare from Trenton-Harper as the words left my mouth.

"Oh, thank you, Mr Macleod. I know I can trust you."

"That goes without saying," added Trenton-Harper with some audacity.

"We'll sit ootside watching Walker and Crouch work on the coach," I suggested. "So she's in the fresh air."

"Oh, yes. She can practise her clarinet and read; get you poor fellows refreshments. Oh, yes. That is a weight off my mind."

Trenton-Harper clapped and rubbed his hands together. "Excellent. Well, you get yourselves off. You're wasting precious daylight."

"This is such a shame," complained Davies as he followed Miss Henshaw out. "We'll try not to be too late back."

"Take your time," Trenton-Harper called after them, before his head darted round, his fierce eyes locked on me. "And what do you propose we do with a teenage girl?"

I whipped aside my blanket, swinging my legs off the bed. "I'll stay behind with her."

"You'll do no such thing," he snapped. "She'll have to come with us. A small dose of laudanum should do the trick."

"Ye'r nawt drugging her!" I jumped to my feet, nostrils flaring.

"Drug who?" Edith stood at the door, her face shaped by melancholy, a small bag in her hand.

"My dear girl. Lovely to see you looking so well," said Trenton-Harper, climbing from his bed, motioning for the girl to come in. "I was talking about my dear aunt back home. Not doing so well, I'm afraid. We're all in a bit of a funk at the moment, eh?"

"Miss Henshaw told me to come find you," said Edith. "They're all heading off."

"Sorry, ye're missing oot," I said, releasing my fists from their angry clench. "It's nawt nice being sick when away from home."

"I wanted to go, but Miss Henshaw said it wasn't sensible."

"Aye, she's right, lass. Ye had a nasty accident."

"Miss Henshaw said my heart stopped, and I was dead for a few minutes." She conveyed the details with a sense of pride.

"Did ye hear that, Mr Trenton-Harper? She died." I enjoyed letting him stew in the consequences of his actions.

"You poor babe," was all the unfeeling bastard could say in response. "Now, can you find some chairs and put them by the coach? There's a good girl."

"Ye drug her and she could die again," I growled through gritted teeth. "Try anything like that and I'll kill ye!"

"You are a melodramatic chap," he replied, stuffing that stupid pipe back in his mouth. "No one's going to die, and I'd rather you didn't kill me."

I claimed my chair with a curmudgeon's huff, sitting hunched with my arms folded. Edith, bless her, had discovered some blankets and insisted we tuck ourselves under.

"I have orders from Miss Henshaw to look after you while you're ill," she explained, ignoring Trenton-Harper's objections, and adopting a hint of Miss Henshaw in her manner. "Now, shall we play I-Spy?"

Crouch and Walker broke off inspecting the coach engine, eyeing Edith with alarm.

"What's she doing here?" demanded Crouch, rubbing his dirty hands on a dirty cloth, jerking his head toward the girl.

"Manners, Mr Crouch!" chided Trenton-Harper. "Miss Edith is recovering with the rest of us. If you work hard, she may play some clarinet."

"Er, what about, you-know-what?" queried Walker.

"Have you found the problem with that engine yet?" asked Trenton-Harper, checking his watch. "If so, perhaps a test run is required? Do us all good to get out of this place, don't you think?"

Walker scratched his head, looking to Crouch for guidance.

"Another ten minutes," answered Crouch, his eyes flitting between Edith and his boss.

"Would you like that?" asked Trenton-Harper of the girl. "A mystery tour."

"Oh, yes," she answered. "But are you well enough to...?"

"To leave the safety of the latrine?" Trenton-Harper completed her sentence, rescuing Edith from the indignity. "Your company has already revitalised us. Is that not so, Mr Macleod?"

"Hmm." My brain scrambled for a way to extract Edith, but I concluded that by my side was the safest place for her.

"Should we tell someone where we're going?" asked Edith, her sorrowful appearance subsiding. "In case the group comes back while we're gone."

"You are a sensible girl," remarked Trenton-Harper. "Mr Walker will tell the caretaker. I think he's the only local about. But let's make this trip our secret, eh?"

"But I don't speak Polish, boss," complained Walker, still not up with the game.

A deep, annoyed sigh left Trenton-Harper's mouth. "Must I do everything around here? Very well. You get that engine running, and I'll speak with what's-his-name."

"Should I bring my clarinet?"

"Ha, a clarinet," repeated Trenton-Harper, trying to hide his exasperation behind a smile. "Well, why not? It's supposed to be fun, after all. Why don't you get on board and leave us adults to get things ready? Mr Macleod can accompany me. One last trip to the you-know-what!"

He gripped my arm, pulling me away. "She's your responsibility," he hissed. "Don't let her off that bus and put the fear of God into her not to talk about today."

"Let go of ma arm!" I snarled to instant effect. "Donnae worry. I'm nawt letting her oot of ma sight while ye're aboot. And what aboot

Kuznetsov? We've nawt seen him since last night. What if he comes looking for us?"

"One hopes his guard is down," answered Trenton-Harper. "Convinced we are as harmless as a girls' orchestra should be. But I'm going to do something most unusual."

"What?" I asked, intrigued by his manner.

"I'm going to tell this caretaker the truth. Well, some truth. If that Soviet barnacle drops in, he'll hear a legitimate reason for our absence, while disarmed by our transparent behaviour." He stopped for a moment in thought. "Having Edith with us will help. Yes, this may turn out for the best after all."

"Aye, who would believe someone could take a wee innocent lass intae danger?" No one on this trip appreciated my sarcasm.

I grabbed a few belongings from our room before finding Edith practising her scales on the coach.

"Ye're a fine player," I remarked, taking the seat in front.

She finished with a dainty flourish, beaming at the compliment. "Thank you. I've played since I was 4."

"It shows." I leaned towards her, my furtive nature unnecessary as we remained alone on board. "I think we got the stomach bug from Mr Trenton-Harper's cups. Chap donnae clean them. If he offers ye a drink, I would politely decline."

Her mouth turned down in disgust. "I don't want to be ill again."

"I have a small flask of boiled water. Ah, speak of the Devil." I may have emphasised the last word as Trenton-Harper's head emerged on the stairs.

"Let us see what wonders Mr Crouch and Walker have achieved," he said, choosing his regular seat behind the driver. "Come along, Crouch!"

Heavy boots clunked up the stairs and our driver appeared, sparing another offended glance at our extra passenger. Walker followed; the doors closed, and the engine roared into life.

"Success!" cheered Trenton-Harper, waving his hat at Edith. "Perhaps a drink to celebrate?"

Edith shot a nervous glance in my direction, which I acknowledged with a faint nod. "I'm not thirsty, thank you, Mr Trenton-Harper."

"Are you sure? Not even to raise a glass for a successful mystery tour?"

"The lass said nae." My glare failed to wreck his grin. "Ye have one for us all."

"Very good, Mr Macleod. That I will." With slow deliberation, he poured half a glass from his bottle, raised his mug and drank it, sighing with exaggerated satisfaction. The rascal had been playing me. "Do you know where you're going, Mr Crouch?"

Our driver grunted. I must have acclimatised to his manner, for I was in little doubt it was a positive reply.

All heads turned as we progressed through the streets of Toruń, intrigue rippling down the long queues outside the shops, our indiscreet bright red coach unsuited for clandestine business. I tried to listen to Edith's tales of her pet dog, Hamish the Scottish terrier, of whom she presumed I possessed an affinity as a fellow Scot, while keeping watch for anyone from the security service on our tail. Ours was a brazen move, fitting for what had turned into a make-it-up-as-you-go-along mission. Please remember, the rules for the Cold War were a work in progress. Suspicion was rife, but paranoia was not yet the default position. Both sides were busy undermining trust, crossing borders to collect intelligence in each other's territory, but Trenton-Harper's assertion we had bored them into negligent disregard felt plausible.

Beyond the city, it was the horse and cart that restricted our progress. Narrow country lanes suited the equine mode of transport, not ours. Crouch cursed behind his wheel, though I suspect the peasants reciprocated with colourful language of their own. I wondered if I too had once trudged along these roads, to and from the fields while under the German yoke, but the horrors swamped the mundane in my memory.

After twenty minutes, we passed a crossroads, and Crouch brought the coach to a standstill in an open area off the road. He turned, map in hand. "If I've read this right, this is the place. No greeting party, though."

Trenton-Harper moved to Crouch's side, surveying the scene through the front window. "We wait," he declared. "I didn't expect balloons and bunting."

"Are we meeting someone?" asked Edith.

"Aye, just some locals," I answered. "Old friends who can show us around." I hated lying to the lass, but what else could I say?

"What a strange place to meet."

She had a point, and we were unmissable in the flat landscape. Of course, this was deliberate. Our friends could spot us from afar, while no one could surprise us.

"Shall I play my clarinet while we wait?" asked Edith, oblivious to Crouch's rolling eyes.

"Why not?" cried Trenton-Harper. He pulled a fresh bottle from a bag. "Feeling thirsty yet?"

"No, thank you. Mr Macleod shared his water with me."

The chance to wallow in my success at outsmarting Trenton-Harper had to wait.

"Someone's coming!" called out Walker. "On bikes."

We crowded at the front, apprehensive about the identity of our guests, except for Edith, who possessed nothing but curiosity.

"It's Tomasz," I said with relief. A young woman rode at his side, her face covered by windswept hair.

"Edith, dear," began Trenton-Harper, grasping the girl by both shoulders. "Will you return to your seat and wait on board while we adults have a chat outside? We shouldn't be that long."

She nodded, compliant and uncomplaining.

"Here's a biscuit for you." Trenton-Harper recovered the item from a folded handkerchief in his jacket pocket. "Stole it from the reception last night."

My heart skipped a beat. Had he outsmarted me? I thought about snatching it, stuffing it in my mouth, watching his stupid grin crumble before I lost consciousness, but Edith had grasped it and was strolling back to her seat.

"It's only a biscuit, old boy," Trenton-Harper whispered to me, the grin back in place. "Thought she might be hungry."

We descended the stairs, shielding our eyes as a gust of wind whipped up grit and dust. Tomasz approached with a wave, his companion combing the horizon for suspicious activity. I found myself doing the same.

"Dzień dobry," cried Tomasz as he applied his brakes, skidding to a stop a yard from us. "Hello."

"Good tae see ye again," I said.

"Dhis Agata." Tomasz introduced his companion.

She kept her head lowered, hair still hiding her features. Another gust of wind swept across the plain, dislodging my hat and blowing Agata's hair backwards, exposing her face. With a small nose, full lips and high cheekbones, I thought her pretty, but before she brushed her hair back, I made out the cause of her shyness: a scar ran up her left cheek into an empty eye socket. She greeted us with a sharp nod; her mouth no longer inclined to smile.

"What news do you have for us?" pressed Trenton-Harper.

"Ryszard Symanski," responded Tomasz, dismounting his bicycle. "Dat name of photo man. Agata know family. I have address."

"Excellent," said Trenton-Harper. "What do we know of him? Not a communist?"

"Nie, but..." Tomasz shrugged.

"But what?"

Tomasz and Agata exchanged words before he turned back to face us. "Ve not have vords to explain."

"I got the gist of what you said," remarked Trenton-Harper. "Everyone wanting power and success is now a communist, so it depends on how ambitious he is."

"Tak, you speak Polish?" He appeared surprised.

"A little," answered Trenton-Harper with a rare modest blemish on his arrogant demeanour. "If he's our man, I'm confident we'll find a lot in common. Get your bikes on board and we'll see what he has to say." He took a step back to the coach, then stopped. "Oh, ignore the schoolgirl. She's looking after us."

I expected to find Edith fast asleep, succumbed to Trenton-Harper's nefarious methods, but she was wide awake, her head buried in a book.

"It really was only a biscuit, old boy," repeated Trenton-Harper on seeing my relief. "Edith, my dear," he continued. "Let me introduce you to Tomasz and Agata. Dear friends who will take us to meet a relative. We may have cake there."

"How do you... do?" greeted Edith, her voice wavering at the sight of Agata's wound.

"You sit behind Crouch," suggested Trenton-Harper to Tomasz. "Let him know where we're going."

I slid back into my old seat in front of Edith. "Are ye okay?"

"Yes, thank you, Mr Macleod. I needed that biscuit. My stomach was rumbling. I've been reading *Great Expectations*." She used the open book as a shield, leaning forward and whispering, "What happened to her face?"

"I suspect something tae do with the war. Are you enjoying it?" I tapped the top of the novel.

"Oh, yes. Estella is my favourite character. We must read it for school, but I enjoy reading. Did you know Charles Dickens survived a train crash?"

The engine started, muffling my negative answer. We were on our way again, with the bikes stacked in the aisle. I straightened, watching the enthused Trenton-Harper conversing with Walker, while Agata sat alone, her sad face lost in thought. As I too wondered what had happened to her face, a finger tapped my shoulder.

"I've got a secret," whispered Edith. She was in good company. Those on the coach held a great many among us.

"Oh, aye. And what's that?"

"Monika's father is a... " She mouthed the last word, but I had already filled in the blank.

I feigned surprise. "A Nazi! How do ye know?"

"She showed me a photo." Edith sat back, swelling with pride rather than disgust.

"Have ye told anyone else?"

"Well, no, it's a secret." Hers was a useful introduction to teenage logic.

"Let's keep it that way," I advised, knowing Monika had likely shared her photo with more than just Edith. "Best we just treat her like a St Agnes girl."

"I've promised to teach her hockey," declared Edith.

"Ye speak German?"

"Er, no, but that's what I told her."

Agata curtailed our strange conversation with a barked command to her compatriot. The coach screeched to a halt as Tomasz translated. "Ve miss turnink!"

Crouch tutted and crunched the gears into reverse, neglecting his mirrors as he manoeuvred backwards. Only a hare had need of evasive action, hopping into the undergrowth. We passed a narrow track, weeds competing with the broken surface for dominance. Tomasz acknowledged Crouch's questioning look with a nod, receiving another tut in reply. Soon we clung on for dear life, thrown upward and sideways on the disintegrating lane. Edith shrieked in joy, her joints more flexible than mine.

A mile on, two farmhouses sat on either side of the track, one neglected, the other tidy, though still in need of a touch of paint.

"Tutaj!" declared Agata, her tone enough to convey her meaning. We had arrived.

"Which one?" asked Trenton-Harper, a hint of disappointment in his features when Agata pointed to the ruinous heap. "Get us off the road, Crouch."

"It looks deserted," commented Edith, as the coach backed into the courtyard. "Creepy."

"Aye."

"But there's someone in. I saw the curtains move."

I too spotted movement, a darkened shape flitting between the grimy rags acting as drapes. "Perhaps it's best you wait here," I suggested to Edith, who required little encouragement.

We disembarked, greeted by decay in all its forms: broken ploughs, a rusting tractor and a dead chicken. A scrawny dog, bound by a chain, barked with half-hearted ferocity.

I shook my head, disheartened by the scene, noticing a face in the window of the farmhouse opposite.

"There's no treasure here," muttered Walker, hands stuffed in his pockets.

"I don't know," confided Trenton-Harper, ensuring our Polish colleagues didn't overhear. "It fits my theory. Wouldn't it make sense for Hyde to go down an obscure, half-hidden track? Who would think to look for the gold in this godforsaken dump?"

"Who wouldn't spruce up their home with that amount of wealth?" asked Crouch.

"There's been a war and a communist takeover, lads," responded Trenton-Harper, growing in enthusiasm. "Not the time to pop to the bank with a shiny gold bar. You hide it away until an opportune moment."

Agata knocked on the door, her ear tilted, awaiting signs of life. I noticed the curtain twitch again, but no one came to the door.

"I wouldn't answer if I saw us loitering ootside," I remarked, as Agata called out to the occupants.

"We can smash the door down?" offered Walker.

"Thank you, Mr Walker," said Trenton-Harper, "but let's stay civilised for the time being."

Tomasz joined us, a smirk across his face. "Agata use nickname vhen baby. Translates as Fat Face." He squeezed his own cheeks.

As I chuckled, thinking of Jean and her chubby features, the door crept open. An old lady peered through the crack, squinting at the face before her.

"I tink this Ryszard's babcia. Er, grandmother," explained Tomasz, as realisation dawned on the old lady's face and she recognised Agata.

She held Agata's face between her hands, her words excited and fond, before they turned to anguish and pain.

"It is sad," translated Tomasz. "She remembers Agata as baby and child but not understand how her Fat Face so damaged. Agata tell her of German bullet."

"That's lovely," said Trenton-Harper, not the least bit interested. "Where's our man?"

The old lady's eyes assessed us, and she called out.

"She invite us in," said Tomasz, motioning us forward. "Ve must respect, before ve get answers." He aimed the comment at Trenton-Harper.

"Absolutely, old boy."

Edith watched from her seat on the coach. I waved before I removed my cap and ducked through the farmhouse door. A chicken greeted me in the hall, perched on a muck-covered chair. It clucked, then hopped to the floor in search of insects between the uncarpeted floorboards. I put my hand to my face, pinching my nose. A pungent mix of beasts and stagnation infused the room with despair. Mould clung to the walls. From a circular stain on the ceiling, a droplet built and then fell, the wood below rotten and disintegrating.

"Reminds me of home," quipped Walker. Or at least I think he joked.

Agata and Tomasz helped the old lady clear a wall-bench in a long room at the rear of the house. It was easy to picture days of old, with family gathered for a feast, laughter and drink, but those days were gone.

"Where's she going now?" huffed Trenton-Harper, as he placed his handkerchief on the bench to sit on.

"She must honour guests," said Tomasz, sweeping dead flies from a chair. "I tell her you English. She has herbata: tea. Agata help her."

"I'm Scottish," I mumbled under my breath.

We sat in awkward silence for a quarter of an hour before Agata led the old lady back with a tray of glass mugs filled with a rich brown liquid.

"Thank ye," I said, my nose twitching over the steaming concoction, eager not to make the same mistake as at the reception. A sip confirmed it was tea, weak but strengthened by lemon and sugar. I sighed with satisfaction.

Tomasz introduced us all to the old lady, now sitting with a noble manner in a chair before us, Agata by her side, their hands clasped together. Trenton-Harper shuffled to the edge of the bench as though trying for a head-start.

"I vill translate for you," said Tomasz, the formalities over.

"Good," began Trenton-Harper. "Madam Symanski... "

"Symanska," cut in Tomasz.

"Sorry?"

"The female form is Symanska."

Trenton-Harper coloured in frustration. "Madam Symanska, where is your son? We would very much like to speak with him."

As the old lady responded, Tomasz translated. "She asks vhich son. I tell her Ryszard. She had five boys. Dhree die in var."

"Yes, yes." Trenton-Harper waved on the conversation. "Where is Ryszard?"

The answer was not instantaneous. A three-way discussion took place between the three Poles, Agata and Tomasz becoming animated.

"What is it?" pressed Trenton-Harper.

"Ryszard in police custody," explained Tomasz. "Dey come in night. She not see for a veek."

"Why?" I asked.

Tomasz shrugged. "Dey not need reason."

"Damn!" cursed Trenton-Harper, struggling not to throw his mug at the wall. "We've wasted a day!"

"Hang on," I said, my hand preventing Trenton-Harper from standing. "Tomasz, can you ask Madam Symanska if her son spoke of his time working during the war? Of meeting prisoners of war?"

"He did," came the reply, triggering a wave of excitement along the bench.

"Has she heard the name Hyde before, Robbie Hyde?" I said the name loud and slow, Trenton-Harper appearing content for me to continue.

She nodded as Tomasz translated, causing Trenton-Harper to quiver in hope.

"I have a photograph of him," said Trenton-Harper, a hand touring his pockets to find it. "Damn, where did I put it?"

"Does she remember Hyde coming tae the house?" Even I grew excited, my hands before me shaping a house.

Again, my question triggered a positive reaction, the old lady chatting away to Agata and Tomasz, the translated reply a simpler 'yes'.

"I knew it were here!" chuckled Walker, rubbing his hands together.

"Can she tell us what happened?"

"I didn't give that photo to one of you?" asked Trenton-Harper while they translated, his jacket off and every corner of his body patted down.

Tomasz cleared his throat, appearing concerned. "Dhere is problem. She say dis Hyde have dinner here."

"Er, okay," I said. "Why's that a problem?"

"She say he come last year."

"Maybe she's just lost track of time," suggested a hopeful Walker.

"Nie," replied Tomasz with a sigh. "She say was after war."

I scratched my chin, assessing the old lady, still in animated conversation with Agata. "Ask her if she remembers a Bud Flanagan."

Tomasz asked the question. I suspected he had come to the same conclusion as I had. The old lady nodded with enthusiasm, a warm glint of recollection in her eyes.

"Well?"

"She say man also visits," answered Tomasz, "and stay for dinner last year.

"Bloody hell," exclaimed Walker. "Fancy Flanagan coming to a place like this."

"You're a flaming idiot," mumbled Crouch.

"Eh?"

"Nae one has visited, lad," I explained. "She's a lonely old lady who donnae want us to leave. Poor lass. She'll agree tae whatever we ask her."

"Found it!" cried Trenton-Harper, the photo of Hyde grasped between his fingers. He showed it to the old lady, oblivious to what had just passed.

"Don't bother, boss," said Walker. "She's loopy."

"What do you mean?"

As I helped Trenton-Harper catch up, the old lady took the photo, studying it while crooning with sweet rhythmic words.

Trenton-Harper stood, brushed down his trousers and swept back his hair. "We have wasted our time, gentlemen. Let us not impose on this lady's hospitality any longer."

We all climbed to our feet, trying to avoid the old lady's eyes, which welled with tears through fear of losing her company.

"What was she saying to the photograph?" I asked out of curiosity.

"Is strange," answered Tomasz. "She repeat name of Zofia Filipekka. You remember, she in family photo I show? Brother of Wojeich."

"Aye, I recall," I said, picturing the traditional family portrait. "Only the mother survived the war. Ask her what she means."

Tomasz shook his head. "It not make sense. She say Hyde live vith Zofia."

"Where?" I grabbed the map from Crouch's hand.

"Don't waste your time, old boy," said Trenton-Harper, edging towards the door. "Her marbles have long gone."

"Show me!" I demanded, thrusting the open map under Tomasz's nose. "She may be senile, but what if there's some truth in her nonsense?"

"Filipeki live here," stated Tomasz, tapping the map south-west of our current location.

"I think it's worth a visit." The gold beguiled others, not me, and yet I now championed the hunt, trying to revive the waning enthusiasm. Perhaps it was something in the old lady's eyes as she studied Hyde's image, but I had a gut feeling.

Trenton-Harper glanced at his watch. "Hmm, it's on the way back. I thought perhaps we'd try Natalia next, but we can do her tomorrow."

"Mr Macleod." A nervous voice sounded from the hallway. "Mr Trenton-Harper."

"Edith?" I called. "Is that ye? We're in here."

The schoolgirl appeared at the doorway, her eyes wide in disgust and fear. Madame Symanska clapped her hands, holding them together as she spotted Edith, her face lifting in delight.

"She think girl her dead daughter," explained Tomasz, trying to restrain the old woman from embracing Edith.

"What is it, lass?" I asked.

"Mr Kuznetsov is here," Edith answered. "With the police."

Chapter 14

How did Kuznetsov know where to find us? Were we followed? I had time aplenty to mull this over as I sat in a dank police cell, the minutes blurring into hours as I awaited answers. In fact, I had time to reflect on the entire episode.

We had followed Edith out of the farmhouse, discovering Kuznetsov awaiting us in the courtyard, a cigarette between his fingers, a disarming smirk on his face. Four police cars blocked the lane, their occupants ripping through the coach in search of incriminating evidence.

"What's all this about?" demanded Trenton-Harper, bluffing his innocence with admirable gusto.

"You not vith girls," stated Kuznetsov. "I vorry. Then I hear you ill and avtobus broke." He patted his stomach, and then the side of the coach. "But you gone. I vorry. Then I find you at house of class enemy." He paused, drawing on his cigarette. The smoke escaped through a grin. "Now, you vorry."

"Your concern for our well-being is most appreciated," said Trenton-Harper. "I left a message for you with that caretaker chap. Did he not pass it on?"

Kuznetsov ignored the question, his attention drawn to Tomasz and Agata, who hung behind us.

"New friends?" asked Kuznetsov, spotting them.

"Cyclists, old boy," said Trenton-Harper, a portrayal of calmness as he filled his pipe. "Gave them a lift. You've seen the state of these roads. We asked the old lady of the house for directions to get us home, and the dear sweetheart invited us in for tea. The generosity of these people is commendable. Reminds me of a trip I once took around Yorkshire. Now, if you don't mind, we should really get back. Can't have the girls worrying about us."

Trenton-Harper's words failed to convince the Russian, the guns brandished by his comrades more convincing on us. They bundled Tomasz and Agata into one car and even took Madame Symanska away, confused and frightened. Kuznetsov ordered us back onto the coach, and then he and a couple of his cronies followed us aboard.

"What's happening?" asked Edith, as we rumbled back along the lane, Crouch driving but under scrutiny from a police officer.

"A little misunderstanding," I replied, trying to appear relaxed for her benefit. "They donnae appreciate people wandering aboot, doing what they like. Seems we ended up at a house of someone they donnae like."

"The old lady?"

"Her family," I said. "But donnae worry. We'll soon be back at the fort."

"So, we're not in trouble?"

"Och, nae," I chuckled. "Why would ye think that?"

Yes, I regretted those particular words as I paced up and down in that prison cell hours later, worrying about the whereabouts of Edith and what the other girls of St Agnes must be thinking. The cell had no window, the only light creeping under the door, but I sensed night had descended. Had someone informed them of our fate? Were they under investigation too?

I had last seen Edith, Trenton-Harper and the others when we pulled up at the police station in the early afternoon. They separated us at the entrance, pushing me along a corridor, ignoring my protests. I listened to Edith sobbing and Trenton-Harper complaining but then silence as the door to my cell slammed shut.

"Donnae worry!" I shouted through the door, not even convincing myself. "We'll be oot soon." More words to regret.

In the darkness, my other senses heightened, each sound triggering a reaction. Muffled shouts filtered through, as too did the occasional scream. Did I recognise anyone? My mind remained undecided, creating nightmare scenarios my rational core fought to dismiss. I had no bed, not even a chair. The floor was too filthy to sit on, the stench an eerie reminder of the cattle carriage I once travelled in through Germany. So, I stood until my knees buckled, sliding to the slime in exhaustion. And when sleep promised to anaesthetise my suffering, a loud bang shook the door, rousing me, confirming a suspicion that they observed me through a tiny peephole. It was at my lowest point, when I confess to sobbing, crying out for Jane, that the door opened. A black shape, surrounded by a halo of piercing light, entered, lifting me to my feet. So angelic they appeared, I remember thanking them over and over.

They carried me to heaven. Or that's how it felt when the blinding light of a new room hit me. A chair occupied the middle, with four spotlights standing in each corner focussed on it. They dropped my sagging body into the chair, binding just my hands. I remember running my tongue across my cracked lips, craving a drink.

"Arrgghh!!"

A bucket of icy water covered me, materialising out of nowhere, and all thought of heaven shattered in the agony. As I gasped for breath, my body in shock, my eyelids squeezed tight, a voice emerged from the white glare.

"The Scottish English teacher."

"Kuznetsov?" I eased my eyelids open a fraction, trying to see beyond the burning light. "Is that you?" I smelt his tobacco.

"Who are you, James Macleod?"

"What do ye mean?" I struggled, trying to lift a hand, seeking respite from the piercing light, but the binding was firm.

"Vhy you here?"

"I'm a chaperone," I answered, my head bent, trying in vain to avoid those lights. "We're just a school orchestra, invited by your governments to tou... Arrgghh!"

Another wall of freezing water hit me, taking my breath away.

"What is it ye want?" I gasped.

"The truth," came the reply. "Vhy you at Symanski farm?"

"Och, we were trying oot the coach. The engine had a problem. We fixed it and went for a test drive. Donnae ye people like tae explore the countryside?" Silence answered my question. "We got a wee bit lost, saw the old lady and I guess she was lonely. What's wrong with accepting an invitation for tea?"

Again, silence followed. I turned my head, straining my hearing to sense movement or a breath.

"Is anyone there?"

I sat like that for an ill-defined time, deprived of all senses, unaware if Kuznetsov or another remained in the room, my mind bewildered, my heart racing.

And then, out of the blue, "Who are you, Mr Macleod?"

I heard a bucket of water slopping and flinched. "I'm a teacher. Here tae look after the girls. My friends call me Jock. I'm married with three children. Nawt the water, please! I was in the West Kent

Regiment, 7th battalion. Captured at Albert in France and held in Thorn." The information flowed from my mouth: part truth, part fabrication.

He fired the same questions again and again, with a disorienting silence between each round, the threat of the ice water ever present. My answers grew longer and more confused each time until I no longer knew what I had said. Finally, the silence stretched for what felt an eternity, and the cycle ended. At last, the lights cut out, leaving me in absolute darkness. I slumped forward in an exhausted stupor.

I stirred to find myself lifted from the chair, a man on either side supporting me as I shuffled from the room. They led me down a series of corridors, up a flight of stairs and into the open air. My brain gave no help, thought replaced by a thick smog, the world a strange blur. The red outline of our coach triggered some recognition. They pushed me up the stairs, down the aisle and dropped me in a seat. I have a vague notion of three other figures already occupying seats, their vacant faces staring out the window, then the rumble of the engine. My next recollection is of waking in my bed at the fort.

Chapter 15

"Where in heaven's name have you been?"

I forced an eyelid open, a blurred world penetrating my throbbing head. A figure stood above me, hands on their hips, the odour my only clue to an identity. "Miss Henshaw?"

"I left Edith in your care, and this is how you repay me!"

"Edith!" I shot awake and upright. It was a mistake. The world spun; a nausea built. I leant to the side of the bed and threw up.

"Disgusting! Have you been drinking?"

"Urghh, nae." I tipped my head back, resting it against the wall, feeling sorry for myself. "That bastard Kuznetsov has been questioning us."

"Mr Macleod, I will not stand for such language nor behaviour. I trusted you, and you let me down."

I laid a hand across my brow, trying to temper the pulsating ache. "Where's Edith? Is the lass all right?"

"Someone dropped her back late afternoon. A stranger! Imagine our concern when finding no one here and then discovering from Edith, when she appeared, what you had been up to. Arrested by the police!"

"Och, we did nowt wrong," I protested. "As long as the lass is safe, then all is good."

"Good?" Miss Henshaw's voice rose an octave. "We're now imprisoned in this god-awful place all day, and they've cut our tour short. We play tonight, but no concert in Germany."

"Sorry, I dinnae think." A fleeting concern at once again finding myself a prisoner in Stalag XXA passed when I realised the other beds remained empty. "Where's Trenton-Harper, Walker, Crouch?"

"Moping outside," huffed Miss Henshaw. "They look worse than you. Mr Davies was no help with you away. I sometimes wonder how he became a teacher. Men!"

On cue, Davies entered. "Ah, James, you're up. Sounds like you had all the fun."

"Mr Davies," chided Miss Henshaw, "this is hardly a matter for levity."

"Quite right, Miss Henshaw," he replied. "Oh, Daphne was looking for you."

The music teacher spared one last glare in my direction and left in a huff.

"That's us even," said Davies, sitting on the edge of my bed. "You saved me from drowning, and I saved you from Miss Henshaw. I just hope Daphne has a problem to keep her occupied."

I tried to laugh, but it hurt.

"What's going on, James? You had us worried."

"Sorry, lad," I answered, wondering how much to disclose. "I donnae know what they did tae the others, but they tortured me."

"Torture!"

"Aye."

"But why? What do they think you're hiding? What on earth were you doing to give them such grounds?"

I decided then to enlighten our Mr Davies about our mission and the dangers shared by the school. "There's something I must tell y…"

"Ah, Macleod, you're awake." Trenton-Harper entered, crashing onto his bed. "You look terrible!"

"Speak for yerself," I countered, his pasty, haggard face pressed into the pillow.

"Did they torture you too?" asked Davies.

"Blah, some robust interview techniques," dismissed Trenton-Harper, accompanying his answer with a moan. "Nothing I didn't use during the war. You couldn't give us a moment alone, old chap? Just need a word with Macleod."

"Oh, sure." Davies glanced at me, seeking assurance I was okay.

"I'll come find ye later," I said, shuffling on the bed, discovering my world no longer spun.

"We're in a pickle, old boy," began Trenton-Harper with Davies out the door. "Did they get anything out of you?"

How was I to answer that? I didn't even know what I had told them. "Nae." Lying to Trenton-Harper carried little guilt.

"Good man. Those electrodes squeeze all sorts out. Walker and Crouch held their nerve too."

Electrodes? I restrained myself from saying it aloud. Had I got off lightly? "What do ye think has happened tae Tomasz, Agata and the old lady?"

"Nothing good," admitted Trenton-Harper, tapping his pipe on his palm. "They won't show any restraint with the youngsters. I just hope they don't sell us out. Perhaps they already have. That's why they're kicking us out."

"So, what now?" I asked, scratching the stubble on my chin.

"I don't know. That's the truth. We're not getting out of here and, quite frankly, I'm spent after last night. Damn! This is a shambles. That gold is so close but beyond our reach. We cut our losses and get back to civilisation and hope it continues to elude Uncle Joe and his gorillas."

I nodded, my addled mind still piecing together the last surreal twelve hours.

"What is that smell?" asked Trenton-Harper, his nose twitching.

"Ah, I threw up," I confessed. "Give me a moment to find my feet and I'll clean it up."

"There's a good chap," said Trenton-Harper, climbing to his feet with the aid of a cupboard. He peered down at a pool of congealed liquid by his feet. "You can clean up mine while you're at it."

Chapter 16

By mid-afternoon I was myself again, on my feet and outdoors. I wandered to the main gates, found them locked, and watched the world pass outside. Across the street sat our coach, no longer accessible or a symbol of freedom. Behind it, a burly man sat on the bonnet of a dark car, his attention locked on me. A sickening shiver accompanied a flashback to the night. I turned away, resting my hands on my knees, drawing in a deep breath.

"Mr Macleod, are you okay?"

My face converted from its sickly pallor to a light-hearted greeting. "Ah, Bridget. How are ye? Goodness, Edith, Monika. Ye caught me by surprise."

The three girls, their hair plaited to match, studied me with concern.

"Edith's told us what happened," said Bridget. "I never liked that Mr Kuznetsov."

"What happened tae ye, Edith?" I asked, steering them away from the gate and the view of our watchers.

"They fed me a cake, asked me some questions and then drove me back here," she said, swelling with pride. "I've now died and been arrested. My essay about this trip will be the best!"

"They didn't mistreat ye?"

"I didn't like the cake," admitted Edith.

I laughed, as much from relief. "And Monika, did ye enjoy messing aboot on the river?"

She answered with a blank look, Bridget taking on the mantle of spokesperson. "It was fun. I fell in, but the water was only so deep." She held a hand above her knee. "We cooked sausages at the campfire and sang songs. Monika played the fiddle again."

"Sorry tae have missed it." How I would have preferred to be there. "And what are ye up tae now?"

"We're exploring," answered Bridget. "Do you want to join us?"

I was about to dismiss the suggestion, but the thought of innocent company, away from the Machiavellian Trenton-Harper and our sinister overlords, appealed. This place of my nightmares was to become my playground.

The girls led me through archways, crumbling outhouses and over collapsed walls. A gate blocked our path, padlocked shut. We backtracked, the girls placing the obstacle into a fantasy narrative.

"The treasure must be beyond," declared Bridget, pondering whether to turn left or right.

"Cerberus lies ahead," cried Edith, grabbing a splintered plank from the ground as her sword, taking the left in the wake of Bridget.

Monika followed behind, somehow absorbed in the adventure, and, in truth, I was too.

A wire fence, the divide between captors and captives, now hindered our way. It lacked the oppressive character of the past, the spiralling barbed wire gone, rust and neglect running along its length.

"There's a gap!" exclaimed Bridget, folding the mesh back from its concrete post. She squeezed through. "Eldorado! We have come for what is rightfully ours."

Her fellow conquistadors wriggled through, leaving me pondering the challenge of following. It was not just the physical aspect; I had to steel myself before entering the prisoners' area.

"Come on, Mr Macleod!" urged Edith. "The Harpies are attacking. We need you!"

"Och, I'm coming." It was not a graceful entrance, the girls clasping my hands to help me through, the wire tagging on my jacket. When I stood, my legs wobbled. I did not know whether they did so from anxiety or fatigue.

"This way!" Edith held her sword aloft, charging past a line of posts devoid of fencing. "Warriors turned to stone. The Gorgons await!"

"The lass likes her Classics," I remarked to Monika.

She smiled back and sprinted after her friends.

"But she's right," I said to myself, pursuing at my pace. "Monsters once lived here."

There was a marked difference beyond the wire. Rubbish piled high filled the space between cannibalised or rotting cabins. No one had sought to preserve or improve it. The scene reminded me of the ghost towns in American Western films, with nature reclaiming a human desert.

"Treasure!" cried Bridget, emerging from behind a heap with a German steel helmet on her head, one side crumpled and torn.

"Put it back, lass," I instructed with a glower, my hands shaking. Our game had strayed too close to reality.

She removed the helmet with disappointment, discarding it where found, but her sour frown soon morphed back to excitement. "Monika, where are you?"

The girl had vanished. I checked my first step toward panic when Monika answered from within a hut, showcasing her improving English. "In here!"

Edith and Bridget ran up the hut steps, giggling at the prospect of whatever lay within. I stood still, my mouth dry, my palms sweating. They would be out in a second, I convinced myself, but silence reigned, and time passed. I built up the nerve to enter, sucking in a lungful of air.

"Girls! Are ye all right?" I pushed my head through the door, which hung on a solitary hinge.

Little had changed inside. Triple bunks stacked tight together left little room to move. A few still housed thin mattresses, the straw exposed by the work of rodents. The stove lay on its side broken, a smudge of soot caking the floor. The girls sat together on a bottom bunk, comforting each other.

"What is it?" I asked. "Are ye crying?"

Bridget looked up with tear-stained cheeks. "Is this what it was like when you lived here?"

"Well, aye. By the end they crammed us in and ye took it in turn tae share a bed." My explanation did nothing to stem the tears.

"It's terrible," sobbed Edith.

"Aye, but we sometimes joked and laughed," I said, hoping to change the mood. I wonder now why I didn't cry too. After all, I knew the brutality that accompanied the discomfort. But soothing the girls took my mind off the past, and as I led them back outside, my anxiety had lifted.

"Let's head back," I suggested to universal agreement. "We donnae want Miss Henshaw on our back."

***

Our secret adventure remained a secret, Miss Henshaw less interested in where we had been and more so in where we were going. The concert approached: the reputation of St Agnes at stake.

I tidied myself, removing the stubble, showering, and polishing my shoes. Without a mirror, it was impossible to tell what legacy of my tormented night remained. I squinted at a window, running my fingers down my chin, satisfied I was at least respectable.

No children escorted us through town this time. We waited at the locked gates; the girls queued with instruments in hand. After a minute, the caretaker appeared with the universal scowl of his profession. He unlocked the gates, grumbling as he pushed their iron structure open. On the other side, several men emerged from nowhere. They flicked cigarettes away, folded newspapers or lost interest in a shop window: their focus on us. The man I had seen earlier on the bonnet of his car stepped forward, jabbering and waving us towards the coach. We complied, intimidated by our silent audience, who gathered from every direction, funnelling us.

With the instruments in the hold and all aboard, they escorted us through the town. Faces that once turned to watch us from the streets with curiosity carried a knowing resignation on sight of our chaperones.

At the theatre, our shadows disappeared, replaced by the shiny faces of the mayor and his entourage. It felt good to feel wanted again. The building contrasted with its grand cousin in Jablonec. Despite a beautiful plaster facade of floral cornucopia, nothing distinguished it as a theatre. Stairs led to an open porch, enclosed by a shallow, ornate wall, with a normal, single door as an entrance. The interior, also beautiful, had no towering atrium, but low ceilings as though it were once a townhouse. Indeed, it possessed a homely atmosphere, and the girls entered with a confidence they lacked under the giant chandeliers of Jablonec. The auditorium was perhaps a third the size of its Czech counterpart, and we took our seats, awaiting the rest of the audience.

Slowly, people trickled in, glancing in our direction, curious and nervous. Trenton-Harper occupied the seat next to mine, reticent and surly. Defeat had deflated that insatiable ego. I closed my eyes, still exhausted, and listened to the growing rumble of the filling theatre.

"Ouch!" I felt a sharp jab in my ribs.

"James." Mr Davies, sitting on my other side, lent in. "Look who's here. The nerve of the man!"

The unmistakable shape of Kuznetsov shuffled down the next aisle and plonked himself down in a seat before us. I lowered my head, a pointless effort to avoid detection.

Kuznetsov turned, his flask in hand. "Ah, Scottish English teacher. I look forvard to trip tomorrow."

"Good gracious, man," said a flustered Trenton-Harper. "We're heading home. There's really no need for you to join us."

"I insist," said Kuznetsov, raising his flask. "You bad habit of getting lost." He took a swig, belched with satisfaction and turned back to face the stage.

Trenton-Harper released a frustrated sigh, his eyes burning into the back of the Russian's head. I, however, stared upward at the ornate ceiling, my initial anger replaced by a fermenting idea.

For the entire concert, my mind plotted: calculating risks, discarding ideas, building options, allocating tasks, factoring outcomes, until all was in place and I sank back in my seat, a broad grin across my face. I hear the girls performed admirably, but I can't remember a note they played.

"What's got you so happy?" asked Trenton-Harper, as we shuffled from our seats toward the exit.

"Are ye willing tae take one more risk tae find that gold?" I whispered, our Russian limpet well out of earshot. "Give that bastard Kuznetsov what he's owed."

"Go on," urged Trenton-Harper, hope lightening his brow.

"Nawt here," I whispered. "I'll tell ye later when we're alone. But there's one condition."

"Oh, yes. And what's that?"

"We tell the girls everything."

He stopped. "Absolutely not! Are you mad?"

"We have tae if they're going tae help us." We locked eyes. "It's ma way or nawt at all."

No reception awaited us after the concert, despite the warm congratulations showered on the girls by our hosts. The secret police now ran the show, and they wished us back under lock and key. It gave me time to persuade Trenton-Harper of my plan, though he had little choice in the face of my stubborn position. I appreciated the early night, even if my mind still raced, playing scenarios over in my head, picturing Kuznetsov's face if we pulled it off. As I practised my speech to convince Miss Henshaw and the girls to help, sleep interrupted, dragging me into its world of abstract disharmony.

Chapter 17

"D on't push, Mildred!" chastised Miss Henshaw as we gathered with our belongings in the fort's courtyard. "Straighten your collar, Anne!"

Kuznetsov awaited us on the other side of the gate, those soulless eyes watching as we massed in readiness. Under a warm sun, he slung his jacket over his shoulder, his cigarette almost burnt to the end.

"Are ye ready?" I asked Walker.

He nodded. "Could do it in my sleep."

I turned to his colleague. "Crouch?"

He sniffed an acknowledgement, and I expected nothing less.

And, finally, our secret weapon. "Miss Henshaw?"

She held her chin aloft. "Girls, once more unto the breach. Your king and country expect you to do your duty." Yes, it was over the top, but I've found music teachers like the dramatic.

The caretaker arrived, mumbled a sad farewell or perhaps a tirade against the British - it was all the same to me - and unlocked the gates. Before he had time to push them open, the girls surged forward. It was a shameful blemish on our great country's reputation for decorum; it was perfect. Miss Henshaw called for order, her voice lacking its usual authority.

Kuznetsov straightened in alarm, flicking his cigarette away, dropping his jacket to the ground. Meanwhile, the girls danced and shouted between our coach and the black security car, chasing each other in circles, wrestling in a playful spirit. Bridget and Margaret even mounted the bonnet, posing for the driver as though models on a photo shoot.

"Enough!" shouted Kuznetsov, seeking support from Miss Henshaw.

"What has got into them?" she pondered from a distance. "Do you suppose it's the local water?"

The Russian blinked in disbelief, unfamiliar with exerting order over teenage girls.

"Leave it to me," announced Trenton-Harper, observing all the mayhem as though a general in battle. "Girls! Calm yourselves. It is time for us to leave."

The order brought instant calm, a hushed peace replacing the chaos. Bridget and Margaret slid off the bonnet, straightened their skirts and joined the orderly queue for embarkation.

"Just letting off steam," I remarked as I passed Kuznetsov. "Dinnae like being locked up."

Walker followed behind. "You dropped your weasel and stoat." He handed the Russian his jacket.

I climbed the coach steps, receiving a wink from Crouch, as he made himself comfortable in the driver's seat. The girls had renewed energy, chatting and laughing as I walked to my seat. With a subtle nod, I acknowledged each for their boisterous performances and dropped into my seat, releasing a deep breath, content with stage one of the plan.

Bridget swung around to face me. "This is exciting."

"Aye, now behave normally! Here comes ye-know-who."

Kuznetsov climbed aboard, receiving a cold welcome. Immune, he sauntered to his seat with a confident air. "Scottish English teacher, again ve meet."

I ignored his attempt to engage as the engine roared and we pulled away, the black car on our tail.

"In Russia ve have saying," he continued regardless. "Bear you fear also bear who lead you to honey."

I had no clue what he was talking about. "Aye, well, in Scotland we have a saying: donnae torture guests!"

"Nyet torture," he objected. "Just questions. Ve must travel many hours together. Let us not depart enemies. In Russia, drink fix all problems." He withdrew his flask from his jacket pocket and offered it to me.

"Och, ye'r right." Who was I to turn down a drink? I tipped the flask to my mouth and sighed with satisfaction. "Slainte Mhath."

Kuznetsov laughed and drank himself. "Za druzhbu." He angled the flask, pointing at the girls. "They are trouble. In Russia, ve not let vomen behave such." He yawned. "You English have much to learn."

"I'm Scottish."

"Da, d…" His eyelids drooped, his head sank forward. Kuznetsov was fast asleep.

With a vengeful jolt from my elbow, I tested my prognosis. He groaned but remained unconscious. I wiped my lips with the back of my hand, removing the residual liquid. Stage two of the plan was complete and ahead of schedule.

"Mr Kuznetsov is away with the fairies," I announced to the coach, receiving a raucous cheer.

"Well done, Mr Macleod," said Trenton-Harper, swaying as he made his way back. "No ill effects for you?"

I found myself under scrutiny. The whole coach strained to see me. "Nae, nawt a drop was drunk, though ma tongue does tingle."

"And what of our tail, ladies?" asked Trenton-Harper of those on the back seat.

"Still there," came a reply.

"Give it time," said Trenton-Harper. "Mr Crouch knows what he's doing."

"May be worth pouring some more down his throat," suggested Walker, nodding at Kuznetsov. "Make sure 'e's out for a while. Didn't have much time to slip a big dose in."

"You're an incorrigible rascal," laughed Trenton-Harper. "But our rascal."

"What I don't understand," said Mr Davies, breaking from his reading book, "is why you have sleeping draught at all."

"Have you not heard Crouch snore?" quipped Walker.

We headed north, away from Toruń. I was not sad to depart. Fresh memories lodged against old, and neither was welcome.

Trenton-Harper tapped on the back of Crouch's seat with impatience. "Time is running out, Mr Crouch."

Our driver did what he did best, remained dour and silent.

An excited scream erupted from the back of the coach. "It worked!"

I scrambled from my seat, gazing through the rear window. The black car had ground to a halt, smoke rising from its engine. Soon, it vanished from sight. I raised my thumb for the benefit of Trenton-Harper.

"Congratulations, Mr Crouch," he said, patting him on the shoulder. "I don't know what you did, but it worked."

From the driver's mirror, I made out a faint curling of Crouch's mouth, daring to believe it might be a smile. Stage three was complete.

"This is the best school trip ever!" decided Bridget, with the most adventurous among her peers signalling their agreement.

I must confess, winning Miss Henshaw's support for my madcap plan came as a surprise. Mr Davies had beamed with enthusiasm as I took him to one side, declaring, "I knew you chaps were up to something!" But the music teacher offered an altogether tougher challenge. I knew just one thing mattered to her: the well-being of the girls. What I asked placed them in the path of danger. And yet she listened with patience, nodded as I pushed my arguments and accepted without opposition. To this day, I don't understand what persuaded her. Perhaps she too seethed with anger at our treatment by Kuznetsov, wishing justice through vengeance? Or, as my Jane suggested when I relayed this episode years later, she considered the girls' involvement in a matter of national importance as an essential part of their well-being, turning irresponsible teenagers into dutiful ladies.

It did not take long to find the family home of the Filipeki, not least because their house was enormous. Shocked by our coach and Trenton-Harper's request for directions, a local peasant confirmed that Madame Filipekka lived in the manor house.

"Madame Filipekka?" asked Trenton-Harper, bowing as a woman opened the main door, his hat pressed to his chest.

I leant on the coach, next to Crouch and Walker, watching the interaction, while assessing the outbuildings and surrounding land. The deserted horse stables caught my attention, but before I had time to explore, Trenton-Harper strolled back.

"Several families now occupy the house. Bloody communists! The Filipek live in the cottage." He indicated the tiny hovel at the far end of the drive.

The girls, pressed to one side of the coach, scrambled to the other side, watching as we traipsed to the cottage.

Trenton-Harper checked his watch. "Another thirty minutes. Any longer, and we'll have company."

"Someone in that house may already have grassed," said Walker. "We'd break their bloody kneecaps in Leyton."

"That fate may befall us if we don't get a move on," remarked Trenton-Harper as he rapped on the cottage door. He checked his watch again.

The door creaked open a fraction; a child stared up from the shadows.

Always one for etiquette, Trenton-Harper removed his hat, addressing the child with a soft, polite tone.

"Babcia!" called out the youngster, the door still open but an inch.

We listened as shuffling footsteps approached, an exchange taking place within. You didn't need to speak the language to know it involved mention of strange men.

Finally, the door opened, sunshine flooding the room. An elegant woman, about my age, in a fine dress, stood before us, the child held in a light embrace in front, his eyes wide with shy curiosity.

"Ah, Madame Filipekka, I pres..." Trenton-Harper stopped, his mouth dropped open, and he swung his head to look in my direction.

My jaw competed in the race, dropping in shock. For the lad, about eight years of age, with mousy-brown hair, was the spitting image of Robbie Hyde.

"Bloody hell!" exclaimed Walker, capturing all our sentiments.

"We're friends of Robbie Hyde," I spluttered. "Do ye speak English?"

"Of course," came a haughty reply. "My grandmother vas from Oxford: Lady Elizabeth Beaumont." Her accent was strong, but understandable. "Vhat is it you vant?"

"Do you know a Robert Hyde?" asked Trenton-Harper. "From the war."

She whispered in the boy's ear, and he vanished into the house. "My grandson speaks a little English too. This is not for his hearing. He believes his father vas a Polish officer killed in the var, not a scoundrel who shamed our family."

"So, Hyde is his father?" I asked, grateful Miss Henshaw was not there to chastise my indelicate approach. "Can we speak to his mother?"

"She is dead," stated Madame Filipekka, hiding any emotion behind her noble facade. "An infection, not a month after the var ended. Vhere is this Hyde?"

"He's dead," I answered. "Shot by the Germans in 1941. How did he and yer daughter meet?"

"I not know," she said, offended by my question. "Zofia said she loved him, but how can this be so? Vorking in the fields under the eyes of the Germans: this is no romance."

I didn't point out that something romantic had occurred. "Did Hyde ever come tae his house? Late one night, with a truck."

She nodded. "I know vhy you come. Take it! It's of no use to me. They've taken my house, my land, my inheritance."

"So, you know where the..." Trenton-Harper struggled to utter the word, now it lay within his grasp. "... the gold is?"

"Who are you?" She teased him with more questions. "Brigands? Chancers? Lawyers?"

"My dear lady," protested Trenton-Harper. "I represent His Majesty's government. We are here to deprive the Soviets of the..."

"The gold," she helped the stumbling Trenton-Harper out. "How noble. But are the people of this land to rot under their yoke? Vhat future avaits my grandson?"

"We can take him with us," I offered with little thought. "He may have family in London." It never crossed my mind Hyde's family had abandoned him.

"No," she said with a protective firmness. "He is vith family. You take your treasure; I vill keep mine."

The lad hid in the shadows, watching from behind a door, his eyes reflecting the light.

"You endanger us by your presence," said Madame Filipekka.

"Tell us where the gold is and we'll be gone," pressed Trenton-Harper, with another check of his watch.

We awaited her response. The silence stretched, her mind considering the proposition. "It is in the icehouse." She pointed to the woods. "I do not have a key. The land is no longer mine, but no one goes there. Not since the Germans massacred our Jews on that very soil. You find cross for dead boy from truck on path."

"Antek," I gasped, remembering the young Pole killed as we escaped with the gold. Dread inhabited my stomach, images resurfacing from days I hoped to forget. This was why the gold never mattered to me.

"Can we get the coach up there?" asked Trenton-Harper, less inhibited by such scars.

"Coach?" For the first time, she stepped out the door, examining our vehicle parked by the manor house. "How many of you are there? You must go! A blind man could see you in that. There is a dirt track behind the stables."

"Thank you, Madame Filipekka," enthused Trenton-Harper, rubbing his hands together. "The British people will not forget your generosity and assistance."

"One moment," I urged, halting our departure. "What's the wee lad's name?"

"Robek," answered his grandmother.

"That's nice. Tell Robek aboot his real father. He was a good man and died saving others. Do ye have the photo?" I turned to Trenton-Harper.

He huffed, reaching into his inner pocket. "Here!"

I spent a moment studying the image, smiling in memory, and passed it to Madame Filipekka. "Keep it for Robek."

She took it, a tear welling. "He is so like my Robek."

"Aye, ye have a handsome lad there."

"Come on, man!" urged Trenton-Harper, tugging at my sleeve. "We don't have time for nostalgia."

"Goodbye, Robek!" I called into the house and thought a faint 'goodbye' answered.

We ran back to the coach, mindful of the silhouetted figures watching us from behind the manor windows.

An expectant audience buzzed as we boarded. "Well?" demanded Miss Henshaw, her usual calm demeanour undermined by the treasure's lure.

"We've found it!" cried Walker, his excitement unrestrained. He pointed to the woods.

"Everyone in their seats!" ordered Trenton-Harper. "We have hard work before us. And not much time."

What a scene that was. The girls whooped and squealed, bouncing in their seats, urging us on. Only Kuznetsov remained unfazed, his dozing body swaying in the commotion. The dirt track limited our speed, Crouch ignoring the baying mob's pleas to go faster, but we did not have far to go.

During this blur, I wondered at Hyde and his secretive life under everyone's noses. How does one fall in love and father a child, when a simple sneeze drew the attention of a gun barrel? Had I not known

Hyde, his disregard for authority, his skills for deceit and deception and his inner pursuit of acceptance and normality, I would have declared it impossible. But the gold we sought was proof of those qualities.

"I want everyone off the coach," instructed Trenton-Harper, the coach stationary at the edge of the wood. "The sooner we find the icehouse, the sooner we're out of here."

Once alighted, we spread out, breaking into small groups, exploring the multiple paths that led through the woods.

"This way, girls," I urged after a few minutes, taking my group of four down a branch to the right. "It may be nowt but a doorway in a mound or slope, but there's a cross outside, a grave."

"Like that?" said Prudence, pointing into the dense wood.

"Er, aye, just like that." A rotting wooden cross, overwhelmed by ivy and surrounded by ferns, led to a dark, rusty gate hidden among the encroaching undergrowth. "Poor Antek," I muttered, before turning to the girls. "Whoever has the loudest voice best let the others know."

"That's me," declared Bridget, with no objection from her peers. "WE'VE FOUND IT! OVER HERE!"

"That's a fine pair of lungs ye have on ye," I remarked.

"I also play the trumpet."

Thorns and tendrils hampered my approach to the gate, pulling at my trousers and laces. I heard the breathless arrival of the others; the men pushing to the front, battling the foliage.

"Is it open?" cried Trenton-Harper, kicking out at a stubborn bramble.

I shook the gate, loosening some of the dead ivy, but it refused to budge. "It's locked."

"A job for Crouch," declared Trenton-Harper. "There's not a lock that man can't pick." Such detail helped fill in the picture of our reticent driver and his past life.

Crouch guarded the secrets of his trade, shielding the lock from view with his torso. He mumbled, cursing the rust, his tongue jutting into a cheek as he concentrated. A loud click declared success.

"Well done, Mr Crouch," said Trenton-Harper, a bubbling excitement spreading through the growing crowd of girls on the path. "I feel like Howard Carter at Tutankhamun's tomb."

"That dinnae work out so well for him," I opined, my audience disinterested in such negativity.

"Matches at the ready, please, gentlemen," urged Trenton-Harper, tugging at the still reluctant gate. "It's dark in there."

Walker pushed forward, lending his strength to the task, snapping the last stubborn tendrils. The gate creaked open.

We entered a bricked tunnel, four small flames flickering in the dank air. I stooped, my hat brushing the arched ceiling, spiderwebs catching on my face.

"Something just ran over my foot!" complained Walker.

Our matches faded together, leaving us in pitch darkness, fumbling for a new match. I swear, our burly bodyguard whimpered.

"Is everything all right?" called Mr Davies from the entrance.

A scratch and phht summoned a new flame and then another until we had light with which to make out our surroundings. We stood at the edge of a domed room, a large circular pit before us. A narrow walkway ran around the rim, and we spread out. I bent to my knees, holding my flame down in the pit. Nothing but soil greeted me.

"It's gone!" cursed Trenton-Harper.

A ladder descended into the pit. I discarded one match and struck another, then reached a foot to the first rung, making my way down.

"Some bloody thief's stolen it," growled Walker.

"Set a matchbox alight and throw it down," I instructed, leaning out from the ladder, my hand digging into the soil. "I need more light."

A blazing mass dropped into the heart of the pit, growing brighter as its contents ignited. I dug deeper and faster, brushing the excess soil to the side. My fingers scratched a hard surface, and I squinted at my labours as the flames from the matchbox exhausted themselves, leaving me once more in darkness.

"Why have you stopped?" complained Trenton-Harper.

"I've struck gold!" Under the faint glow of the matches above, a warm yellow shimmered through the soil.

"Yeehah!" yelled Walker, grabbing Crouch in a bearhug.

"Well done, Mr Macleod!" cheered Trenton-Harper, with a near hysterical laugh.

Despite my loathing for the gold's allure, I joined the laughter and cries that celebrated its discovery. What strange noises reached those waiting outside I don't know, but Mr Davies entered, enquiring in a timid voice if we were quite ourselves.

"Quite well, Mr Davies," declared Trenton-Harper. "We have a treasure to take home."

As news filtered outside, the triumphant outpouring increased an octave or two.

"What now?" asked Mr Davies, shouting over the cheers.

"We make those girls earn their keep," answered Trenton-Harper, the match held before his face showing off a broad grin. "Have them lined up at the door. We men will pass the bars out; the girls will run back to the coach carrying one each, then rejoin the back of the line."

"On their own?" queried Davies. "What if they come across a bear? They have them here, you know?"

"Then I suggest they run fast," snapped Trenton-Harper, earning a snigger from Walker. "You are a wet blanket, Davies. We didn't win the war fretting about bears. Time is of the essence, so run along."

I could not see Davies's reaction, but heard his footsteps crunch back down the tunnel.

Walker and Crouch leapt down into the pit, helping me clear the remaining soil, until a carpet of gold warmed the entire room with its radiance.

"It's cold," complained Walker as we passed the bars down the chain, but we were soon hot from our labours.

I had climbed out of the pit, stooping in the tunnel, using my long reach to pass on the precious load. A sports day atmosphere consumed the woodland; the girls raced through with a competitive spirit, cheered on by their friends. It was hard to judge time at a moment such as that, but it did not take long until the pit once more had a covering of dull, brown soil, the gold hidden in the coach.

We hurried back to our vehicle, sweaty and filthy, but bubbling with smug satisfaction, the unconscious Kuznetsov slumped in his seat, ignorant and out-thought.

Back in our seats, Trenton-Harper stood in the aisle, not for the first time, trying to quieten the girls' excitable cacophony. "Ladies! Ladies, please!"

"Girls!" Miss Henshaw's voice delivered the silence.

With a gracious nod of gratitude to the music teacher, Trenton-Harper continued. "His Majesty's government thanks you for your help, but having performed beautifully at two concerts thus far, your greatest performance must come next. We carry a valuable load, but you must act as though it's not there. Do not mention it to anyone, including each other. Even when safe in Blighty, we must keep this our secret." This triggered a groan. "Yes, I know, you all want to brag to your families and friends about how we rescued the gold but…" He turned to Miss Henshaw. "I apologise for my bluntness. People will lose their lives. If the Soviets discover we used this trip for clandestine business, they will shoot the locals who helped us. You heard what they did to us in their police cells. Can you give me your assurance to keep it a secret? God save the king!"

A raucous affirmative cheer erupted, the girls bouncing in their seats.

"Easy on those seats," cautioned Trenton-Harper with a playful wink.

For those wondering where our stash now lay, I ask you to recall my delight at the raised seats when I first joined this journey, so advantageous for my gangly legs. Each of us sat above at least three bars, secreted in a discreet cavity custom-built beneath the padding. How the girls delighted at the idea they would guard our treasure from the safety of their seats.

Only one person felt compelled to grumble amid the joyous atmosphere. "Sit still!" ordered Crouch, studying the map spread across the dashboard. "You try steering this thing with all that metal weighing us down."

"Don't steer, man," joked Trenton-Harper, retaking his seat behind the driver. "Set a direct course for home!"

Chapter 18

Our route veered west towards the German border, our course anything but straight. I remember I sat there, Kuznetsov dozing by my side, with a feeling of great contentment. Knowing Hyde lived on through a son brought a sense of closure. I pictured my old friend's face, his eyes gleaming at the sight of the gold, and chuckled: what a brilliant hiding place! Did plans to recover the gold swirl in his head before a bullet cut his life short? What would he make of our scheme to deliver it to the British government?

"Is he really a killer?" Bridget popped up before me, inspecting the placid face of Kuznetsov.

I turned to the Soviet, his mouth ajar, a small dribble of saliva running down his chin. "Er, I guess so. Life seems tae mean less in Russia. They rule through terror, nawt the law."

"Can't we kick him off the coach?" Bridget examined the passing countryside. "With some water, of course."

"Nae, lass," I answered, despite some sympathy for the idea. "We may need him. Best he stays with us, thinking all is as it was."

"I suppose you're right," said Bridget, wrinkling her nose as a final judgement on our unwanted guest. "Were you really a prisoner in the war? I think you were a spy, operating behind enemy lines?"

"Just a poor wee suffering prisoner. It was a dull life… except when it wasnae." I presented my most enigmatic smile.

As she scrutinised me, her eyes narrowing, Kuznetsov mumbled, his shoulder jerking in a spasm.

"Our friend is stirring," I whispered. "Let everyone know. Quietly, now."

It took another half hour before Kuznetsov's opened his eyes. He pinched his forehead between finger and thumb and groaned. The first question he asked came out in Russian.

"Are ye all right?" I asked. "Ye've been dead tae the world and mumbling in yer sleep."

He glanced at me, confusion etched across his face. "Vhere are ve?"

"Oh, still in Poland," I answered. "The engine seems to struggle on these roads." I folded my arms, trying to appear as nonchalant as possible. "Been asleep myself, so nae idea what towns we've gone through."

Kuznetsov checked his watch, shaking his head at his lost time. He pulled himself up, grimacing and putting a hand to his side. "Rib hurt."

I rubbed my elbow, which carried a matching bruise. "I'm nawt surprised. My body feels like it's had a round or two in the ring with Joe Louis after this coach journey."

"Vhy you so dirty?" The Russian's eyes fell on my hands and sleeves, as he reached inside his jacket and pulled out the flask. "Empty?" He held it upside down, shaking out nothing but a droplet.

"Nae wonder ye slept so well." I rubbed one hand against the blind side of my seat, trying to clean off as much soil as possible.

"Hmm." A disconcerted frown joined a disappointed pout. "I fill up next town. Now, I find from driver vhere ve are." He stood, rubbing his eyes with his knuckles.

I made way, watching as he swayed down the aisle, gripping each seat as he passed. A wave of silence followed from the curious girls.

Had he his wits about him, he may have noticed. I urged a return to teenage normality with the universal hand signal for blethering.

"It's very hard to talk when ordered to do so," commented Bridget in a restrained voice.

"Ye seem a natural." The lass reminded me of my Jane, never one to leave a silence unfilled.

"My mother says I talk too much, but I think other people don't talk enough." With her elbows balanced on the back of her seat, she rested her chin on her hands, contemplating where her line of thought might go next. "What did Mr Churchill say? Meeting jaw to jaw is better than war."

I had a quote ready myself from Mr Lincoln on the merits of saying nothing if you had nothing to say, but Bridget had declared jaw.

"I would like to be on the radio when I grow up. Can you imagine all those people tuning in just to listen to what you have to say? I could combine talking and music. Or, yes, I could interview famous people. Princess Elizabeth was on last year. I'm not sure I would like to be a princess. Well, maybe the clothes and dances but not the ceremonies. Do you think she got told off at school for talking?"

Our Soviet secret service agent saved me. "Fifty miles to Gorzow," said Kuznetsov, returning to his seat.

"Oh, aye," I said. "How far is that tae the German border?"

"Imperialist and borders," he sniffed.

"What's it like in Russia?" asked Bridget, not to be denied her platform. "Is everyone really happy, like in the posters, or do they pretend?"

The question caught Kuznetsov off guard. "Er... Ve make paradise for vorkers. No exploitation. It is honour to toil and sveat on this path to freedom from you bourgeois imperialists."

"Oh, no, we're middle-class," corrected Bridget in all innocence. "We're very happy, though my uncle Wilfred – he's a banker – is always miserable. Working with money must be depressing. Imagine sitting on all that wealth and not being able to spend it."

I shuddered in alarm, glaring at the girl, unaware if she played a dangerous game or not. She rambled on, oblivious of the knife edge on which she balanced.

"You talk too much," stated Kuznetsov in a rare moment of silence as Bridget caught her breath, an icy stare accompanying his words.

Bridget laughed. "And that's how Mr Macleod and I started this conversation. Isn't that funny?"

I'm not sure our Soviet companion was amused, but the coach juddering to a halt distracted his attention.

"Roadblock!" announced Trenton-Harper. He leaned into the aisle, aiming his next sentences at Kuznetsov. "You want to make yourself useful and have a word with your comrades? The sooner we're through, the sooner we're out of your hair."

It was only at this point that Kuznetsov took an interest in what lay behind us. "Vhere is Pobeda?" he demanded.

"Eh?"

"Car! Vhere is escort car?"

I feigned ignorance. "Och, I think they left us ootside of Toruń. Were they meant tae keep up?"

Kuznetsov released an exasperated snort, cursing in Russian.

"Ye won't get intae trouble, will ye?"

He answered me in his own language, departing to engage with the sentries from the roadblock.

"And that's why we keep him with us," I whispered to Bridget, as we watched the barrier raised and Kuznetsov return, our coach uninspected.

Chapter 19

We passed through Gorzow without incident, crossing the Warta River. Again, we were on old German territory, now part of Poland. Its heritage lay in ruins, with only the odd building disclosing its Germanic origin, all else a wasteland.

"Will we go through Berlin?" I asked of Kuznetsov, as we approached the German border.

"Nyet." A reticence had consumed him since discovering the absence of his colleagues.

"Good," I said.

"Vhy? Vhy good?"

I shrugged. "It symbolises everything aboot the war and Hitler. I'd prefer tae forget."

"I not understand you, James Macleod." Kuznetsov assessed me with his sunken brown eyes. "Your friends..." He waved a finger towards the front of the coach. "They not simple driver or education man, but you, you remain mystery."

"That's what ma Jane says too." My bravado was at odds with the fear welling within.

"I think you not teacher." He nodded, content the pieces slotted together. "Nyet, but I believe you prisoner in Toruń. So, vhy you come back? Vhy all hands dirty? These questions trouble me."

My laughter may have exposed my nerves. "Ha, ye do sound like my wife."

Kuznetsov sniffed in amusement.

"What happened tae Madam Symanska and the other Poles ye arrested with us?"

"She home," answered the Russian. "Simple old woman. I not think she vell." He tapped the side of his head.

"And the youngsters?"

"Da, young make mistakes. Not problem. Ve educate them. They become good citizens. All is good."

My smile hid my doubts. "I hope ye give them their bicycles back."

"Ah, ve at border." Kuznetsov climbed to his feet. "I fill my..." He tapped his jacket and grinned.

"Flask?"

"Da, I fill my flask vhile search of avtobus."

"Search?" I tried not to sound shocked and hoped the thud of my heart was not audible. "Will it take long?"

Kuznetsov shrugged. "Not long if you tell them vhere to look."

He left me shaking, undecided if he suspected something.

A Soviet guard ordered us off, anxiety gripping each face as we left our seats.

"I'm scared," confessed Bridget.

"Aye, donnae worry, lass. We'll soon be on our way." My record of reassuring promises was not good.

Even Trenton-Harper's grin possessed a fragile character as we congregated under the watchful Soviets. He puffed on his pipe with an unnatural intensity, his hands locked behind his back.

Miss Henshaw, as mother hen, huddled her chicks together under her wings, distracting them with her mix of discipline and encouragement.

"I've never been good at these sorts of things," confessed Mr Davies, cast out from the female corral, picking at his nails. "Bit of a dicky bladder, if I'm honest." He tilted his head in and whispered. "They won't harm the girls, you know, if they find you-know-what?"

I wanted to reassure him, but the truth was I didn't know what would happen. "Just act naturally."

"I consider myself a capable actor," he remarked. "Once contemplated a career on stage. Can you see me as Hamlet or perhaps Lord Windermere?"

"Och, aye." Having seen neither play, I soothed his ego with a lie.

Only Crouch appeared unperturbed by our situation, his usual sour face buried in a book.

"What ye reading?" I asked him, trying to pass the time in idle chatter.

He tilted the book cover up, refusing to acknowledge me even with eye contact.

"Ah, *Great Expectations*. Edith's reading that too. Ye'll have tae discuss it with her. I think her entire English class has it on the curriculum. Where is she?" I stretched my neck, trying to spot her amid the girls. "There she is. Edi..."

"Don't!" Crouch grabbed my arm.

"What is it?"

With a grudging sigh, Crouch rotated the book, his eyes shooting left and right. Normal, unassuming pages faced me until he turned several at once, exposing a cavity cut within the bulky tome. Inside rested a small revolver.

I gasped before he flipped the pages back to portray a harmless book once more. "That Dickens is full of surprises. What do you intend to do with it?"

"Nothing," mumbled Crouch. "Unless I have to."

I counted the Soviet guards, all armed with submachine guns. "Donnae do anything stupid! There'll be a bloodbath if ye draw that."

"Piss off!"

It seemed the sensible thing to do, so I slipped away, shaking my head, returning my attention to the coach and its infection of border guards. A glance at my fob watch told me they had been at it for thirty minutes. They had opened the bonnet, emptied the hold, and searched the wheel arches and beneath. What they did aboard I couldn't say.

Ten minutes later, Kuznetsov appeared, his flask in hand, a smile on his face. "All is good. Ve go."

A collective sigh of relief washed through us, nervous chatter morphing to boisterous as we started to re-embark. Until a scream left the mouth of Miss Henshaw. I pushed past the girls, leaping up the stairs.

"Look what they've done?" exclaimed the music teacher.

The padding from multiple seats spilled out where a blade had sliced them open. Again, I sighed in relief. They had got close, but our secret remained safe.

"Well, they've made a right mess," remarked Trenton-Harper from behind me. "But nothing a needle and thread can't fix. I don't suppose you have any, Miss Henshaw?"

"I... It's the principle, Mr Trenton-Harper! You cannot defend vandalism," she cried.

I put a hand on her shoulder. "We must take our medicine and bear it. The sooner we're oot of here, the better."

My words earned me a despoiled seat, Miss Henshaw adamant her girls deserved comfort. She reserved a poisonous stare for Kuznetsov, though held her tongue as he selected his old, unblemished seat.

I was glad to be away from the Russian, even if my rump complained more than usual as we pulled away from the border, a new security detail following in our wake. Another few hundred miles and we would be beyond Soviet reach. I felt beneath my seat, running a finger along the smooth, angled cover that hid the gold, thanking the individual who had designed such a clever hiding place.

"How about a song?" suggested Miss Henshaw, her eyes still sending daggers at Kuznetsov. "I know just the thing."

It was hard to judge what our Russian made of our rendition of 'Rule, Britannia'!

Chapter 20

I calculated we were north of Berlin when we pulled over for a break. A dense forest offered the opportunity for privacy and shade from the hot afternoon sun. The girls vanished to one side of the road, and us gents on the other. With essential needs met, I strolled back to the road, a cigarette in my hand.

"You've done us proud, Mr Macleod." Trenton-Harper appeared from behind a tree, buttoning up his trousers. "Inspired thinking. I was ready to give up, you know?"

"I had an aunt, nawt right in the head, but her nonsense always had a grain of truth. Ma gut said there was something tae what the old lady was saying. Why link Hyde and the girl? There had tae be some connection. So, I followed ma gut."

"Lucky you did, my dear fellow. Lucky you did."

I paused, leaning against a tree, dislodging a pine needle from my sock. "We're fast using up our luck. That was a close call at the border."

"I was sure they'd rumbled us," confessed Trenton-Harper. "Don't really fancy a holiday in Siberia."

"Aye, well, yer man nearly made it worse with that gun."

"Gun?" Trenton-Harper blinked in surprise. "What are you talking about? Who?"

"Crouch," I answered. "A revolver stashed in a book."

"A gun?" repeated Trenton-Harper, scratching the back of his neck. "How very strange."

"You dinnae know aboot it?"

"Of course not. Could have scuppered the entire operation before we even entered France, if discovered. Damn fool! I told you he has this habit of finding his way into trouble." A forlorn branch found itself the victim of Trenon-Harper's wrath, breaking with a sharp crack. "I'll be having words with Mr Crouch."

Back by the road, the girls rested under the trees, sharing a drink from the large water canteen. Miss Henshaw sat with Monika and two other girls, their discussion in a mix of German and English, an impromptu lesson.

For the first time, I noticed how the chassis of the coach sagged, weighed down by its precious load. All these little clues existed, awaiting discovery by the keen eye. However, a far less subtle incident exposed our secret.

No blame must rest with Monika. She had not understood Trenton-Harper's warning to avoid discussing the gold. We rightly assumed Kuznetsov had little grasp of German, but never did we consider our linguistic cousin might share familiar words. I do not know what the girls discussed, but three innocent words leaked out: gold im bus. These may have drifted away, lost to the wind, but Kuznetsov stood close by, his suspicious mind always on alert. Even then, things may have passed unnoticed, but the other girls reacted, shushing loudly, declaring a secret divulged.

He flicked away a cigarette, swooping on the girls as though a bird of prey. "Vhat you say? Gold on bus? Tell me! Tell me!" His eyes glowed as he turned towards the coach and back to the girls.

They froze in fear.

"Don't be ridiculous, you stupid man," snapped Miss Henshaw. "We are teaching each other phrases. You obviously misheard."

"Silence!" His eyes remained locked on the trembling Monika. "Vhy gold?"

As she muttered a reply, Kuznetsov straightened, an arm raised, alerting his colleagues who sat watching from their car.

"I vish to talk more vith this girl," he announced, lighting another cigarette. "I think she has much to say."

"Now, steady on!" cried Trenton-Harper rushing over to intervene. "You are not questioning our girls. I will not allow it."

Kuznetsov answered the declaration with a whip of his arm, a hand striking Trenton-Harper across the face. "Ve go back to border. Have closer look at avtobus."

The two Soviet security agents stood behind Kuznetsov awaiting orders, while Crouch, Walker and I presented a united front behind Trenton-Harper, who nursed his bruised cheek.

"I don't understand why you're taking a few words from a Dutch youngster so seriously," said Trenton-Harper.

"Dutch?" queried Kuznetsov. "Not Sviss?" His eyes turned to me.

"I may have got ma facts confused," I mumbled, knowing this was checkmate.

Kuznetsov snapped an order. One agent pulled a gun, triggering gasps and screams from the girls, which soon turned to angry shouts as the other agent grasped the sobbing Monika by the arm, dragging her to her feet.

I stepped forward, mimicking my compatriots, only to have the gun angled in our direction.

"Back!" growled Kuznetsov, drawing his own gun from an inner pocket. "I disappointed, Scottish English teacher."

I don't have a tale of a heroic charge, where I tackled Kuznetsov, grabbed his gun and saved the day. Things took an altogether unexpected and messy turn. The gun pointed at my head convinced me the game was up, and I stood there helpless, glowering back at the Russian. Meanwhile, Monika had decided to resist, fighting off her abductor, dragging her feet. Her screams inspired her teenage peers, who threw themselves at the unsuspecting agent. I doubt our Russian had heard of a banshee before, but I can think of no better way of describing the attackers. One assaulted from behind, leaping to cling with arms around his neck, while others yanked on his clothes, the sound of shredding material adding to the mayhem. Blood dribbled from his cheek, fingernails slashed, tufts of extracted hair flew into the air, as shoes battered the fellow's shins. He didn't stand a chance.

Kuznetsov stared in disbelief, screaming in a strange mix of Russian and English, trying to bring order. Having failed, he raised his gun and fired it into the air.

I flinched, taking a step back, as did those around me, but not our banshees. Immune to fear or bewitched by their bloodlust, they continued their attack; the victim prostrated and whimpering.

Like all cowards, Kuznetsov delegated the worst jobs. With a barked order, his subordinate levelled his gun at the scrum of girls.

"Stop!" cried Kuznetsov. "Or ve shoot."

As the rebellion continued, his mouth shaped to give the order. Walker and I scrambled forward: once more into battle. It was ambitious and foolhardy to think we might cover ten yards before the words left his mouth.

BANG!

I shielded my face with my hands, skidding to a halt. It crossed my mind the bullet may have had my name on it, but with the time required to digest the thought, I knew it wasn't so. With time frozen,

I gaped in trepidation at the girls. Not one lay prone or bloodied; instead, they emerged from their madness, adjusting hair and attire, transfixed stares locked past Kuznetsov.

Confusion filled Kuznetsov's face too. I followed his eyes as they turned, falling on the would-be executioner. A trickle of blood ran from the agent's mouth, his eyes wide in shock. The gun dropped from his hand. His legs wobbled, then collapsed.

"Someone shot him!" screamed a girl, setting off a volley of similar responses.

I struggled to make sense of it, turning to find Trenton-Harper and Crouch as bewildered as I, the latter's hands gripped tight but no gun in sight.

"Who fired?" I demanded, swinging around, searching both the woods and the watching crowd.

Kuznetsov's head jerked back and forth, his gun hunting the source.

"Put the gun down, Ivan!" came a voice from behind the coach.

"Mr Davies!" exclaimed Miss Henshaw, as the deputy head emerged, a revolver pointed at the Russian.

"Be quiet, you annoying woman!" snapped Davies, removing his glasses and throwing them to the ground.

"What's going on?" demanded Trenton-Harper.

"I *will* shoot you, Ivan," continued Davies, ignoring the Englishman. "I'm rather a good shot, no? So, drop the gun!"

Kuznetsov complied with a hiss.

No one moved. All eyes followed Davies, trying to equate the unassuming man with his new persona as a killer.

"Collect their guns, Walker!" instructed Davies.

"Yes, boss."

"Boss? What the hell is going on?" demanded Trenton-Harper again. "Walker?"

"Oh, you are a wet blanket," said Davies, bending to check the pulse of the shot agent, his eyes and gun still aimed at Kuznetsov. "He'll not bother us again."

A gasp escaped Miss Henshaw's mouth.

"And your girls have done a fine job of incapacitating the other one," continued Davies, jabbing the cowering agent with his boot. "Vicious little kitties! Tie them up, Walker... the Russians, to be clear," he added with a chuckle.

"I don't know what's going on, nor like it," stated Trenton-Harper, taking a step toward the coach. "But let's get out of here and out of this godforsaken country."

Davies steered his gun at Trenton-Harper. "Change of plan, old chap," he said in his best imitation of the government man. "A little earlier than planned. This is what we call a hold-up in my trade."

"Your trade?"

"An outlaw, robber, bandit, thief. You choose."

"I knew you were no deputy head," interjected Miss Henshaw with a haughty sniff. "A waste of space!"

"Guilty as charged," replied Davies with a smirk. "But I know some good forgers. You should really double-check who you employ." He turned to me. "Oh, Jim, you look so crestfallen. Don't you remember what you said? 'Trust nae one.' Wise words. I told you I was a fine actor.' "

"You even had me fooled, boss," chuckled Walker. "All that star-watching rubbish."

"One must invest fully in such roles," declared Davies, as though on stage and us his fellow thespians. "A sleeping draught or foppish behaviour is but a small sacrifice when treasure is involved. This is how Robbie would have wanted it. Why do you think we're here?"

"Hyde? What's he got tae do with it?"

"Who do you think he ran with before the war?" Davies's voice had lost its clipped middle-England accent, a hint of the London commoner sneaking in.

"Me and Hyde were like brothers," offered Walker, tugging on the knots binding Kuznetsov's hands tight together.

It made sense, even as I shook my head in disbelief. Some unguarded comments from Walker resurfaced in my mind, Hyde's name mentioned with an over-familiar tone, clues I had ignored.

"Hyde's achievement was the talk of the underworld," explained Davies, enjoying the stage. "And, as one of our own, it's only fair the gold belongs to his family. Just needed a little help to get to Poland. Thanks for your help on that, old boy." He winked at Trenton-Harper.

"But it was Crouch who told me about the gold?" said Trenton-Harper, a painful realisation dawning on him. "Crouch!"

Our driver shrugged. "They pay more."

"You traitorous scum!" spluttered Trenton-Harper, his face crimson with rage. "You'll hang for this."

It was not the right moment to remind him of his words about trusting no one in his business.

"Ha, capitalists," laughed Kuznetsov.

"Gag him!" instructed Davies.

"So, what now?" I asked. "Ye cannae leave us here."

"Oh, but we can, and we will," replied Davies. "Don't worry. By the time you're found, we'll be safe. They'll send the girls home, and you'll get a few months before Percy's friends get you out. Can't promise they'll treat you well."

"But ye risked yer life tae save Edith from drowning?" I tried to bring sense to this nonsense. "Stopped them from shooting the girls? Why, if ye now abandon them tae danger?"

"And why ensure that psychopath didn't miss the coach in Jablonec?" added Trenton-Harper, pointing at Kuznetsov to eliminate any doubt as to which psychopath he referred.

"You're a fool, Percy. A stuck-up toff with contempt for anyone who didn't row for their university. The first thing Ivan would have done if left behind was have you all brought back and sent home, but you couldn't help yourself – getting one over on the simple Red." Davies bent by Kuznetsov's side, uttering in his ear. "I hate them as much as you commies, but my kind aren't hypocrites." He straightened, walking along the line of schoolgirls, the silent audience in this horror show. "We never harm the fairer sex. Our mums would kill us!" He shared a laugh with Walker. "And we don't like those who do." He swung around, ran back to Kuznetsov and planted a boot in his midriff. "You communist pig!"

The brutal act stirred further tears among the girls, who huddled in small groups, finding some comfort with each other.

Miss Henshaw, emboldened by Davies's words, expressed her disgust with a swing of her bag at her ex-colleague's head.

He ducked, avoiding the assault, and gripped the music teacher by her wrist. "But we keep our ladies in line." He cocked the gun, aiming it between Trenton-Harper and me. "Which one will it be, Miss Henshaw? There are consequences for misbehaving."

"I'll not play your games. You brute!" declared Miss Henshaw, struggling to break free.

BANG!

"Arrgghh!"

"Oh, my dear God!" screamed Miss Henshaw, falling backwards as Davies released his grip. "You shot Mr Trenton-Harper."

I confess to some relief it wasn't me but hurried to assist poor Trenton-Harper.

"My bloody arm!" he cried, clasping one hand over the seeping wound below his shoulder. "Avoided getting shot during the whole of the war, and now this."

I removed my jacket, pushing it down against his flesh to stifle the bleeding.

"Lucky it wasn't your head," growled Davies. He turned to the girls. "Don't feel sorry for him. He made Walker push Edith into the river."

That put the cat among the pigeons. The wee lasses didn't know what to do, torn between tears, anger and fear.

"There's a first aid kit on the coach," said Miss Henshaw, as clear-minded as always. "We need to treat the wound."

Davies gave permission with a flick of the gun. "Be quick. We ain't sticking around." He motioned Crouch forward. "Do what you have to do."

As ominous as the words sounded, the command related to putting the agents' car out of commission, something we knew Crouch was a master of.

Miss Henshaw returned with a tin, her once-bound hair down, fluttering in the wind. "Edith, help me. You're a Girl Guide."

The girl approached Trenton-Harper with an ambiguous expression, and I feared what she might do as he lay there vulnerable and in pain.

"We'll take over now, Mr Macleod," said Miss Henshaw, her hands replacing mine on my jacket. "I have some training from the war."

"Glad tae hear it," I said, backing away, examining my blood-stained hands.

I need not have worried about Edith. She showed an integrity lacking in us men, cutting away Trenton-Harper's sleeve, while Miss Henshaw kept one hand pressed to the wound, the other pulling together gauze and bandages.

"I owe you an apology, young lady," said Trenton-Harper, his eyes lowered in shame. "It is true I recklessly endangered you for a distraction, but please believe me when I say I never intended to harm you. A little wet, maybe, but harm, never."

"You're forgiven," said Edith, her face screwed up in concentration as she reached Miss Henshaw's fingers with her scissors.

"Right, let's have a look at this wound." Miss Henshaw removed my jacket and yanked apart what remained of Trenton-Harper's sleeve. The thick red blood flooded down his arm. "Elevate it!"

Trenton-Harper squeaked in pain as Edith raised his limb, holding it straight, reducing the flow.

"The bullet went straight through. That's the good news." Miss Henshaw washed the wound with some water, a gauze pad at the ready.

"And the bad news?" I asked.

"Arrgghh!" screamed Trenton-Harper.

"This will hurt," she answered, having applied a pad coated in alcohol. "Now, the gauze and bandage please, Edith."

It was absorbing work, so much so that the coach engine starting caught us off guard.

"They're getting away!" yelled Bridget.

"One thing at a time," urged Miss Henshaw, the first revolution of bandage secure.

"There goes the gold," sighed Bridget. "Now I know how King John felt on the Wash."

I chuckled when I discovered the meaning of her reference later in life, but things appeared grim as the coach pulled away.

"We're in a bit of a pickle," Trenton-Harper stated, while grimacing as Miss Henshaw secured the bandages tight.

"Aye," was all I could think to say to that understatement.

Chapter 21

As the growl of the engine faded in the distance, there was work to do. We had a wounded man, two Soviet prisoners, a dead body and traumatised girls. I was not feeling so great myself. Only Miss Henshaw carried herself as though a normal day in the countryside.

"I've buried the body," I said, brushing the pine needles from my hands. It was a shallow grave, inviting the creatures of the forest to disturb it, but with no spade, a covering of fallen needles was all I could offer. "Will the girls be all right?"

"Once tidied and respectable," answered Miss Henshaw. "We women may react with tears, but lest you forget, we've hearts of lions. That wretch can verify such." She peered down at the battered Soviet agent. "I will remind the girls of our greatest monarch."

"And what do we do with our captives?" asked Trenton-Harper, resting against the flat tyre of the car, his certainty and authority a shrunken wreck.

"Good question." I crouched, plucking the gag from Kuznetsov's mouth. "Well, what do ye think?"

A Russian curse flew at me, followed by a more understandable order. "Free me!"

"Nae, lad. Ye're a dangerous scamp. How far is Berlin?"

He laughed. "You not valk. My people catch and shoot you. Free me. I speak for you. Trust me."

It was my turn to laugh. "Ha, I'm nawt trusting anyone ever again."

"Then you…" The replaced gag reduced his sentence to a muffled complaint.

I glanced at my watch and up at the sun. "South is that way." I pointed through the forest. "Our best bet is tae make our way tae Berlin. Get off this road and intae one of the Western Allied sectors."

"You think we can make it?" asked Trenton-Harper, a hand placed on his sling. "Are you sure Berlin lies to the south?"

"Maybe nawt directly," I confessed, aware my proposal carried enormous risk, "but a city like Berlin sticks oot. Roads, rivers, people: they all gravitate to the city."

"I don't know," mulled Trenton-Harper. "We have no food. Davies was right: they'll send the girls home. It's just you and me who must pay a price for this fiasco."

"I'm nawt going back tae prison!" I exclaimed.

"Miss Henshaw," said Trenton-Harper. "Your thoughts? Will the girls be up to walking to Berlin, wherever it may be?"

"We stick to this road," declared Miss Henshaw, pointing westward.

"But they'll spot us," I objected. "It's a miracle nowt has passed us in the last hour."

"We stick to this road," repeated our music teacher in a calm, authoritative voice. "You must trust me."

Despite my earlier declaration, I did. My faith in humanity not yet exhausted.

"I stay," muttered Kuznetsov as we prepared for our walk, on his feet, his gag discarded.

"Ye're coming," I countered.

"Nyet."

A resourceful girl named Alexandra resolved our impasse, employing the pin of her brooch in that most sensitive of regions, Kuznetsov's backside. It was a rare moment of levity, watching the cold-hearted thug scamper down the road, yelping with his hands tied behind his back, Alexandra pursuing and encouraging with a timely prod. His compatriot required no such persuasion.

We marched down the quiet road, neither as ordered as my march eastward in 1940 nor as disordered as westward in '45. Trenton-Harper languished at the rear, weakened by his blood loss. I walked with him, realising the foolishness of my plan to walk to Berlin. Miss Henshaw led the girls with the enthusiasm of an explorer, keeping them occupied with questions, facts and encouragement.

"I'm getting that woman a medal when we get home," said Trenton-Harper. "Formidable!"

A horse and cart approached us, a middle-aged man behind the reins. His bemusement at this troop of foreigners turned to friendliness as the girls greeted him with passable German, Monika establishing a brief conversation. The bemusement returned at the sight of the bound Russians, and the imploring Kuznetsov crying out a scattering of German words among his native tongue. The man sneered and spat in Kuznetsov's direction, passing by with a mutter.

"Monika tells me the farmer mentioned the coach passing," called out Miss Henshaw.

I acknowledged with a nod, wondering what merit such information possessed.

"Perhaps veering," added the teacher. "Though my German is not good enough."

"Fascinating," I muttered out of earshot.

"There's no love lost between the Germans and Russians," remarked Trenton-Harper, over his laboured breathing. "That may be to our advantage."

"Aye, but there is reward in betrayal," I answered, feeling the strain of our brisk walk myself.

"You preach to the converted, Mr Macl... Oh, to hell with deception - Jock. Was I really such a fool to be played? I thought I knew them. We rescued an informant from Yugoslavia together just last year."

"That gold corrupts the mind," I stated. "Destroys all who covet it."

"You may be right, old chap." Trenton-Harper placed a hand on my shoulder. "But do you know what upsets me most?"

I awaited his answer.

"They stole the girls' instruments! Did their music not stir your soul?"

"All were very good," I replied, unwilling to bring my soul into it. "You'll see them right for replacements?"

"Oh, the least His Majesty's government can do," promised Trenton-Harper, coming to a halt. "Perhaps a break is in order? A little lightheaded, don't you know."

"Aye." We already lagged a distance behind our youthful companions, but I recognised the poor man had nothing left.

We reclined on the grass verge, Trenton-Harper rasping under a sweat. It was impossible not to think back to the winter of 1945, when a roadside rest brought both relief and danger. Only the spring sunshine differed. I watched the column of girls disappear around a corner, wondering at the odds that we might have the energy to catch up.

"You must be cursing me," said Trenton-Harper between deep breaths. "Dragged you into this shamble, and now I can't even keep up."

"I've cursed ye plenty over this last week," I admitted. "But nawt for getting shot. We all got played by Davies, or whatever his name is."

Trenton-Harper sighed. "That's me finished. If we make it out of here. I won't..."

"Mr Macleod! Mr Macleod!" Bridget appeared around the corner, sprinting back to us, her arms waving.

I jumped to my feet, a foreboding hitting my gut. "What is it, lass?"

"We... We..." She struggled for breath.

"Take yer time."

"The coach," she gasped. "It's... It's around the corner." Her hand flapped cooling air toward her face, before eking out one last word. "Crashed!"

"Crash?" I echoed. "How? Did you hear that, Trenton-Harper?"

The government man struggled to his feet. "There's hope!"

"Miss Henshaw and the others are finding out what happened," continued Bridget, drawing air through her nose. "They sent me back to get you."

"What!" I cried, slapping a hand to my brow in disbelief. "They're still armed. I donnae care what they said aboot nawt harming women, that gold makes them desperate. And what if there's a police patrol?"

Bridget shrugged. "I was just told to get you, because I'm the fastest. Did you know I won both the 100 and 200-yard sprints at sports day last year?"

"Aye, thank ye, Bridget," I gripped her shoulder, as I did with my boys when encouraging their focus on important matters. "Ye're tae stay with Mr Trenton-Harper. I'll go on and discover what's happening. If I donnae come back in half an hour, get help from the next passer-by who comes from the other direction. Do ye understand?"

She nodded, disappointment forcing her brow to drop.

With no time to spare, I ran off cursing Miss Henshaw under my breath. Soon, I was fighting for that breath and eased myself to a fast walk, my legs and lungs burning as I pushed up the slight incline to the bend in the road. Trees ringed the inner curve, hiding the view beyond. Atop the brow of the hill, the road flattened, continuing its arc through the woods, before opening to look down on a shallow valley. Not 100 yards on rested the coach, angled off the road, its front buried within the foliage of towering shrubs. I picked up my pace, discarding any thought of danger. The girls mingled around the coach door, Miss Henshaw nowhere in sight.

"Is everything all right?" I called out when in range.

A chorus of responses merged to become indecipherable, but the mood was unmistakable: they were thrilled.

"What happened?"

I don't think a satisfactory reply came, but I heard one intriguing response: "Miss Henshaw's a genius."

Pushing my way through the girls, I grabbed the handrail at the base of the coach steps, pulling myself up. There was Crouch, slumped forward over his steering wheel. "Miss Henshaw?"

"Ah, Mr Macleod. Bridget found you." She appeared in the aisle, looking down at my confused face.

"Are ye all right? What's going on?" By this point, I could see Davies and Walker, either side of the aisle, both collapsed in their seats.

"I've a small confession," began Miss Henshaw, a rare smile breaking across her face. "While collecting the first aid tin, I may have exploited the situation to our advantage. You must forgive my generalisation, but I know men and their weaknesses. Wallowing in their triumph, I knew they could not resist a drink to celebrate. Mr Walker had kindly left his jacket on his seat. I had seen him sipping from that flask – disgusting habit! Out of spite, I simply planned to empty it, taking away a little joy. But what else should I discover in those pockets but his sleeping draught."

A smile had already broken out on my face.

"I'm not proud of my immoral actions," she continued, before adding with a flush. "Well, perhaps a little proud. I hope I didn't add too much. They are still breathing."

I laughed. "Ye are a genius, Miss Henshaw!" For a mad moment I considered planting a big kiss on her lips but thought better of it.

"But what now?"

"Well, as a man, I fancy a drink tae celebrate." I allowed a second for my joke to settle, winking to dispel any doubt I might be serious. "Let's see if we can get the coach back on the road. The damage doesn't look too bad. There's just one problem."

"Which is?"

"I cannae drive." Before the war, I once drove a friend's car, but it didn't end well. Too many pedals and things to do at once.

"You soldiers never appreciated us WAAFs," said Miss Henshaw. "I drove fuel tankers for part of the war. Can't be that different."

"Are there nae ends tae yer talents? We'll send a couple of the girls tae collect Trenton-Harper and Bridget. Then I suggest we aim for Berlin."

***

"I don't know," mulled Trenton-Harper, tucked back in his seat on the coach under a blanket, revived a little by a sugar-loaded drink of squash. "They're British citizens. We know what will happen if the Soviets get their claws into them. And I want to see them brought to justice by the country they betrayed."

"It's what they planned for us." I was feeling unforgiving at that moment, ready to dump our dozing bandits in the German countryside to fend for themselves. "We donnae have the rope to bind all, and how do we keep five under watch? It's either the Russians or the crooks?"

The crunch of a gear change made me cringe, Miss Henshaw still familiarising herself with the beast.

"Kuznetsov's an ideological zealot," said Trenton-Harper, glancing over to the Russian, bound and gagged in the seat across the aisle. "If we point a gun at him to make him lie for us at the next checkpoint, I think he'd take the bullet."

Those deep-set eyes flickered in our direction. Our Russian knew we discussed him.

"And if we release him, he alerts the authorities, and we'll ne'er get through. Can't leave him tied up. We'd need the rope for the others." I worked my tongue around my mouth in thought. "There is something we could do tae discourage his zealotry."

"Do tell."

"Er, Miss Henshaw is nawt going tae like it."

After a little persuasion and a ten-minute stop, the coach pulled away again. The girls crowded at the rear window, howling and screeching in hysterics. Miss Henshaw's complaints fell on deaf ears. If the girls respected her more than ever, they no longer saw her as their teacher. The rebellious heroine had spawned rebellious disciples. I peeked over the huddled teenagers, chuckling myself at the sight of the two naked Russians, abandoned in the road, their clothes under my arm.

Chapter 22

The closer we got to Berlin, the busier the roads became. Soon we mixed with troop lorries, horse and carts and the cars of those lucky enough to have access to fuel. What a sight we must have been: our bright red coach mingling with the dull green and black vehicles, our cargo of slumbering villains, energetic schoolgirls and hidden bullion. Miss Henshaw drove at a cautious pace, unfamiliar with the roads, this strange habit of foreigners driving on the other side, and the sluggish coach.

We faced a dilemma. Where were we heading? Yes, Berlin, but none of us knew the city or what awaited us. All around the once-great metropolis lay territory under the control of the Soviets. We stood out like a sore thumb, turning the heads of all we passed. Perhaps Kuznetsov had convinced some poor farmer already he was no madman, protected his modesty, and called through to alert his masters.

"Our fuel is running low," stated Miss Henshaw.

"How low?" asked Trenton-Harper, a touch of his former confident self resurfacing as the mission found itself back on track.

She tapped on the dashboard, squinting at the dial. "These things aren't accurate. Wouldn't like to say. We could run out in a few miles or fifty."

"I'm going to say a brief prayer for fifty," remarked Trenton-Harper. "Anyone care to join me?"

A silence filled the coach, luck no longer enough. We called on our faith.

With the city on the horizon, we drifted westwards, Trenton-Harper convinced our trajectory led to friendly territory. His optimism vanished with a couple of words from Miss Henshaw.

"Roadblock!"

"Damn!" cursed Trenton-Harper, our music teacher no longer concerned by a slip of the tongue. "What do we do?"

"Put yer foot down!" I cried. "Hang on tae yer seats, girls, and keep yer heads down. They'll be shooting at us."

"Are you sure, my man?" Trenton-Harper's words had hardly left his mouth when the coach jerked forward.

Our engine competed with its load, struggling to accelerate, but we gradually built speed. From my vantage point, I saw the faces of the guards. They noticed us with mild curiosity, clocking our foreign shape and number plate, building to focussed intrigue, before our speed registered and alarm took over. Two military vehicles blocked the road, angled against each other. There was no way through without taking damage. The guards struggled to raise their guns, flustered and unprepared.

"Brace yourselves!"

An almighty bang confirmed impact; the two cars spun and shattered as our coach ploughed through. The girls screamed. Miss Henshaw screamed. I may have screamed. Our momentum carried us through. I heard the crack of gunfire, single rifle shots. If they hadn't known of our approach before, they knew about it now.

"Is everyone okay?" I shouted, relieved to find all were safe.

"Whatsh going on?" Walker stirred, fighting to keep his eyelids open while his brain sensed the drama.

Uninclined to explain the last few hours or our current predicament, I ignored him. Instead, I scrambled to the back of the coach, urging the girls to keep their heads down. Chaos filled our rear view, traffic building up behind the wreckage.

"We're oot of range," I declared, making my way back to the front. "Well done, Miss Henshaw."

She didn't answer. Her knuckles were white, gripped around the steering wheel; her neck jutted forward, eyes locked on the road ahead.

"How much further?" asked Trenton-Harper, his own features drained of blood.

"I donnae know, but we can expect more barriers." A picture of the Czech border formed in my mind, with its hedgehog obstacles and tanks. Berlin and safety seemed so close, yet so far.

"Drugged!" Davies had awoken, echoing his last conscious memory.

"Sorry, boss," mumbled Walker, who grappled with his bindings.

"You slept well, I trust?" asked Trenton-Harper, enjoying his revenge. "We tied your ropes particularly tight, Davies."

Still too befuddled to comprehend, Davies groaned a response.

"Mr Trenton-Harper." Edith stood in the aisle, Monika behind her.

"You may wish to stay in your seats, ladies," said Trenton-Harper. "Things are going to get rocky."

"Monika has a question, which I think I understand." The coach swerved, overtaking a cart, sending Edith and her friend into the adjacent seat, the occupants pushing them back.

"Well, hurry. What is it?"

"How did Mr Davies intend to enter Berlin?"

Trenton-Harper's eyebrows lifted in surprise. "That's an excellent question. Thank you, Monika, Edith. Now back to your seats."

Fortune was again on our side. Of our criminal triumvirate, the most malleable had regained his cognitive functions first.

"Walker, you traitorous scum," began Trenton-Harper, with a tact I thought a little misguided. "I'll take the death-penalty off the table for you if you tell us how you planned to enter Berlin."

Walker glared back.

I intervened. "Come on, lad. Hyde was ma friend too. He told me aboot his life, growing up on the streets of London. Ye donnae always get a choice in life but, when needed, he did the right thing." I took a deep breath. "He sacrificed his life for me and our comrades. They dinnae always treat him well, but he took those bullets for them. Ye can do the same and live. Help these girls get home safe."

Davies mumbled from behind, still unable to get a coherent sentence out.

"Ye saw his boy," I added, sensing my words were affecting Walker. "Hyde lives on through him. Donnae ye want that too? If we're caught, then they'll track the gold back to Madame Filipekka."

"Please, Mr Walker!" Bridget appeared, a welcome intervention, as fluttering one's eyelashes was never my strong point. It triggered a mimicking chorus from her friends, which not even Holmes' nemesis, Moriarty, could have ignored.

"Crouch has a map," muttered Walker, disconsolate at grassing. "There's a country road that leads into the city. The locals come and go with no one batting an eyelid."

"Good man!" declared Trenton-Harper, ignoring the whining complaint emerging from Davies. "And where's this map?"

"Dunno. That's the truth."

Little drama accompanied our search for the map. With a polite 'excuse me,' I slipped my hand into an inner pocket of Crouch's jacket, found a compact, folded sheet of paper and extracted it without stirring its owner.

A helpful red line mapped the road we sought, and I held it up for the benefit of Miss Henshaw.

"That's all very well," she said, her eyes flicking from map to road. "But I've no idea where I am now."

This popped our bubble, eliciting a curse from Trenton-Harper, followed by a telling-off from Miss Henshaw.

"Crouch will know," I said, my voice more confident than I felt. "He seems a natural on these foreign roads."

"Except he's asleep." Trenton-Harper was less than helpful.

"Use the smelling salts in the first aid kit," suggested Edith.

"Pinch him!"

"Slap him!"

All helpful ideas from the girls, but Edith's appealed most. I wafted the vial under Crouch's nose, causing a spluttering tremble and incoherent moan.

"Come on, Crouch!" I urged. "We need yer charm for a wee job."

"Don't help them!" ordered Davies, finding his footing in the conscious world. We recycled the gag used on Kuznetsov, much to Davies's displeasure.

"What's going on?" muttered Crouch, recoiling as I waved the vial under his nostrils once again.

"If you'd prefer to avoid the hangman's noose," said Trenton-Harper, looming before the bewildered man. "Then you will assist Miss Henshaw in navigating."

The dozy Crouch struggled to lift his head, all his effort required just to keep his eyelids open.

"This is useless," complained Trenton-Harper.

"Fill him with coffee." To our surprise, Walker offered this gem of an idea. I like to think my earlier words converted him, but I suspect self-preservation played its part.

Trenton-Harper donated his supply of coffee, the girls mixed it in a mug of cold water, and I tipped the contents down a reluctant Crouch's throat, pinching his nose to force him to swallow. The violation did as much to wake the crook as the caffeine. I'll refrain from sharing his next few words. Needless to say, Miss Henshaw objected, while the girls giggled.

Convincing a sourpuss to help you is no simple task, especially when they've perfected the art form over a lifetime. Crouch struggled in his binding, demanding release, urged on by the mumbling Davies.

A bang, crack and shattering of glass, topped off with the screams of the girls, brought our perilous situation back into sharp focus.

"They're behind us!" cried Alexandra, cowering on the aisle floor, amid the broken glass of our rear window.

"Those at the back, move forward!" I urged, spotting two police vehicles in our wake, a man leaning from the front window of one with a handgun. "Keep yer heads down."

We had no chance of outrunning them, our cumbersome vehicle already at its limit. They crept nearer, one bullet lodging in the ceiling, another in the back of an empty seat, not a minute before occupied by a schoolgirl. Even with a change of mind from Crouch and Berlin but a mile away, we were out of time.

"Can ye see them in yer mirrors?" I asked Miss Henshaw.

Her eyes shot up and then to her right. "They're about 30 yards behind." She rocked in her seat, urging the coach to go faster. "And there's more of them. Military vehicles. They're catching faster. But..."

Bang!

The coach shook and rocked, sinking at the rear left, setting off another round of screaming. I recognised the sensation. They'd shot out a tyre. At our speed, it was a miracle Miss Henshaw kept control. The wider road helped as we veered into the other lane, thankfully clear of oncoming traffic.

"Best pull over," shouted Trenton-Harper over the grating roar from the road. "We've done our best, but let's not risk the girls' lives."

Not for the first time, Miss Henshaw ignored sound advice.

I was conscious of one of our pursuers overtaking us but focussed on hanging on as our coach continued at speed with its erratic, swaying path.

"What colours are the French tricolour?" asked Bridget.

With my life or freedom in the balance, I felt justified in telling our talkative schoolgirl to shut up, but before I made a fool of myself, I spotted the source of her curiosity. On the road ahead, a jeep cut across in front of us, displaying on either side of its bonnet two blue, white and red tricolour flags.

I dared to edge to the back of the coach, sticking my head above the rear seats. Despite the sparks flying from our back wheel, another jeep rested tight behind us, this one adorned with the stars and stripes. We had gained an Allied escort.

The police cars dropped back, unwilling to fire on a military convoy, and I felt bold enough to give them two fingers, and a friendly wave to our American saviours. Heaven knows what they made of this craggy Scot peering through the back of the coach.

At the time I write this, such a brazen venture by Allied vehicles into the Soviet bloc is impossible, the borders sealed shut, the hatred fixed, the rules of engagement established. But in April 1948, all was fluid, though I dare say we helped solidify it.

As we approached the border post, the French sector on the other side, the Soviet guards aimed their guns, but none had the authority to start a war. We made sure they spotted the girls, who waved hats and handkerchiefs from the window vents, a virtuous school party returning from its planned tour, albeit with a crumpled bonnet, a blown-out tyre, shredded seats and shattered windows. Without our escorts, a night in the cells beckoned for ignoring their roadblock, time for Kuznetsov to find clothes and a phone, and for our escape to unravel, but those jeeps were our free pass. If they had known what lay hidden under our seats, what a showdown would have awaited us. Trenton-Harper went so far as to claim we may have triggered World War Three. But as they opened the barriers, with a grudging scowl and salutes for our guard of honour, I knew we were safe.

Chapter 23

You have never seen celebrations like it. Coil a spring as tight as you can, then let it go. Those girls led the party, hollering and cheering, hugging, laughing and crying. Trenton-Harper buckled under the strain of success, blubbering and tittering with a hint of madness. There was even a touch of respect on the face of Davies, though Crouch maintained his granite scowl. While Miss Henshaw tried in vain to lead the national anthem, her voice cracking with emotion, her choir otherwise engaged. As for me, I laughed seven years of guilt loose, howling until my stomach ached. The French guards boarding the coach must have thought we had escaped an asylum.

The strange thing is, they appeared to be expecting us, rather than treating us like nuisance tourists rescued from misadventure. A representative from the British army, Captain Aldwick, greeted us.

"I want you chaps in our zone a.s.a.p.," he disclosed, out of the hearing of the French and Americans. "Don't want news of the cargo leaked to old Frenchie. They'll be wanting a cut."

Of course, the government knew of our cargo, but I still didn't understand how news had reached Berlin. I thought of asking Aldwick, but the man was too busy convincing the French authorities to send us on our way.

A French medic examined Trenton-Harper's wound, nodding with satisfaction at the work of Miss Henshaw and Edith, while an engineer replaced our tyre, gesticulating with Gallic melodrama at the lasting damage caused by our escape.

Amid the joy, one sad event occurred. It was time to say farewell to Monika, whom the Americans promised to whisk away and fly off to reunite with her father. In a few days, we had taken Monika into our hearts. The girls never asked questions, at least not the cynical kind, accepting her, befriending her and then losing her. From the high, they crashed, their tears lamenting a unique camaraderie.

"Goodbye," said Monika, as she held out her hand to me. "Dank you. I enjoy playing at fort."

I laughed, shaking her hand. Of all the things she remembered, it was running around amid the ruins of my old prison camp. Yet from the ordeal of the trip, those carefree moments are the memories I treasure too. "Ye take care of yerself, lass."

I think she still writes to Edith and Bridget, and is now married with three children, living in some desert city in the heart of America.

Captain Aldwick got his way, expediting our departure, taking over the driving from a grateful Miss Henshaw. "Not an easy beast," he commented, pulling onto the streets of Berlin. "I'm surprised a woman managed her."

He was not the first man to underestimate Miss Henshaw, joining a growing club of which I had once been a member. But within that coach, he found only admirers.

"She drives far better than you, old chap," stated Trenton-Harper. "And under fire too!"

A chant of Miss Henshaw's name spread through the seats, as though she had captained the girls to victory in a hockey tournament and scored the winning goal. The music teacher blushed, trying to temper the noise with a finger to her lips.

"She's a very fine driver." In a journey full of surprises, nothing shocked me more than such praise coming from Crouch. Unable to force a smile himself, Miss Henshaw acknowledged the compliment with a silent 'thank you'.

"My apologies," said Aldwick, our message received. "I meant no disrespect." He sought refuge in tales of life in Berlin, the increasing pressure from the Soviets, food shortages and fears for the future. It was all a little gloomy, if I'm honest.

Few cars hindered our journey across the city, past ruins and building sites, sombre faces and tented communities. As a sanctuary, it had a lot to be desired.

Finally, we entered the British zone, the destruction as complete, but somehow the Union Jacks and familiar uniforms made me feel safe and welcome.

"I bet you all want a decent cup of tea," said Captain Aldwick, heaving the handbrake up, our destination reached.

"Aye, that and a pint," I responded, making my way off our trusty red steed. I patted the scratched, glossy paintwork, thanking her for getting us out safely.

"Jock, my friend."

I turned in surprise, recognising the voice. "Konrad! What are ye doing here?"

My dear old German friend stood before me, a few extra wrinkles on his face since I last saw him as we went our separate ways from the Fallingbostel prison camp. "I get your letter," he answered. "You in trouble again."

"Aye, I have that habit." We hugged, our bond from surviving the death march in 1945 unbreakable. "I donnae know why I wrote it. Maybe I couldnae tell Jane, but I wanted someone to know if I dinnae come back."

"It is lucky you did, Jock. I now vork for British army intelligence, hunting Nazis. It is big risk you take. I tell my people to votch for you. They hear from friends in Poland. Ve ready for you."

"Ah, Trenton-Harper, Miss Henshaw," I waved the government man and teacher over. "I want ye tae meet a friend and the reason we got our escort." I put an arm around Konrad's shoulder and squeezed. "I've missed ye."

Trenton-Harper gripped Konrad's hand, shaking with vigour. "Much obliged, old chap. A friend of Jock's is a friend of mine. I fear more bullet holes would now decorate my body without your help."

"Who is Jock?" asked Miss Henshaw, offering her hand to the ex-prison guard.

"My dear lady," said Trenton-Harper with a chuckle. "There is much to tell you, but first I have good news. A flight is arranged to take us home. They want us out of here before the Soviets wake up. I think the girls will enjoy that."

Miss Henshaw looked uneasy. "But I've never flown before."

"Och, ye'll be flying it yerself before we land."

Epilogue

A government car dropped me at home. I pulled my holdall from the back seat, thanked the driver, and stood staring at my house. My treasure awaited inside, but I wondered how they would greet me. I had left to find myself, to confront my guilt at Hyde's death, to unlock an eternal peace. As I trudged up the front path, I knew peace still evaded me, but I had eased my guilt, finding a new plane on which to exist. One where I accepted the pain, the memories, the life I had before me.

"Dad!" Dick, my eldest boy, appeared from the side of the house. "Mum said you'd been away. Some jolly, I bet."

"Dick, ma boy. Still nawt qualified for the police?"

"Give me time," he responded with a grin. "I've asked the crooks to take things easy until then."

"They're probably all be abroad," I said, recalling my farewell with Davies, Crouch and Walker as the Military Police escorted them away. I never found out what happened to them.

"We're around the back. I want you to meet my new girlfriend. She's training to be a nanny. Mum's blown all the rations on cakes. I hope you're hungry."

I followed him down the path, a warm glow generated from talk of home, family, cakes and new love.

"Jane!" I cried at the sight of them all picnicking on the lawn. "I missed ye."

"Jock!" She climbed to her feet, that hesitant glint in her eye.

"I'm back," I said, dropping my holdall, engulfing her in my arms. "This time I'm really back. I cannae promise nawt tae be a fool again, but I'll nawt keep another secret from ye. We can be a family again."

"I love ye." She didn't have to say anything more.

"Hi, Dad," said Tom, my wee Jean cradled in his arms. "Jean says…" He blew a raspberry, holding her tiny hand in his and waving at me.

"And I missed ye too," I replied, kissing Jean's forehead, and squeezing Tom's cheek until he squirmed.

Jean's face lit up in recognition before the hum of an airplane overhead distracted her.

"An Avro York," remarked Tom, always a keen identifier of planes.

I paid no heed, enjoying the company of my family. Little did I realise, those very planes would soon be the lifeblood of Berlin, ferrying essential goods into the city once Stalin blockaded the roads and railways. Did an insignificant incident at the northern border of the French zone push our Uncle Joe to such drastic action? The history books blame the introduction of a single currency across the Western sectors, but I don't suppose he was happy when old Kuznetsov reported what we carried on that coach.

"Dad, can I introduce you to Elsie?" An elegant young woman stood by Dick's side with a shy smile.

"Pleased tae meet ye." I offered my hand, clasping her delicate fingers. "Ye'll have tae forgive the state I'm in."

Tom leaned in, whispering in my ear. "She's a talker. Worse than Mam."

"We donnae talk enough," I said, remembering Bridget's words. "Now, I must wash and change before the worms think I'm their home."

"Let me give you a hand with that," offered Tom, lifting my holdall. He cursed, dropping it back onto the floor. "Blimey, dad, you got a brick in there?"

"A brick, ye say? Ha, something like that. Just a wee memento from Poland."

The End

Author's Note: The History

The three adventures from *In the Face of the Foe* are works of fiction, a chance to celebrate the bravery and endurance of those who spent the war as prisoners, and explore the lasting legacy of their suffering. However, I set these fanciful tales within a loose framework of historical reality.

In 1939, on the outbreak of the Second World War, the Royal West Kent Regiment divided its two territorial battalions to form the 6th and 7th and 4th and 5th Battalions. While they fully equipped and provided advanced training for the latter two, fighting at Oudenarde and Nieppe and evacuated at Dunkirk, they committed the 6th and 7th to guard duty, leaving them lacking in preparation. During the Phoney War period in April 1940, they transferred the 6th and 7th to France to help move supplies and build airfields and railway sidings south of Rouen.

When a full-strength German armoured division broke through the French defences at Sedan in May 1940, cutting the British lines of communication, the 7th Battalion found itself as part of an improvised force with instructions to hold back the advancing Germans. A series of actions took place, with the British pushed back by the overwhelming enemy superiority until they reached the town of Albert (c. 20 miles north-east of Amiens).

Meanwhile, the 6th Battalion, amalgamated into a mobile column, pulled back along the chaotic, refugee-filled roads until they reached Doullens (c. 20 miles north of Amiens), where they had orders to hold back the Germans.

The outcome for both ill-prepared battalions was inevitable, with about 1000 men of the 6th and 7th killed or captured.[1] I use the term 'sacrificed' in book one, implying their worth to the army was perhaps less than those rescued at Dunkirk. While I can level criticism at the lack of preparedness afforded these battalions, I will leave to the professional historian the analysis of whether they were engaged for practical reasons of locality or deemed expendable against the greater strategic aim of saving the army. To learn more about the estimated 27,000-40,000 British soldiers left behind after the Dunkirk evacuations, I can recommend Sean Longden's excellent book, *Dunkirk – The Men They Left Behind.*

For those captured, prisoner of war camps awaited them for the next five years. The Germans sent detained officers to Oflags, dedicated camps suited to their status, and the rank and file to stalags. With artistic licence, I incorporated both into one camp for a brief period to foster dramatic opportunities within the story and to coincide with Operation Barbarossa (June 1941), allowing the Germans to plunder and transfer the gold back home.

Toruń (referred to as Thorn in book one and two, reflecting the German designation), birthplace of Copernicus, was home to many stalags, incorporated within the old fortifications. It is situated halfway between London and Moscow. They housed a range of nationalities, including British, Russian, Yugoslav, and Polish. The

---

1. The Queen's Royal West Kent Regiment official history

Geneva Convention allowed nations at war to use captured soldiers below the rank of sergeant for work, and local industry and agricultural land, confiscated by the occupier, exploited and benefited from the toil and sweat of the prisoners and local Poles.

The Nazis looted occupied countries, stealing priceless works of art, industrial machinery, forced labour and precious metals. It is an area that still causes rancour, with many items never returned, their location a mystery. It also provides a reservoir for the imaginations of writers and treasure hunters. Tales and myths are plentiful about hidden Nazi loot, moved and stashed as the Reich crumbled. Legends have grown, such as the Wałbrzych Gold Train, a shipment purported to be in a tunnel somewhere in Poland. I am happy to add a new legend with the Toruń bullion heist, but stress this comes purely from the author's imagination.

There were around 170,000 British prisoners of war (POWs) held in Europe by the Germans and Italians during the Second World War. Despite the constant worry of loved ones, those languishing in POW camps were not the priority of governments desperate to win a war. The endeavours of the Red Cross maintained a prisoner's connection to home and hope. With the success of D-Day in June 1944 and the failure of Germany's Operation Barbarossa and subsequent retreat from Russia, the defeat of Hitler became inevitable. And with the war's end in sight, minds could at last turn to planning for peace, at which point politics muddied the water, with prisoners becoming pawns in a bigger game.

The ferocity and brutality of Operation Barbarossa sowed the seeds for an equally monstrous revenge when the Soviets invaded Germany. Fear of this shaped Nazi policy for their prisoners. Germany's national borders stretched further eastwards than they do today (the post-war settlement saw Poland's borders shifted westwards and Russia kept parts of old eastern Poland). With prison camps spread across Germany and occupied Poland, the fast-advancing Red Army soon came within their range. Beyond the still deluded Hitler, other Nazi leaders recognised the value in seeking a negotiated peace with the Western Allies, hopeful they might even join them to fight the Soviets. While there is no concrete evidence to prove the Germans organised the transfer of POWs westwards to use as bargaining chips, this is the accepted explanation by historians. The forced march westward also included many inmates from the eastern concentration camps.

Stalag XXA in Thorn/Toruń was one of the furthest east. At its peak, it housed around 10,000 prisoners, with another 10,000 in sub-camps. Its British, Commonwealth and American inmates left in January 1945, either walking west to Fallingbostel, between Hanover and Hamburg, or to Southern Germany, splitting into manageable columns of about 250 men. The Russians liberated the camp at Thorn/Toruń on 1st February 1945. Originally established to host those building the nearby concentration camp of Bergen-Belsen, the Germans later converted Fallingbostel into a Stalag, making it one of the largest by the end of the war.

Many of the incidents I describe on Jock's march across Europe, such as the friendly fire, the atrocities, nightmare train journeys, the hunger, the cold and the despair, happened to some poor POW somewhere. Many chose not to talk about their experiences, but there is an excellent non-fiction account, researched and written by John Nichol and Tony Rennell, called *The Last Escape*. In their book they refer to a statement made to the post-war courts by an English prisoner of war from Stalag XXA about the march through northern Europe, saying, 'the privations suffered and the mistreatment described were extreme.' There are no official figures for the numbers who died during these marches and conditions and casualties will have varied for each route.

An estimate puts deaths at around 8,000 plus. I highly recommend *The Last Escape* for those wishing to discover more about this little-known part of the war.

Life for returning POWs was difficult. All within society had suffered in this total war, while culture, often steered by government, had focussed on victory and successes. POWs were a reminder of failure and defeat. Only during the 1950s did cinema, for example, draw on the experiences of POWs, building a troupe of the plucky Tommy who never surrenders, attempting to escape at every opportunity. There was also little understanding of the mental trauma of combatants and captives, Post Traumatic Stress Disorder as yet unrecognised, while mental health was a taboo topic for society. Men, therefore, suffered in silence, turning to alcohol and other means to bury their torment, sometimes venting through anger and violence. For returning Soviet POWs, their fate was truly terrible. Surrender was a betrayal of the revolution, and many found themselves in the gulags or worse.

At the Yalta Conference of 1945, Stalin, Roosevelt and Churchill agreed to the post-war settlement for Europe. But while the Western Allies recognised the right of the Soviet Union to occupy the east of Germany and Poland etc, they naively hoped democracy would return once more in the countries of central Europe, with the Red Army soon withdrawing. As early as March 1946, Churchill recognised Soviet contrary intentions, warning of the 'Iron Curtain' rising across Europe. Stalin manipulated local elections, merging democratic socialist parties with communist parties; votes counted for the former, allowing the latter to take power, then destroying any rivals with typical Soviet brutality.

In the immediate post-war period, Europe also experienced a momentous shuffling of its people. Ethnic Germans, whose families had long lived in central Europe, befell the vengeance of the liberated nations, attacked, murdered or forced out back to Germany. Elsewhere, refugees, prisoners and soldiers all returned home, many discovering their homes no longer existed. In this chaos, shortages continued and worsened. The Soviets stripped the countries under their occupation - whether or not a victim of Nazi aggression - of their industrial equipment, hindering economic recovery. I can strongly recommend *In the Ruins of the Reich* by Douglas Botting, as further reading on this overlooked period.

In early 1948, your familiar Cold War watchtowers or walls were yet constructed, and some fluidity for populations and foreign parties to travel across borders remained (I suspect this didn't stretch to school parties). Each side would send vehicles across to collect intelligence of military strength and movements, closely monitored by the other. Access to Berlin for the Western Allies, an island in a sea of Soviet-occupied Germany, always relied on the goodwill of the Soviet Union, and since 1946, Stalin tested the will of the West, limiting, closing and opening the routes into the city. From March 1948, Stalin upped the ante, shutting off access for longer periods and harassing Allied planes. This resulted in a collision on 5 April between a Soviet jet and a British Airlines Viking plane, killing all aboard and increasing tensions still higher. When the Allies tried to stabilise the German economy by introducing a new single currency, the Deutsche Mark, across their three zones in June 1948, the Soviet Union reacted by blockading West Berlin, setting off the first major crisis of the Cold War.

I hope this brief historical overview provides a helpful context for the adventures of Jock Mitchell and an appreciation of the many who endured the war in captivity and their families.

***

Writing dialogue in the vernacular is an exercise fraught with danger. It is a case of 'you can't please all the people all the time'. To capture every accent and nuance may leave the dialogue incomprehensible to some, while to have none undermines the character. Including a sprinkling provides the flavouring without, I hope, creating corny stereotypes, but I apologise if my compromising leaves a bitter taste in any local's mouth.

Charlotte Ward, an Oxford University language student, expertly translated the German dialogue used in *A Place More Dark*, for which I am most grateful.

***

To support independent authors, please leave a review online. They are an invaluable source of feedback and help other readers learn about new authors.

Also, if you liked my take on the past, why not sample my view of the future with my award winning novels, *Liberty Bound* and *Where Liberty Lies*.

With appreciation,

Nathaniel M Wrey

www.nathanielmwrey.com

www.facebook.com/nathanielmwrey

About the Author

Nathaniel M Wrey is a contemporary British author known for his imaginative storytelling and thought-provoking narratives. His work often explores themes of identity, society, and the human condition, blending elements of science fiction, speculative fiction and historical fact to create immersive and engaging tales. His first novel, *Liberty Bound,* published in 2020, achieved critical acclaim, winning a Readers' Favorite award, while its sequel, *Where Liberty Lies* (2023), won multiple awards, including a Global Book award, a Bookfest award, a North American Book award, a Literary Titan Gold Book award and a Royal Dragonfly Book award. Nathaniel has also written a children's book, with illustrations by Helen Cochrane, under the name Nate Wrey, called *Mooge: the Prehistoric Genius.*

Having studied history at the University of Reading in the UK, Nathaniel has worked as a civil servant for over 25 years, largely in the area of health and nursing. His literary influences include the social commentary of George Orwell, the adventures of John Buchan and the foresight and imagination of Ray Bradbury and John Wyndham.